I0817803

DARK SENTINELS BOOK TWO

JACOB CRAWFORD

The Assassin, Book Two of the *Dark Sentinels* series

Published by Ravenhart Press, 8635 W. Sahara Avenue, #677,
Las Vegas, NV 89117
www.ravenhartpress.com

Edited by Tim Baughman, Jr. – www.thattinywebsite.com
Cover & interior design by Caitlin Greer - authorcaitlingreer.com
Cover art initial concept by Matt Davis,
and final design by Caitlin Greer.

Hardcover ISBN: 978-0-9996106-6-4
Paperback ISBN: 978-0-9996106-5-7
eBook ISBN: 978-0-9996106-4-0

First Edition

P.E. Crawford

For my father, who I miss dearly.

E.V. Jacob

For everyone who helps me fight my Shadows.

And from both of us...

For everyone who has suffered through 2020.
This book was written years before, but still somehow resonated with it.

ONE

"I see dead people."

"That's very funny, Rosalind," Dr. Thompson said, scribbling something on her notepad.

I wished I could see what she was writing. Maybe, 'stubborn and obnoxious,' or, 'weird, possibly delusional.' In my defense, she *had* asked what I thought my current biggest stressor was, but I was sure my answer sounded more like an annoying teenager taunting her than the admission of truth it was. Whatever she thought, she was writing it down.

Or maybe she was drawing. I was.

The subject of my sketch was the forest. Ford's van parked near the trail we'd taken to the clearing. I couldn't stop thinking about that day, so I was just trying to focus on the non-horrific parts of it.

"I know this can be uncomfortable," Dr. Thompson

said gently, surprisingly patient despite all my lashing out. "But it doesn't have to be. First sessions are usually quite awkward. But I think it will get better with time."

I didn't say anything, and she settled back into her seat, watching me calmly.

"I wasn't kidding," I finally said, not taking my eyes off my sketch.

"About what?" she asked.

I knew she wanted me to say it—to tell her that I was seeing ghosts, and that I'd meant the statement in all seriousness.

My mouth was open to respond when I saw young man standing behind her. Tall, a little heavy, wearing a black Offspring shirt. He looked to be around my age, though who knows how long ago that had been. My breath caught in my throat and I watched him, waiting for him to do something.

Like so many of the other ghosts, though, he just stared at me. After a moment, he faded and disappeared. A sharp pain on my left hand alerted me that I was picking at my fingers again, my thumbnail nervously scratching against the cuticle of my ring finger until a little bead of blood appeared beside my nailbed.

My breath hitched. I'd have thought I'd be used to ghosts by now, but they could still startle me. I looked back at Dr. Thompson, checking her reaction.

She had turned to look over her shoulder, then back to me.

"Did you see a ghost just now?" she asked. The seriousness of her tone disarmed me. I wondered if there was any chance she actually believed me, or if she was just pacifying me, trying to get me to cooperate by pretending to understand. That seemed like the more likely option, so I didn't say anything. Not exactly a vote of confidence on my mental state, but I was too unnerved to care.

Our escapades on the mountain had been dubbed the 'Area 51 Breach' by the internet, as everyone seemed to think it had something to do with the military base (an idea Ford had eagerly latched onto, despite knowing the truth). This whole notion seemed really stupid to me, since Area 51 was something like a hundred and fifty miles from where *our* incident had occurred in the mountains, but no one seemed to care that this made no sense—Area 51 existed in the general vicinity of Las Vegas, weird stuff had happened and was continuing to happen in Las Vegas, and so a nonsensical theory was born.

Such was the internet.

At least no one knew that we were at the heart of it, but between the fire that burned at an inexplicably high temperature, the strange sounds reported, the bright lights in the sky, and the things residents of the mountain community had reported seeing in the forest—all of which had some shaky video evidence from fleeing residents—the whole 'aliens vs. government testing gone wrong' debate had gained a lot of traction, and theories were popping up all over the place.

For me, I just tried to focus on keeping my own life together. Since that day, I'd been seeing spirits *everywhere*. Before, they'd mostly been at my house. I'd had a few incidents away from home, but now it was a regular part of my day. I had managed to close the portal that had somehow opened up there, but apparently the energy-blast that was sent out in doing so had released a massive amount of paranormal...stuff.

That was actually the least of my worries, though. The ghosts didn't really do much—open a few doors, turn over a few chairs, break a glass here and there. And that was just the uppity ones; most of them stared at me. It was creepy, but largely harmless.

The real problem was the spike in violent crimes. The dramatic increase in missing persons cases. The storms and power outages that kept striking. The way hundreds of people in the area were reporting inexplicable activity that had the cops scratching their heads.

The past week had been a stressful one, considering I felt largely responsible for everything that had gone wrong. I still wasn't entirely sure *how*, but at least my attacker's words had started to make some sense.

She's too dangerous.

I had thought that was ridiculous. Now I understood. Not quite *why*, but at least *how* I could be dangerous to others. And I hated it. I hated the little voice in my head that kept saying, *you should have just let that Shadow kill you, to spare everyone else.*

I shoved that thought back immediately, refusing to consider it any further.

"No," I said to answer her question. "Just a headache."

She nodded, shifting slightly in her seat. "Rosalind, our hour is almost up. We haven't gotten very far, which is perfectly fine. We'll go at your pace. But before you leave, would you be willing to tell me why you agreed to therapy? I know your father didn't force you—you came here willingly, even if you appear less than enthusiastic about it."

I put my pencil down and looked up at the doctor. She was a little older than my dad, with streaks of silver mingled in with her blonde hair. She had a gentle face. Kind eyes that crinkled when she smiled. Her demeanor was gentle and supportive. But I really didn't think she believed me.

"I came here because my father was worried about me," I admitted.

"Is that the only reason? For your father?" I smudged my finger across the sketch to blend my lines a little and create a smoother shadow.

"Yes," I said absently. "I came to appease my father. That's all."

"So, there's nothing you hope to gain from these sessions?" she pressed, her tone still unnervingly calm.

I looked up again. "Not really. I have problems, sure—everyone does—but in all honesty, Dr. Thompson, I sincerely doubt you'll be able to do anything about mine."

She smiled. "Whatever troubles you, Rosalind, I promise I can help."

I laughed, then stopped myself.

You and what army? I wondered.

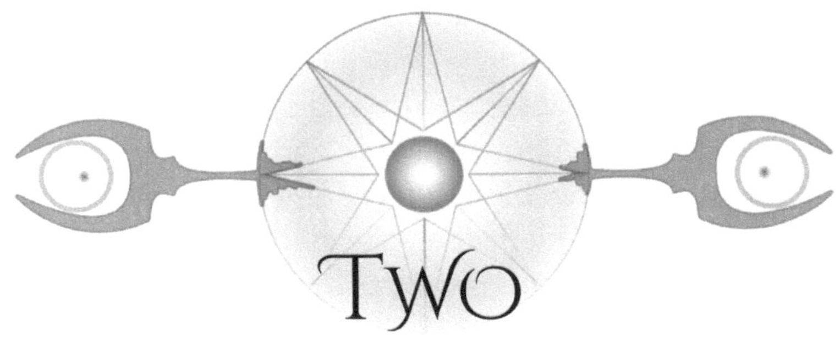

I held the flashlight steady while Emily typed away on her computer. Beside me, Derek was taking pictures, making notes. He was a little awkward, with one arm still bound in a cast, but he seemed to have gotten the hang of maneuvering with his broken arm. I felt bad, but he insisted I shouldn't.

"There," I said, looking toward a darkened corner and trying to focus.

Derek followed my direction, nodding as he caught sight of the ghost on his screen. It was less apparent to me when they appeared on camera, since I could see ghosts even without the aid of technology. I could see them much more clearly now, and they were noticing. Some of them were curious about me, some almost seemed relieved, while others didn't seem all that thrilled about my new ability, but what could I do? I didn't exactly love it either, but here I was.

The ghost in the corner snarled and withdrew further. This one was stubborn and hard to pin down. The house we were in was old, but not old enough to warrant generations upon generations of ghosts. Las Vegas doesn't have old buildings the way Europe does, or even the East Coast—a fact Emily complained about often.

Now, though, it seemed age of the building was irrelevant. No one had ever died on the property. There had only been two owners since it was built, and as far as we could tell, they'd both lived happy, peaceful lives. The second owner still lived here, as she had for almost thirty years, and she'd never had any kind of paranormal disturbances until a week earlier.

They'd gotten so bad in that time, she'd temporarily moved out.

Her church's priest had come to try and exorcise the house. That hadn't worked. He'd called in other priests from other churches, but still the presence lingered. Emily was her last hope.

Or rather, *I* was.

"Okay, Roz—do your thing," Emily said.

I hesitated. 'My thing' was apparently banishing ghosts, but I still wasn't completely sure how I did it, and I didn't feel particularly confident that I'd be able to call up that talent when I needed to. I didn't have the best track record, though I had been getting a *lot* of practice lately.

I squeezed my eyes shut and focused on the ghost. I could still feel him—it was almost like seeing him, but worse—as he moved closer.

I 'saw,' with my new senses, the wavering light of his energy, something I'd begun noticing I sensed not only with ghosts, but with people. People, though, were overwhelming and unsettling in a way, like I was intruding on them. Ghosts, while still upsetting, at least fit into the 'weird stuff' box in my head. And their...whatever I was seeing...seemed diffused, softer. I focused on the strange, bright energy of the ghost, ignoring the much brighter presences of Emily and Derek, and imagined it dissipating. Vanishing. Slipping away into wherever it was that ghosts belonged. It wasn't this world, but I didn't really know where it was, and I couldn't worry about that now.

Go back, I willed him.

His image flickered, dimming.

Then, he shouted, launching at me, clearly seeing me as an attacker. I screamed and swung at him instinctively as he charged me. My concentration broke and the action had no effect. He wasn't solid, but he could touch me, so when he hit, he knocked me back into the wall. I smacked my head hard, my vision spinning.

"Roz!" someone shouted, and I felt hands grab me and try to pull me away.

The room was still out of focus, but I was able to pick out the ghost's energy. It was moving closer, stronger and more corporeal now.

I raised my hand to the ghost and concentrated, ignoring everyone and everything else in the room. I put all my power, all my energy into that moment—into that ghost. I pushed as hard as I could with my mind, with the new, unfamiliar part of my consciousness that somehow dispelled spirits.

The room darkened around me. My stomach churned with a sudden wave of nausea and my head throbbed so hard I lost my footing, sinking to my knees.

I mentally pushed at the ghost again, and I could feel it slipping away, pushed back behind whatever barrier divided the living and the dead.

I shuddered, slumping to press my forehead against the cool tile floor. Emily was the one who'd grabbed me, and she stumbled under my weight.

"Did it work?" she asked.

Derek checked his EMF detector, then looked up and nodded, crossing the room to us. Emily helped me to a sitting position, and I pressed my fingers to my temples.

"You okay, Roz?" Derek asked.

I nodded. "Yeah. Sure. I think," I said, my vision still spinning.

They sat with me while I collected myself, taking slow, measured breaths. After making sure I wasn't about to pass out, they got up and packed away their equipment while I rested, chattering excitedly about this latest ghost expulsion.

I didn't mind having a moment alone—in fact, it was kinda nice to just sit in silence for a minute. Not that I would have objected to having Hazel or Ford there, but they were both busy today. Ford was working, and Hazel had a date with Sean. They were hanging out as much as they could before he took off for some camp he went to every year. She'd almost cancelled to come with me on this job, but I'd insisted I wouldn't unlock the door to let her in if she *did* show up, so she had agreed to keep her date.

I didn't want everyone's lives to be as overtaken by the ghosts as mine had been.

Emily and Derek were a different story—they seemed to love it.

"That one was harder, wasn't it?" Emily asked, coming over to me.

I nodded, testing whether I could stand without the aid of the wall.

"Yeah..." I said. "It really didn't want to go."

"This seems to be a pattern; every ghost is worse than the last," Derek commented. He looked at me. "Any theories?"

I shrugged. "You're the ghost experts. I'm just..."

I let it hang. I didn't know what I was.

"Maybe we should be more careful next time," Derek said, glancing at Emily. She looked at me, then at the cast on Derek's arm. While we hadn't encountered anything quite as violent as the ghost that dropped Derek from twelve feet in the air, we'd faced a few challenges in our busy week of ghost removals, and it was getting harder for me, not easier.

Emily frowned, but nodded.

"Yeah. We had another one scheduled for this afternoon, but maybe we should do it tomorrow," Emily said, glancing at me. I must not have looked all that great, because Derek nodded in agreement.

"Which one?" I asked.

"What?" Emily replied.

"The other...expelley-exorcism-whatever thing we had scheduled for today. What's the case?"

Emily blew absently at her bangs. "Uh, next one's a banshee." She looked more serious than I was used to, and I wasn't sure if it was because she had just changed her hair—it was all her natural black again, and shorter, though still long enough to brush her shoulder blades. The bangs were new, too, and now she wore it in a serious and professional ponytail on jobs, which made her look older and more sophisticated—or because things had become so much more serious in our lives.

Hopefully it was just the hair.

"A banshee. Must be my lucky day. Who's it haunting?" I pressed.

Emily glanced up at me. "Just...this woman."

Her tone bothered me. She was leaving something out. "*And*?"

Emily sighed. "And her two kids..."

I leaned against the wall. "Well, we shouldn't put that off."

"Roz," Derek said, his tone surprisingly gentle. "I don't really think that's a good idea."

"Why not? I don't think it's a good idea to leave them in a house with a screaming ghost. That sounds horrible."

"Yeah, but..." he looked at Emily for help.

"It's just..." Emily started, adjusting her bag on her shoulder. "You've been pushing yourself *really* hard this past week, and—"

"This is my fault, Emily," I said.

"No! Stop that!" Emily snapped, hitting me lightly with a strap from her bag.

"That's not fair to you, Roz," Derek said in that same gentle tone. His brow was furrowed with worry.

"It is! It's my fault and it's my mess to clean up. If I hadn't..." I shook my head. "I still don't know exactly what's going on here, but I know I caused it, so I'd better make it right. Plus, no one knows better than me how awful it is to live with ghosts in your house. I can't leave *kids* in that mess, okay?"

Emily scowled. "It's *not* your fault. But...fine. I won't cancel just yet, but I *am* gonna check in with you before we go, and if you're not up for it, I'm calling it off until you're at full capacity. And I get to make the call so don't even argue with me."

"Fair enough," I said.

Her phone chimed again, and it was a notification sound I wasn't used to. Emily checked it, her mouth twitching briefly into a grimace, and then she put her phone away.

"What was that?" I demanded. I was becoming so paranoid that I was freaking myself out, but I couldn't seem to stop.

Emily looked up at me, seeming to weigh her words before saying, "Possible new mission. But...it's a weird one. Nothing like we've ever dealt with before. Not even sure if..." she shook her head. "Never mind. How about this: You go home and rest, and then I'll tell you about it. But *only* if you rest."

I felt like a pouting child when I grumbled, "Fine," but Emily only chuckled and patted my shoulder. I was still curious what this "weird" case could be, but I was honestly too tired to keep badgering her, and she was clearly too determined to look out for me. The brat.

They drove me home and I contemplated whether I had enough stamina left to go all the way upstairs to sleep on my bed. Banishing ghosts was tiring work, and the sofa was so much closer.

Just as I was getting a blanket to curl up with, I heard the doorbell ring.

Frustrated, I threw my blanket onto the sofa and went to the see who it was. I must have been exceptionally tired, because there was no explaining why I just opened the door without even checking to see who was there.

"Oh, hello," I said to the woman standing on our porch. I was surprised to see her there, as if the ringing doorbell hadn't signaled to me that someone would be waiting outside. For a wild, panicked moment, I wondered if she was a ghost, but everything about her indicated she was human, so I tried to get my emotions under control.

She smiled. "Hello. My name is Elixabete Otxoa, I was sent by the agency." She spoke with an accent I couldn't place, though it had a musical quality to it.

"Hi," I said, still a little startled. She had dark, olive skin, with twinkling black eyes and an impish smile. "Um," I stuttered. "You...the agency sent you?" I asked, brow furrowing. My father had mentioned hiring another housekeeper, but I hadn't expected anyone today.

"Yes, they said you needed a housekeeper? Said you were having a bit of trouble finding a good fit?"

I blushed a little, wondering how in the world I could explain that in a way that wouldn't make us sound like troublemakers.

"Um, right, yeah, for some reason...that has been kind of an issue," I said. So much for eloquence.

Elixabete's smile broadened. "Well, I'm the one they send in for special cases," she said, adding a wink.

Oh, that makes me feel so much better, I thought as I recalled all our past housekeepers.

"Right. Um. Can I see your paperwork?" I asked. I didn't get any weird ghostly-sense from her, but I had become suspicious of everyone. Besides, normal people could be dangerous all on their own.

She nodded and handed me an envelope. I opened it and skimmed the documents. Everything was in order. Trying to look like I also had my life together, I smiled and stepped back, letting her inside. I guessed her to be in her mid-thirties, short and curvy, her long hair in a neat bun.

"Glad to have you here, um, Elixabete? Is that right?" I asked, checking the paperwork again.

"That's it!" she said brightly, looking around the house. "Your home is lovely."

"Thanks," I said, taking a look myself. It actually was, but I hadn't had much time to appreciate that lately, and it was kind of a shame.

I gave her a quick tour, explaining where everything was. As I showed her around the second story, Elixabete put a hand on my shoulder, stopping me in my tracks.

"Rosalind," she said gently. "If I may say so, you seem tired. Why don't you go back to whatever you were doing before I arrived, and I'll get started with what you've shown me so far. If I have any questions, I'll find you," she said with a reassuring smile.

"O-okay," I said, returning her smile.

I shook myself a bit, trying to clear my head. I didn't know what I'd tell my dad if this housekeeper left, too, but I couldn't worry about that now. I had to get some rest so I could go back to fixing all the problems I'd caused by going up to the mountain and...doing whatever it was I did. I'd closed the portal, I knew that much, but something else had happened, too. And it was causing even more of a mess.

I collapsed onto my bed and drifted off for a while.

The soft buzz of my phone woke me. I grabbed it, still half-asleep, and pulled it to me.

It was a text from Ford. I checked the clock and saw that I'd slept for almost two hours. This surprised me—sleeping didn't usually come easily anymore. It was good I'd woken up; I needed to get ready for our next job. I rubbed my eyes and opened the text.

Hey, how'd it go today?

I reoriented myself so I could type, *Eh*

That bad, huh?

Not really. I just hate it, I sent back.

Ford responded in his usual style: *Right. Having a superpower. SO lame*

I don't have a superpower, I replied.

Ford's indignation was palpable. *Well I know I can't send ghosts away WITH MY MIND*

I rolled my eyes, *You poor deprived soul*

lol

I thought perhaps he was done, but then I received, *You still going to take care of the banshee?*

Apparently he'd been in touch with Derek or Emily. I sighed and texted back: *Yes*

Cool. Can I come?

Sure. I stared at my phone, suddenly suspicious, and sent a second text. *Why?*

I want to test a theory

I rolled my eyes. *What theory?*

He sent an angel emoji.

Ford. I hoped the severity of my tone could be conveyed via text.

You'll all-caps at me

I scowled. *What is it?*

...aliens

IT'S NOT ALIENS!

SEE!?

I laughed, despite myself. *Whatever. It's at 3. I'll have Emily send you the address*

Excellent

I got up then and decided to check on Elixabete.

She was happily cooking in the kitchen. When she spotted me, she gave another broad smile.

"Hello, Rosalind! Can I fix you anything? Tea? Coffee? A snack?"

I shook my head. "No, thank you, I just want to make sure you're doing all right."

"Everything's just fine," she said.

I nodded. More awake now, I noticed that Elixabete wore a collection of bracelets and necklaces adorned with crystals and intricately-carved symbols. They reminded me of the kind of thing Aunt Fiona's new-age hippie friends wore.

"Well, I've got a load of laundry going, and dinner will be ready in about half an hour. I also noticed that there are still some unpacked boxes in the guest rooms, so if you'd like me to take care of that, I can."

I blinked. "Oh. Okay. Uh, I'll ask my dad."

She nodded and returned to her cooking, humming softly to herself.

I studied her movements. She seemed very relaxed.

Very at ease. That didn't mean anything, though. She'd only been here for a couple of hours. I had tried expelling the ghosts around my house, but it didn't seem to work long-term. I hadn't seen the foreign ghost for a few days, or Diego since that first night, but the creepy old woman, the girl from the theatre, and a few new ones were keeping up with regular appearances, despite my best efforts to banish them. Despite knowing that I was at the epicenter of this, I didn't fully understand what was happening; I only knew one thing—it meant no one here was safe.

Well, save for my father, who seemed to repel ghosts naturally. I still didn't fully understand that, but my mother's journal confirmed it; ghosts left him alone. Maybe Elixabete had that same...whatever it was.

Either way, I hoped Elixabete would at least get enough cooking done to last us a few days before she left and never came back. This would be three strikes at the agency, and they might not want to send any more of their people to us after that.

I turned away. I couldn't worry about Elixabete today.

I had a banshee to get rid of.

Three

The woman, our client, was waiting for us, framed in the door. Her face was drawn and pale. I watched her from the car for a moment before getting out, dreading what I had to do next. It didn't matter how often I did this; my stomach still dropped every time.

"Hello, Julia!" Emily called, making her way up the path.

I put my phone away—I'd been reading yet another article about the strange spike in crimes lately—and grabbed some equipment, following Emily up the path. The house was small, a little older, but very well-maintained. It had an almost whimsical look, different from most houses in Las Vegas. At least, compared to the ones I'd seen in the month I'd lived in the city. Which was a lot, actually, as Emily had me on assignments all over town.

"Aww, this place is so cute," Hazel said. She took out her phone and snapped a few pictures.

"Hazel, what are you doing?" I asked.

"It's for my inspiration board!" she said.

I shook my head and crossed the little yard to the homeowner, taking a moment to mentally push away any stray ghosts who might be drifting towards me. I seemed to attract the now, and I didn't need any extra ghosts getting in my way during an...extraction. I didn't want to think of these as exorcisms, it was too weird.

"Julia, this is Rosalind, one of my associates," Emily introduced me as I approached.

I glanced at her sideways. I'd more or less gotten used to Emily's professional demeanor when on a job, but still. 'Associate' or 'ghost-whispering weirdo'—same thing, I guess.

"Hi, Rosalind," Julia said. She had all the signs of living in a ghost-infested house: She was jumpy, her left eye was twitching, she kept looking around for the next attack, she was pale with dark circles under her eyes, and she had a few bandages on her arms.

Julia looked me over, then glanced between Emily and I. "No offense, but...what can you actually *do* about this?"

I couldn't blame her; a bunch of teenagers didn't seem like the right crew to evict a malevolent spirit.

I looked at Emily for the answer, as I was *not* good at selling my skills.

"I know it's hard to believe, but I promise you, we've done dozens of spirit removals and have a one-hundred percent success rate," Emily answered.

Derek walked over then, nodding to Julia as he

passed, lugging bags of supplies.

I looked back to see where Ford had gotten to. He was still by the van, talking to someone on his phone. He looked agitated. I watched him hang up and stuff his phone angrily into his pocket. His face was unusually serious.

When he turned and saw me looking at him, he flashed me a big smile, and I tried to return it before looking back toward the house.

"I'm...gonna go get set up," I said, excusing myself in a desperate attempt to escape having to try and explain my weird powers.

Emily kept talking to Julia while I followed Derek inside. He sat down and began meticulously setting up his equipment.

The second I was through the threshold, the presence I'd gotten a vague sense of became far stronger. I shivered, head spinning a little in the wave of energy that hit me as I stepped inside. When I stopped feeling dizzy, I looked around. There was a lot of broken glass—windows boarded up with a few jagged shards left in the frame, picture frames stacked in the corner, their glass fronts missing, some of the pictures torn. I was sure there were cups and glasses missing from the cabinets.

Two kids were sitting on the sofa. One—the girl, about eleven—had a big bandage on her face, the type they put over gashes that need stitches. I glanced at Derek's cast, fidgeting uncomfortably at the memory. He ignored my concern, too busy rubbing down the table with a sanitizing wipe.

"You know that does nothing, right?" Emily asked as she set her bag on the floor.

"Makes me feel better. That's something," he muttered, arranging the EMF detector and thermometers on the newly-cleaned table in careful patterns. They went from largest to smallest, but there was some other order to them, too, though it didn't make sense to me.

I set down the bag of equipment I'd brought in and returned my attention to the kids, who watched us curiously, fearfully. The boy was younger, about Diego's age. My stomach knotted when I saw his nervous little face. I hoped I could help this little boy before it was too late for him.

"Jodie, Bobby, come on," Julia called. The kids got up and followed their mother out, lacking the liveliness and curiosity kids should have.

"Can you really do this?" the girl, Jodie, asked.

"Uh..." I shifted awkwardly. "Yeah."

Hazel patted me on the arm as she walked inside. "Roz is a natural."

"I'll get whatever's in your house out," I promised, a little less confident in my own ability than Hazel seemed to be.

She nodded and pulled her brother along.

The tension in the air was palpable. I could feel the itch of paranormal energy strung throughout the house. I couldn't see or hear anything yet, but I felt it the way you feel a storm in the air before it hits. The smell of ozone and the foreboding pressure of the air pressed down on me.

Ford stepped inside and Julia took her children, driving off. We were alone in a stranger's home.

"Why are you guys still setting up all this

equipment?" Hazel asked as she sat down on the sofa. "Isn't Roz basically a human ghost detector?"

"It's my process," Derek said, distracted. "Besides, Em still wants to gather data."

Ford nodded. "As do I."

I ignored them. Ford was still obsessed with finding a scientific explanation. Emily and Derek just wanted all the data they could get to back up their grant proposal. At this point, I figured they'd either win the grant, or get us all in trouble with our parents. Maybe both.

Emily reached into one of the bags and pulled out a bunch of things that looked like big black tactical headphones and passed them out.

"Here, these are electronic earmuffs," she said as I studied mine. "They'll let us hear each other talk, but any sounds over twenty-two decibels will be reduced any anything over eighty-two decibels will be cancelled out—at least, mostly. Should stop the banshee from rupturing our eardrums or anything like that," she said.

"Good thinking!" Hazel said, still excited about this.

I frowned. "Em, ghosts can mess with electronics, what if the banshee breaks these?"

She tapped the casing around the ear-covers. "Even if the tech is completely busted, these are still decent hearing protection. Way better than going in unprotected." She showed me how to turn mine on and put a pair over her ears.

"Fair enough." I put mine on, too, and turned the little dial to power them up. I heard a soft hum, but nothing invasive, and when the others spoke, I heard them as if through a speaker.

Derek, having lined all his little devices up neatly,

began switching them on. The sensors immediately came to life, lighting up or beeping or doing whatever else they did. I spotted a rush of information feeding into a computer screen. The cameras and sound recorders were up and running, humming softly in the background.

"We've got a presence," Emily whispered.

I closed my eyes. The energy was moving, swirling. I couldn't make sense of it, not mixed with what my eyes were seeing, but I could tell it had noticed us, and it wasn't happy we were here. I picked up a slight static in my headphones as it moved around us and hoped they wouldn't short out.

The presence was strong. Aggressive. I could 'see' my friends, too—I was starting to realize that some of the energy I felt was from other people—but they felt different from the entity. Familiar. So unassuming I could almost miss it. I usually did.

Now, I was far more concerned with the jagged, unfamiliar energy whipping around the edges of the room.

I could feel it circling us like a vulture. The ghost moved too quickly for me to pin it down. I tried to concentrate, but the effort made my head throb.

"Got a temperature drop," Derek reported. "That was fast."

A loud cry snapped me out of my daze, cut off by the headphones as the screech rose in pitch until it became distant and weak. I opened my eyes. The detectors and readers on the table were going wild, readings coming in fast.

"Roz?" Emily asked tightly.

"I can't pin it down..." I answered.

"Wind speeds at thirteen miles per hour," Derek reported as the air swirled, blowing back my hair and rustling the pages of his notebook.

The problem with my supposed 'power' was that I needed to concentrate to make it work. Hard to do in general, but especially when everything in the room was flying about. Plus, I had no idea how to control it. Sometimes it worked, sometimes not so much.

I knelt down as the wind picked up, causing lamps and remotes to soar through the air. In the kitchen, cabinets opened and closed violently. I didn't expect this torrent from a banshee, and it was throwing me off my already shaky game.

"Rosalind!" Hazel shouted. "Now would be a good time for...your...power-stuff!"

I curled up on the ground, shielding my head, desperate for a moment of silence that would let me clear my mind.

Not happening. Push through.

I squeezed my eyes shut, concentrating as best I could on the chaotic energy causing this whirlwind. As I did, it coalesced, and all at once it was before me, coming right at me.

I opened my eyes and screamed. I saw the mangled face of the vengeful spirit racing toward me. And it seemed like it was visible to the others, as well, because I heard several yelps of surprise.

It was grotesque—less human-like than most ghosts, more vaguely humanoid in shape, but overall distinctly *different*. It had a gaunt, long form and gleaming black eyes, wide, like two shining marbles set in its chalk-white face. Its body was skeletal, draped in wispy grey smoke and mist that hung form it almost like cloth. I couldn't see most of it, as it seemed to blend into the shadowy smoke surrounding it, but its face was clear, and I met its dark eyes as best I could.

I tried to hold it in my mind and push back, but I couldn't get myself to focus.

A shriek began to build in the room, swirling around me and echoing on all sides, and though the sound was dulled, I could still feel the power of it in my bones. The pain in my head lessened and the room abruptly went silent. I had fallen, and now sat up, greeted with a familiar but still dreaded sight: Darkness.

I looked around, turning fast and clambering to my feet. I stood, crouched, braced for another attack. It was Julia's house, but dark. The furniture was more or less in place, though it had a stillness to it that made my skin crawl. This had happened before, and every time, it was trouble.

"Hello?" I called into the eerie silence. The quiet swallowed up my voice. I was alone. The realization weighed heavily on me. All I could hear was the soft hum of my headphones, barely noticeable in my own world, now prominent in the oppressive silence.

"Hazel!" I called. "Ford!"

Something moved behind me and I spun around. The banshee. It wasn't screaming now, but I recognized it from before. It hovered at a distance, eyeing me and growling a low, eerie sound.

I swallowed hard and sank slowly to my knees.

"It's okay," I whispered, holding my hands up. "I'm not here to hurt you. I'm here to help."

The ghost snarled and recoiled further. I didn't know

why it was so afraid of me, but it was acting like a frightened animal now. I took a deep breath of stale air and scooted closer, assuring the banshee that I was friendly.

Meanwhile, I was barely keeping from panicking. I hadn't slipped into this darkness since before the incident on the mountain. I was on a job, with a very powerful and violent ghost, and I was completely cut off from my friends.

I was only a few feet from the ghost now. I could feel its growls in my bones.

"Hi," I whispered. Its black eyes—almost invisible in the darkness—seemed to stare at me, though I couldn't imagine how it could see. Maybe it felt energy, like I did.

Most of its body had a hazy, fuzzy quality, like it wasn't quite there. Like I was seeing it through water. There was less smoke swirling around it here, and that made it look small, helpless.

I reached out, slowly, and it snarled, screeching at me. I quickly withdrew my hand, keeping my eyes locked on the ghost. It eased forward, circling me slowly.

"What do you want?" I asked softly. I was still trying to help these spirits whenever I could, but it was hard when I had no idea how. I didn't think I could just will this one away, and I also didn't think it had enough of a grip on reality to know why it was vengeful anymore. In all likelihood, it had forgotten its human life and was simply consumed by anger and pain. I'd seen a few of those, but this was the most intense case yet.

It flickered and disappeared, and I blinked, initially too stunned to be horrified. Had it gone back up to where my friends were? Had it gone farther down, to some even emptier dimension I couldn't reach?

I did my best not to panic, closing my eyes and feeling out for the banshee. I could feel a lot of vague ghost energy in my general vicinity, but none matched the aggressive feel of this particular ghost.

While I was feeling it out, I heard—in my mind, not with my ears—an inhuman screech. The headphones did nothing to dull this cry, and I felt it like it was stabbing into my skull. Not the banshee's cry; something else. Something *worse.* I could see flashes of forest around me, even with my eyes closed. I opened them, looking around the darkness, but I could still see the forest in my mind, almost like it was overlaid atop my actual surroundings.

And the worst part was I recognized it.

These were the woods around the clearing where the portal had been opened, where I'd fought the Shadow, where I'd nearly died in a massive forest fire.

The trees around me were charred and blackened, but not completely destroyed, and I seemed to be running, panting and gasping for air, fleeing further from the damage of the fire and deeper into the untouched woods.

Behind me, that awful scream rang out again. It sounded almost like the shriek of a hawk, but too loud. It rattled in my bones. I felt the sound in a wave of terror that shot up my spine and prickled across my skin. Suddenly, the banshee was almost a welcome alternative.

And then I was back in the darkness, stumbling to catch my balance, panting and shaking from a horrible vision. I didn't know what to do with it. Last time I'd had one of these, it had come true only a few weeks later. Was this a peek into my future? Was I going to be chased through the woods by some horrible nightmare monster?

I didn't have time to worry about this, because the banshee reappeared. In a blur of movement, it leaped for me, tackling me to the ground and shocking me with how solid it felt. I screamed and pushed back with all my strength, sending it sprawling back.

Home, home, home, I thought frantically.

The banshee raced at me again, screeching.

"Rosalind!"

I toppled over, all semblance of grace lost. Three shifts in one minute was more than I could take. My eyes burned and my head spun from shifting from falling in darkness to hitting the ground in a brightly lit room full of noise and movement and people.

"Are you okay?" Hazel demanded, pulling me up.

"I—what happened?" I asked, looking around frantically for the banshee.

"No idea," Emily said. You just started shaking and fell over.

I blinked. That was interesting. I sat up and pulled the earmuffs off. "So I wasn't...gone? At all?"

"Uh..." Derek said helpfully. "No?"

"Oh," I said, pushing my hair more or less into place. "Well. That really clears things up."

"You're a mess, Roz," Ford said, also apparently feeling super helpful.

I swatted away a few remaining stray hairs. "Yeah, well, you would be too if you got dragged into a bunch of different nightmares where a banshee tried to eat your face and a monster chased you through a forest."

Everyone just stared at me.

I coughed away the smell of the burnt forest still lingering in my nose and stood up.

"So anyway," I said. "Get any good readings?"

The lights began to flicker before anyone could answer, and I spun around instinctively.

"Still getting them, in fact," Derek said.

The banshee materialized before me. She moved forward, slowly, as if she wasn't sure what she wanted to do with me. Her motions were jerky and uneven and reminded me of a malfunctioning robot. I fumbled with the earmuffs, slipping them back on in a hurry.

"Roz!" Hazel screamed.

The specter reached me and, in a swift movement I couldn't see, had her hands around my neck. And then, she began to scream.

I clawed at her. My friends moved towards me, but ducked when her scream pitched up and shattered several lightbulbs, sending glass flying like shrapnel through the room. In her distraction, I placed my hand on her shoulder and concentrated.

I'm sorry, I thought.

She screamed, thrashed, but couldn't get away. I had the power this time, and she had made too much contact with me—it was a mistake I could use.

Be at peace, I wished, hoping that was really what happened to the poor lost souls when I sent them away.

Let go.

A brilliant light shone, mixing with the banshee's cry. And then it stopped.

I opened my eyes and looked around.

She was gone.

I closed my eyes again and felt for her. No, it wasn't a mistake this time—she was nowhere I could sense. I sighed and slumped to the ground, too exhausted to stay standing. Ford caught my arm and eased me down.

"That was incredible!" Emily said.

"Readings are off the charts!" Derek added. "Tapering off now, but we peaked a few times there."

"You okay?" Ford whispered to me.

I nodded. "Yeah...yeah. I'm fine. Just...woozy."

Hazel was by my side, looking concerned and excited. I let Ford and Hazel help me to the sofa. I didn't even sit, opting instead to lie down, eyes closed, ignoring everything. The others assured me that I didn't have to worry about packing up—my job was getting rid of the ghosts, they'd take care of the equipment and cleanup. I still felt kinda bad, but this time I was so sick and exhausted, I couldn't even attempt to help.

When everything was packed up, and we'd cleaned up as best we could, Julia was called back to the house. She didn't seem to care that she needed to replace half her lightbulbs, she was just relieved that it was over.

After that, we went to the café where Derek worked. His shift started in an hour, so we had just enough time to go over what I'd seen and summarize the job before he'd have to start work.

It had started to rain while we were in Julia's house, and the downpour continued, as we sat in the café, making the sky unusually dark. We'd passed three accidents and one miscellaneous police car, sirens on, racing in the opposite direction. There was still so much chaos, and I couldn't help but suspect ghosts as the cause.

But I had to focus for now, so I did my best to explain what had happened in the darkness with the banshee, and the strange vision I'd had. It was a challenge. Making sense of it was still hard for *me*, and I'd been there. Emily listened intently. Derek took copious notes. Hazel got excited and kept interrupting with theories or ideas to add.

And Ford? Ford just looked like he was taking this new information and fitting it into his 'this is aliens' puzzle.

Personally, I wasn't in the mood to theorize or sort out data. I was shaken. I kept seeing the forest, the charred remains of trees, the blur of leaves as I ran. I kept hearing the screeching howl of the beast chasing me.

Emily was very curious about the vision.

"Did it sound like any animal you've heard before?"

"No."

"How far was it from you?"

"I don't know."

"Did you see any landmarks or signs to let you know exactly where you were?"

"Nope," I said, rubbing my eyes.

"Em, that's probably enough for today," Derek said. "I've got to get ready for my shift, anyway."

She made a pouty face, but agreed.

Ford drove us all home after that. When it was just the two of us left, he turned to me.

"Hey, so, you wanna tackle that journal again? We'll take it easy, maybe just one page? I have some theories..."

I was torn. I wanted to, and yet I never wanted to again.

"Yeah, we should," I said.

"Only if you're up for it."

"Yeah. Not today, though."

"Cool. Text me when you are."

I nodded, mumbled a goodbye, and got out. I watched him circle the cul-du-sac and pull into his garage as I made my way into my own house.

Elixabete was still there, doing laundry. The house was *spotless*, and smelled fresh and clean.

"Elixabete?" I called out, still a little uncertain of the pronunciation. I wondered what language it was, and where she was from. No doubt my father, the conversationalist and friend of everyone, would find out and tell me.

"Hello, Rosalind. Did you have fun with your friends?" she called from the laundry room.

"Uh...yeah," I said. Thinking about it, I started to giggle for some reason. It wasn't funny, not really, but I couldn't stop myself.

Elixabete came over holding a basket of fluffy, fresh-from-the-dryer towels neatly folded.

"That's good," she said. "Are you hungry?"

I nodded. I hadn't eaten at Leone Café, as I'd still been nauseous, but now I was famished.

Elixabete put the basket by the stairs and led me into the kitchen, where I could smell something delicious cooking.

She heaped a bowl with food and told me to sit at the island. I did, inspecting my meal. A wonderful-smelling stew served over steaming white rice.

"This is good. What's it called?" I asked as I tried a bite.

"Marmitako, my mother used to make it. It was my favorite meal as a child."

I was so hungry, I scarfed it down, finishing it within minutes.

"Wow, you did like it," Elixabete said with a laugh.

I nodded. "It was delicious."

"Do you want more?" she asked.

I shook my head, getting up and rinsing my plate in the sink. "No, thank you, I'm...not feeling well. I think I'll lie down for a little while."

She smiled. "Let me know if you need anything."

I thanked her again and went up to my room.

Despite how tired I was, though, I couldn't sleep. My body was exhausted, but my mind was racing. I couldn't stop thinking about the vision. Before, I'd had dreams that ended up coming true. That had been bad enough, but this time, it wasn't even a dream. And it wasn't the Shadow, or anything like it, it was some horrible, mindless beast that seemed intent on killing me.

I had been afraid the ghosts might kill me, and that thought had been horrifying. Now, though, I had a new fear—that some hideous beast from another dimension would rip me apart.

I laid there, listening to the rain and willing it to lull me to sleep. Slowly, I began to relax.

Then my phone buzzed and I groaned. I had given my friends a specific vibration pattern, so I'd always know it was them, and that's what I'd just heard. It was Emily, with a short text that chilled me to the bone.

Remember that new case I mentioned? Got a lead on

it. I think it's related to the vision you had today.

I sat up, suddenly wide awake and shaking from adrenaline at the mere memory of how that had felt. With trembling hands, I typed back: *What is it?*

Can't be sure yet, but it's not a ghost. I think it's some kind of actual monster, and I think it's attacking people.

FOUR

All paranormal creatures, I had discovered, were horrifying.

No matter what I looked up, they were all awful. Emily didn't know exactly what this was, but there was some creature in the mountains scaring hikers and making inhuman sounds. Basically, all we knew was that it wasn't a mountain lion or any normal animal that lived up there—it was something new, and it had appeared right after the fire.

So I researched everything. In large part because I didn't know what actually existed anymore. Ghosts were real, and I'd more or less accepted that, but if other things were real...that somehow seemed even more unbelievable. And terrible.

I'd also discovered that searching 'paranormal monsters' was not a narrow enough filter—I was getting bombarded with information about *everything*, from every culture and mythology, and by the end of my attempt to do some research, my head was spinning.

All I had were more questions. What was this thing? A demon? An ogre? A goblin? A wendigo? A chupacabra? Which of those were real, and which were myths? Were they *all* real?

And, more pressingly, what was I supposed to do with any of these? I had just barely figured out ghosts and now...whatever this was...existed. And I had to get rid of it, apparently.

I sat on my bed, laptop open, doing research and generally stressing myself out. I had band-aids around three fingers on my right hand and two on my left from picking until I bled. As I did my research, I fiddled with a stress ball to try and keep myself from picking anymore.

Beside me, my phone kept buzzing. I grabbed it and turned it to silent, deciding I didn't want to deal with whatever the others were saying just yet. I needed to wrap my head around this whole monster concept by myself before I started sorting through their ideas.

The problem was I really didn't think there was anything I could do about this. I dealt with *ghosts*, monsters or demons or whatever were...I had no idea, but there was a part of me that wanted to argue that they weren't the same as ghosts, and therefore I couldn't—perhaps even *shouldn't*—try to deal with them.

Speaking of ghosts...there was one in my room now, not visible to me, but simply pulling books from my shelf and letting them drop. I still wasn't entirely sure *why* some ghosts acted like this, but from what I could gather it was just boredom and frustration and the desire to do *anything*.

"Please stop that," I said absently, focusing on pushing the spirit away. I felt the subtle change in the room as they left, but couldn't tell if it was from my efforts or of their own accord.

There was still so much I didn't understand. But at least no more of my books would get thrown on the floor.

When I could no longer stand to keep researching paranormal creatures, I closed my computer and set it aside. Then I laid back, checking all my messages. One was actually from my dad telling me about some fashion show Veronica had this weekend, and telling me I could invite my friends. I didn't really want to, but if I was going to get dragged along to it, I may as well have my friends with me. Technically, I knew I could tell my dad I didn't want to go, and he'd respect that, but I hated to disappoint him, so I resigned myself to just going and bringing some backup.

The rest of my messages, as I'd suspected, were all on the group chat. The other four were discussing various monsters—what each of them suspected this was, how to deal with it, tactics, logistics, and how to get rid of it. With a few semi-relevant memes thrown in the mix. I was supposed to invite them to the fashion show, but I'd do that later—they were way too hung up on this new task. Hazel brought up the very good point that this wasn't our jurisdiction. Ford brought up the even better point that demons or whatever almost definitely didn't exist. Derek seemed to agree that this might not be for us, but Emily was adamant that we at least check it out.

Roz? The last text said. It was from Ford, and despite

being only one word, it almost seemed like he was asking me to decide. Like it all hinged on me.

I closed my eyes against that thought. It still gave me chills. The words of the Shadow echoed in my mind once more.

She's too dangerous.

I typed out my response and hit send.

No.

Emily replied as I was sitting up and stretching with, *:(*

No way Em. I can't handle this, I shot back. I was already scared of taking my friends with me into ghost territory. After reading about the various kinds of monster this could be, I was certain that if any of them were real, and we messed with whatever this was, we'd all end up dead.

Can we at least check it out? she begged.

And get killed? No thx. Weren't you just telling me to work less and relax?

We don't have to DO anything to it, I just want to investigate.

I wasn't dragging my friends into any more danger. I still remembered the sound of Derek's bone breaking. The pierce of Emily's screams as she fought against an angry spirit. The terror on Hazel's face whenever a chill entered the room.

I remembered Ford's face, tight with fear and orange in the blazing light of the fire as he pulled me away from the flames.

No. I'd clean up the extra ghosts around town, that was my responsibility, but not monsters. I couldn't handle real monsters.

Against all odds, I slept well.

I woke to my alarm, instead of ghosts, and laid there for a moment—first confused, then relieved—just enjoying waking up like a normal person.

Then I remembered that weird paranormal monsters apparently existed, and that kind of killed the mood.

While I was brushing my teeth, Hazel texted me, asking me to pick her up so we could meet Emily later. There was some update she wanted to give us in person, apparently. Which was a bad sign.

I agreed to it then put it out of my mind, blasting some music while I got ready instead.

My dad was in the kitchen making coffee when I got downstairs, and I sat with him for a bit. I wasn't usually a big coffee fan, but we had a new coffee maker and my dad was having a lot of fun trying out new lattes and cappuccinos and other concoctions, so I was making it a point to try them.

"How do you like that one?" he asked.

"It's good," I said, and it was true—probably because it was more milk and sugar than coffee, but still.

He smiled, sitting down across from me. "What's today looking like for you?"

"Gonna go pick up Hazel and meet up with some friends," I said.

"Good. Good, have fun. I'm glad you two are getting to spend so much time together."

I nodded. "Yeah, me too." It was true. As stressful as the past few weeks had been, I didn't know what I would have done without Hazel. Not only had she helped me deal with all of this, but she had introduced me to Emily and Derek.

Even Ford, I realized. I might have met him on my own, being his neighbor, but I doubt I ever would have talked to him beyond required pleasantries had she not taken me to that party.

It was odd to realize, but all the friends I had here were thanks to Hazel.

Which is really all my friends in general, I thought. I hadn't been particularly social since high school started, so I hadn't had anyone to leave behind. Which made leaving easier, I think. I was tired of Los Angeles. I was tired of the memories I'd had there, and the life I'd lived there. I wanted to be somewhere else, to start over, to be near Hazel. And somehow that had led to me having friends. Even if things were ridiculous and stressful now. That wasn't even that new—things had been stressful before. The main difference now was it was weird and supernatural.

Considering this, I almost felt like it was a worthy trade-off. Besides, I likely would have had all these issues anyway. Best to do so with a support system.

We finished our coffee, and I gave my dad a hug before leaving.

My car was parked in the driveway, since we had been sorting through boxes in the garage. So I went through the front door, nearly running into the person standing there.

"Ah! Oh! Sorry!" I cried.

"It's all right, Rosalind," Elixabete said with a laugh.

I stopped dead in my tracks. "E-Elixabete? What are you doing here?" I blurted out.

She raised her eyebrows. "I'm scheduled to arrive at nine, aren't I?" She said, checking her watch.

"Uh," I laughed nervously. "Right. Of course. That—that makes sense. That you're here. Now. Sorry."

"Are you going out?" she asked.

"Yeah, just...just visiting with some friends," I said, still fumbling over my words. "Here, let me introduce you to my dad."

I led her inside and called my dad out of his office. They shook hands and started chatting, and I knew they'd be fine without me, so I ducked out with a quick wave to both and headed outside, closing the door behind me.

But rather than head to my car, I stood on the porch, staring at the closed front door, wondering why, at the absolute height of my house's ghost infestation, Elixabete was returning for a second day of work, seeming perfectly confident and happy.

Shaking it off—or, I guess, setting it aside for later—I got in my car and drove to Hazel's. She directed me where to drive from there. I didn't know the area perfectly yet, but I knew it well enough to know where this was.

"Why are we meeting them at a grocery store?" I asked.

Hazel shrugged. "Emily wanted to see us, in person, *now*, and that's where they are, apparently."

I decided not to keep asking "Why?" like a sugared-up toddler and just park the car, following Hazel inside.

"She says they're by the cereal," Hazel said, checking her phone.

I followed her through the unfamiliar store. We

spotted them halfway down the aisle. Derek was reading the back of a box, one hand on the grocery cart beside him. Emily sat in the cart, legs crossed, typing away madly on a new phone. Not her phone—that was perched beside her on a bag of rice, and instantly recognizable by its shiny purple case.

"Why are you in a shopping cart?" I asked her as we approached.

She looked up. "Derek got a new phone."

I raised my eyebrows. "...I feel like I'm missing crucial information here."

Emily returned her attention to the phone. "Derek got a new phone, and it needs to be set up. He doesn't want to set it up, so he asked me to do it. I said okay, but then he needed to go grocery shopping and I tagged along because if his phone isn't set up *now*, I can't properly antagonize him at all hours of the day. And I *know* he'll forget to do it for a least three days if I leave him to his own devices. *But*, I didn't want to walk around looking at a phone and bumping into stuff, so I said I'd set up his phone if I could sit in the grocery cart while he did his shopping, which is why I'm in here like a five-year-old."

"Good thing you're about the same size as one," Derek said.

Emily rolled her head around to glare at him.

"What?" he said. "You are."

She threw a bag of chips at him and he caught it, laughing.

"I'm sorry, I thought there was something important you had to tell us? In person? Immediately?" Hazel asked, failing to hide her amusement.

"Right. That," Emily said, repositioning herself so her legs dangled over the side of the cart. She kept working on Derek's phone while he pushed the cart along. We followed, listening to Emily.

"Our local mountain monster? It attacked someone. Like, *really* attacked someone," she said.

"What?" I whispered.

She glanced at me before continuing. "This woman, Tricia Schmidt." Emily grabbed her phone off the bag of rice to show me the article, complete with a picture. The woman was pretty and smiling, with thick red curls going everywhere. According to the caption, it was her last posted picture before she went missing. For a second, my heart raced—at first glance, she had reminded me of Rowan. They didn't *really* look alike; their faces had completely different shapes and features, and Tricia had much kinder eyes. Upon first seeing her, though, the shock of red hair and pale skin reminded me of the terrifying professor, and how I'd been avoiding contacting her for days now.

Then that shock passed, and the headline—*Local Woman Missing, Presumed Dead from Mountain Lion Attack*—hit me full force. My knees wobbled.

"Apparently she went for a hike," Emily went on, "and...well, they found a portion of her backpack...and a lot of blood...the pros say it doesn't really look like a mountain lion attack, but they don't know what it could be. We don't get a lot of mountain lion attacks here so...it's probably whatever's new to the forest."

I couldn't meet her eyes. I couldn't move. My heart was hammering. I hadn't wanted to deal with this, I had wanted it to just disappear, and now someone was dead.

And I didn't know how to handle this, but I probably *was* the only person who stood a chance.

"I..." my tongue felt dry and heavy, like sandpaper in my mouth. "I don't know how to get rid of a...a...whatever this is! What am I supposed to *do*?"

"Well, that's why I want us to talk strategy," Emily said. "So we can be prepared. Trust me, I don't want to get hurt or die, either—I just think if we go into this ready for the fight we're facing, we can win. We can figure this out, Roz."

She sounded so hopeful and confident, and I decided to just lean on her certainty for now. Maybe it would rub off on me. We walked along in silence beside Derek for a while as he gathered groceries, steering us towards the produce section.

"Have you had any dreams regarding this?" he asked.

I shook my head.

"Well, keep an eye out for them—you seem sensitive to...psychic things," Emily said, back to working on Derek's phone.

I made a face. "I'm not psychic."

"You might catch glimpses, though," Derek said. "It's not uncommon for people with a sixth sense to experience a little psychic awareness or develop some basic psychic abilities. It's kind of like how a lot of psychological disorders and mental illnesses go together, or even cause each other—seeing ghosts is related to ESP in a basic sense. You've already had semi-prophetic dreams; I'd be surprised if you didn't have more. It's like...paranormal comorbidity," he said, dropping a bag of oranges in Emily's lap.

Emily looked up at me. “Speaking of which, what *have* you been dreaming about?”

“Not much. The ghosts. The fire,” I looked away. “My mother.”

Emily nodded sadly, but Derek gave me a look I couldn’t quite place. All I knew was that ever since learning she was dead, he’d started getting a little weird whenever I mentioned my mother. But not weird like most people did, where they were awkward and uncomfortable, which made it all the more confusing.

“Are we really the right people to deal with a...weird forest monster?” Hazel asked.

Derek headed toward the self-checkout and we trailed along beside him.

“Who else can?” Emily asked. “I know it’s risky, but I’m sure if we make a game plan, we can handle this.” she said, climbing out of the cart as Derek loaded up bags.

“Need help, Derek?” I asked, wondering how much his arm impeded his day to day tasks.

“No, thanks. I got it,” he assured me.

“Derek has a very precise method for bagging groceries,” Emily said, as though this was something she was quite accustomed to. She was still messing around with his new phone.

“I—okay, look,” I said, still nervous. Pacing and shaking and wringing my hands as I spoke, “I’m not saying I don’t want to help because I do, I do! I just...” I ran my hands back through my hair. “I don’t know what to *do*, Emily!”

A mom with a toddler in her cart turned to look at me with mild concern.

“Roz. Hey.” Emily said, catching me in my pacing and

gripping me by my shoulders, forcing me to look her in the eye. “You have powers,” she said, dropping her voice low so the other shoppers couldn’t hear us. “I have knowledge. We have the organization king over there,” she nodded towards Derek. “And no one’s got more spirit than Haze.” She laughed, adding almost as an afterthought, “And he might be kinda ridiculous, but I can’t deny that Ford’s damn smart. We can do this. I know we can.”

I wasn’t so sure about that, but I didn’t argue.

We made arrangements to go up to the mountain—a prospect which terrified me—and investigate this monster business.

FIVE

After dropping Hazel off, I took a moment in my car to call Ford while parked.

"Hey, Roz," he said.

"Hey. That monster? It...things are getting worse. So I have to do something. Are you free to meet up and discuss strategy tomorrow?" I wanted to tell him about the attack, but I couldn't seem to say it.

"Yeah, I should be. What made you change your mind?"

I drummed my fingers on the steering wheel watching some kids playing up the street. They had hockey sticks and roller blades, and a few wore Golden Knights jerseys or shirts. They laughed and raced around, and I wondered if any of them had ghosts or other terrible things in their homes.

I couldn't bring myself to answer Ford's question.

"Can we meet in person?" I asked.

"Sure. But I can't now—give me like, half an hour. Where do you want to meet?"

"You pick," I said, rubbing the bridge of my nose. "I don't have any decision-making juice left."

He laughed. "Okay. Uh...oh, I know! There's this little waffle place I like. You sound like you need sugar. I'll text you the address."

We hung up and a moment later his text with the restaurant's info popped up. I went straight there, blasting music the whole way. I had brought my notebooks with me since Elixabete was in the house, so at least I would have something to work on.

I sat in my car, waiting. I didn't feel like dealing with strangers without Ford. He was a great buffer. He could chat with people and be friendly and I could just sit there quietly, not participating.

Outside, the wind picked up and clouds started to gather overhead. They weren't enough to completely block out the sun, and no rain started, but the day darkened a bit and I stared up at the clouds. It had been doing that a lot lately, and I wondered if that was normal—Vegas was mostly known for being hot and dry and sunny.

When I saw Ford's van pulling up, I gathered my notes and went over to meet him. The waffle house was actually pretty close to the café where Derek worked. I followed Ford into the pretty little restaurant. It had a kind of industrial feel, with exposed beams and concrete floors and metal framework. I loved it. I could see an art studio blooming from this, or even a house. Someone like Ford would probably like a house like that. He could fix and take apart engines anywhere.

We sat down and a friendly waiter came over. I mumbled a simple order of tea and left the rest to Ford. When the waiter departed, Ford turned to me.

He waited for me to say something, but I couldn't come up with a good way to start this conversation.

"So," he said when I remained silent. "Why did you want to meet up?"

I sat back and looked up at him. May as well just tell him.

"It killed someone," I said.

Ford's eyes went wide. He was quiet as I recounted what Emily had told me.

The waiter brought our drinks and we fell silent. When he left, Ford leaned across the table toward me.

"Rosalind," his use of my full name took me by surprise. "I'm really starting to worry about how much you're blaming yourself for what's happening."

I gave a half-hearted shrug. "I know. Hazel is too. So are Emily and Derek. But...it's fine. We can worry about that later—right now, I need a strategy for *how* to deal with this...monster...without getting *us* killed."

"Is that why you have all your notes?" he asked.

I had actually just grabbed them out of habit. I looked down at them, then decided this might not be a bad place to start. "Uh, yeah," I said.

We spread out some of my notes, and I opened my journal to the short list of capabilities I'd noticed or discovered. They were, essentially, *draw ghosts to me*, *send ghosts away*, and *open/close portals*.

I had no idea how any of these things could aid in getting rid of a monster.

"Do you have any theories on how to use my..."

"Superpower?" he offered.

"Sure. That. How do I get rid of actual *monsters* with it? Not ghosts, actual horrible monster things."

Ford drummed his fingers on the table, frowning in thought. "Well...you can send things away," he said, tapping the where I'd written out that exact thing. "I know a ghost isn't an actual living creature, but...could you pull that off with this? Like, sending it to another dimension?"

"Maybe?" I said. "But what if I can't? What if I can't and it kills us?"

"Fair," he said, shifting in his seat. "Definitely don't want that. Are there any weapons we could take? In case your powers can't do anything?"

"I think most paranormal stuff is vulnerable to silver. And fire. But...I don't want to mess with fire," I added quickly.

"So I shouldn't bring my flamethrower?"

"No, I'd prefer you leave that at home," I answered.

"So we're back to portals then. You open a portal and banish it to another dimension, boom, no more monster."

I fidgeted. "I guess so? But...what if I just send it somewhere else where it can hurt more people? I don't know what's out there...do you know anything about dimensions?"

Ford shrugged. "No—not a *ton*. I mean, no one does, really. There are a bunch of theories and some research, but it's not something we've really figured out yet."

I gnawed on my lip and thought of Rowan again. She had asked me to follow up with her, but even thinking of approaching her terrified me. I didn't know if I even wanted to ask her about this, since it was kind of outside her realm of expertise. She theorized about other dimensions; I was actually dealing with them.

Ford scanned over my notes. Seeing it all mapped out like this, with the prospect of fighting an actual monster, made me more nervous than ever.

"So...we'll get some silver weapons and formulate a plan. Speaking of which," he tilted his head to one side. "Why aren't we discussing strategy with the rest of the gang?"

I sighed. I didn't have a clear, logical thought process for this, I'd just felt like it. "I dunno. No particular reason. I didn't actually intend for us to start planning, I just didn't want to talk about it on the phone. But it can't hurt to start theorizing, right?"

He nodded. "Fair enough."

"Do you think weapons and...whatever I can do...will be enough?"

"Maybe."

The waiter brought our dishes and I turned the plate, analyzing the chocolate-and-berry covered waffle before me. I had honestly forgotten Ford had ordered something for me as well, and now that I was feeling slightly less sick, it seemed appealing.

"You know," Ford said, picking up his fork and poking at his own dessert. "We haven't had a chance to properly discuss this 'dimension' business you've been getting up to. What's that all about?"

I took a sip of my tea, just to buy myself time. "Well, what I've gathered from my mother's notes...ghosts are just...in another dimension. Or..." I rubbed the bridge of my nose. "I don't know, but since they used to be human, I imagine...it just...it just *feels* like they're in a dimension right next to ours, you know? And that's why some people can see them. Because they're like...our neighbors. Like...maybe they're in the house next to us...and I can just see them because I'm...by a window? Or a door, I guess. That's stupid, but you know what I mean."

Ford nodded slowly. "Right. That's actually not a bad explanation for ghosts. Human life-force energy, soul, whatever you want to call it...getting, what, stuck in this other dimension?"

I nodded. "Exactly. I think. Anyway, that would also explain why they keep coming to me. I'm not just seeing them, I'm attracting them. Like I'm—I'm a way *into* this dimension. Which...I guess is where some of them want to be."

Ford nodded. "Any clue as to why?"

"Well, I am...opening the door, or whatever. I'm acting like, well," I pointed to the word 'portal' in my notes.

Ford smirked. "From our very first séance."

We both fell silent for a second.

"This is actually super-scientific, Roz," Ford commented.

I shrugged. "Just makes sense. Besides, that's what it feels like."

"Yea, well if feelings can lead you to this, then your feelings seem pretty on-point."

I watched him shuffle through my notes, muttering to himself.

"Emily must hate this," he commented.

"Why?" I asked.

He kind of chuckled. "She doesn't think ghosts and things have a scientific explanation. She thinks it's just 'paranormal' and that's that."

I rolled my eyes. "Yeah, well, don't gloat. Science hasn't answered many questions here. It's given me a bunch, though."

"That's pretty standard," he said. He held up a rough sketch I'd done of several tall, pale, faceless figures.

"The mannequins," I said. "Or...whatever. That's what I call them, anyway. Those are what I've been seeing. Actually, I've only seen them twice, but it was..." I shuddered.

Ford studied the drawing. "They're not ghosts."

"No," I frowned. Then I nudged him under the table with my foot. "They're *not* aliens."

"I didn't say anything."

"They're *not*."

"Maybe they are, though."

"No. Aliens are from space," I said.

"So...what's something from another dimension, then? 'Aliens' seems like a pretty good term to use."

"*No*, okay?" I said, but I was laughing by then.

He snickered. His eyes fell on my mother's journal. "And your mother could do the same things you could?"

I pulled her journal to me and flipped through a few pages. "Yes. But I don't think she ever fully figured it out. Not to this degree."

"She didn't have any help," he said softly.

I nodded, and we fell silent for a moment as I contemplated my mother, and all she'd been through. Then I remembered that my mother *had* known someone who was trying to help. Maybe I could try to find them.

But that was a project for another time. When there wasn't a monster or demon or whatever to deal with.

Ford and I talked a little longer, going over my notes. He had some book recommendations and a few documentaries he thought would be helpful.

"When do you want to present our 'plan' to the group?" Ford asked.

"Okay, first of all," I said. "The air quotes? Not helping me feel more prepared. And secondly...I guess tomorrow. No sense putting this off any longer than we have to."

He nodded. "Okay. Well, let's call a meeting." He pulled out his phone and sent a text. My own phone buzzed in my purse.

We paid for our food and Ford helped me gather up my notes. Then he walked me to my car.

"Heading home?" he asked.

I shrugged. "Might just drive around. Clear my head. Thanks, by the way. This...it helped."

"Good, I'm glad," he said.

I turned to get into my car, then stopped and looked back at him. "Hey, Ford?"

"Yeah?" he asked, glancing over his shoulder.

"...You don't *actually* have a flamethrower, right?"

He grinned that impish grin and said, "That's for me to know and for you to find out."

"That sounds like a threat," I said, raising my eyebrows at him.

"No! Of course not!" he laughed. "It's...an invitation?"

"To burn stuff?"

"Why you gotta be so logical all the time?"

I laughed and turned away, "Whatever. Later, Ford."

He laughed and we went our separate ways.

I ended up doing what I'd told Ford I might—driving around, listening to music and trying to think about normal things.

The problem was, I barely even remember what 'normal' thoughts were. What had occupied my mind before all this started? What had I spent my time doing? I remembered liking time alone, and laughed, realizing I hadn't felt truly alone in weeks—there was always someone or something there with me, and even if they weren't being aggressive or frightening (many ghosts were pretty gentle and harmless, actually), they were always *there*.

I couldn't fully remember the person I'd been prior to all this; the picture of my life before was strangely fuzzy. It felt like a dream that was slipping away after I'd been jolted awake. I made a mental note to ask Hazel what I'd been like before all this, because as ridiculous as it sounded, I was forgetting.

The strangest part was that it didn't feel necessarily *bad*, it was just surprising to realize.

The truth was, as bad as this was, and as much as I wanted all the ghost stuff to stop...I didn't really want to go back to before. I hadn't been happy before. I hadn't been happy in so long that it seemed like something for children—something I had almost written off.

But I was finding that, even though things were confusing and stressful now, I was...getting closer to happiness. My dad and I had more time together. I liked

Las Vegas a lot more than Los Angeles—the traffic alone was enough to swing things in Vegas' favor. I had friends. I was learning interesting, if frightening, things.

Things had changed so much in just a few weeks. Since moving here, my life had done a complete flip, and there was a strange hope there. It wasn't exactly a joyful feeling; I couldn't honestly say I was *happy* with this, either—I was stressed and tired and frustrated and I wanted to put a stop to the bad things, especially the bad things happening to others. I was scared things might keep getting worse. Sometimes, I was scared I would *die*, or something would happen to someone I cared about. In a lot of ways, things were harder. But if before I was mostly numb, now I was alive. Electric. Aware and moving and feeling something, even if it was bad a lot of the time. It was *something*, and that was better than nothing.

I missed painting lessons. I could paint if I wanted to, but it wasn't the same. I didn't just miss painting, I missed talking to Joanne. I missed her calm presence. She always seemed like she was unbothered by everything, and it made me feel calmer, too.

My dad had dinner with Veronica tonight. He was still insisting they weren't dating, but they sure were hanging out a lot. It meant I didn't really need to head home—Elixabete had cooked enough that there were leftovers for dinner, so she wouldn't be preparing anything. If I stayed out long enough, I wouldn't even see her before she left, and after how today had gone, I preferred not to see *anyone*, least of all someone who freaked me out.

The sky was darkening, and a strange fear washed

over me—fear of the monster in the woods. It was silly; I was nowhere near the forest, and every time I had visions of the creature lurking in the mountain, it was among the trees. But still, the fear twisted in me, like I was out there with it. Like it was hunting *me*.

Home again, I sat in my car a while longer. I wasn't sure what emotion I was feeling, but somehow, after talking things over with Ford, it didn't seem as catastrophically hopeless as it had before. Someone had still died, though, and that knowledge sat in the pit of my stomach like a stone. The only way I could even *begin* to find peace with that was to make sure that creature couldn't hurt anyone else.

My phone buzzed and I sighed. Without even looking, I knew it was Emily, and I knew it was about the monster.

SIX

"You have to admit, it's kinda exciting," Hazel said.

I stared at her, not sure what to say.

"I mean," she went on, clearly trying to convince me. "It's just...life was so *boring* and *ordinary* before. Now there are ghosts and mysteries and problems to solve...it's kinda cool! It's like something out of a story!"

"Haze..."

"It's an adventure, Rosalind!"

I shook my head. "I just don't see it that way. To me, it's more like 'a bunch of problems and weird stuff'."

"Well, no one else at school is having a summer this eventful, I can tell you that," Hazel said, taking a sip of her coffee-chocolate-sugar concoction. I chuckled. I couldn't quite match her enthusiasm, but I also couldn't deny her the excitement. If she was enjoying it, good—at least someone was.

We were all at Derek's work again, and it was a slow day, so he was lingering around us as we talked, only leaving when he had to deliver an order or help a customer.

"Here," Emily said. "Another report of a loud screech heard up around Rainbow Canyon."

Derek had stepped away but veered towards us just then, carrying a tray of food and drinks with his good arm, and added. "That's pretty consistent with the other sightings."

I frowned. "How many sightings have there been now?"

"Can I have that cake?" Emily asked.

Derek rolled his eyes. "If you order your own. This one is not for you. Also, Roz asked you a question."

Derek went back to work, and Emily returned her attention to me.

"We're up to nine. I'm guessing it's hungry because it seems to be getting more daring, at least it seems that way from how many incidents there have been the past couple days."

I nodded. "What kind of reports?"

"Mostly sightings—reports of a seeing a large being moving through the forest, or hearing a loud screech." Emily said, pulling up a few articles she'd saved. "One person claims to have been chased by something, they described it as a living tree with claws. Whatever that means. But I guess they didn't see it well because that's all we got—his report was dismissed as an alcohol-induced hallucination."

"Was the guy drunk?" Hazel asked.

Emily shrugged. "I have no idea. But my guess would

be no; the rest of his testimony seems level-headed and he was out there with his kid. I mean, it's not *impossible* a dad with a five-year-old on a forest hike was drunk, but it doesn't seem like you're gonna be getting trashed at nine in the morning when you have a kid with you."

"One would hope," I said.

Ford sat forward "We were thinking silver knives to fight this thing off, in case Roz's powers aren't effective."

Emily didn't look up from her typing, but said, "That's a good idea. Most supernatural entities *are* vulnerable to silver."

"And almost everything is vulnerable to knives," Ford added.

"Yes. Splendid," I said. "So...what, we just load up with some *silver knives* and go....fight a monster in the woods?"

"Like a movie!" Hazel said happily.

"Stop enjoying this," I begged her.

"Where do we get silver knives?" Hazel asked, ignoring me.

Emily opened a new tab and searched 'pure silver knives' which turned up a very broad and varied selection of knives, all of which were ridiculously expensive. We went to a few more specific sites, including Amazon and Etsy, but the selection was slim.

"Of the three categories we need—real silver, affordable, and able to arrive anytime this week—it doesn't seem like anything checks all the boxes," Emily said in annoyance, gnawing on her lip.

"Are there any local places where we can go?" Ford asked.

Emily narrowed the search, looking for places that

sold silver cutlery in Las Vegas. After what felt like an eternity of digging, we found a little shop that bought and sold real silverware.

"I might be able to modify a knife," Ford said.

"What do you mean?" Emily asked.

"Like if all we can get are...I dunno, butter knives or cake servers or something. I have tools, I've done some basic metalworking before. I could probably fix it up, make it into something we could actually fight with."

Emily considered this, then looked at me. "That could work."

It sounded ridiculous to me, but then again everything was ridiculous, so I shrugged. "I mean, why not?"

Ford grinned, genuinely excited, and I smiled back despite myself. His joy was annoyingly infectious.

Derek's shift ended and he came to sit with us, bringing with him a tray of each of our favorite orders.

"Hey, thanks man!" Ford said.

"Thank you," I said, accepting the chai latte he handed me.

Hazel squealed in delight at her mocha cappuccino, and Emily turned to him expectantly and said, "Well?"

He grinned. "What? You think I brought you something?"

"I think you're too obsessed with fairness to actually leave me out."

Derek chuckled and produced a plate with the cake she'd been eyeing earlier, which had been hidden by the angle he'd held the tray at.

"Yay!" Emily said, swiping her finger through the puff of whipped cream before returning to her work. "Okay, let's buy some silver knives."

"Uh...what?" Derek asked, looking between us.

Emily waved her hand, "For battle!"

Derek looked at me and I couldn't help but laugh. Ford took pity on him and caught him up on the plan.

"Have you been listening to *East/West*?" Emily asked as she typed.

"No, honestly I've been avoiding it," I admitted. Even though it was a world-wide broadcast, it was based in Las Vegas, so it had been mostly about the 'Area 51 Breach' and the various weird occurrences around the Valley.

"It has been talking about this a lot," Emily said gently.

"I was afraid of that," I said.

"I haven't listened much either," Hazel said. "I've been busy at the shop."

Emily picked up her fork and took a bite of her cake. "That's what I'm here for. Anyway, the reason I ask is because they interviewed a mythical creature specialist on there and discussed a bunch of different possibilities. But apparently one of the main ways to stop most mythic beasts is fire and, well, I know that's no one's first choice."

Hazel and I both shuddered. The boys, who had been talking amongst themselves, seemed to tune back in and glanced over.

"No fire, please," Derek said.

Emily shook her head. "No fire. Though I do think we should have *some* controlled burning supplies, just in case."

"Do any of us know how to *do* a controlled burn?" Hazel asked.

I took a big swig of my latte to avoid saying anything about fire in forests.

"That's what *research* is for!" Emily said brightly, taking another bite. I was honestly impressed with how cavalier she could be, even in the face of all this.

"I'll take that," Derek said. "My family goes camping a lot, I know some of the basics of how it works—mostly for safely starting campfires and whatnot, but I have some experience at least."

"Perfect," she said.

"What can we do?" I asked.

Emily glanced at me. "You, champ, don't need to do anything. Just get some rest and charge up those superpowers."

I rolled my eyes, but she ignored me for the last bite of her cake.

"*But* if you insist, I suppose someone does need to go buy those silver knives."

"Cool! I can do that," I said.

"I'll go with you!" Hazel said.

"And I'll make sure I have what I need to turn them into actual weaponry," Ford said.

Emily nodded, closing her laptop. "Good, we've got a plan then."

Weirdly, I felt good having a clear-cut task before me. Go to a store, buy a thing. It was strangely comforting how *possible* it seemed. How normal and manageable it felt.

It was also a great way to ignore the lingering stress from everything else in my life that was *not* normal and manageable, particularly this whole 'fight a monster' thing I'd gotten myself into.

Hazel was in my car, joining me on my drive across town. I had let her select the music. I wasn't familiar with whatever song she'd put on, but I was enjoying it.

We were technically outside of Las Vegas now, in a neighboring town called Henderson. It was where the store Emily had found was located, and it claimed to carry a large selection of silver cutlery, so it was looking like our best bet.

I parked in front of store and looked up at the big sign advertising that they would buy and sell anything silver. Hazel jumped out and made her way to the door, looking back at me expectantly. I reminded myself that this was a quiet, normal errand.

To get a knife. To fight a monster.

"Normal," I said to myself, getting out of the car.

Inside, a man sat behind the counter, looking to be preoccupied with a large silver platter.

Hazel and I perused the displays, looking for anything that could be turned into weaponry. Ford seemed pretty confident in his ability to modify any generally knife-shaped apparatus into a silver knife for hunting, but the whole thing still seemed pretty far-fetched to me.

I had a weird realization as we walked the store, looking at various antique silver pieces: Ghosts were tied to antique things.

Not that this necessarily mattered for me—I got ghosts no matter where I went or what I did—and not that I just came to this brilliant conclusion on my own. I came to it because I saw a ghost, felt them, on the other side of a tall glass display. We locked eyes. It was a woman, probably in her forties, looking tired. She'd died from sickness; something that wore her down for years before taking her. I looked at the items in the display case, then back at her, trying to sense if she was tied to one of these, or if she was just drawn to *me*. Her presence wasn't very strong, and she wasn't particularly solid-looking. I could see through her, and not all of her was visible—a weak presence that drifted in and out.

There was a silver hair clasp in the display case that tugged on the edges of my mind. It was hers, and frankly it was beautiful. She didn't seem angry or in need of much, but I felt something from her.

I tried to push her back, but it didn't seem to work. She wasn't troubling anyone, though, and didn't seem very troubled herself, so I decided to let her be. I could feel her trailing behind me, but she didn't feel like she wanted anything, she just seemed curious. Sometimes, that's all they wanted—to investigate me. Usually, they left after a while.

I let the ghost trail me through the store, oddly unbothered by her. I wasn't sure if it was a good thing or a bad thing that I was getting so accustomed to the presence of the undead around me, but either way, I was. And at least, for me, it was nice not to be terrified every time one of them showed up.

"These are so pretty," Hazel commented, having found the serving knives. There were several that could fit our needs. I didn't know how adept Ford was at metalworking, but it I figured it wouldn't hurt to get a few extras. We asked to see a few options and picked out the ones that looked best.

As Hazel asked about some silver brooch she wanted to get for her mother, another knife caught my eye—it wasn't a serving or dinner knife, it was an actual weaponry-type knife. It had a little fold-out blade, about four inches, and a beautiful, simple polished wooden handle. I tapped the glass and looked up at the shop manager, who was standing back watching Hazel admire the brooch.

"How much is this?" I asked.

I wasn't sure why, but I wanted it.

When we left, we had several old knives—cheaper for being damaged, tarnished, and generally unpretty, which wasn't what we needed them for—and I had my little pocketknife. I kept fiddling with it, running my thumb along the polished handle. It was going to be completely useless against whatever we were facing up on the mountain, but I didn't really care.

When we pulled up to Ford's house, I found his garage open, waiting for us. He smiled when he saw us and waved us in.

"Hey!" he said brightly. "You got the silver?"

I held up the bag with the knives and Ford's grin widened.

Hazel had to get back home, but I stayed to watch him work.

He took the bag and looked through it, then set it down and started carefully removing knives, laying them out and considering them.

"Can you work with those?" I asked.

"Should be able to," he said. "They might not be pretty but they'll work for our purposes."

I sat down and watched him gather tools. "Well, that's all I care about."

"Can you cry on demand?" he asked.

"What?"

He grinned. "You know, add a tear to the forging of a blade and fortify it with magic or something," he said. "I mean, I think you're supposed to use blood? But that seems extreme so we can stick to tears."

I snickered. "I cannot cry on demand, sorry."

"Ah, well," he said, returning to his task.

"How do you even know how to make stuff out of silver?" I asked as he selected the first knife to work on.

"Couple years ago, one of my mom's like, heirloom chains broke. And I asked her if I could fix it instead of her sending it in for repairs," he said, setting to work on the first knife. "So I learned how to do basic metalworking for like, jewelry repairs and stuff. And it was kinda fun. For her birthday that year I made her a pendant to go with that chain, since it didn't have one. That evolved into being able to fix car parts and stuff myself, which was helpful and saved a lot of time. Never done so *much* silver, but I figure the principle is probably the same."

I shook my head. Ford was an eternal enigma.

He worked for a while, clearly getting lost in what he was doing. I liked watching him slip into that focused state of mind. There was something peaceful about it. I supposed it was like when I got really into a drawing—where all you're thinking about is that moment, and the task you're working on, and you lose all sense of time or other people or anything that's weighing on you.

As I watched him, I realized I hadn't had a moment

like that in a while. I had come close while painting with Joanne, but since it was a lesson, and I wanted to do well, I always kept a bit of that edge.

I should do something about that, I thought, making a mental note to do something purely for relaxation and enjoyment later. As I considered what to do, I pulled my new knife from my pocket and looked at it more closely. I wasn't sure why I liked it so much—I had never been particularly interested in knives, nor had I owned one beyond just...having knives in the kitchen to cook and eat with. I think my dad had a couple old collectible things from the Civil War, but they were non-functional, sitting in display cases and looking cool.

"So. How's today been?" Ford asked.

I looked up, pulled from my thoughts, but continuing to fiddle with the knife.

"It was nice, actually," I said. "Saw a couple ghosts but nothing dramatic. Got boba with Hazel, got lost in Henderson, bought some silver cutlery."

He glanced over his shoulder, smiling. "Yeah? Sounds like a calm day."

"It was," I said, realizing it only now. The thought made me smile.

Ford was quiet for a moment, but somehow, I could feel that it wasn't the same kind of quiet he'd been before. He was still working, but there was something different about his demeanor now. He wasn't 'in the zone,' he was troubled by something, and I frowned, uncertain what could have happened in the brief time since I'd last seen him relaxed and happy.

"Have you seen your therapist lately?" he asked.

"Yeah, I had an appointment with her earlier this

week," I said, still playing with the knife, but a little more aware of his tone, the set of his shoulders, the way his movements had become more mechanical.

He was quiet for a moment, then said, "Do you like her?"

"She's nice," I answered carefully. *Where is this going?* "I kinda feel like there's not as much she can do for me, what with all the ghost stuff being the main problem. But she is nice. And she listens, that helps. Plus, she's given me some ways to deal with my anxiety. And my mom stuff...at least as much as I can tell her."

He nodded. He was unusually quiet and serious now, and I glanced up from my knife to look more closely at him,

"I'm thinking...maybe I should find someone for myself," he said, his voice softer than I was used to.

The admission caught me off guard, and I didn't want to say the wrong thing or accidentally discourage him.

"Oh. Yeah?" I said, trying to sound both nonchalant and compassionate.

"Yeah. I..." he picked up one of his tools, but just held it quietly for a moment before looking over at me. "I should probably tell you something. Just in case it ever comes up. Also, I know a lot of your drama, so it only seems fair you know some of mine." He added that last part with a little smile, trying to joke. "I've been wanting to tell you. But I didn't want to like...pile on when you were having really bad days, you know?" he said, his voice becoming quieter, almost a whisper at the end.

"Oh," I said. "Do you want to tell me now?" I asked.

He glanced at me, a shadow of his old smirk crossing his face. "Well. I thought I would. But now I don't want to ruin a *good* day," he said with a weak laugh.

I almost rolled my eyes teasingly, but I caught myself just in time. Something was bothering him, and he was worried about it, and about me, and I didn't think making fun of his internal struggle was the best move. He was opening up to me, and I knew when I admitted I was vulnerable and someone made fun of it, it kinda hurt my feelings.

But Ford likes *to joke around, maybe he'd feel* better *if I teased him?*

Great, now *I* was going in circles.

I decided to just keep it simple. To not deflect with a joke just because I was uncomfortable.

"It's okay, Ford, you can tell me whatever it is. You won't ruin my day." I smiled, but my mind was racing trying to figure out what he was talking about, and hoping I was saying the right thing.

He tried to keep his expression light, but I could see worry there. "Are you sure? It's kind of a downer."

"Yeah, I'm sure." I leaned forward a bit. "What's wrong?"

Ford looked at me for a moment, then returned to his work. We were silent for a little longer before he cleared his throat.

"Right. So. I had an older brother—Alexei—he was six years older than me. But...uh, he died. When I was ten."

My heart sank. I clutched the little folded knife in my hands like a lifeline. I had never, ever seen Ford like this. It wasn't just that he was serious—I had seen that before. This was...devastated. He seemed smaller. Meek. Lost. I mentally scrambled, momentarily unsure what to do.

"I-I'm so sorry, Ford," I said softly. It was a stupid,

empty, generic response and suddenly I felt a little more sympathetic for all the people who'd said similarly bland things about my mom. Their placations seemed less disingenuous now that I was on the other side of it. There just...wasn't anything else to say, at least not that I could find. It was hard to know how to respond to tragedy. It made me more emotional than I would have expected, but I knew what loss felt like. And I knew how hard it could be to tell someone about such a loss, especially if you were sharing it because you felt like you *had* to, not because you were ready to yet.

And with that, it hit me why exactly Ford was telling me this.

Oh.

He went on, and I didn't try to interject with my realization.

"Yeah. Sorry. Just...I've been thinking about it for a while. I hope—I hope he doesn't come see you. But if he were to turn up, I'd want you to be prepared. I didn't know when to bring it up, but once I went to that séance and realized all this...ghost stuff was real...and we started figuring out that ghosts are drawn to you...I realized that I was gonna have to tell you, because he might show up. And I'm sorry, I wanted to tell you sooner, but then weird stuff kept happening and I never knew how to bring it up, then we found out about your *mom* and everything just kept getting more..."

"Hey," I said, gently interrupting. "It's okay."

He glanced at me. "I'm sorry I didn't tell you sooner."

I shrugged. "You didn't have to tell me at all. It's not information you owe me, Ford. I mean, I definitely appreciate knowing—both as your friend and because I'd definitely rather be prepared for your brother showing up one day, but...I didn't tell you about my mom right away, either. I get it. Don't feel bad."

"I know. Just seemed...relevant."

I tilted my head to the side. "Is that the only reason you told me?"

He looked over, almost surprised, then chuckled, returning to the knife he was working on. "No, I guess not. I don't ever really talk about him—half my friends don't even know. The ones who do heard about it from older siblings or parents. I guess I just...wanted to get to tell someone myself. On my own terms. Plus, you're one of the few people who...*gets* it."

I nodded. I knew what he meant.

"Well," I said. "I—thank you, for trusting me with this." Then I added, "And, you know, for the heads-up."

He laughed, more earnestly this time.

"Hypothetically, would you...ever maybe *want* to talk to him?" I asked. I was trying to be gentle, but I also wanted to make the offer, in case he was too nervous to ask. The idea of Ford being nervous still felt alien to me, but I knew better than to assume that people who seemed happy and confident never felt bad feelings, and thinking he couldn't be nervous or vulnerable wasn't fair to him.

"...I don't know, actually. Part of me *really* wants to, but part of me..." he glanced over. "Is it stupid to say part of me is scared?"

I shook my head. "No. It's scary. I still don't know how I feel about seeing my mom. I—" I sighed. "It's complicated."

"Yeah. It is. I mean, I miss him a lot. And...I thought

I'd start to get over it and be able to...talk about him...and maybe even talk *to* him...but whenever I think about him, it's like..." his voice was thick, and he stopped.

"It's like it's hitting you all over again," I said softly.

He nodded. We both fell silent for a beat, and I carefully looked down at the knife in my hand, giving him a moment to collect himself.

"But, uh, yeah," I added casually after a moment had passed. "My therapist is nice."

"That's good. I only went for a little while after he died, but I refused to participate. Wondering if now maybe I should try again..."

"It might help," I said.

"Yeah...yeah..." He was quiet, thoughtful, for a moment. Then he shrugged and went back to working on the knives. "I should really finish these, huh?"

"Yeah. I mean, whenever. Thanks for doing this, by the way. And...thanks again for telling me."

He flashed me another smile—rueful and wounded—but genuine.

We fell into another comfortable silence, if a bit heavier than before. But I didn't mind. I liked sitting in silence with someone, and I wanted to give Ford a little space if he needed it, even if we were still in the same room. I needed it—I had to take a moment to process what he'd told me.

I wasn't too surprised to learn that Ford had an older brother—I had seen him in a family portrait hanging in the living room—but I had never asked about him. Mostly because Ford had never brought him up. But I had assumed it was more that they didn't get along. I knew Ford clashed with his father a lot, and I suppose I'd just figured it was the same kind of thing with his brother, who seemed old enough that he'd be off at college anyway.

This was...so much worse. I felt bad for even thinking that now.

I had so many questions, all of them bouncing around my mind, but I couldn't bring myself to ask any. I was still haunted by Ford's expression. I watched him, thinking of all the times I'd been an emotional wreck and he'd comforted me, or cheered me up, or been strong for me. And all this time, he was carrying his own pain.

I hoped I could return the favor someday.

He finished the knives, and I was surprised by how...*cool* they were. They didn't look like store-bought perfect knives, but there was a raw, rugged craftmanship to them that made them strangely beautiful. He'd wrapped their handles in leather, and polished them to a fine sheen. They were sharp, too—he had demonstrated by cutting a piece of paper and holding it up for me to see.

He was so proud, and frankly, he had every right to be.

"These are *awesome,* Ford, thank you," I said, taking the one he handed to me.

"I got these sheaths online," he said, tossing one to me. "Not sure they'll fit perfectly, but I tried to size them about right."

I shook my head. "You have so many weird skills."

"I'm a man of mystery and intrigue."

I laughed. "That you are."

We loaded the knives into his van, next to all the shovels and trowels and other such things. It felt strange.

Like we were characters in some weird adventure movie about to go fight a monster.

Isn't that exactly what we're doing, though?

I shuddered and closed the van. The sooner this was over, the better.

SEVEN

"Here, Monty, Monty, Monty."

"I'm pretty sure that's not how you're gonna find whatever's up here, Ford," Derek pointed out.

"You don't know," Ford countered.

"More to the point, why are you saying 'Monty'?" I asked.

"Monster, Monty, I dunno, it seemed fitting," he said.

Hazel giggled nervously while Emily ignored us all, serious and focused on the mission.

I was supposed to be 'sensing' the monster. Problem was, I didn't know how to. This power was still new, and I only really had any experience with ghosts. And I wasn't even that good with *them*.

I was getting something, though. I couldn't identify it, but I took that to mean I had my guy. Kneeling down helped me stabilize when I got dizzy. I placed my hands on the still-warm earth and closed my eyes.

Again, I was able to access that strange extra-sight I sometimes got into. Before this, I had used it mainly on ghosts, but it might help me find the monster. Since we were at the edge of the forest, I could faintly sense the life-force of everything in the vicinity. The trees, the little woodland critters, even the air carried a charge I could pick up on. But all that was dim compared to the energy of people.

I could 'see' each of my friends, moving about, giving off a soft yet powerful glow. I could tell them apart from their energies—Hazel's was warm, and very familiar. Even though I was only becoming aware of this now, I could tell it was a presence I'd known all my life.

Emily's was brilliant, bright, driven. She was strong.

Derek was quiet, but steady, withdrawn. Like he was trying to keep himself from shining too brightly.

And Ford. Ford wasn't as familiar as Hazel, of course, but he still felt like someone I *knew*. Reliable. Safe.

When my head stopped spinning, I opened my eyes. Sight felt strange after what I'd seen, and for an instant, it almost felt...limiting. Inferior. I realized, with a strange little jolt, that the sensation had reminded me of when I was dealing with that banshee, and everything had gotten...weird. These abilities were becoming more and more confusing as time went on, which was the exact opposite of what I wanted them to do.

As I expanded my search, I locked on to something deeper in the woods. Something more sentient than the animals of the forest, but not quite in tune with the humans.

In fact...it felt *off* from everything around me. Like

music playing out of key. An instrument in the orchestra that was wildly out of tune.

"There," I whispered, nodding my head in the direction of the foreign presence.

Emily started off into the woods. Hazel and Ford followed, whispering excitedly.

"Be very, very quiet—we're hunting monsters," I heard Ford stage-whisper.

"Whatever you say, Elmer Ford," Hazel said, just to annoy him.

Derek looked back at me. "You coming?"

"Y-yeah. Just..."

Derek raised an eyebrow. "I can almost guarantee there won't be any fire this time."

I gave a strained laugh and stood up, wiping my hands off on my jeans.

"That's not as reassuring as you might think," I said.

"Well. I did say *almost*. The chance of fire is low, but never zero."

This laugh was a bit more earnest, and I looked down the path to see where the others were.

We walked quietly after the rest of the group. They weren't far ahead, but we were all trying to be quiet, just in case whatever we were after had good hearing. The high, noon sun was bright, even under the cover of the trees. After a while, we broke from the path and wandered into the forest.

"Hey, can I ask you something?" Derek said, a bit haltingly. His voice was low.

I couldn't imagine what he'd want to ask me, but I got the feeling he'd deliberately hung back to speak with me.

"Uh, sure. What's up?" I asked.

He looked at the others, then down. "Did...your mother's suicide...was it a shock, or...did you kind of see it coming?"

I blinked. Of all the topics he could have brought up, that was one I would have never guessed. Or, more accurately, I hadn't expected it to come from somewhere so *vulnerable*. This wasn't work-related—it was personal.

"I'm sorry," he said quickly. "That was...a weird question. I shouldn't have—"

"No, no!" I caught myself, lowering my voice. "I mean...it's okay. I just didn't expect you to ask that. But I don't mind."

He looked a little relieved.

"And, to actually answer your question, well," I started, wondering how to respond. "Yes and no. I mean, part of me, now, is wondering if she killed herself. I mean," I shook my head. "Sorry. My therapist wants me to say 'died by suicide' instead. Anyway. I'm not sure anymore if it was that or...or if someone—some*thing*—killed her but for a whole year, I really believed that she had, and...I don't know. I mean, I was shocked at first, but not as shocked as you'd expect, you know? Like, I'd have been completely thrown if it was my dad. I would never expect that. I wouldn't believe it if he did. But with her..." I shook my head. "I didn't see it coming, that's for sure. I *was* shocked. Horrified. But I don't know. After, it kind of fit. In a really horrible way."

He nodded, and I had to work very hard not to ask him why he wanted to know. We were silent for a moment, and suddenly, I felt compelled to throw out another little piece of information, almost more for myself than him. I hadn't said this to anyone—not my therapist, not my dad, not even Hazel or Ford—and I got the sense that, if anyone I knew could relate, it would be Derek.

So I said, "I have a confession: It sounds horrible—absolutely *awful*—but...I was..." I sighed. It was hard to say aloud. "I was a little...relieved...when my mother was gone."

I glanced at him. The words were so hideous they made me wince, but Derek didn't look judgmental, or even surprised. In fact, he looked a little relieved himself.

"Really?" he asked.

I nodded. "Yeah. And I hate even saying it. It took me most of the last year to even admit it to myself, but...yeah. And it's not because I didn't love her. Or because I was glad to be rid of her. I loved her so much...and I wish she was still here. I think I always will. Just...she was so *unhappy*. She was in so much pain. My mother's life was difficult, and I know she loved me and my dad, and I..." my voice was shaking now, but I pressed on. "I wish she could have stayed with us. But...she was in too much pain. And...I miss her. So much. But I didn't want her to suffer anymore. To be so miserable. Suicide—death—it was...it was a kind of release, and one of the few ways she could have any power in her own life. Or at least, I *thought* it was."

He nodded, remaining quiet while he processed my words. I thought about how I didn't know anymore if it had been her choice, or another tragic thing that happened to her. The thought made everything feel fresh and new all over again.

"What did she have? Other than a ghost infestation?"

he finally asked, itching absently around the edge of his cast.

I scanned around for the beast, but it was still moving deeper into the woods. Too far to sense with anything other than my strange abilities.

"She was diagnosed as manic-depressive. Narcissistic personality disorder. And one doctor thought she was a paranoid schizophrenic, but knowing what I know now, I'm almost positive it was the ghosts, and not hallucinations."

He nodded, silent again.

"My dad," Derek finally said. "He's...he has schizophrenia."

"Oh," I said softly.

"He's a good dad. A good person. And he has a lot of good days. But the last few months have been rough. He's been struggling, and there's nothing I can really do to help him, and...it's hard to see him in pain."

I nodded, watching him.

When he remained quiet, I offered another little thought, one of those thoughts you don't always let yourself have. "It can be...challenging...and scary...to love someone who's...struggling like that," I said carefully.

"Yeah."

We were silent again, and I considered this new information. It explained a lot, and it made me sad. I knew how hard it was to watch your parent go through that, and how isolating it could be. There had been times when I felt like my family was the only one experiencing any of that stress and strain. And at least I was really close to my dad—I didn't get the feeling Derek had that with his mother.

"Sorry," he finally said. "Didn't mean to be so depressing."

I shook my head. "No, no, it's...nice, actually. Most people don't get it."

He gave a hollow laugh and nodded. "Yeah. Don't I know it."

When he said that, I thought of Hazel. And Ford. I looked ahead to see him glancing back at me, and wondered if I wasn't giving him enough credit. He had lost his brother, after all. I didn't know the circumstances, but it still wasn't really fair to make assumptions. Maybe he *could* understand, if I took the time and had the courage to explain. Maybe if I wasn't so afraid of how people might react, I could actually tell Ford...and maybe he'd understand.

I glanced at Derek, then back at Emily.

"Have you ever talked to Emily about this? I know you've known her for a long time."

He shrugged. "A little. She knows my dad's...not well. But...I try not to bug her with this stuff."

I nodded. *Trying not to bug people*. Those words struck a nerve in me that made my stomach knot. I realized I'd started to tear up a bit and blinked rapidly, trying to clear them away before I dared speak again.

We shouldn't feel like we were bugging people, especially since they probably wanted to help us. It was just such a hard thought to internalize.

"I think—"

A screech pierced the air, and I ducked instinctively, covering my ears. We'd brought the headphones we used for the banshee, and we all put them on, scrambling to get them in place before it sounded again. Up ahead, I saw Hazel, Ford, and Emily doing the same.

"Come on!" I hissed, gesturing toward the others.

Derek and I ran towards them, keeping our eyes trained on the treetops ahead.

"What is this?" Hazel asked.

The sound died down, and slowly, we uncurled from our defensive crouches.

"That's it, that's the monster," I whispered.

Emily nodded.

Derek and Emily had their phones out, cameras on. I was struggling to concentrate, but the screech had thrown me, and my racing heart was pounding adrenaline through my body, leaving me shaky and half-panicked.

"Can you pick up on it?" Emily hissed.

I shook my head. I *could* feel something, but there was no way to pin it down, let alone send it away. I had my silver knife in a sheath on my belt, like some kind of wild hunter.

Another, shorter cry pierced the air. The forest was eerily quiet, but I could hear bursts of movement rustling leaves, punctuated by moments of silent stillness.

"Where is it?" Derek whispered.

I didn't want to say, 'I don't know,' so I closed my eyes and scrambled around with the energy. The signatures of my friends were wild and distracting, hyped up with fear and anxiety.

My eyes snapped open. I whirled around, and there it was. Without my strange new sense, I'd have never been able to spot it so quickly—it would have snuck up on me.

Even so, my eyes could barely pick it out.

It was tall—ridiculously so. Its skin was an ashen brown-grey, which, paired with its wiry height, made it blend in remarkably well with the trees, like it was designed to camouflage into the forest. There even seemed to be a kind of mossy, greenish fur growing on parts of it, lending to the treelike look of its body. At first, I couldn't see its face, just it's narrow, angular limbs.

But following the lines of those limbs, I eventually found it.

I wished I hadn't.

The creature's face was monstrous; huge and sharp, with distorted features and eyes that seemed to have a dull, red glow. Its mouth was overflowing with gigantic fangs, and a massive, sharp branch-like crown grew from its head, in keeping with its tree-theme.

Its eyes were fixed on me, and my stomach turned so violently I feared I might throw up.

"I don't see it," Emily whispered.

I pointed a shaking hand at the beast before us. "There," I barely choked out.

I wasn't sure the others had spotted it, but I didn't dare look away now that I knew where it was.

Beside me, Derek's good hand moved to the knife at his hip. I could just see him out of my peripherals, unclasping the hilt and gripping it tightly. I wondered what the hell he was planning to do to this massive creature with that little knife, but he seemed ready for the fight.

The monster—whatever it was, it didn't seem to fit the description of anything I'd read about online—was still, watching us. After a few seconds of tense, fearful stillness, it launched. Derek slashed out with his knife, but I was faster than both of them. I'd locked onto the monster's energy the second I'd found it, and now, I mentally pulled it down, dragging it to another dimensional level.

I made a mistake, though—I went with it.

My head spun a bit, but I forced myself to focus. I was in that weird dark place, with a dry, barren ground beneath me and sparse, dead trees all around. The sunlight was gone, and the creature stood before me, looking mildly confused, insofar as that hideous face could express anything.

I scrambled back as it came towards me, and I struggled to mentally detach myself from it. I could drag myself back up to my own world, and leave it here, and then our problem would be solved.

I slashed at it with my knife as it darted closer, stumbling away. With my connection to it severed, I concentrated on moving back to my dimension.

Just as I began my ascent, though, I felt a piercing pain. The creature's clawed hand grasped my leg, digging into my skin. I screamed, losing concentration, but not before I'd already pulled both of us back up.

"Roz!" Hazel cried.

Ford and Derek sprang forward, slashing at the beast but missing as the shockingly fast creature dodged them. Emily ran to me, cutting at the hand that gripped me.

It lashed out, knocking Derek back and slashing Ford across the chest. Hazel shocked me by launching forward and stabbing wildly at the beast, but it kicked her with a jagged foot, and in the frenzy, I could see that it had narrowly avoided impaling her with its sharp claw. It lunged after Hazel as she darted out of its reach, toppling to the ground in its mad dash to reach her.

I decided to ignore the knife and utilize my powers. Forcing the pain and terror aside, I pushed the creature away with all my might. Its hand shot out and gripped me, pulling me towards its mouth and digging claws into my flesh.

Emily slashed it across its face, and it let out a piercing cry that sent me reeling. It released me, slashing towards Emily, but she was too fast, ducking and rolling away across the forest floor.

With it focusing on her, I had just enough time to concentrate. I pushed it down, gripping the roots of the tree I'd fallen against to anchor me to this dimension. The creature was huge, and solid, and certainly not a ghost. It took every ounce of strength I had, but I could feel it working—the monster was slipping down, down, away from us.

My eyes squeezed shut in concentration, forcing the beast away. I struggled against it, and finally, I felt it slip past this dimension, into the one below.

I collapsed against the tree trunk, and for a moment, I just sat with my eyes closed, taking slow, shaking breaths, trying not to throw up from overexertion.

"Is it gone?" I croaked, opening my eyes slightly. I tried to focus my mind enough to feel it, and found I couldn't sense its presence anymore.

"Um...kinda," Hazel said.

I sat up shakily, leaning on Hazel and taking my first real look around. Derek, Emily, and Ford were all standing around the still, sagging form of the beast.

I stared at it in horror.

"I...I thought I sent it away..." I whispered.

Emily brushed her messy hair from her face, turning wide, wild eyes to me. She whispered, "I think you did...but...just its spirit...like the ghosts."

I couldn't tear my eyes from the corpse. I hadn't sent it away; I had ripped its spirit from its body and sent *that* to the dark place, leaving the empty, dead husk behind. Its hideous face was still aimed at me, eyes dark and blank. My stomach rolled, and this time, I did throw up.

Hazel held my hair back and rubbed my shoulders while I collected myself. I was still shaking, still weak from pushing myself so hard, and still horrified by what I'd done. I had never considered that aspect of my powers, and it terrified me. What if I'd accidentally done that to one of my friends? What if I somehow did that to myself?

"I might've spoken too soon about that fire," Derek said, glancing at me as he took his headphones off. I looked at him in confusion, then looked at the monster again, the realization dawning on me.

"You're going to....burn it...?" I asked.

Ford appraised the body with an oddly serious manner. "Probably the best option."

"Hazel, why don't you take Roz back to the car? We can take care of this," Emily said.

"No!" I snapped.

They all looked at me in surprise.

"I mean..." I said, clearing my throat. "I'm fine. I don't need to hide. I can...I can help."

"Man, Roz, let us contribute *something*," Ford said with a weak smile. "You gotta beat the monster and dispose of the body?"

I rolled my eyes and stood up shakily, using Hazel for support. We cleared away all the dry leaves and twigs, anything that could burn. Ideally, we'd move it to a more open area, but there was no way, even working together, that we could move the beast. It was huge, probably fifteen feet tall, maybe more when it was at its full height. It was hard to gauge it, curled awkwardly on the ground, slumped and still.

"Are you okay? Is that bad?" I asked Ford, pointing to the rips across his shirt.

He looked down, then back up, nodding. "Yeah. I'm fine. It just grazed me—I'll clean it up when I get home but it's not bad enough to need stitches."

"It's just dumb luck that it didn't disembowel you," I said. I surprised myself with the bluntness of that statement, but how close he'd come to getting seriously hurt really freaked me out.

"Yup. But it didn't happen, so we're okay, yeah?" he said gently. "We'll bring some armor along next time."

He was joking, but I couldn't get into the spirit of the teasing with him. I just nodded and went back to clearing the area.

Looking at the monster was still hard for me. I focused on the ground around it, trying not to look too hard at its crumpled form.

Ford and Derek made the trek back to the van to get a couple shovels. We dug a little pit and threw some of that dry foliage on it to start the flames. Ford had enough supplies in his van for his little gardening business that it wasn't as hard as I'd anticipated. He even had a fire extinguisher for if things got out of hand.

It took a long time to dig the hole, and longer still for

the creature to burn. The smell was horrible—we had to step back a good deal, though we weren't willing to go too far, lest the fire catch the trees.

I hadn't looked at my phone in some time, but I could see the sun sinking lower in the sky, and I knew we'd have to get home soon.

While it burned, I caught a glimpse—a *feeling*—of something that confused me. Another human. My head snapped around, but I couldn't see anyone. I frowned—the presence was...odd, somehow, and too far and faint for me to fully read.

I decided to keep an eye out for any wandering hikers. We were in a pretty dull, quiet part of the forest, lower on the mountain than Echo, away from the neighborhoods, and less likely to encounter any other people, but I still stayed alert.

When it had burned enough, we buried it. The whole thing was long and draining, and by the time we were ready to head home, I felt like I might need to sleep for three days.

The sun was setting, casting deep orange light over the mountains and tinging the clouds overhead pink. To the east, the sky was already darkening, and I could see the shimmer of a few particularly bright stars just starting to peek through the emerging darkness.

As we moved away from the woods and back to the van, that feeling from before bubbled up again. I stopped and turned back, gazing into the forest. There was something back there that definitely felt human. But it felt like something *different*. I couldn't place the sensation, though. Human, but...off. Like seeing an old rotary phone in a high-tech lab. Not otherworldly, just misplaced. I closed my eyes to feel out the sense in a more accurate way.

There—just at the edge of the woods. There was a person, or at least something that *felt* an awful lot like a person.

And they were...watching me.

My eyes snapped open. I stared into the woods, where I'd felt the presence. Thick plant life blocked my view, but I was sure I could feel someone staring right at me.

And the scariest part was that I knew it wasn't the Shadow. It wasn't even another monster.

It was something new.

Eight

It would seem like an easy task, to be on time to a neighbor's house, but I'd somehow managed to get caught up listening to *East/West* podcasts and lost track of time. Not that Ford would mind, but I didn't like to be late. Today's episode had been about some weird occurrence in Arizona where a woman who'd gone missing twelve years earlier had suddenly turned up, unaware of the passage of any time, the same age she had been the day she vanished, and completely confused by the whole thing. She apparently had no explanation for where she'd been. It was eerie stuff. I was just glad I hadn't encountered anything like that.

Granted, I still hadn't slept well. I wasn't having *nightmares*, per se, but I kept seeing the forest. It almost reminded me of the dreams I'd had of the clearing before the fire, which scared me. Last time I'd had dreams that felt like that, I'd ended up almost dying. But these dreams were somehow more detached. Which, frankly, only worried me more.

I'd had an appointment with my therapist that morning, and I was grateful we'd decided to take the weekend off, because if I hadn't had a little down time to recuperate, I wasn't sure I'd have been able to convincingly say, "Nothing much," when she asked me what I'd been up to in the past week.

Thankfully, getting ready for school next month was enough of a topic of discussion that I was able to keep us on that for a while. I didn't even have to make up my concerns; starting a new school was always a bit nerve-racking.

After that, I'd gone home, gathered my ghost notes, and listened to some podcasts. Which led me to being late, despite having planned this day out to have plenty of time between meeting with Dr. Thompson and meeting with Ford.

I adjusted my bag on my shoulder as I reached the bottom of the stairs and called, "Bye, Dad!"

"Have fun, kiddo," he replied from his office. He'd been working from home a lot more lately, even foregoing a couple business trips that had come up. He claimed he was pushing a couple of the younger partners to be more active and was perfectly able to do everything he needed to from home, but I knew he was doing it to be around me more. And he knew I knew. And neither of us called the other out on this, but there was something comforting in that unspoken agreement.

He still encouraged me to spend time with my friends, though. If he knew why, exactly, I saw them as much as I did, he'd likely change his mind on how healthy this was for me. I didn't dwell on that, though; I had more pressing matters at hand. My mother's journal and my own notebook were stuffed in a tote bag, tucked tightly under my arm, as I headed out the door. Shaking myself out of it, I crossed the cul-du-sac and went to Ford's house.

We were going to go over our monster hunt—Ford's words, not mine—and see what we could learn from it. He had brought up the very unsettling fact that there could be *more* creatures like it that we might have to deal with, and I hated that I hadn't thought of it *and* that it was a distinct possibility. And since we still didn't know what that thing had been, specifically, we thought it might be smart to try and sort it out.

"Roz!" his mother greeted me cheerily. She pulled me into a tight hug.

"Hi, Mrs. Abramovich."

"*Please*, call me Maisie," she insisted, leading me inside. She had a lovely British accent that I always liked to hear.

Philip, Ford's younger brother, was lounging on the sofa playing a game on his phone while Olivia, or 'Oops' as Ford called her, built a tower of foam blocks in front of a television showing Elmo and some other fuzzy characters I didn't know.

I found myself thinking of Ford's brother—of how the family would be if he was here, if I would have met him, and what he would have been like. I wondered how much it weighed on his poor mother, and if she'd ever mention him to me, or if that was something she'd prefer never to speak of. For my part, I wouldn't bring him up, though I did catch sight of a family photo hanging on the wall featuring the two parents and their three boys.

"Hey," Ford said, coming down the stairs, pulling me back to the moment.

"What are you kids doing today?" Maisie asked.

"Ford's helping me with some research," I said, holding up my tote bag.

She told us to get some snacks and went back to keeping an eye on Olivia.

Ford and I went to the library (he had a *library* in his house) and sat down at the big mahogany table.

"Guess what," I said as we sat down.

"Huh?" he asked, setting his laptop on the table.

"Our new housekeeper *still hasn't quit.*"

"It's weird that that's so weird," Ford commented.

I took out my mother's journal and my notebook, spreading out my papers. "Right? But...it *is* weird, isn't it? She's...she's fine at our house. And she keeps coming back."

He nodded. "Maybe she hasn't seen anything."

"Maybe," I said. "But there have been plenty of ghosts around."

"She might be like your dad? Like, she repels them naturally?"

I considered that. "Maybe? I mean, my mom made that sound really rare, so it'd be weird if my dad *and* Elixabete had that ability."

"Oh, maybe she's like...a Men in Black agent who fights ghosts and stuff!"

"Ford, please focus," I said. I did not want to get derailed by another one of his silly theories.

I opened my mother's journal and we started going

through it, looking for any mention of monsters. It was a lot harder to decipher than I'd thought it would be when we'd first started this project. There were articles clipped from newspapers, magazines, or printed out and taped in place. They didn't appear to relate at first, but Ford seemed to be able to understand a lot of the pieces, even if he didn't quite get how they fit together as a whole.

"I can't get over how...scientific this all is," he said, not for the first time.

"I can't get over what a *mess* this all is," I said.

"A mess, yeah, but..." he held up one of the articles. "Quantum mechanics? That's pretty heavy stuff. Or this piece on the holographic universe theory? This clipping is from like, twenty-five years ago, *way* before it was really public knowledge, or even a generally acceptable theory. She was *digging* if she found this stuff back then."

I tapped my pen on my notepad. "What do you think it all means?" I had a lot of theories, but I'd developed a habit of asking him for his thoughts—I liked to hear his untainted ideas, to see if they meshed with my experiences at all. If he observed or suspected anything that matched with my experiences, it meant there was credence to it.

"I dunno. Was your mom a theoretical physicist?"

"No, she was an actress," I said, followed by a muttered, "and not even a very good one."

Rowan is a theoretical physicist, though.

I dismissed that thought immediately. I had only met Rowan Fallon, a new professor at the local college, once, and she gave me the creeps. Not to mention the way her research correlated so strongly with what I was experiencing made me uneasy. Damn scientists and their explanations for everything.

Ford chuckled. “Well, then, looks to me like she was searching for a scientific explanation for her ghosts. Like...oh, I don’t know—”

“Don’t say it,” I warned, pointing my pen threateningly at him.

He held up his hands. “I wasn’t gonna!”

“You were,” I said, eyes narrowed.

Ford resumed flipping through pages. After a moment, he whispered, “It’s aliens.”

“It’s *not* aliens!” I exploded, barely audible over his laughter.

We went through a few more articles, then moved on to her personal writings. Some were journal-entry style pieces. Others were weird—strings of numbers, a series of coordinates, equations even Ford couldn’t make sense of. They seemed random, and the written entries gave almost no context or explanation.

We looked up the coordinates, but they weren’t leading anywhere specific. Random, empty fields, some nondescript lake, an unremarkable mountain.

“What if we plot them out on a map? See them all at once?” I asked.

Ford took a moment to set it up, then turned his computer so I could see the screen.

I frowned at the formless squiggle they created. “Well...that was unhelpful.”

He nodded, but didn’t say anything. I wished we had more to work with—it certainly seemed important, but I just didn’t know *why*. I rubbed my temple as the headache that always came with this research became impossible to ignore.

"Maybe these are like...places where something weird happened? Or where other portals were?" Ford suggested.

I shrugged and slumped back in my seat. My head was killing me. I massaged my temples.

"So. This project seems to be more confusing every time we approach it," Ford said. I noticed him rubbing his own temple, like maybe he was developing a headache too.

"My mother was insane," I said bitterly. "What do you expect?"

He glanced at me, a little alarmed. "You okay?"

I sighed. That had been unnecessarily harsh. "Yeah. I guess. Sorry. I didn't sleep well."

Ford was quiet, typing something on his computer. The air in the room shifted and—almost bored—I turned to look towards the disturbance. A middle-aged woman with ashen skin and a confused look on her face stood on the other side of the table from us. Ford hadn't noticed her, which probably meant she wasn't very strong or aggressive. I balled my hand into a fist and closed my eyes, pushing her away. I held my breath until she was gone, then exhaled slowly. I had a bad habit of not breathing when I sent ghosts away, but at least I was conscious of it now.

Ford glanced up, seeming to realize something was off. He cast his eyes towards where the ghost had been, then towards me, a questioning look on his face.

"I'm just tired," I waved him off. It wasn't a lie—I had been tired for weeks.

"Right..." he didn't seem convinced, but he didn't argue.

"I mean," I went on, circling back to the topic, even though I wasn't really enjoying it. "I don't know what to do with my mother anymore. Like, how I *think* of her..."

"Do you still think she killed herself?"

I didn't know how to answer that. I'd been wondering about her death already, and while the journal didn't offer many explanations, it definitely made me feel less certain that her death had been suicide.

I remembered finding her. She'd overdosed on pills, or at least, that's what we'd been told. That's how it had *looked*, but...

I closed my eyes. I could still see that mountain of a man, wreathed in flames, yelling at my mother's ghost. He knew her. He tried to kill me. It wasn't outlandish to think he killed her.

I almost laughed. No part of my life qualified as 'not outlandish' anymore.

"I don't know," I finally answered Ford. "Maybe not."

He nodded. "Can you ask your grandparents about some of this stuff?"

I shook my head. "My mother didn't really have parents."

"What?"

I shifted in my seat. "She was put in foster care when she was really little. I never found out when, or why. I mean, I don't know if her biological parents died, or just couldn't raise her, or if they lost their rights to her for some reason...anyway, she was shuffled around to a few foster homes over the years, but she never settled down anywhere. She got a scholarship to Stanford, and was on her own after that." I shrugged. "I mean, until she met my dad."

Ford's eyes were wide. "I did not know that. That's... mysterious." He grinned.

At first, I didn't know what he meant. Then I rolled my eyes.

"Oh my *God*, shut up!"

"I didn't say it!"

"You *thought* it."

"Your powers don't include mind-reading, you don't know," he countered.

I shook my head.

"Anyway," he said nonchalantly. "Alien abduction. It could happen. It could *have* happened."

I hit him with a stack of papers. "My mother's parents were *not* abducted by aliens, Ford."

"You don't *know*," he insisted.

I laughed and started packing up the papers and journals.

"Anything else weird going on in your super-weird life?" he asked.

I shrugged. "Other than the surprisingly normal problem of not liking my dad's girlfriend-who-he-swears-isn't-his-girlfriend? No. You're up to date on all the weird."

"Cool. Except I haven't met this girlfriend-who-he-swears-isn't-his-girlfriend, so I do feel a little out of the loop."

"Don't," I said. "You're not missing out, trust me."

"No!" Ford said, pounding his fist dramatically on the table. "I must know more about this not-girlfriend person! It's...my constitutional right!"

"Oh, is it now? Explain your reasoning," I said.

Ford thought about this for a second, then said, "No. I plead the fourth."

"The right to not quarter soldiers in your home?"

"I've made my choice."

I raised an eyebrow. "Well. I'm pretty sure the founding fathers didn't include 'have all available information on Veronica' in the whole 'unalienable rights' thing, but okay."

"That's not in the Constitution. That's the Declaration of Independence, Rosalind," Ford said in mock disgust.

"Nerd."

"Unamerican!" he said loudly.

I hit him with my papers again. "Whatever!" I laughed. "Anyway, I don't even know how I'd arrange for you to meet her, so you might have to just let this one go."

Ford drummed his fingers on the table, clearly trying to think of a way he could make this work.

I sighed. "There is this...fashion show," I mumbled.

He raised one eyebrow and tilted his head ever so slightly. "There's a what now?"

"A *fashion show*," I said, enunciating it more clearly. "Veronica invited us. I guess...I guess you could come to that. We have a couple extra tickets."

His face brightened. "*Perfect*. My rights are finally being respected."

I rolled my eyes. "Don't make me regret this."

"Now where's the fun in that?"

I hit him with my notebook and we both laughed. It was nice to goof off with Ford, even if it still all centered around my weird life.

Sitting there, I realized there was one thing I hadn't updated Ford on—my nightmares.

"I do keep having this dream," I said, almost like I was answering a question he hadn't asked.

He looked over at me. "Yeah? What kind?"

"Same as before. I'm in the forest, running. But...it's not a nightmare about the fire. It's about the monster. It was different last night, though. It was just...being in the forest, cold and alone..."

Ford watched me, his face serious again as he listened.

"I've never been a big 'dream interpretation' person but...I dunno, I feel like it means something. At first I thought these were about the *monster*, so I thought it'd stop after we..." I couldn't finish the sentence. "So...I don't know why it's still happening."

"You had a...vision-type dream before the fire, right?" he asked.

I nodded. "Yeah. Yeah but that was different. That one didn't really change. This one...this one keeps changing. Like, not only was it just quiet and lonely, but it felt like I was closer to town. Like I wasn't as deep in the woods."

Ford didn't know what to make of that and I couldn't blame him. I shook my head, almost regretting having brought it up, simply because I didn't like thinking of it.

"What about, um...what about crime rates?" I asked.

"Ah. Well," Ford said, pulling up a new page on his computer. "It's about the same as before—an increase in violent crimes, and people going to the hospital, but it's holding steady. Hasn't gotten *worse*, but hasn't really gotten better."

"What am I supposed to do about that?" I asked, more to myself than Ford.

"Nothing, Roz. That isn't on you," he said, his voice surprisingly soft.

I nodded. I knew he was right, but I still felt like if anyone could resolve this, I could. The crimes and hospital visits were, I guessed, the result of all these new ghosts showing up, and other than continuing to go to houses and get rid of ghosts, I didn't know what to do.

Outside, the sky grew grey.

"Does it always rain this much?" I asked. I had noticed a few big storms recently—they would form suddenly, pouring rain down for a bit before clearing away.

"I mean, it's technically our monsoon season," Ford said. He caught my expression and laughed. "Okay, that sounds dramatic. It's called 'monsoon season' because of how the storms form, but they aren't anywhere near as bad as real monsoons, but yeah, it rains a little more during that time."

A crash of thunder punctuated his words, and he glanced over at me.

"Not as much as it has been this year, though."

I wondered if that was because of the events on the mountain or if it was just a coincidence. Hopefully I hadn't messed up the weather, too.

"The rain's good, though," Ford said. "We've been going through a drought, this helps."
"Well, that's good" I said, a little relieved that, if this somehow *was* my fault, at least it wasn't a *bad thing*.

My dreams of the forest came to mind and I found myself worried about weathering the storm with no cover. But I was here, I was safe, and I refused to worry about something I had no proof would hurt me.

I hung out at his house for a little longer, but we didn't make much more progress in our research. His mother insisted I have lunch with them, so I stayed for that. No ghosts interrupted me, though I would occasionally feel the flicker of something lurking just beyond my awareness. It felt harmless enough, though, so while it made me a little uneasy, it wasn't enough to ruin my afternoon.

When that was done, I headed home. My dad's study was empty, so I guessed he had ended up going to the office after all. Elixabete was still there, busily working, but I realized I wasn't quite sure what she was doing. I watched her, looking for tools; duster, rag, vacuum, but she had none.

She seemed to be muttering to herself. I crept closer, but I couldn't understand her words. The language was unfamiliar, and strange-sounding.

As I approached, I saw there *was* something in her hand. I didn't know what it was, something small and gleaming.

"Ah!" Elixabete exclaimed, turning to see me. "Oh, Rosalind, you startled me. You're so quiet, like a ghost."

I laughed. Probably a lot harder and slightly more hysterically than I should have. "Sorry," I said. "I didn't mean to startle you. Um...what are you doing?" I added, hoping I sounded casual.

Elixabete held my gaze and smiled, though it was a strange smile.

"Just looking to make sure everything's in order," she said. I took a quick glance at her hands, but whatever I'd seen that gleamed and shone before was gone.

She smiled and made her way to the kitchen. "Are you hungry?"

"No, I ate at Ford's, thanks."

I watched her, trying to read her expression, but there was nothing to tell me what she'd been up to. I'd already asked what she was doing, and she'd brushed it off. Her demeanor was casual and relaxed, a little confused by my question, but otherwise amicable.

I didn't trust it.

"Well. Sorry to interrupt you," I said.

She waved her hand dismissively. "No, no, please. Let me know if you need anything. Did you have fun at your friend's house?"

"Yeah. I did."

"Wonderful."

We were silent for a moment and if she didn't think I was weird before, she certainly would now.

A faint beeping signaled that the washing machine was done with a cycle, and Elixabete took the opportunity to escape my general strangeness.

"Ah, let me get that," she said, excusing herself and heading down the hall.

I watched her go, the fake smile falling away and leaving me gnawing on my lip uncertainly.

"Any of you ghosts got any dirt on her?" I asked the empty room.

No one answered. Not right away, at least.

Nine

With Elixabete on the other side of the house, I darted into the corner of the room where I'd initially seen her.

There was nothing unusual. A little table with some pictures and some ornate box that had been in my family forever. Everything was normal.

I knelt down and inspected the ground. Nothing.

I peered over at Elixabete. First Veronica, then Rowan, now her. Maybe I *was* just paranoid.

Probably something I should take up with my therapist.

I watched Elixabete curiously as she headed upstairs. She struck me as odd, and the fact that she kept returning here had me wondering.

While I was studying her, the temperature of the room dropped. I shivered and turned to see what kind of spirit had arrived.

I saw nothing.

Odd. I knew sometimes ghosts could remain unseen, but that didn't seem to apply to me anymore.

I scanned the room, trying to feel out the presence.

I kept searching, eyes closed, going by feel, but I couldn't pinpoint the presence. I could tell *something* was there—I could feel it, I just couldn't get a lock on its location. Like hearing someone talking in an echoey room, not knowing where the voice originated from.

Finally, it dissipated, and I was left wondering what that had been about.

I opened my eyes and found myself face-to-face with the ghost-girl from the silver store.

My stomach clenched and the shock jolted me, but I didn't scream. She watched me for a moment, then turned and walked away. Her motions were jerking, shaky, awkward. I watched her retreat.

She disappeared, and a loud *crash* on the second floor made me jump. I raced to the stairs, calling, "Elixabete?"

"Yes?" she asked, poking her head out of the guest room. Diego's room.

She didn't look hurt, or even startled. Her face was serious, though. It almost seemed concerned.

"I—I heard something fall. Are you okay?"

"I'm fine. Did anything happen to you?" she asked.

I thought of all the housekeepers we'd had in the short time we'd lived here. I thought of their fearful faces, their uncertainty. None had ever asked about *me,* or how I was doing—they'd all been so afraid, so in a rush to get out.

What's her deal?

"No, I'm fine." I stopped, then added. "It got kind of cold all of a sudden..."

Elixabete was well-guarded. She didn't let much by. But something in her eyes looked to me like recognition. Like she knew what that meant, at least in my case.

"I did set the air conditioning a little colder, since I was moving about so much. Should I warm it up a bit? Are you too cold?"

"No, that's all right," I said, still trying to read her face.

When she returned to work, I went to my room. I sat down to draw, thinking it might calm me. I drew Ford's sister; she was a little ball of joy; it made me smile.

The light in my room was low, with the windows closed. I pulled back the curtains to let in a little sunlight. I heard a soft rattle when I moved them. I looked up in time to see something small falling toward me.

"Ow!" I yelped. It hit my nose and bounced to the floor. Rubbing where it had struck me, I knelt to see what it was. A small, smooth stone lay on the floor. It had a wavy pattern in its colors, creating a gradient from light orange to a dark brownish-orange. I looked up. There was a little ledge above the tall windows of my room, formed by the decorative molding that framed the glass. I picked up the little stone and studied it, then stared at the ledge again. It was small enough to sit up there, I figured, and not be seen from the ground.

In my distraction, I had missed the presence of a ghost. The girl from the silver shop was back again, watching me expectantly, her face serious as always.

"What?" I asked. I looked at the stone, then back at her. "This?"

She faded away, and the room warmed a bit.

I sighed, then turned my focus back to the stone. It was a crystal. I rolled it in my hand. It was carved with something, a symbol, though I didn't recognize it.

The sun caught the little crystal and lit it up briefly. My mind went immediately to the thing I'd seen in Elixabete's hand downstairs. It had glittered, a lot like this.

I pocketed the little stone and raced downstairs. I went to the corner and searched again. Behind the picture frames, in the tiny drawer at the front of the table...

I opened the little ornate box and found another stone. Similar to the one from my room, but this one was light green.

There was a different symbol carved into this one. I recognized it, though I couldn't remember where I'd seen it before.

I went back to my room and got out my mother's journal, flipping through the pages until I found the one I was looking for; a collection of carefully-drawn symbols and their associated meanings.

I found the symbol from the green crystal.

The stone, I guessed, was jade. The symbol looked like a rectangle that was open on the left side, with some extra lines crossing through. There were little triangles at a couple of the corners and ends of lines, and overall I didn't understand what the drawing was supposed to be of, but it looked old. It wasn't in my mother's notes; mostly, there were a lot of circular, geometric looking patterns on that page.

I sat there with the little crystals in my hands, then I

glanced down the hall. Elixabete was still working in Diego's room.

I inched down the hall and stood in the doorway, peeking in. She had a basket of cleaning supplies, but seemed to be ignoring them. She stood on a step, placing something on the ledge of this room's window.

I withdrew silently, wondering what she was doing, and most of all, *why*.

My phone buzzed in my pocket, making me jump. It was just my dad, texting me that he'd be home soon and informing me that we'd been invited to my Aunt Fiona's for dinner.

Downstairs once more, I combed the house, searching for more of the little crystals. I found two—one in the kitchen and one in my dad's office. I held them, studying them. Pulling out my phone, I took a picture of them, making sure to capture the symbols.

Then I put them back. I wasn't ready for Elixabete to realize that I was on to...whatever she was doing.

I sent the picture of the crystals to Ford, Hazel, Emily, and Derek in the group chat, asking if any of them knew these symbols or what they meant. I gave no context, and offered none of my own research, just the picture and my question.

I kept the one from my room, I had almost put it back—I'd been pulling a chair over to stand on—when it occurred to me that whatever she was doing, I wasn't sure I wanted it in my house, least of all in my room. So I left it in my pocket, not sure where to put it just yet.

I took my journals and hid them. I didn't trust this woman, and I didn't want her digging around in my stuff.

I got a text and checked it quickly, but it wasn't one

of my friends. It was Joanne.

Finally back in Vegas! When are you available for a lesson? :)

I typed back, *Anytime. I'm free the day after tomorrow, if you are.*

She didn't answer right away, but that was fine. I sat on my bedroom floor, turning the crystal over in my hand while I stared off into space. The symbol etched in its surface felt like a little web of lines under my thumb. No form or shape or meaning, just random grooves.

The slam of a door pulled me from my daze. I got up and went downstairs. Elixabete was there, sweeping the front entry way. It was the first actual cleaning I'd seen her doing today, aside from apparently throwing a load of laundry in the wash. Not that the house was that messy, or that I wanted her to be breaking her back working all day...it was just odd that she *seemed* so focused and busy, but not with any of the stuff she claimed to be doing.

My father walked in and greeted Elixabete with a smile. They chatted for a moment. The crystal, I realized, was still in my hand. I slipped it back into my pocket, hoping Elixabete hadn't noticed.

I'd have to figure out a way to convince my father to fire her. Maybe *I* could fire her, without him even knowing. Housekeepers had been quitting left and right, he wouldn't suspect anything.

He came over and gave me a little hug. "Hey, honey, how was your day?"

"Good," I said. I was about to say more when Elixabete cut in.

"Mr. Weissmandl? I have a request."

"Yes, Ms. Otxoa?"

She put her tools aside and stood before him, tiny, yet oddly imposing.

"I know you travel a lot for work, and your daughter is often on her own. This is also a large house with lots of work to do to manage it effectively."

"That's true..." my father agreed tentatively.

"I noticed a room downstairs—off on its own, very private. If you are interested, I would like to stay on, but as a live-in housekeeper. I believe I can serve your family best this way."

My heart sank. Well, so much for firing her on the sly.

TEN

Elixabete went home for the evening, promising to arrange the live-in agreement with the agency. My father was thrilled. We'd finally found a housekeeper who wanted to stay. She even wanted to move in.

And I had to grudgingly admit, she was good. She'd made a strong case, playing on my father's emotions and fears—the new house, me alone, a big city, and him working high-profile cases that could make us a target. We even had that additional room downstairs, which she'd so helpfully pointed out.

And what could I say? She had nannying experience, CPR and emergency training, and fifteen years of positive recommendations from past employers. I had some rocks I'd found around the house. I couldn't even be completely certain it was Elixabete. We'd had a slew of other housekeepers come in and out over the past month. And a bunch of ghosts. And Veronica. I still wasn't sure about her, and now that I knew ghosts were real, I'd decided *anything* was possible.

Speaking of ghosts, with so many spirits around, who knew what they were up to?

Besides, my judgment was already in question. My dad still didn't believe in the ghosts. I couldn't blame him, really. He hadn't seen any, ever, despite the house crawling with them.

"You're awfully quiet tonight," my dad said. I was sitting with him in his office while he filed away some documents.

"Sorry."

"Don't be," he said. Being a lawyer, my dad was big on word-choice. He didn't like me to apologize when I hadn't done anything wrong.

"Anyway," I said. "Um...how's work? Not too stressful, I hope?"

He chuckled. "I wish. Things are...going along, though not without a few bumps."

The air shifted a bit, getting colder. My dad didn't seem to notice, but I glanced around, looking for the cause.

I spotted nothing, and remembered the same thing happening earlier.

What is that? I wondered.

I still couldn't sense anything specific, though I knew for certain something was *here*.

I closed my eyes and tried to pinpoint the energy, but I couldn't. It frustrated me.

My dad carried on with our conversation like nothing was happening: "So, is Joanne back yet?"

I shook the anxiety off and returned to fiddling with the toys on his desk.

"Um, yeah, I think so. She texted me earlier. We're talking about my next lesson."

"Good," he said. "I'm glad you're having those lessons."

"Me too." They were the only normal thing left in my life.

I missed Joanne. I hadn't seen her since before everything went *really* off the rails. She'd texted me a couple times, but she was busy with family, and I didn't want to bother her while she was with her sister.

Once my dad was done with his work, we left for Aunt Fiona and Uncle Naagesh's house for dinner.

The Balasubramanian household was a lot louder and livelier than mine (even when my house wasn't full of dead people). Hazel and Haldi were both high-energy people, which they had apparently inherited from my aunt. According to my father, she'd had a similar temperament to Hazel when she was younger. I had no idea how Uncle Naagesh kept up with those three, but he seemed to do so happily.

We were greeted with a lot of excitement and chatter when we arrived. With Hazel, Haldi, and Aunt Fiona all going at once, it sounded like there were ten people talking.

"Housekeeper update," I whispered dramatically to Hazel, amidst the buzz of excitement. Sure, I could have kept that to myself until I could actually *tell* her, but it was much more fun to hint at something and watch her squirm with curiosity for the rest of the night. I can be kind of mean sometimes.

"What are you two whispering about?" Haldi interrupted, bouncing over in that happy-puppy manner of his.

"Your *face*," Hazel said, putting her hand on his forehead and shoving him away like he'd been on her nerves all day. "And how *ugly* it is."

"Well, no, because we wouldn't whisper—that's no secret," I threw in for fun. I didn't have siblings, so I had to borrow Hazel's for my amusement.

Haldi put a hand over his heart. "Oof, ouch, Roz. That is just *cold*."

Aunt Fiona had some pre-dinner snacks out. My dad and uncle were already talking, taking a seat at the island to snack on samosas and pita with hummus. They didn't always cook up both Indian and Jewish traditional foods, but Aunt Fiona knew I loved both, so she tended to make a point of it when we were stopping by.

Aunt Celia and Uncle Mitch hadn't been able to make it—my little cousin Leah was sick, and they didn't want to leave her with a sitter, so it was just the six of us. So it stood out a little more when Hazel dragged me away from the rest of the group, no doubt to question me about Elixabete. Haldi interrupted again and I laughed; his timing was perfect.

"So. Roz. Heard about how people are seeing ghosts in the forests on the mountain?" he asked.

I went from amused to anxious in an instant. My insides churned, and I swallowed the knot in my throat, choosing my words carefully, even though I knew it didn't matter what I said, Haldi had no idea what I was up to, or that my house was haunted, or that we'd recently hunted a monster up there.

"Uh, right, I did hear something about that," I said.

"Right after that Area 51 Breach. Seems a little...suspicious, doesn't it?" he asked, raising his eyebrows.

I made a face. "Suspicious how?"

Hazel shoved him away again. "Suspicious *nothing*. Haldi has no theories worth hearing."

He grinned, ignoring her and ducking out of her reach to stand next to me.

"I think it has to do with Area 51," he said.

I rolled my eyes. Maybe he and Ford could start a club.

"Think about it!" he went on. "The fire, it was so weird. If you read the reports—"

Mention of the fire paired with my already stressful memories of the hunt made my head spin. I clenched my fists, hoping no one noticed I was swaying slightly. My breathing became shallow and rapid. I moved back toward the kitchen, turning to the snacks, trying to look like I was just surveying my options.

"You guys were up there, right? When it happened? Did you see anything?" Haldi pressed on.

"Ugh, Hal, I already told you, *no*! Get out of here!" Hazel said, shooing him away.

"Mom!" he cried.

"Hazel, be nice to your brother!" my aunt called from the pantry. I stared at its glass door, remembering when I'd smashed it to save Emily. A moment later, it had been intact like I'd never broken it.

I'd thought of my time on the mountain a lot in the past week. I still didn't know what happened. I knew it had something to do with dimensions, but the technicalities of it still completely eluded me. Plus, when we'd been up there for the monster, I'd sensed... something...in the woods. Something new.

"Are you okay?"

I looked over at Hazel, only then realizing that I was looking *up*. I'd sunk down a bit, my shaky hands gripping the counter.

Haldi was still there, looking a bit confused. Hazel's brow was knit with worry.

"Yeah, yeah," I said quickly. "Just, um, I'm gonna sit down."

"I'll get you some water," Hazel said.

I went to the little breakfast bar just off the kitchen and sat down, taking slow, deep breaths. The words, "*I think you're dealing with PTSD*" bounced around my skull. Dr. Thompson had weaseled it out of me that I hadn't just *seen* the fire, I'd been *in* the fire, and only barely got out alive. I didn't tell her it was largely my fault that that...*man*...had started it, since I wasn't sure how to explain that detail.

Any mention of it made my knees wobbly, so she'd given me some breathing exercises to do when I was feeling weak or panicky. By the time Hazel brought me my water, I had calmed down significantly. My hands were still trembling, though.

"Should I get Mom?" Haldi asked.

"No, I'm fine," I said quickly.

He watched me for a moment longer, then gave a halfhearted shrug. He opened his mouth to speak when his father cut him off.

"Haldi, come here. Tell Uncle Geoff about that debate team thing you have coming up," Uncle Naagesh said.

"I am a lawyer—I can give you some tips," my dad added.

Seeming to forget us, Haldi left to join them, and Hazel let out a sigh.

"Sorry. He's become convinced the fire was a military thing and that we might have seen something up there."

"Yeah, let's keep him away from Ford," I said.

Hazel laughed, then grew serious again. "What about the housekeeper?" she demanded.

I told her how Elixabete had not only continued to return, but requested to live in the house as a full-time housekeeper.

"That's super weird," Hazel said.

"Right? I don't know what to think. Everyone else runs...why not her? It's gotta mean something."

"Maybe she's like your dad? Like, she repels them or something?" she whispered.

I shook my head. "Ford suggested that, too, but..." I pulled the crystal from my pocket. "She's leaving *these* around my house."

Hazel took the stone from me and turned it over in her hand. "Oh yeah, you texted us about this..." she looked up at me. "How many?"

"No idea. A bunch. I only found a few, but she was at the house alone all day, she could have put them all over by now."

Hazel nodded, still examining the crystal.

"Where were the ones you found?"

"This one was on my windowsill, up high. I think."

"You think?"

"Yeah. I think one of the ghosts knocked it down. To show me."

"And the others?"

I told her where I'd found everything, and she frowned in thought, still studying the crystal.

"Do you have a theory?" I pressed. She'd been quiet for too long.

Hazel shrugged. "It actually sounds like she's setting up a crystal grid."

"A what?"

"A crystal grid. They can be small or they can be around the whole house, like, specific crystals at major points around the house and in each room. My mom set one up here, actually. They're for protection, safety..." she looked at me. "This looks like agate, it's for driving away spirits and protecting against psychic attacks. Doesn't exactly seem sinister."

I accepted the crystal as she dropped it back into my palm, glaring down at it.

"Why would she set up a crystal grid in my house?" I wondered.

"I literally just told you, it's for protection—"

"You know what I *mean*," I interrupted. "Why would she be *helping me?*"

"No clue. Maybe she's actually nice? Eat something, you're still pale."

"Yes, *mother*," I teased.

"Speaking of which...heard anything?"

I frowned. "No. Not since...you know."

Hazel nodded. Then asked, tentatively, "Have you tried to reach her?"

"Kind of? I mean, I know I can do *something* with these ghosts, but I'm not very good at it yet."

"Maybe we should try another séance."

I shook my head. "No. No way."

She looked down. "Yeah...maybe not the best idea."

"Anyway," I said, taking a samosa and nibbling on it. "I don't really want to talk to her, so it's probably for the best."

"Don't you have a million questions for her?" Hazel asked.

"Yeah, but..." I shook my head again.

"Still mad?"

I sighed. "Madder than ever. She never told me *any* of this stuff and I..." I didn't even know where to begin with that. With how it had hurt me. Hurt *her*. It was a mess in my head.

Hazel nodded and fell silent. I gnawed on the inside of my cheek.

Ford texted me to say that he didn't know anything about the crystals and symbols, but he would look them up. I decided to just say *thanks* and save Hazel's info about crystal grids for later.

The rest of the evening went smoothly, and Hazel and I talked about normal things. Non-paranormal discussions now felt weird to me. Stuff like Hazel's upcoming birthday and Haldi's various summer camps. It was so...ordinary. But nice. Aunt Fiona asked how I liked my therapist, but she had a way of speaking that didn't put me on-edge.

I had another session coming up with the doctor, and I wondered what I would tell her. While I answered my aunt's question, I spotted the ghost of a little girl hiding behind Hazel's sofa. I tried to ignore her as I spoke. It was distracting, and a little unnerving, but certainly not the worst thing I'd endured so far. 'Normal' didn't last long in my world anymore.

"Hey," Hazel said when the adults had gone back to talking amongst themselves. "Do you want me to come over and check out the grid?"

"Sure. Do you think it'll help?"

"It might," Hazel said. "I feel like I've seen that crystal's symbol before. I'd like to see the rest."

So Hazel went home with my dad and I. The two of them talked about Hazel's tennis lessons and her plans for the next year of school. I slipped my hand into my pocket and ran my finger along the engraving on the stone, lost in thought.

At home, I showed Hazel where the other crystals were. We waited until my dad went to his room to hunt around for others.

I made a little map of the house to chart where each crystal was. They all had unique carvings, and I used those to document them all.

Elixabete would be moving in soon, so if we were going to investigate, now was the time.

I found myself wishing Ford was with us. He knew so many weird, random facts. And even though this was more Hazel's department, I knew his presence would have been calming.

Emily texted us while we were gathering crystals, replying to my earlier message about them. I told her what we were up to and sent the rest of the pictures, as well as the map. Then Hazel and I sat on my bedroom floor, placing the crystals on the map I'd drawn in their respective spots. There were over 30 crystals total, in different shapes, sizes, and colors. Some had engravings, but many were just plain crystals.

When everything was in place, Hazel put her chin in her hands and stared at it for a while, her face scrunched up in serious thought.

"Does any of this make sense to you?" I asked.

"Not really. I don't know a *ton* about crystal grids, just that they exist and their basic purpose is to be helpful. But this pattern seems...different. Complex. I don't really recognize it."

I bit my lip and checked my phone. All I found there was the same confusion I'd seen before.

"We're missing something," Hazel said suddenly.

"What?"

She tapped the center of the paper. "The center crystal. The one that, well, if you believe in crystal grids and the like, it's the one that 'powers' all the others. Charges them up, I guess."

I frowned. "How did we miss it? We looked everywhere."

"Well, for starters, I forgot about them until we sat down," Hazel said. "And also, it might be hidden more carefully. It would be bigger, too, so maybe she had to resort to a different tactic."

I stared down at the map. None of this made sense to me, and now I felt even more lost and confused than I had before. Snapping a few pictures, I disassembled the map and made a note in my journal to look for the center crystal.

My dad came and said goodnight to us, and reminded me about seeing Dr. Thompson in the morning. The thought made my stomach knot, but I forced a smile.

When he'd gone to sleep, we put the crystals back. As

we did, we hunted around for the center piece. According to Hazel, it had to be in the middle of the house. We searched every room that could even remotely fall under "center" status, but found nothing.

"Why is the center crystal so important?" I asked.

"Because," Hazel said, climbing around on my countertops in search of crystals hidden high up in or on the cabinets. "The center crystal doesn't just charge all the rest, it provides direction. It will determine the *exact* purpose of the grid."

My phone buzzed and I checked it to find a message from Derek.

I think those symbols are Sumerian

How can you tell? I sent back.

Been looking at old languages online

Do you know what they mean? I asked.

Not yet. E will help

Wait, what are you volunteering me for? Emily responded.

Research, Derek said.

Emily replied with, *That's your department. I'm the visionary*

Derek sent back a gif of Regina George saying *"whatever."* I chuckled at their exchange and slipped my phone into my pocket.

Hazel climbed down, shaking her head. "I got nothing."

"Where else could it be?" I grumbled. Then, I looked up and sighed.

"What?" she asked.

"Question: Does it have to be *dead* center, or just close?"

Hazel considered this. "Close should work. More 'in or around' the center. Why?"

"Then I bet you anything it's in my dad's room."

Hazel frowned.

"Well," I muttered. "I guess we'll have to find it in the morning."

"What time does Elixabete get here?"

"Nine."

Hazel nodded. "That should be enough time."

My phone was buzzing again. I checked it to find messages from Ford.

Looking into crystal grids. Pretty sure Elix is a witch

You said that about Joanne, I countered.

There can be more than one witch, Roz

Weirdo

They don't seem bad, tho. The grids, he said. I could almost hear his attempt at lightheartedness and comforting calm through the text.

None of this weird stuff is ever GOOD

Nothing is good or bad, but thinking makes it so, he texted back.

Don't use Shakespeare to rationalize your stupid theories

Hazel and I finished putting the crystals back and I tucked the map into my journal. At least I knew where most of them were now.

It wasn't that late, so we stayed up talking for a while. I was researching the symbols Derek had mentioned. I found some things that looked similar, but not the exact symbols from the crystals. And the meanings were sketchy, hard to understand.

"It's cold," Hazel said. The tinge in her voice told me

she had also forged an association between 'cold' and 'ghosts.'

I'd felt the cold, but hadn't said anything. I was still, eyes unfocused, trying to determine where the ghost was.

Nowhere. It was the untraceable presence—the one I felt but never saw. The one whose energy seemed to come from everywhere and nowhere at once.

It was faint, too. I only caught it when I really concentrated.

The room's temperature returned to normal, and Hazel, who had tensed up, sat back, at ease in the restored warmth.

I, on the other hand, still sat at attention. The presence was subtle, easy to miss, and almost seemed to have faded, but I could still sense *something* there.

"Roz?"

"Do you see anything?" I knew she couldn't, but I wanted to see where her eyes went. Hazel didn't have my ability, but she was still good at feeling things out—better than me at recognizing and understanding her instincts, that was for sure. Maybe she'd get something, and I could use it to calibrate my own sense.

She whirled around, taking stock of the room, looking first at a blank spot of wall by the window before turning and scanning for the ghost.

I focused on the spot where Hazel's eyes had first fallen. If I squinted, I could almost see a darkness there. A...blurring around the edges of...

Of what? There was no shape I could discern.

Just like that, the presence evaporated completely. Hazel was watching me, face drawn.

"Are you okay?"

"Yeah...just...thought I saw something. Probably just another random ghost," I lied, not wanting to spook her.

Hazel and I spent the night reading about rare types of ghosts and other beings that can follow a person, as well as crystal grids, and I had to say, I much preferred the crystal grids. So I was trying to think of those instead of whatever this new presence I kept sensing was. But thoughts of it—and the fear that it might be something similar to the Shadow that had hunted me before—still kept me up half the night. When I finally fell asleep, my nightmares about the forest fire now included the figure of a monster lurking in the darkness, hungry eyes watching me. And something else. Something smaller.

The dream shifted to a cold, clear night with the stars and half-moon shining overhead. I was standing by where we'd parked to search for the monster, but rather than a fire or a beast, I saw only dark, silent forest. Within the trees, that *something else* lurked. I could feel it. It beckoned to me, drawing me to the darkness. Not malicious, not dangerous, but still...mysterious.

When I woke up, I could still feel the chill of the mountain air on my skin.

ELEVEN

I drove Hazel home the next morning after getting only a few hours of sleep thanks to staying up late, theorizing and researching. We'd managed to check my dad's room, and found a crystal Hazel called 'orgonite' hidden under the back corner of his dresser. I'd asked her what it was. She'd admitted that she wasn't sure, but she could find out. So I was waiting for an explanation. Googling it just told me that it was a pseudo-science, new-agey type thing, which only frustrated me. I decided to wait for whatever Hazel might come back with.

As I drove home, thinking I might stop at Starbucks just to break up the monotony of the day, I heard the multiple notifications of a ton of texts coming in. Probably Emily and Derek discussing the crystals; Hazel had sent a few updates that morning.

I got my tea and went home, where I found Elixabete

carefully polishing the bookcase in my father's office. I wondered if she was putting more weird little crystals around.

"Hello, Rosalind. How are you today?" she called over when she saw me.

"Good, good. How about you?" I asked.

She smiled and nodded. "I'm well. I spoke with your father and the agency about the new arrangement—I should be all moved in by the end of the week."

"That's great," I said.

"I think so. Can I get you anything?" she offered. Why was she always offering things to me? Was that normal? She was a housekeeper not a...butler or whatever.

"No, thanks," I said, looking over and thinking with dread how she'd be living here soon. What would that be like? I went up to my room and decided not to worry about it now.

I kept wondering if other entities were going to show up. Other things like the monster we'd fought...or worse. *East/West* talked about all this stuff; chupacabras, mothmen, changelings, even, yes, aliens. But that didn't mean it was all true. Just because ghosts existed, that didn't mean every other mythological or supernatural thing was real, right?

The logic sounded flimsy, but I decided to stick with it. Or, perhaps, cling to it.

It occurred to me that I *could* find out more...by asking the ghosts. Specifically, my mother. Her journal gave no mention of werewolves and vampires and other creatures, but maybe she knew *now*.

I locked my door and got out my mother's journal. My own journal sat beside it.

Emily had started using summoning circles in our work, and I'd gotten pretty good at drawing them, since Emily had zero talent with, interest in, or patience for drawing. It usually fell to Derek and I, and with his arm still broken, I always volunteered.

Not wanting to ruin my floor, I laid out a large piece of thick paper. I drew out the symbols, referencing the notes in my journal. For me, a summoning circle wasn't necessary. I could summon ghosts all on my own. Hell, I was unintentionally drawing them to me at all times, even when I didn't want to. But the summoning circle gave me a measure of control that I lacked; it was less about gathering them here and more about organization. With the circle, my energy was focused, and the ghosts showed up in a specific spot, not 'somewhere in my general vicinity.' I didn't want any surprises.

I had no way of keeping spirits and other paranormal things away from me—Emily and Derek had tried methods from stories and lore, like salt and iron, but they had no effect. It seemed to work on them to some degree, but not for me. The only thing that came close to keeping them at bay was my father's presence.

I sat before the summoning circle, flipping through my notes. Beside me, my phone buzzed, but I ignored it, setting the notebook aside and taking a deep breath.

"Okay," I said, purely for my own benefit.

I closed my eyes and concentrated. I felt the little ache in my temples, but I pressed on, focusing on one specific person—my mother.

It was hard to think of her and keep my focus steady. Emotions flared up, and I frowned, trying to keep my mind on my goal. I hadn't seen her since the mountain, and we hadn't really been able to talk, seeing as she was fighting with the Shadow and trying to save my life. And before that...

I rubbed the heels of my hands into my eyes. I didn't want to think of the time I'd seen her before that. I needed to concentrate, and this train of thought was going to completely derail me. So I took a moment to breathe and collect myself, and to get my mind off all the turmoil that had surrounded us. That wasn't relevant now.

When I had finally calmed down enough to try again, I rearranged myself, closed my eyes, and concentrated. At first, nothing happened. This was normal—ghosts could be skittish. I waited. Slowly, the sense of a ghost settled on the room.

Opening my eyes, I checked the circle. My mother's ghost wasn't there, but someone else was. Keeping the surge of fear down was hard, but I'd had a lot of practice lately, so I was able to maintain.

"Hello," I whispered. The ghost before me—a young man in tattered overalls who looked like he was from the 1920s—flinched and faded a bit, but he didn't respond.

"Um...I'm trying to find someone. M-Miranda? Miranda Weissmandl? Do you know if she—"

He faded, and I huffed in annoyance. The room was clear of ghosts once more, and I settled back down to try again.

I went through several tries, pulling up various random ghosts who weren't able to help me much. When they were willing, I did my best to help them, but I was very aware that I was using up time and energy on things that weren't my objective, and soon I'd be too tired to deal with my mother, even if I did find her.

I cleared the room again, focusing. Unfortunately, as I tried to summon my mother, thoughts of that night on the mountain popped into my head. Then the monster. Then, that strange energy I'd sensed...the one I'd dreamed of...

I opened my eyes, intending to start over, only to find myself in a blank white void.

I gasped, looking around, but before I could fixate too much on this strange new occurrence, I spotted a boy—probably around my age—sitting just before me, mirroring me. His clothes were worn and tattered, and looked like they were from some long-passed era.

He looked just as surprised as I was to be here.

For a moment, we just stared at each other in mutual shock and confusion. He wasn't a ghost, I could tell that immediately. He was alive. He was human. And he was...

It clicked suddenly, where I'd felt this feeling before. It was the energy calling to me in my dream. The one I'd felt the day we fought the beast.

"It's you," he said in awe.

"You were on the mountain," I said, similarly stunned.

"Where are we? What is this?" he asked.

I shook my head. "I don't know. Who—"

The void around us began to crumble, and before either of us could react, it was gone. I was sitting on my bedroom floor again, head spinning.

Ghosts were showing up rapidly now, like I'd blown a hole in a wall instead of just opening the door. And they weren't restricted to the circle anymore—they were everywhere, all around me, pressing in on me.

I withdrew, scrambling back, but I bumped into still more ghosts, cold and not fully solid. It felt like moving through Jell-O. I yelped and dove to the side, but they were all around me. Cold hands gripped me, pulling at my hair and clothes.

There were too many to count, and they grabbed at me desperately. I tried to focus and push them back, but my heart hammered and my mind raced. The ghosts had me, and they were pulling me down. I could feel myself *descending*, slipping, almost like falling. A scream escaped me, tearing at my throat. I thrashed, all powers forgotten. Too thrown by everything that had happened to concentrate.

"No! No!"

I didn't want to go down into their world. I didn't like it there.

But I could feel my grip on my own world slipping away. I couldn't hold on. Cold rushed all around me until I was consumed. My vision was going dark. It was happening too fast and I couldn't focus enough to push them away. Terror gripped me—they were going to get me this time. Their grip became harsher, more corporeal, and I could feel claws digging into my skin. It felt like drowning in a cold sea, with dozens of desperate hands clutching at me, as if I could save them, but instead they were just drawing me down as well.

From far away, I heard pounding on my bedroom door. The whirlwind of sound swallowed up Elixabete's voice, but I knew she was there. Pulling myself back was like clawing up the side of a well while something tried to drag me down. I heard a loud *bang*, and the voices of the ghosts rose from frantic chattering to a cacophony of wailing and howling.

A brilliant light filled the room, paired with a piercing, metallic screech.

All at once, the ghosts vanished. I fell to the floor hard enough to knock the wind from my lungs. For a moment, I just lay there, confused. My head spun, recalibrating to my surroundings.

"Rosalind! Rosalind, are you okay?"

Elixabete knelt beside me, checking me over with surprising precision.

"I'm—I'm fine," I said. "How did you...?"

"Shh, tell me where you're hurt. And how badly. Do I need to get you to the hospital?"

"No, no, I'm okay. I hit my head, but it wasn't hard. I'm fine."

She continued looking me over, checking my pupils, pulse, and breathing until she was sure I wasn't seriously injured. Then she helped me up and ushered me downstairs, muttering about tea and ice packs.

Elixabete had me sit at the kitchen island while she worked. I was given a cold press for my head, which had started throbbing. She prepared me a strange-smelling tea, which she claimed would help with my headache. Then she sat down beside me with a tin of ointment that carried a sharp, medicinal scent. She dabbed it on my scrapes while glanced curiously at the cup of tea she'd set out.

"What happened up there?" I finally asked.

She kept working as she spoke, "I don't know, I just heard you screaming and came to see if you were okay."

"And...?"

"And I found you lying on the floor. Must've been a bad fall; you've got a few scrapes. Did you have a seizure or other such episode?"

"No..." I said. "I was taking a nap. I think I just...had a nightmare."

I watched her. If she was lying, she was good at it. I couldn't figure out how to ask her how she'd banished the ghosts, but I was almost certain that's what she'd done.

The grid. The ghosts. Who is *this woman?*

"Well you must have some dreadful nightmares. Here, drink this," she said.

I took the cup and sniffed it cautiously. It had a rich, rosy scent. I swirled it around, considering it. Odds were she wasn't trying to poison me, but I couldn't be sure of anything with Elixabete.

"What is this?" I asked.

"Rhodiola. It'll calm your nerves."

I sniffed it again, then took a cautious sip. It was good, actually. The rosy flavor, paired with a little tartness, was pleasant. I drank a bit more while Elixabete finished up with the scrapes on my arms.

"Where did all these come from?" she asked, indicating the older burns and bruises from the fire. I even had lingering shadows of the gashes from when the mannequin-looking things attacked me in my bed.

I shuddered. I was glad I hadn't had an incident like that in a while. Remembering it made me think of Ford's alien theory. I wondered what he'd make of all this.

"Rosalind?"

"What? Oh, sorry. I got them on a hike. I fell. Clumsy," I muttered.

"You really must stop falling, Rosalind."

I laughed weakly. "Yeah..."

"And your fingers?" she asked, eyeing the band-aids.

"Bad habit. I kinda...claw at my hands sometimes," I admitted.

"Ah. Nervous habit?"

I nodded, and Elixabete dropped the topic, continuing her work in silence. She finished patching me up and looked me over once more.

"Are you all right? Is there anything else I can do for you?" she asked.

I shook my head. "No, no, this was...very helpful, thank you."

She nodded, but she was still watching me closely. I was about to start feeling uncomfortable when she finally said, "Well, I have some work to finish upstairs. If you need anything, just call for me."

"Okay. Thank you."

"And Rosalind?" she said, stopping me just as I was getting up.

"Yes?" I asked, unsure what she might want.

"Take the rest of the day off, won't you? I know you're working on a project with your friends, but it seems to me you've been pushing yourself a bit too hard. Everyone needs a day off—I'd suggest making this yours."

I didn't know what to say to that, so I just nodded. She smiled at me and went back upstairs, where she was working on unpacking the remaining boxes in Diego's room.

I decided to take Elixabete's suggestion and give myself the rest of the day off. In part because, at today's appointment, my doctor had talked about wanting me to have more down time. She was concerned my anxiety would lead to burnout, and since she didn't even know half of what I was dealing with, I had to conceded that she was probably right.

So I curled up on the sofa and watched movies. It was the closest I'd come to feeling calm and relaxed in a while, and while it was nice, I couldn't shake the questions about Elixabete. Everything she'd said indicated to me that she knew more than she was letting on, and while her actions *seemed* helpful, I kept wondering if that was to lure me into a false sense of security, or if it was genuine.

I had a thermos of tea and a bunch of shows to catch up on, and for a while, I tried to just forget about mysteries and conspiracies and even ghosts. I tried not to wonder about the white void, and the boy I'd seen there, who I'd sensed on the mountain. I pulled a sketch pad from the little bag I carried with me everywhere and started sketching, trying to draw him. I wanted to capture the nothingness of the void, but it ended up looking like I'd just drawn a picture of a boy and decided not to include a background.

It was a strange day, and no amount of attempting to relax could make me forget it.

Being back in Joanne's studio calmed my strained nerves. It felt familiar and safe, and paired with having taken most of the previous day to just veg around my house and marathon shows, it made me feel like I actually was getting a break, even if it was incredibly hard to tune out the worry in the back of my mind.

"I'm so glad we can resume our lessons," Joanne said as I skimmed my sketchbook for designs I wanted to paint.

"Me, too," I said. "How was your trip?"

Joanne laughed and shook her head. "Well, my sister is...my sister, as always, so that was...interesting."

I glanced at her. "Do you guys not get along?"

She sighed. "I suppose you could say that my sister and I have differing viewpoints on most things. I love her, I do, I just don't understand her."

I kept Joanne talking about her trip for as long as I could, but of course, the conversation eventually came around to me and how I'd been in her absence. I told her the mundane stuff. Finishing up registration for school, starting therapy, and our interesting new housekeeper.

"And the ghosts? Any more trouble with them?"

I focused on my canvas. "No."

Joanne didn't say anything, but she knew I was lying. I could tell.

I painted the clearing from the mountain. I'd sketched it when we'd returned, and for some reason, I couldn't stop thinking about it. I figured since it had been wiped out by the fire, it would be nice to have a way to remember it. This attitude kind of surprised me—usually, I'd want to forget all about the place where I'd been attacked by ghosts, had a giant try to murder me, and nearly burned to death all in the space of ten minutes. Instead, I was obsessed with it.

"That's beautiful. May I ask what inspired it?"

I didn't like the aspen tree I was working on. I stepped back, wondering how much to share while I pretended to contemplate my technique.

"Just...somewhere I saw on a hike."

"It's lovely. Simple, yet...emotive."

I smiled. "Thanks." I loved the way Joanne talked. Flowery and elaborate. I went back to trying to fix my tree.

"I heard about the fire on the mountain," Joanne said.

"Oh. Right. You have a cabin up there," I said.

She nodded. "It's far from Echo, though, so it was safe. Sadly, a lot of homes weren't. I have a few friends who live up there full-time, and some lost everything they had in that fire."

My stomach twisted. I tried to hold on to what Ford and Hazel kept telling me—that it wasn't my fault—but every time something reminded me of the devastation others were enduring, it came back to me.

Hands trembling too much to keep painting, I set my brush aside and pretended to be wiping paint off my fingers. That was when I caught sight of the ghost. She was a little girl, clutching a stuffed bear. Her wide eyes watched me.

I concentrated, but the second I felt myself push against her, she began to scream. Not just scream, though—*wail*. Like the banshee.

I clapped my hands over my ears and let out a cry of pain that was swallowed up by her screeching. Joanne looked alarmed, then covered her own ears, searching for the source of the sound.

I sank to my knees as the pitch increased until it was so deafening, I thought my head might split open. Then, the sound changed. The ground started to shake as the scream became so cacophonous that I thought I might pass out.

The glass dome around us cracked, and I realized what was about to happen. Joanne's hand—stronger than I would have imagined—gripped my arm and pulled me to the door. We practically fell down the little spiral staircase just as the glass dome shattered.

The sound was impossible, breaking through even the ghost's wail. I curled up in a ball, shielding myself from the shards that fell.

The scream stopped, but my ears were still ringing, my vision spinning. I was so dizzy, I couldn't see straight. The world was a tilting blur.

"Rosalind! Rosalind!"

"What—Joanne? Are you okay?"

She nodded. "I think so. Are you?"

I pushed myself up and brushed my hair out of my face. The glass had mostly missed us, thanks to the angle and the stairs, but my hip throbbed painfully from the fall.

"Yeah," I said shakily. "Thank you, you acted quick."

"What in the world was that?"

Trembling, I stood and climbed the stairs, broken glass crunching under my shoes.

"Rosalind, no! Be careful!" Joanne cried.

I reached the top of the stairs, a breeze rustling my hair.

The dome was annihilated. The metal framework that had supported it still stood, but it was an empty skeleton. Everything was covered in glass. All the canvases were ripped to shreds. Easels lay in splintered ruins on the floor.

The ghost was nowhere to be seen. I turned in a slow circle, searching for the ghost girl and taking in the devastation. My eyes landed on my canvas, still standing on a broken, slanted easel. It was torn up, but what gave me pause was the big hole in the center of the clearing. I could see the open sky through my painting.

It looked like the light that had opened up in the clearing and spilled out destruction.

TWELVE

The others were busy for a few days—other friends, their families, errands and work and the like—and it was, frankly, a welcome rest. I had no ghost banishing missions. I had no monsters in the woods to fight. And, for the most part, I had almost no ghosts around the house.

I slept. A lot.

It would have been perfect, except I kept having stupid ghost dreams. Or at least, that's what I figured they were. They weren't *bad* or *distressing*, but they reminded me that there was another mystery to solve.

The one that kept repeating lately was a dream of that blank white void I'd found myself in when I'd tried to summon my mother to me. More specifically, the boy I'd seen there.

He was afraid, and lost, and that was the most I could

sort out. He didn't know where he was. He wasn't a ghost, he was alive, I knew that much. We couldn't communicate much, but I tried to help whenever he appeared in my dreams.

I always woke up immediately after the void dreams, and I always felt particularly...*strange*.

When I woke up Monday, after a weekend that had all blurred together into 'sitting on the sofa with my dad watching shows' and 'napping', I had a message from Emily claiming we should all meet up and plan our week.

I was glad Emily was around to be organized and driven—I much preferred her just telling me where to go and what to do than me actually having to figure it out.

I showered and dressed and felt a bit like I'd finally woken up after being in a bit of a stupor for the past couple days. It had been nice to withdraw from the world for a bit, but it was also nice, now, to clean up and put on 'leaving the house' clothes and have somewhere to go, something to do.

My dad was just leaving when I went down, so we said goodbye and I wished him a good day at work. I peered around, looking for Elixabete, but was unable to find her. I gave up after a few minutes and got in my car, heading to the café where Derek worked, which was starting to feel like a second home.

When I got there, Emily was already all set up at a table, laptop out, notes beside her. She smiled when she saw me, waving me over.

"Hey! How was your weekend?"

"I became ever so slightly like the ghosts we hunt," I said.

"What?" she asked.

"I was basically dead to the world," I said.

She chuckled. "Well, you probably needed that."

I nodded. "Yeah, it was nice. So. What do you have for us this week?"

"Not too much, actually," she said. "A couple banishings, but they seem low-key. Nothing we can't handle."

"Good."

Derek stopped by, dropping off a tea for me.

"Oh, thanks. Do I just pay at the register?" I asked.

"Nah," he said. "Emily ordered it for you."

"Aw, thanks Em."

"You earned it," she said. "Plus, last week was rough. I'm gonna...try not to schedule that much stuff in the future. Especially if we have a big monster. Big monsters get their own weeks from now on."

I snickered, nodding. "Good call."

I sipped my tea while Emily worked on her grant, checking her notes and occasionally asking me questions.

"Are you including the...mountain...monster thing?" I asked.

"I'm considering it," she said. "But I'm not sure if I should. Especially since we don't know what exactly it was. Then again, maybe it's good—we might have discovered something *new*."

Hazel arrived, with Ford coming a little after. It occurred to me that the two of them didn't *really* need to come to these kinds of meetings, but Emily always included them and they always showed up. It was weird. But nice.

"One thing I do want to do, whenever you're up for it, is an interview," Emily said to me.

"Uh, sure. Do you want to like, record me?"

"Would you mind that?"

I was honestly a little camera shy, but I knew personal testimony could be really valuable to her proposal.

"Oh, can *we* do interviews, too?" Ford asked.

"Yeah, why not?" Emily said.

"If we don't have anything to do today, we could work on that," Hazel said.

"Do we have to?" I asked. I sounded a little whiny, even to myself, but I decided I had the right to whine a bit. "I just...I don't...feel like doing more work today. We never do anything *normal* together. I just want to hang out with you guys like we're...regular friends."

I realized after I said it that I wasn't sure if they considered me a real *friend*, and more to the point, I actually wanted them to. Hazel did, of course—that I was secure in. And I suspected Ford did. But I had this underlying fear that I was just a project to Emily and Derek. That they were nice to me just because they were nice people, but that outside all this ghost stuff, they wouldn't actually *want* to hang out with me.

"I second that," Derek said, almost like he was responding directly to my internal fears. "We've been working really hard lately, we deserve a break. And to at least make some attempt at normal human interactions. We can't have *everything* we do together be ghost stuff."

"I am also on board with this," Ford piped up.

Emily laughed and closed her laptop. "Okay, you guys make a fair point. Let's do something normal."

"Awesome," I said. "Thank you."

Hazel finished her drink. “What did you have in mind?”

“Uh...” I said. “My idea was ‘hang out’. You guys have to help me out from there.”

Hazel turned to Emily. “Roz is socially challenged.”

“How about GameLand?” Ford asked. “On the Strip? It’s got a movie theatre nearby, could be fun.”

“Yeah, okay,” I said.

“Can we go today?” Hazel asked. “Derek, when do you get off work?”

Derek raised an eyebrow. “Twenty minutes ago. I can’t sit here chatting with you guys when I’m on the clock.”

I snickered at that.

“Fair point,” Hazel said.

“If you guys are all free, we could go now,” Ford offered, sounding like he wanted nothing more than for us to all take off and play arcade games.

No one had anywhere they needed to be—Emily decided she could work on her grant later, Hazel had blocked a few hours for this, and Derek didn’t feel like going home just yet. I also had the day open, so we piled into Ford’s van and he drove us east.

The Strip was abuzz with life and activity. It always was, but today, we were part of it.

“I haven’t been here in *forever*,” Derek said, looking around.

“Me, either,” Emily added.

I had been on the Strip a few weeks back with my dad, but I hadn’t stopped to really pay attention to how much it had changed in the last few years. Not that the new casinos were a surprise; the Strip was ever-evolving.

My dad had been a little concerned about me going, but since we were a group of five, and since he'd met and liked all my friends, he'd just told me to have fun and be safe.

"Anything else weird with the housekeeper?" Hazel asked.

"*No*," Ford said dramatically. "No weird-talk, remember?"

"It's not weird-talk, it's life talk," Hazel countered.

"About her weird housekeeper, which falls under 'weird,'" Ford said.

I tried to keep things light: "Nothing else has happened...yet."

Ford threw up his hands in mock frustration. "Were you not the founder of Normal Day?"

"Yeah, well," I said, shrugging. "If we don't have *any* weird today, we couldn't have invited you."

Ford shook his head disapprovingly, but Hazel giggled.

We were in GameLand, at the rock climbing wall. Emily had scampered up like a little spider. The rest of us were still making our way to the ledge at the top.

Rock wall climbing hadn't been on my to-do list for the day, but Ford had suggested it, and I'd decided to try being a little more spontaneous. Hazel had said that my life was an adventure—better to embrace it, I guess.

Ford was the second one to the top. I was right behind him. He offered me a hand and I took it, pulling myself up beside him. I could see the whole establishment from there. It was a huge space, with several stories featuring every arcade game in existence, as well as a restaurant, pool tables, bowling alley, rides, and of course, the rock climbing wall, which rose through the four levels of the arcade, meaning we were surrounded by shoppers and gamers as we climbed.

Derek was taking his time, helping Hazel, who was afraid of heights and almost quit several times. I hadn't expected him to be able to climb, but he was managing surprisingly well with his cast, even though he hardly used his left hand, and was distracted by Hazel. He was patient and encouraging, and got her all the way to the top. I leaned over the edge and pulled Hazel beside me. She sat at the top, a little shaky, but laughing, catching her breath. Ford gave Derek a hand and we sat there, admiring the view, even if it was just an indoor view.

With all of us having completed the climb, Emily stood up and hit the big button at the top of the wall. A loud, excited siren sounded, and everyone within earshot—on all levels of the arcade—cheered.

Hazel and Emily whooped and hollered victoriously. Ford joined in, loud and boisterous. He bumped his shoulder into mine, and I laughed, giving a little shout.

"That was pathetic," Ford said.

"Hey, don't shame my celebratory tactics," I said.

We sat up there for a moment longer before rappelling back down. I went slow, staying with Hazel. Ford and Derek raced to the ground, all but falling the whole distance. Emily took a nice, moderate pace and landed lightly.

Once down, we wandered around. We played some games, but I wasn't very good at those. Derek suggested pool, so we played that for a while.

We got lunch, then looked around some more.

"We could check out Xerxes," Hazel suggested,

indicating one of the newer casinos, which I'd never been in.

"Nah, that place is lame," Ford said. "But in The Venetian's shops there's a bookstore you'd like, though, Roz."

"Okay, we can go there next," I said.

We passed street performers ranging from musicians to people dressed like movie characters, taking pictures for tips, club employees handing out passes, tourists taking pictures and carrying three-foot tall souvenir beer mugs at varying levels of fullness. The tourists were decked out, or super casual. Either way, they were *everywhere*.

We reached the Cosmo and Hazel announced she needed to go in, leading the way to the shop she was seeking. There were stores and art pieces, a multi-story chandelier encompassing an entire restaurant, and of course, even more people.

There was some place that rented nice dresses for special events that Hazel had to visit. I expected the boys to be bored or complain, but Derek just played on his phone, chatting with Emily while she browsed.

Ford got into it, though. He found a feather boa and wrapped it around me. Then he searched until he found a plastic tiara.

"Having fun?" I asked, adjusting the tiara so the teeth weren't digging into my scalp.

"I'd be having more fun if there were...what are they called? Opera gloves?"

"The long ones that go all up your arms?"

"Yeah," Ford said.

"Yeah, those are opera gloves. Which you're

concerned with because...?"

He shrugged, grinning.

I laughed and shook my head while he took a pair of sunglasses covered in rhinestones and carefully placed them on me.

"Okay! Sorry guys, had to check my homecoming dress," Hazel said.

"You reserved one already?" I asked. "It's early July. Why are you *renting* a dress, anyway?"

"Because it's cheaper than buying a dress you'll wear once, so you can get a cooler dress. You should get yours, Roz."

"I like how you think I'm going," I said, peering over my sparkling sunglasses.

"I like how you think you have a choice," Hazel shot back with a wink.

"I like how no one's commenting on Roz's attire," Derek said, snickering.

"Well, I *don't*," Ford huffed. "I worked *hard* on that look."

"Oh, you did not," I laughed.

Click!

I blinked. "Did you just take a picture?"

Ford was looking at his phone screen. "I'm making it your contact picture."

I tried to snatch his phone away, but missed. I took off the random accessories and put them back. We left then, taking the chandelier-draped escalator down to the ground floor.

Just before I stepped off, a sharp pain struck behind my left eye.

I missed my step getting off the escalator and Hazel

caught my arm. She let go quickly as I rubbed my temple, pressing my fingers into my eyes.

Why now? I wondered.

Something felt wrong, and I was almost afraid to look around and see whatever ghostly presence had decided to pay me a visit.

I took a deep breath and opened my eyes.

I blinked. I closed my eyes, then opened them again.

Slowly, I turned, taking in the scene around me.

There was no one else around me. Not my friends, not the tourists, not the hotel employees, *no one*.

But nothing else about the scene had changed. I was still in the Cosmo. I was standing exactly where I had been—at the bottom of the escalator, under the chandelier, about to head out the giant glass doors to Las Vegas Boulevard.

I looked up at the escalator. It was still running, humming softly in the absolute silence of the completely empty casino.

"Hello?" I called. My voice echoed off the walls, and I realized how big the building really was.

After a moment more of looking around, I felt a shiver running up my spine. I had to get out of there. I rushed to the towering glass doors, shoving them open. Outside, a little breeze rustled my hair, but I was faced with an identical expanse of emptiness.

All the casinos and stores were in place. Everything was where it should be. Even the sun was shining brightly overhead.

But the streets were silent. There wasn't one car, and the traffic lights changed for empty intersections. Televisions played to deserted bars. The sidewalks, walkways, restaurants, shops—they were all empty. All eerily still.

I was struck by the sheer scale of the Strip. Las Vegas Boulevard, the street that the Strip was built around, was *huge*. Wide and long, with huge asphalt squares where it met with other roads. They were like vast, black rivers of impossibly still water.

And the casinos! They towered above me, absurdly tall, gleaming like gems in the late-afternoon sunlight. They stretched out along the empty street, modern palaces of steel and glass and stone, all color and light.

On billboards and signs all along the street, lights flashed and blinked and twinkled, advertising shows and restaurants and new shops or clubs. It would have been amazing if it wasn't sending chills down my spine. It was so unsettling. So *wrong*.

I walked slowly down the street, looking around. I could see the Bellagio a little way up the road, its fountain show playing enthusiastically for no one. The music the water danced to echoed off the high walls of the casinos around me.

My headache hadn't eased, but now it stabbed at me, far more intense than before. I stumbled, leaning against the wall of the Cosmo. When the pain subsided, I resumed walking. I wasn't sure where I was going, but I needed to do *something*.

I didn't sense any ghosts, but something about this whole thing felt paranormal. It didn't feel the same as the dark place—and it certainly looked different—but it had a similar tinge. Because of this, I thought perhaps I could get out of...wherever I was. But when I concentrated and tried to return home, nothing happened. I couldn't get out. This realization made my stomach twist.

Movement up ahead caught my eye. “Hey!” I cried, hurrying after it. The figure, which I couldn’t make out from this far away, disappeared.

My vision got a little blurry as I ran, unsure if I should call out or try to sneak up on the figure. I darted forward, and for a split second, my vision went completely out of focus.

The blare of voices, footsteps, music, sports scores, cell phones, cars rushing by, and planes flying overhead hit me all at once. But loudest of all was the horn of the taxi that way racing toward me.

I fell back, disoriented by the sensory-overload. Someone grabbed me roughly and pulled me out of the street as the taxi screeched to a halt. Had I not been pulled away, it would have hit me. The driver screamed at me, but I barely heard her.

I stumbled and fell against whoever had grabbed me, still trying to process the sudden rush of input. My head spun, my knees wobbling as I tried not to throw up or pass out or both.

“...get over here? Roz? Roz!”

Slowly, Ford’s voice came into focus, registering as familiar.

“What happened?” I asked.

Ford’s usual humor and good mood were gone. He was pale and shaking, his breathing rapid and uneven. He was still clutching me, eyes wide.

“Are you kidding me?” he said. “I was hoping *you* could answer that question!”

I looked around at the once-more busy street, totally bewildered.

"I...I was...it was empty..." I whispered.

Ford watched me, clearly confused. He nodded and gestured for me to follow. We walked away from the street, which I hadn't realized I'd stepped into. Ford leaned against the wall of some shop.

"Are you okay?" he asked.

"Yeah, are you?" I watched him closely. He was still pale.

He nodded. "That just really scared me." He seemed to remember something then and pulled out his phone. "Sorry," he said as he typed. "Gotta tell the others I found you."

"What happened? On your end, I mean?" I asked.

He went to put his phone away, but it started buzzing right away. He kept watching me, though, almost anxiously.

"You just disappeared. You kinda...you tripped, and Hazel grabbed you, but suddenly you were just *gone*."

I nodded. That made sense. Then I made a mental note about how wrong it was that, in my mind, any of this made sense.

Ford went on: "We looked for you, we knew it had to be ghost stuff, but we weren't sure what to do. So we split up. Then all of a sudden you were standing in front of me, waking into the street..." he shook his head. He was still clearly freaked out.

"ROZ!" Hazel hit me hard enough to knock me into the wall. "Oh my God, I was *so* worried about you!" she said in a rush.

A few seconds later, Derek joined us, looking anxious and asking a million questions. Hazel still hadn't let go of me, and Ford was uncharacteristically quiet, still watching me like he expected me to vanish again.

When Emily found us, she had me recount exactly what I'd experienced. We went over it about four times. By the end of it, it didn't even sound real to me anymore. It was like one of my dreams, only I wasn't waking up in my bed. I'd woken up in the middle of a busy street and almost died.

Once Ford calmed down a bit, he started spouting off theories. All scientific, all driving Emily crazy.

"You've *seen* the ghosts!" she said.

"I'm not denying that. I'm just saying there *has* to be some kind of science behind it."

I tuned them out. My eyes were closed as I tried to piece together what had happened. A strange desire swept over me—to go back to UNLV and talk to Rowan. I hated that idea, because frankly, that woman had terrified me, but she understood so much more than I did. Trying to collect my thoughts, I pulled out my phone and opened my notes app.

"What's that?" Derek inquired, probably as bored as I was of listening to Ford and Emily bicker, again, about ghost versus aliens.

"Just some notes on what happened today," I said.

"Any theories?" he asked.

I put my phone away and grabbed the crystal from Elixabete's grid that I was still carrying in my pocket. "I'm not sure yet," I said.

It was a lie—I had a pretty clear theory taking shape, and I didn't like it.

THIRTEEN

I drummed my fingers on my desk, staring at the blank email. When I'd made the decision to write to Rowan, I had figured I'd know what to say when the time came, but here I was, as lost as ever.

Maybe this was a terrible idea. I never had to speak to that scary woman again, so why force it? Any updates would only lead to follow-up questions, and I didn't know if I wanted to deal with that.

At the same time, though, I was already in over my head. I was going to need to talk to *someone* who knew about dimensions, and Rowan was probably the person who knew the most. Even if humanity didn't have *much* understanding of the science behind dimensional shifts, Rowan was still my best bet. And after that incident on the Strip, which felt like I'd fallen into some halfway point between dimensions, I needed help. Especially since I had no idea how I'd gotten into, or out of, that place.

I stared at the blinking cursor. The fact that Rowan had moved to Las Vegas a week after I had still bothered me. Why had a world-renowned genius physicist with a specialization in the exact problem I was experiencing suddenly drop her entire career and move to the same city I had? It's not like the local university was the leading research facility for dimensional travel or anything. She'd had offers from around the globe, from the most prestigious schools, scientific institutes, fellowships, and foundations, and yet she'd taken up residence at a state college.

It was unsettling, and I couldn't help but feel a bit suspicious.

I sighed and started typing.

Rowan,

My name is Roz, I'm the girl who came in with questions about a portal.

I frowned at my first sentence. What a wordsmith I was.

You asked for a follow-up, so I'm writing to let you know that I was able to successfully close the portal. Thank you for your instructions.

I bit my lip. What should I say next? Should I just leave it at that, or let her know more weird stuff was going on? Part of me was desperate to tell an adult who might actually be able to help about everything that was happening. I knew she couldn't really solve my problems, but there was a nervous ache in me that wished so badly for someone else to know what to do. To be able to help. I felt like a small child, wanting the grown-ups to fix it.

I ended up chickening out on telling her anything of substance.

I hope you're enjoying living in Las Vegas.
Thanks,
Roz

I sighed, looking at my pathetic, largely pointless email. I hit "send" before I could overthink it. There were still spirits showing up, which Ford pointed out meant there was likely another portal open somewhere. This thought was distressing, but hopefully with practice, I could get good enough at closing them that it wouldn't go as badly as last time. And I was still having dreams of that...void...that nothing place. That was new *and* unsettling.

On my desk beside me was a page of my journal where I was doodling various spirits I'd seen, or places that were popping up in my dreams. That white void was one of them, with the mysterious boy I'd encountered there. The most recent episode of *East/West* was playing in my ear, and discussing, once again, the 'Area 51 Breach' and the mess of supernatural beings and phenomenon that had spilled out since it happened. A few were cases Emily and I had already dealt with, or were on our list. Luckily, that part of the show wasn't *too* long, and Chad transitioned to callers talking about tulpas in Maine, which I logged away as, 'yet another thing I hoped I never had to deal with.'

I yanked my earbuds out and closed my laptop. I was too restless to sit around my room, researching and wondering. I headed downstairs, let Elixabete know I'd be going out, and got in my car. I had no destination, but it was nice to drive.

It was still early enough in the day that Ford was likely working. Emily had told me she was going somewhere with her mother, and I knew Derek was taking an extra shift today.

But Hazel, while she was also working, would be available. I headed towards the Apothecary, certain Aunt Fiona wouldn't mind me stopping by.

The shop wasn't too far from my house, and Las Vegas traffic was nothing like Los Angeles traffic, so I got there quickly. I pulled up and looked at the familiar sign. Inside, it was all crystals and chakra maps. There were gems, dreamcatchers, books on every metaphysical topic in existence, and every imaginable incense.

"Welcome to the—oh, hey, Roz!" Hazel chirped from behind the counter.

I walked over to her and stood by a display of Himalayan salt crystals. "Hey, Haze. How's work?"

She shrugged. "Slow day. Last people in here were some college girls looking for weed. They seemed disappointed we weren't *that* kind of apothecary," she said with a laugh.

I snickered. Apparently, they had been dealing with a lot of that recently.

"So," Hazel went on. "What brings you in today?"

"I dunno, just needed to get out of the house," I said,

fiddling with some malas on the counter.

We talked for a while, and I looked around at the new items on display. It was always fun to come in here. She was about to get a chair for me to sit with her behind the counter when the door chimed behind.

I turned with vague interest to the newcomer.

"Welcome to the Apothecary!" Hazel said to the guy who'd walked in. I couldn't really see him around the displays between us, but what from what I could see he looked disheveled, and a bit bewildered. My first thought was that Hazel was going to have to send another pot-seeking would-be patron away, but as he looked around, he didn't appear to be looking *for* something, just *at* everything.

A strange twinge of familiarity hit me, and I shifted to see him better.

Hazel seemed to get the same unusual sense from him that I did. "Um, can I help you find anything?" she asked.

I did a quick scan; he wasn't a ghost, that was obvious, but there was something...odd...about his energy. I found myself staring at him, frowning, trying to sort out why I felt like I recognized it.

It clicked into place very suddenly, and my heartrate skyrocketed before my mind could even process why. He was the boy I'd seen in the void. The same presence I'd felt on the mountain.

The energy I'd felt in my dreams.

"You," I whispered, stunned.

The boy turned to me and blinked in surprise, jumping back slightly. "I..." he stammered. "You're the girl...the one I saw in my vision."

"Who are you?" I asked, taking a few steps forward.

"M-my name is Yarin." He spoke with a light German accent.

"What are you doing here?" I asked, my brow furrowing in confusion. But not fear, strangely—I knew I didn't have to be afraid.

"I-I don't know. I don't know where I *am*. Or..." he looked around, bewildered once more. "Or how I got here..."

I watched his shocked face, glancing at Hazel uncertainly. She shrugged and I turned back to the boy. Yarin.

"You were in the forest before," I said. "You were watching me. I felt you. And you were in that...void... place yesterday. But...how are you *here*?"

He fidgeted, looking uncomfortable. "W-well, I recognized you. F-from the first time I saw you. I woke up in a forest...and there was a fire...a-and..."

My eyes widened. Hazel gripped my arm, letting out a little gasp.

Yarin went on: "Wh-when I saw you in the forest, a-and after you fought the beast, I...I wanted to ask you for help. I don't know where I am, or how I got here, a-and you...have the same," he frowned, seeming to think for a moment. "The same abilities I do, yes? To...I do not know the word for it. To visit the afterlife? And return here?"

I looked at Hazel. Her eyes were wide.

"You...you see spirits?" I asked.

He nodded. "Yes, yes. But I also...sometimes I...can go to where they are..." he frowned. "But I'm not very good at it. I have gotten stuck there before. I worried my brother so..." he ran his hand through his hair. "That is why I need your help—I need to find my brother. He's in danger, there are..." he looked around, almost like he expected someone to jump out and grab him. When he spoke next, his voice was lowered in a fervent whisper, "We were captured, and I'm not sure how I escaped, but I can't leave him there. I have to go back for him. Please, where am I? I know I'm not in my homeland, this place is...strange..."

Hazel and I exchanged another perplexed look. "You're in Las Vegas," I said. "In Nevada—the United States?" I added when I saw no recognition in his eyes.

He reeled at this. "The United States!? *America?* How did I get here?" he cried. He looked around, as if to confirm this fact, then froze when his eyes fell upon the display rack of agendas that read 'Three Year Calendars.' Aunt Fiona was a fan of them, so she tended to keep them in stock year-round.

Yarin went pale at that, freezing in place.

"Yarin?" I asked after a few seconds of him staring at the calendars in horror.

"It's...it can't be..." he whispered.

It was only then that I looked past the disarray of this attire and realized what else had looked strange about his clothing: It looked *old*. Like it was from another time.

"Yarin? What year did you expect it to be?" I asked, looking between him and the calendars.

He looked at me, shaking and pale and full of fear, and whispered, "1942."

FOURTEEN

It had taken a while to calm Yarin down. Hazel had ushered him to the back room and let him use the bathroom to clean up. We'd found some clothes in the shop that would fit him and let him change—he was a mess from hiding out in the forest for several days. After that, Hazel gave him some tea and a protein bar that they sold in the shop. I lingered around while she soothed him, feeling generally useless. I'm not great at comforting people in distress.

The situation had only gotten weirder the more we'd learned about it: Yarin was sixteen, but had been born in 1926. He was from Germany, but spoke English because he'd lived in England for a few years with an aunt. After explaining that, he'd clammed up and was sitting in what I could only assume was total shock, mechanically sipping his tea.

Hazel had to step out to take care of some customers, leaving me alone with the traumatized stranger.

I fidgeted. I didn't know what to say.

Yarin mumbled something that I couldn't quite make out.

"I'm sorry?" I asked.

"This place. I...I knew something was wrong. Everything looked so..." he shook his head, brow furrowed. "I just never thought..." he looked down at his mug of tea.

We were silent for a moment.

"My brother," he said, looking up at me. "He is—was," Yarin winced at that. "Was...only seven. I need to find him."

I looked frantically towards the front of the store, where Hazel was ringing someone up. I definitely should *not* be the one to tell this kid that his brother might very well be dead by now, and at best would be an old, old man.

"Uh..." I said. "I...I might be able to help?" I had no idea why I would make such an offer when I didn't know how to follow up on it, but he just looked so miserable. I studied him for a moment, then remembered something he'd said. "You said...you said your brother was in danger? That you were captured? Why? What happened?"

Yarin looked up at me, almost like he'd forgotten I was there. I couldn't imagine the turmoil he must have been going through. I tried to use my best friend psychic abilities to call Hazel back.

"We were staying with this couple...two doctors...they were helping us after our parents died but...they were not trustworthy. They hurt us..." his voice trailed off.

"That's...awful..." I said softly. I looked desperately back towards the front of the store, wishing Hazel would return. I was not equipped to deal with this. I didn't know what was happening, or why, but I knew I was far, *far* beyond what I could reasonably handle.

Was he just some poor soul suffering a serious delusion that made him think he was a time-traveler? No. I'd seen him in my visons, in the void. He'd talked about having the same powers as me. He was telling the truth—he was from another time, and somehow, he had been pulled here.

The email I'd sent to Rowan earlier popped into my head and I almost burst out laughing. Now *this* was a good question for her.

That thought derailed as soon as it arose, though, as I realized that I had to be careful who I told about Yarin. I looked down at him, sitting hunched on a little office chair, staring at everything with a mixture of fascination and horror. Best case scenario, he'd end up in the same system that had left my mother with trust issues and an assortment of psychological problems. And worst-case scenario? He'd be locked in an institution for the rest of his life.

No, that wasn't the worst-case scenario—the *absolute* worst was someone believing him about his abilities. The government claiming him and scientists studying him like some kind of specimen. And frankly, I didn't think I could trust Rowan with this information, not when that possibility was on the table. I barely knew her, but she'd felt ruthless, and I wasn't prepared to test that with Yarin's freedom.

But what was I supposed to do with him? I didn't know why, exactly, I had decided that this, too, was my problem to solve, but here he was, and he certainly didn't know what to do. Someone was going to have to do *something*.

My head dropped to my hands as I tried to control my breathing. I was spiraling, I could feel it. This was too much.

Once I'd managed to get my breathing under control, I pulled out my phone, typing up a message to the others: *New weird development. Found a kid from Germany in 1942 with no memory of any time passing between then and now, or how he got here.*

In the main shop, Hazel said a cheery, "Have a nice day!" as the door dinged. A few seconds later, she was by my side again.

"What do we do?" Hazel asked.

"I have no idea," I responded. We were standing a bit away from him, huddled together, talking in barely audible whispers.

"Is this guy for real?" Hazel asked, eyeing him nervously.

"I don't know how to explain how I know this, but yes. He's telling the truth," I said, watching him curiously. "I sensed him on the mountain. I...I saw him in some kind of vision. He's from the past."

"My mom will be here soon," Hazel said, looking at her own phone. "We have to get him out of here."

"Okay," I said. "When's your shift over?"

Hazel glanced out at the store. "It's a slow day, I could leave as soon as she gets here."

I nodded. “Right. Um. Should we meet up with the others?”

“I mean, what else can we do?” Hazel asked.

I glanced back at Yarin, feeling guilty for talking about him in front of him, but he was so checked out and vacant, I didn’t think he’d even noticed.

My phone buzzed and I checked the message. It was from Derek, asking a multitude of questions.

“What’s that?” Yarin asked. His voice was hoarse and weak, but he was looking with confusion at my phone.

I glanced at him, then back at my phone. I had no idea how to explain the device in my hand to someone from the forties.

My phone buzzed again. *This is some Captain America level weirdness right here.* That was Ford, of course. I laughed, despite myself, then turned back to Yarin.

“Um...it’s a communication device,” I said. I felt weirdly dorky saying that, but it was the best description I could think that wouldn’t confuse him. ‘Phone’ definitely wouldn’t sum it up correctly. “I can send messages to my friends and they can send them back to me.” I decided not to bring up the ten thousand other things it could do—the poor boy was already overwhelmed.

He looked confused, so I switched to my thread with my dad, where I wasn’t actively discussing Yarin’s fate with people making comic book references, and showed him the screen. He stared at it with wide eyes. “Remarkable. How long does it take?”

“Uh, it’s instant,” I said, and his eyes widened in response. Turning back to Hazel, I said quietly, “Okay,

I'm gonna get him out of here. We'll figure out where to meet up and you come by as soon as you leave work."

She agreed and I went to Yarin, speaking gently. "Hey, I'm gonna take you to meet up with some of my friends so we can help you, okay?"

He nodded, setting down his cup of tea and following me out of the back room. I led him to my car, feeling very weird about having this stranger in my car alone with me. But I pushed that anxiety away and focused on the task at hand.

I said goodbye to Hazel and got into my car, Yarin looking around, no doubt taking in the differences between the cars he was used to and the ones of today. He studied the seatbelt and the buttons for the radio and temperature control with interest that almost seemed to pull him from horrified to intrigued.

Before we drove off, I checked my messages. Emily had responded, too, first with, *!!?!??!?* and then with actual words: *How did you even find this guy? Are you sure he's telling the truth??*

I glanced over at Yarin, then wrote back, *Yes, trust me. He's the real deal*

Yarin was watching me with curiosity, but he didn't say anything. Emily wanted to do a group call, but I asked her to stay on text. I didn't want to alarm him any more by having three other people's voices coming from the tiny black rectangle in my hand.

We decided to once again meet at Derek's work, since he was just finishing up a shift. He grabbed us a table at the back where no one would bother us. Once we arrived, I steered Yarin to the front counter.

"Are you hungry?" I asked him, certain he must be famished.

He nodded emphatically and looked at the selection of foods before him, seeming overwhelmed. Realizing this could take a while, I asked a few questions to get a feel for what he might like, and made some suggestions. He ended up going with a simple cheese sandwich and a black coffee. Luckily, it was Derek processing the order, so I didn't have to worry about trying to seem like the situation was normal.

"This place is...similar to a place I used to visit back home," he said. "But also quite different," he said, his eyes lingering on the modern card reader and register.

"Yeah, it does kind of have that style," I said, watching him take in the room.

"What is that?" he asked of the card reader.

"Um. A way to transfer money to pay for stuff," I said. I kept phrasing things in the weirdest ways, and it was throwing me off, but it felt like the only way to explain what must have felt like a completely alien world to Yarin.

We sat down and I gnawed my lip impatiently. I had wanted to take today to catch up on research, maybe work through a plan for the caseload Emily had for me, or prep for her interview, but instead I suddenly had a wayward time traveler on my hands.

Yarin seemed to notice my distress. "Rosalind?"

"Yeah?" I asked, trying to collect myself.

"Are you all right?"

"Yes, yes, sorry. I'm just...trying to figure out what happened to you," I admitted.

"As am I," Yarin said.

Derek brought Yarin's order and he dug into his food hungrily, and I was relieved that this, at least, was a problem I could easily solve.

As Yarin ate, my mind drifted back to the *East/West* episode about the woman from Arizona who'd gone missing. I grabbed my phone and did a quick search, pulling up an article about it and skimming over it. She had vanished without a trace twelve years ago, and had been found recently with no memory of the time that had passed, and no signs of aging. She was even wearing the same clothes she'd disappeared in—apparently she had walked back to her home only to find another family living there.

I looked at Yarin—it sounded eerily similar to what had happened to him.

The geography was just a little...off. A mystery I still couldn't make sense of. When I resurfaced from the dark place, I came back to the exact same place and time I'd left.

Yarin had moved through time *and* space by a considerable amount. And not knowing why that happened terrified me, because it meant I didn't know how to avoid it.

Derek came back a few minutes later to join us.

"You okay, Roz?" he asked as he sat down.

"Yeah. Just...worried."

He nodded, then held his hand out for Yarin to shake. "Hi, I'm Derek Vega," he said. The absurdly normal interaction made me giggle and they both looked at me in confusion.

Tentatively, Yarin shook the hand offered to him. "I'm Yarin Sapir. It's nice to meet you."

"Likewise. Rosalind tells me you're not from around here," Derek went on, in the most casual, conversational tone I'd ever heard from him.

I had to fight not to laugh—this whole thing was so ridiculous.

"No...I'm..." Yarin frowned, looking around. "What is that?" he asked. I looked in the direction he was pointing. He was staring, perplexed, at someone's laptop.

"Um, that is a computer. But a very small one," Derek answered. Yarin stared at it in surprise, leaning a bit to get a better look.

"How is it so small?" he asked.

Derek explained some technical stuff I wasn't quite tracking on, then glanced at me and added, "Roz? You sure you're good? You look a little...frantic."

I nodded, trying wave him off reassuringly, not trusting myself to speak yet. I was teetering somewhere on the edge of laughing and going completely catatonic. I didn't know why *I* felt so overwhelmed when poor Yarin was the one displaced in time, but here we were.

Emily saved me by rushing in just then, plopping down beside me and looking at Yarin in disbelief.

"You're a time traveler?" she blurted out.

Derek sighed. "This is Emily. She has no filter. Emily, this is Yarin."

Her arrival gave me a minute to calm down. I didn't want to get panicky, so I did some breathing exercises from my therapist. While I did that, Emily tried to ask Yarin an assortment of questions, but Derek suggested we let the poor boy finish his meal and settle in a little more before we started figuring things out.

Ford joined us not long after, and surveyed Yarin.

"Steve Rogers himself," he said with a grin.

"Who?" Yarin asked, looking even more perplexed than before.

I sat forward. "He's a movie character who also traveled from the 1940s to the modern day," I said. "This is Ford, another of our friends."

Hazel arrived last, and Derek got one of his coworkers to get the rest of us food. Everyone had a million questions, and for some reason, they all thought I might have answers. I had none.

"How did you find me?" I asked Yarin. He'd seen us in the forest, that was dozens of miles from the Apothecary. He'd seen me in the void, but that was...nowhere, from what I could tell. And how had he known *exactly* which store to go into?

Yarin flushed lightly. "Well, I followed your energy."

I blinked. I guess he wasn't kidding about having the same powers as me.

"Her *energy*?" Emily asked, taking copious notes.

Yarin nodded. "I can...I can sense an individual's... spirit, I suppose. It's not much different than sensing a ghost, really."

"That's *amazing*, I had no idea that was a thing. I knew Roz could sense *paranormal* stuff but I never thought of applying that to *people*. I mean...I suppose it makes sense? A ghost is just a person without their physical body, so...we all kinda have ghosts inside us?"

"Definitely new," Derek said.

"Actually...I can do that, too," I said.

They all turned to look at me.

"You developed a new ability and you didn't tell me?" Emily asked.

"Keep it down, Em," I hissed, looking around.

After a while, we managed to piece it together: Yarin had very similar abilities to me, which he'd discovered shortly after his parents died. He didn't say how it happened, and none of us pressed him for details.

And yes, he had been evading the Nazis. The idea that I was speaking directly to someone who had lived through that, seen it, lived in real fear of it...it was a little much. And now that my stress-induced giggle fit had ended, I was sobered by the reality of what Yarin had endured.

"After my parents died," Yarin said softly, "my little brother and I ran away. We had family in England, and I thought...I thought if we could get there, we'd be safe. But it was hard to travel. We didn't have much money, and we had to keep ourselves hidden."

Ford immediately began searching for Yarin's brother, Seth Sapir, online. Emily wrote down everything Yarin said. Hazel kept asking questions about his well-being, like where he'd been sleeping and what he'd been eating. Derek answered his questions about the modern day and what had changed with surprising gentleness and patience. And I...just sat there, stunned, taking it all in.

"What do you remember?" I asked. "What's the last thing you remember before you ended up here?"

Yarin was quiet for a moment, then said. "A couple took us in, as I said before. My brother and I. They said they would protect us. They were doctors. And they...they tried many things on me, I suppose to see what my abilities were. I-I realize now that that's why they agreed to take us in. I don't know how they knew I could communicate with spirits, but they did...they wanted to use my ability for something, and they used my brother as a...a hostage. To keep me there. So they could...try and use those abilities..." he didn't elaborate and we didn't push for more details. I could only imagine how hard this was for him to recount.

"I don't know what the experiments were, only that they hurt. During the last one, I actually thought I might die," his voice was soft and shaky now, and we'd all gone completely silent.

"I...I found myself in that..." he looked at me. "The dark place. Where the spirits are."

I nodded. I knew the feeling.

"I didn't know how to escape, but I was away from the doctor, so...in a way I felt relieved. But I was worried about my brother. I thought if I could get back, and sneak in without them seeing me, I could get him and we could escape. I wandered around for a while, trying to find my way out, and then...then a bright light appeared, and pulled me to it. And then...I was in the forest, and a terrible storm was raging. The wind and lightning and fire startled me, and I ran into the trees to hide. I thought...I thought I was back in my own time, but very quickly I realized I was no longer anywhere familiar."

"How long were you in the dark place?" Emily asked.

Yarin shook his head. "Not long, perhaps an hour? It's hard to keep track of time under such conditions, but it didn't feel like much time passed...but...then a passage opened, pulled me through, and I was in a forest, and there was fire...so I ran."

"You said that you sensed me that night?" I pressed. "How did you know that I was like you?"

"I could sense each of you there," Yarin said. "At least, I could sense there were other people around me. None of you felt familiar, not only as strangers but as...as people from another time. I couldn't tell *that* at the moment, but...I felt something different. I knew I hadn't sensed anyone else like me before, certainly not anywhere near the doctors. I knew someone else like me must be near. You disappeared too quickly for me to follow, but when I felt you return to fight the...the beast...I vowed not to lose sight of you."

"You were running from that thing," I blurted suddenly. "That...that monster."

He nodded. "It chased me more than once, but I could sense it, so I could usually keep a good distance, and I knew where to hide to avoid it."

Yarin's ability to sense energy was *much* more refined than mine. On the other hand, he seemed to have a harder time with moving between the dimensions than I did, and that seemed to be what trapped him. But over so much time? I shuddered.

We sat in silence after his story. Hazel was teary-eyed, and the rest of us were too stunned to say much.

"I just want to find my brother," Yarin whispered. His eyes lit up and he looked at me hopefully, though I could still see a sheen of tears threatening around the edges. "Do you think you could send me back?"

That almost made me cry. "I...I don't know, Yarin," I whispered. "I don't know how."

His face fell, and he looked down, nodding. "I know...it may well be impossible."

"I will try, though," I said in a rush. I had no idea how I might go about this, but I couldn't stand the thought of him never seeing his brother again. "I'll do everything I can."

We didn't know what to do with Yarin long-term, but Ford said he could stay with him for a couple days, at least until we figured something else out. None of us wanted to try and explain this to our parents, and we were afraid that if word got out, Yarin would be taken away. If we stood any chance of helping him find his brother, and possibly get back to his own time, we were going to have to keep him close.

After that, we went home, my mind still reeling from finding another person, aside from my mother, who could do what I could do. We didn't have much of a plan, but we had a brand new problem to deal with, and a new fear—getting lost in time and never being able to find my way home.

FIFTEEN

At home, I glanced across the street, watching Ford lead Yarin into his house. I was so tempted to drop by for dinner and see how Ford was going to explain Yarin to his parents. It wasn't that I thought he'd choke—knowing Ford, he'd tell a flawless lie. I just wanted to see what it was.

But I had to stay home; my dad was expecting me for dinner, and I was still trying to keep up the appearance of normalcy with him.

So I sat on the sofa, flicking through pictures on Instagram. I hadn't drawn much in my sketchbook lately, as I was mostly drawing ghosts or visions or dreams or weird symbols in my journal, rather than just fun or creative ideas.

I went back to my home screen, only to notice my email had a little red circle showing three unread messages. I tapped the icon, strangely torn between hoping Rowan had answered me and hoping I never heard from her again.

I did, in fact, have a message from her. I opened it nervously and read:

Roz,
Glad to hear it was successful.
Keep in touch,
Rowan

I frowned at the brevity of it, but was glad she hadn't asked any follow-up questions.

On a whim, I went to the UNLV website and looked up Rowan. I was curious what classes she was teaching in the coming semester. She was listed on a few graduate physics classes with descriptions I couldn't even understand. Seemed about right for her.

Continuing on this vein, I searched her again, seeing if any more articles had been posted. A few more had cropped up speculating as to why she had moved, but she had refused comment, so it was all just guesswork and rumors. And I knew that every field had rivals who were ready to pounce on you and tarnish your reputation if they had the chance, so I couldn't take anything said by her colleagues too seriously. Rowan was strange and mysterious, and didn't seem to make many friends, so I doubted anyone around her knew her true motives, and she clearly wasn't broadcasting them. Even my dad had detractors among other lawyers; until I had facts, speculation and rumors from people who might just hate her for being better at her job than they were wasn't much to work with.

I decided to stop puzzling over her. Unfortunately, the next thing I came up with to think about was Elixabete.

There were too many weird women in my life. Rowan. Veronica. Elixabete. I chuckled to myself as I remembered that, were I to say this to Ford, he'd insist on adding Joanne to the list.

Then again, I was turning out to be rather unusual myself, so maybe that was just how it worked—I was strange, so I got more strangeness drawn to me.

My dad arrived, and we had dinner—he asked Elixabete to join us, but she said she had an errand to run and she'd be back later in the evening. I tried not to dwell on what errand Elixabete might be on, for all I knew she was visiting a friend, or taking a break, or just out on a date and it was nothing to be worried about. Not that she'd have to lie about any of that, but maybe she liked to keep her work and personal life separate. She had *just* moved in a few days earlier, and we weren't her family, so the idea that she wasn't sharing every detail with us was...quite normal, actually. It was probably nothing, just a normal activity that I had no reason to be suspicious of.

Still...

We caught up on shows after dinner, and I took the opportunity to draw. I even forced myself to draw things that weren't related to ghosts or ghouls or anything else paranormal. After a while, it didn't feel forced, it felt natural, and I slipped back into our old routine comfortably.

My dad got tired around ten and went up to bed.

Briefly, the memory of the big case he was working flitted through my mind, and I wondered if I should ask him again about it. Maybe things had calmed down, and he'd tell me now?

But I didn't ask, I just told him to sleep well and packed up my drawing stuff, figuring I'd go hang out in my room before turning in. For once, I wasn't actually tired, and while I didn't want to destroy my sleep schedule, I did want to enjoy the feeling of being awake and creative and unbothered by paranormal activity.

As I was getting myself a cup of tea to take upstairs, I heard the front door open. My heart raced until I remembered Elixabete, and sure enough when I rounded the corner, it was her.

"Hello Rosalind, are you heading up to bed?" she asked.

"Yeah," I answered. "Did you have a nice evening?" I asked. It felt kind of lame but I couldn't help it, I was curious. Besides, what errand kept you out until past ten? I knew Vegas was a twenty-four hour town, but it still seemed kinda strange.

"Nice enough," she said. "More productive, I'd say. Well, I'll let you get some rest—I should get to bed myself. Have a good night, Rosalind!"

"Good night," I said, heading up the stairs and watching as she locked up and set the alarm. It was strange, having her here. It was stranger still to wonder why she seemed so...unusual.

Dismissing that thought for now, I went upstairs to finish my sketches and drink my tea. After everything with the monster and Yarin, I just wanted a few quiet, normal hours.

I had completely forgotten about Veronica's fashion show. My dad reminded me as I came downstairs, and I feigned awareness, pretending this information hadn't entirely vacated my brain the moment my dad first told me about it.

So I reminded my cousins and Ford—all of whom had remembered on their own because they did smart things like put events in their calendars or generally commit information to long-term memory—and went to get ready. It wasn't until late afternoon, but I didn't have much else to do for the moment.

Hey, what are we gonna do for Yarin while we're all gone? I texted Ford, worried about our wayward time traveler.

No worries. Got him covered, Ford responded.

I frowned at my phone, torn between amused and annoyed. I knew what he was doing—he was giving a vague answer so I'd have to ask what 'got him covered' meant and then he could go on one of his elaborate explanations.

It was weird how well I could know someone after only a few weeks. Then I remembered his brother, and how my mother had had all the same problems I have but I hadn't known it until now.

It was also weird how *little* you could know someone, even after a long time.

What are you doing with this poor boy? I sent back, giving in to his wish for an audience for whatever scheme he'd cooked up.

I'm hiding him in my attic

I rubbed my face in agitation. *Really, Ford?*

What?? I can't just keep him here as an unexplained house guest forever. My mother loves him but she's GOING to ask questions if he just never leaves

So you're going to hide him in the attic like one of those people you see on the news who secretly live in someone's house?!

Hey, it works for them, he replied.

I rolled my eyes and typed out: *It very much does not*

Well what else should I do with him? At least no one is looking for him

I held my phone, staring down at it. I had no idea what to suggest. If any of our parents realized he didn't have a home, they'd call the authorities. They wouldn't do it to be cruel, they'd just think that was the right thing to do, the way to find his family and get him home.

I sighed and responded, *Idk. I guess that'll have to do for now*

Don't worry, he's got a sweet setup

Ford then proceeded to text me several pictures of the attic, which I had to admit he'd decked out pretty nicely. I wasn't sure if it was already set up to hang out in from before or if he'd done something ridiculous like staying up all night getting it ready, but it was comfortable and spacious, with peek-a-boo windows that let in light and plush pillows and blankets. There was even a kind of bed setup—maybe an air mattress or the cushion of a futon—a miniature, free-standing air conditioner, and beside the bed, a massive stack of books. Yarin was in one of the pictures, sitting on a heap of pillows by a window and reading. He was clean and changed, and looked quite peaceful.

Got him some food, too

I was still uncertain. *What if someone hears him?*

Then I'll have a lot of explaining to do, but I told him if they do find him to just tell my parents he was abandoned and I'm helping him out, just in case. Doubt they will, though. This part of the attic is over my brother's room, and no one really goes in there anymore. Even has a bathroom he can sneak down to use.

It wasn't going to work forever, but I supposed for today, it would be a good place for Yarin to hide and rest and have a little time to process everything that had happened to him.

I hated that we were going to this stupid fashion show, but at the same time, I wouldn't have known what else to do with Yarin right now. Maybe he just needed a day off, too. He seemed very happy reading the books Ford had left for him. I hoped he was relaxed and comfortable. I knew how stressful this could be, and having a couple days of down time had made me feel a lot better. I wanted him to have that, too, especially after all the horrors he'd endured.

I told Ford I'd see him outside—my dad was driving us all together, and we'd be picking up Hazel and Haldi on the way—and slipped my phone into my pocket. I spotted the little knife I'd bought and tapped my fingers against my purse strap, debating. Events like this tended to check purses, sometimes even have metal detectors. I didn't want to risk losing it, but for some reason I liked having it with me.

Sighing, I left it behind and headed downstairs.

The fashion show was loud and crowded, taking place in one of the large convention centers at the Wynn, where tall, thin women with overly-serious faces strutted down the runway wearing outfits and shoes no one would ever wear in real life. I tried not to pout about a perfectly good evening—one where I could have caught up on some research or gotten a little extra sleep or even just played on my phone for a few hours—being ruined by frivolities.

Where we sat was shrouded in darkness, while the stage was so brightly lit it almost hurt to look at. Everyone around me was resplendent in their high-fashion glory, looking like...well...like the kind of people Joanne would hang around with.

I wondered idly if she'd ever participated in fashion shows or modeling. She was certainly tall enough to be a model, and based on the pictures I'd seen, she had once been a perfect match for what designers and agencies looked for. She seemed to like standing out and dressing extravagantly.

The models were prancing along before me. I glanced up at the runway. It wasn't even that I didn't like fashion and the people who promoted it—I did, actually; it was like a 3D painting, a living, moving tapestry of color and cloth created by other artists—I just didn't like *her*.

Speak of the devil.

Veronica came down the runway in a long, flowy turquoise gown that brought out the sea-green in her stupid eyes. And it made her hair shine in contrast like spun gold. And she looked gorgeous and I hated it. So I sat, pouting, thoroughly refusing to have a good time.

Ford was having fun, but Ford was *always* having

fun, so that didn't actually offend me as much as it might have.

Haldi also seemed to be enjoying himself, taking lots of pictures and grinning from ear to ear. Emily and Derek would have had fun, too, if they hadn't been too busy to attend. Hazel was beside me having a blast, and she kept elbowing me, telling me to smile and relax.

But I couldn't. I was officially in a *mood* and everyone insisting I get out of my mood was only making it worse.

When I wasn't thinking of how horrible Veronica was, I was scanning about the room, closing my eyes and practicing that new 'energy sense' I had. I couldn't stop thinking about it ever since Yarin had used it to find me. It was shaky at first, latching on only to people I knew well—my father, Hazel, Haldi, Ford—but once I got it started up, it became overwhelming, picking up on everyone with no limits, until I felt like I was drowning. I opened my eyes and massaged my temples.

"Do you need a pill?" my dad asked. He'd taken to carrying migraine medication everywhere he went in case I needed it. 'Migraine' was the official diagnosis, but I knew no pills would really help.

"No, I'm okay, thanks," I said, discreetly pressing two fingers into my right temple until it was over.

When the fashion show had ended, my dad said, "Come on, Veronica said we could go backstage." He sounded a tad too eager for my liking.

I grumbled in compliance and followed the group back, trying to figure out how to shut down this 'energy sense' now that I had switched it on. I could see *everyone* in the room twice now—through my normal, eye-based vision, and again through my what-is-happening-to-my-brain vision.

Since I couldn't shut it down, I decided to try and focus it. Maybe that would alleviate some of the overload I was experiencing.

I zeroed in on my father, since I'd never tried this around him before. He had a steadiness to his energy that immediately calmed me. It was very familiar—the most familiar of anyone I'd ever seen, though that wasn't surprising. But it was like I could see it clearly now. It wasn't just an inkling, it was *strong*.

I switched to Haldi. He was hyper, like Hazel. His energy abuzz with excitement and joy.

As I analyzed my cousin, it occurred to me that I might be able to use this to help me figure out Veronica. I wasn't sure how; it didn't allow me to read minds or even see things like intention, feeling, or anything else useful, but I was definitely getting *something*, and that was worth looking into, even if it didn't make any sense to me yet.

So when we were backstage, I sought out Veronica and locked on to her.

Her sense was ordinary in many ways, but I only noticed that because I'd been so busy observing ghosts and other such paranormal beings.

She had a *strong* presence. That was the first thing I noticed. Dominant. It blocked out others easily, overpowering the rest of the models and even my friends. Apparently, she was just really egotistical. Probably a narcissist.

I wonder what my mother's presence felt like.

I pushed that unwelcome thought away quickly.

When I compared Veronica's energy to the other

models, I saw a clear difference. The rest of her coworkers were...well there was no set 'type' for them, but there were similarities among them that seemed pretty constant. And while some where haughty and others were bubbly or energetic, they all had a similar *tone*. Veronica reminded me more of...

Actually, I couldn't place her. I was new at this, so it wasn't too surprising, but it still frustrated me.

Veronica was chatting with a few work friends as my dad and I stood beside her.

"I'm so glad you could make it to the show!" one of the girls said excitedly.

"Yeah!" another chimed in, patting Veronica's shoulder. "We haven't seen you in *forever*."

They went on for a bit about getting coffee together, or going shopping or something, and then Veronica broke away to talk to my dad. I was distracted with reading energies. They talked a little, and all the while, I tried to use this power, whatever it was, to read her mind. But it didn't work like that—not even close. I couldn't even get a sense of what she felt or wanted or intended—it was too vague and new for me to understand.

She turned, her cool blue eyes locking on mine, and I tensed, turning away. *Stupid, that was so obvious.* I should have played it off like I'd just happened to be looking at her, instead I had basically admitted that I'd been string daggers at her, and had been for a while.

I furrowed my brow, trying to switch this new sense 'off' again. It wasn't helping me, and if I kept it up I was going to give myself another headache.

We left, dropped Hazel and Haldi off at their house, then drove home.

SIXTEEN

The dome on Joanne's house wasn't fully repaired yet, but she had another, smaller studio in her back yard, which is where she led me when I showed up for my painting lesson.

"For when I need to feel a little more...isolated. Connected to the earth," she said to me, leading me into the small, shed-like space. It was very different from her dome—that had felt lofty and ethereal. This place, with its wooden walls and quaint little windows framed with lace, potted plants and rose bushes, felt like a small country home.

"This is so cute," I told her. I'd never seen it before, as it was tucked away between some tall trees.

She laughed. "Different from my usual style, but it..." she glanced at me. "To be honest, it reminds me of my mother."

"Oh. That's nice," I said, ignoring the clench in my gut.

We painted with watercolors, which I had mistakenly thought were overly simplistic, but now realized *were* an art form of their own. I had to concentrate on my work, which was wonderful, really.

"So, are you ready to start school in the fall?" Joanne asked.

"Eh. I guess," I said.

She gave me a side-long glance. "You don't sound very convincing."

I actually laughed. "It's not that I mind school. It's just...I don't know, I guess I've had kind of a hard time settling in here. I'm not sure how well I'll do if we add school into the equation."

Joanne chuckled. "You're a bright and strong young woman—you'll do spectacularly."

I wished I could believe her.

My painting for this project was Chinese-inspired: A young woman in monk's robes sitting under a large, yellow ginkgo tree, with leaves falling all around her. I hadn't intended for it to, but it had ended up with a kind of *Avatar: The Last Airbender* vibe. I liked it.

When we finished for the day, we sat on her porch enjoying some lemonade. Joanne's yard was so dense with greenery, it almost felt like a piece of the rainforest.

"Tell me, Rosalind, are you concerned about school for any other reasons?"

I shook my head. "No, I do fine in school. I'm sure it'll end up being no big deal."

"What do you enjoy most?" she asked.

I turned my glass of lemonade in my hands, letting

the edge of the drink touch just below the rim of the cup.

"History. And any art classes I can get, of course. I do okay in math. English...I love to read, but I'm not much of a writer."

"What would you like to do? When you're older, I mean."

I thought about how to answer that. I had a tendency to go back and forth. On the one hand, I had plenty of technical and organizational skills, all of which could work well for fields like law, politics, or medicine. Not that they appealed to me. Medicine, maybe, but in all honestly, I was a bit squeamish.

Alternately, I often found myself drawn to what my grandmother would call 'unrealistic' options. Painting and drawing and art in general. If I could do *anything*, it would probably be illustrating graphic novels. Or animation. Or doing promotional art. Or something along those lines. Last year, my dad had encouraged me to look into some internships, but I'd pulled up a few sites and then...never done anything with them. I hadn't applied, or even really found out what was out there.

"I don't really know," I answered honestly. With all that had happened since the move, I had genuinely forgotten about my future, or making any kind of plans for it. Probably because, even before all this, thinking about it had felt overwhelming and stressful.

"That's all right," Joanne said, looking out over her gardens and sipping her lemonade. "It's not something you need to stress over now—you're sixteen. Be young. Have fun. You'll find what you're meant to do in the living of your life."

I looked at her. In a world of adults telling me to

figure my life out in advance, her words were rare, and precious.

"Thanks," I barely managed.

As I was leaving, I saw a tall, attractive young woman entering Joanne's house. She wore a very stylish, tailored grey pantsuit. Her skin was dark and her hair was trimmed short in a neatly-sculpted afro. She was incredibly professional, and seeing her in Joanne's colorful, cluttered house was a kind of amusing juxtaposition. Especially with Joanne standing there in her paint-splattered overalls and peacock-patterned blouse.

"Joanne!" the professional woman said. "I have your dry cleaning, your groceries will be delivered this evening, I booked that flight for you next month, and we have three new artists to consider for the gallery." The words came out quickly, in a clipped, serious tone that threw me out of the serene quiet I'd found in Joanne's backyard.

"Hello, Danielle. Thank you," Joanne said, smiling.

Danielle looked up, saw me, and frowned. I had a feeling I wasn't on her itinerary, and that she didn't much care for things that weren't on her schedule somewhere.

"Oh!" Joanne exclaimed. "Where are my manners? Danielle, this is Rosalind—she's a student of mine. Just moved in next door. Rosalind, this is Danielle, my personal assistant and professional life-saver!" Joanne said affectionately.

Danielle had seemed stand-offish at first, but I guess once she knew how I fit into Joanne's life, she warmed up.

"Hello," she said, smiling and shaking my hand. As soon as she was done, she turned back to Joanne and began talking about the various artists petitioning for spots in her gallery.

I said goodbye quickly, not wanting to intrude on business matters, and went back home. Elixabete was cooking dinner, which I was used to seeing mid-afternoon by now. She made these old-school homemade meals that were entirely from scratch, and required tons of prep.

"Hello, Rosalind. How was your painting lesson?" she asked.

I still thought of the crystal grid or whatever it was whenever I saw her. It made me uneasy.

"It was good," I said. I sat down at the counter, still not brave enough to outright ask what her deal was. She'd just lie like she had with the crystal, anyway. So instead, I said, "What does that symbol on your bracelet mean?"

She glanced at her wrist, then smiled. "It's called the flower of life. It represents creation."

"It's beautiful," I said. I wasn't lying—the pattern was simple, yet lovely.

"Thank you," she said with a smile.

Normally, I'd shut up at this point, but I was still hoping to get some information. Anything.

"Um, it looks like the kind of thing my cousin Hazel would really like. Where did you get it?"

Elixabete nodded. "She likely would. You can find them all over. I received mine as a gift for my fifteenth birthday."

I studied the old leather band. It looked *very* worn. Old. Much older than it should—she couldn't be older than forty.

"Was it a family heirloom?" I pressed.

She nodded. "It was my mother's, before me. She died when I was young."

"Oh, I'm sorry," I said, a bit taken aback. "My mom's dead," I blurted out. Then I wanted to slap myself for being so awkward.

Elixabete glanced at me and nodded solemnly. "Yes, your father told me."

"How, um...how did you lose your mother?" I asked.

Elixabete set down the bowl of diced vegetables she was holding. "She got sick," she said. "Cancer. It was long, and slow."

We were silent.

"How old were you?" I asked, almost forgetting I wanted to get information out of her.

"Eight when she got sick. Twelve when she died."

"I'm sorry," I whispered.

She smiled sadly, her eyes distant. "I'm sorry for you, too," she said softly.

I looked away. I wasn't sure how to proceed with my interrogation now. There was that energy-sense thing. I wasn't great with it, but I figured I should at least give it a shot.

I tried to slip into that mental space. It was harder to get into now—my head was aching—but I felt a faint light from her. Steady. Strong. And...something else. Something I couldn't place. It didn't scare me, but it was curious.

I shocked myself by realizing that what she reminded

me of was the distinct, unique energy I'd felt from *Veronica.*

It faded as my concentration broke, and I massaged my temples. That revelation didn't help my trust of Elixabete at all. Veronica was still an enigma to me in so many ways, none of them good. And Elixabete...well, I was still on the fence about her, nice as she was.

I sighed. My powers, or whatever they were, were *way* more trouble than they were worth.

My dad came home and we sat down for dinner. Elixabete joined us this time, and she my dad talked while I mostly listened, which wasn't unusual for me, I tended to prefer listening. He had another trip coming up next week. He'd be gone for four days, but he seemed less anxious than he had for his last trip. Granted, I was in therapy now, behaving (as far as he knew) much more calmly, and we had Elixabete around.

Not that her presence necessarily put *me* at ease, but my dad trusted her. I glanced at her, wondering if I should, too. He was a pretty good judge of character. Usually.

I thought of Veronica and sighed. Maybe he wasn't. Maybe I wasn't. Who even knew anymore?

When I finally went up to bed, I found I couldn't sleep, but not because of ghosts or nightmares or shadow demons. It was because of how confused I was.

What were these powers I had? Where had they come from? Why? How?

I knew I'd inherited them from my mother, but that didn't really answer my questions. It just added another step. Where had *she* gotten these powers from? And why?

Thinking about my mother woke an ache deep in my core—one I'd never find relief from. I knew, because in the year since her death, it hadn't once subsided. I could bury it. Or ignore it. Or just deny it existed, distracting myself from it, but I couldn't actually escape it.

I rubbed at my eyes and tried to breathe, slow and even, to calm my nerves. Accepting that I couldn't sleep, I got up and flipped through the pages of the journal again, searching for answers I knew weren't there.

When I realized it was 3:30 am, I groaned. Tomorrow was going to suck. I switched off my light and set the journal aside, hoping I could get a couple hours of sleep before breakfast. I tugged my curtains shut against the sunrise that would come too soon, glancing up at the spot where I'd found the first crystal.

Another mystery, but one for later.

SEVENTEEN

"I talked to Elixabete a bit more today. I'm so glad we finally found a good fit," my dad said as he prepared coffee for us. "And I think it's going to be good with her here full-time."

"Yeah," I said. I wasn't sure what else to say, because I didn't think it was all that great.

"I like her," he went on. "She's very intelligent, very interesting. Turns out cooking is a passion of hers, so I asked her to make us some Basque dishes."

"Basque?" I asked.

He nodded, handing me a cup. "Apparently there's a sizeable Basque community in Northern Nevada. That's where she's from."

"Oh," I accepted the warm mug and took a sip. "I've never heard of...any of that."

"You should ask her about where she grew up."

I wasn't surprised my dad knew all this stuff about her. He'd probably had multiple conversations with her already, and learned a ton about her, while I'd been researching ghosts, listening to *East/West*, and generally getting into trouble.

It made me feel a little guilty that I hadn't taken the time to get to know her, but I still wasn't sure I trusted her, so that wasn't helping me connect. I mostly just wanted to spy on her, but I was afraid she'd have some means of finding out, and then who knew what she'd do. I realized I was being paranoid, but in my defense, my life had gotten very odd very fast.

I rubbed my eyes—it was too early for this. I needed to think of something else. I ended up skimming through our group chat, looking for a distraction. We had been discussing Yarin and what to do with him. I felt bad, talking about him without including him, but he didn't have a phone and still seemed to be a little overwhelmed by this whole thing. Not that I could blame him, I was overwhelmed, too, and I was still in my own time. I had no idea what we were going to do with him long-term, but for now he was camped out in Ford's attic. I knew that couldn't last, but at least he was safe and fed for the moment.

Despite this more pressing and important concern, Elixabete still occupied my thoughts.

It was a quiet morning, my dad had gone upstairs to get ready for work. Elixabete seemed to be upstairs, as well, though I hadn't seen her when I'd left my room.

I stood in the kitchen, sipping my coffee, almost unsure what to do with myself. It was an odd sensation, realizing I didn't know what to do when I wasn't around someone else or working on a project. As an only child, I'd always been *good* at being alone. Feeling out of sorts on my own was alien.

As if on cue, my phone chimed. A text from Ford.

Good morning, Scooby Gang. We're still on for lunch today, right? I didn't write it down so I'm not sure if it's today or tomorrow

Yup, today, noon. You're bringing Yarin, right? Emily responded.

I wondered how Yarin was doing, hiding out in Ford's attic like some refugee. Which, technically, he was.

I didn't have anything to do until it was time to go to lunch, so I sat on the sofa playing on my phone. It wasn't the best use of energy, but it was a simple one, and I tried to enjoy those moments as much as possible whenever they came up.

In that peaceful quiet, where I had some time to just *be* without worrying about anything too major, a new worry managed to surface in my mind: I was starting my junior year at the end of the summer, and at this rate, the summer would fly by with no time for preparation or any real relaxation.

I groaned, sinking further into the sofa. Why did I have to think of that now? I didn't want to worry about school, but now I was, along with the added worry of how I was ever going to balance a full workload from my classes alongside all this ghost nonsense.

My dad came down then and greeted me, ruffling my hair a little as he passed. I turned, clambering up on my knees to look over the back of the sofa at him as he moved through the kitchen.

"Dad, am I all registered for school in the fall?" I asked.

He looked up, a bit surprised, and nodded. "Yes, of course. I've been copying you on emails with your school counselor, and you should have all your login information if you wanted to get into the system early and start preparing or getting familiar with things."

I nodded, relieved, glad my dad had covered that for me. I *had* noticed a lot of emails from my dad that had looked important, but I realized I had just been skimming past them to look for ghost-related things. I had intended to catch up on them soon, but kept forgetting to. It was an endless cycle of 'open my email for a specific reason, see a bunch of other stuff to read through, promise to get caught up after I did whatever I'd originally intended to do, then getting distracted and moving onto the next thing without actually ever catching up' I'd accidentally gotten caught up in.

At least I was registered. I opened my email and looked through the various updates. I had my class schedule and teacher information. I knew what day I started. I just had to manage to be ready for school in a couple months. Not even, really—we were in early July and school was set to start late August.

All of this was making me anxious.

"Do you want to go shopping for school supplies soon?" my dad asked, carrying on the conversation. "I've been meaning to ask but I keep forgetting."

"Yeah," I said. "Yeah that'd be great." I wasn't even really focused on what I was agreeing to, I was just trying to keep from getting too worked up about how soon school would start and how little school was even registering for me as a thing anymore. My life had become consumed by the paranormal and I wasn't sure how to tell the ghosts to back off because I had to work on a school project or study for a test.

"Sounds good. Okay, well, I have to get to the office—I was hoping to work from home but I've got a client flying in for a meeting, I should at least make an appearance," he said.

"Okay. Have a good day at work," I said.

He kissed the top of my head and left, and I settled back in to flick through school-related emails and try not to worry about how I'd balance that. Maybe I should ask the others. After all, they might not be as caught-up in this as I was, but they were pretty busy with all the ghost-related activities.

Another, even worse thought hit me then: What if my friends couldn't keep helping me once school started?

Why even wait for school to start, actually—they were really busy with all my drama and they didn't need to be. Surely they needed to do their own things. Surely they couldn't keep helping me navigate my life.

I opened the group chat and looked back at some of our conversations. It was an active chat, lots of discussion happening. It hadn't hit me until right this moment how much I relied on them, their support, just their general presence. If that went away...if that faded like it so often did...

I thought of what few friends I'd left behind in LA. I had barely heard from any of them, and when we did share a message or a meme, the conversation seemed to die before it ever really started.

I knew Hazel wouldn't abandon me, but she could get

busier and need time for herself. That was entirely fair. That was *normal*. And under normal circumstances, I'd be fine with it. I'd want the time for myself, for other activities, for hobbies and whatever else. But now...now I felt like I needed her. She was a lifeline and I was clinging to her.

As for the other three? They had just met me, they had no reason to be so devoted. Sure, Emily and Derek were interested in ghost research, but they had lots of data at this point. And things had gotten dangerous more than once. Hell, Derek had broken his arm. He had a job. He had a lot of responsibilities at home. Emily had told me about her many extra-curriculars and school activities.

What happened when they needed to focus on their own lives, and their own responsibilities, and their own interests, and had enough ghost info and didn't need me anymore?

What if Ford got bored with this, or scared? What if he just got tired of dealing with constant ghost issues? With me freaking out and turning to him for comfort and distractions?

I closed all my apps and put on some music. I needed to calm down. I was going to slip into a full-on panic attack if I didn't stop obsessing, but I still hadn't figured out how to *stop* obsessing and I was uncertain that was even a possibility.

A text from Ford interrupted me and pulled me back to the moment, derailing my downward spiral. It was a text just to me, not on the group chat.

Hey, I'm getting ready to go. Got Yarin. Want me to pick you up and we can drive together?

Yes, please

A shaky breath escaped me. Driving there with Ford and Yarin would be good.

I put my mug in the dishwasher and finished getting ready, just in time for my doorbell to ring. It surprised me.

Curious, I headed downstairs to find Elixabete already at the door. She smiled up at me and said, "Rosalind, your friends are here."

At the door, I found Ford and Yarin standing there waiting for me.

"What—" I started. I had been expecting a text.

"Yarin said it was rude to just text a lady that we had arrived, and that we should go to the door and pick her up properly," Ford said, grinning.

Elixabete chuckled. "How polite! Would you boys like to come in for a moment?" she offered.

"I'd love to, ma'am" Yarin said. "But I'm afraid we have a lunch to get to."

He was so proper, it made me smile.

"Um, thanks," I said to them. "Elixabete, I'll see you later, we're just grabbing lunch with a few friends."

"Have fun," she said, waving us off. I stepped outside and closed the door.

"She still being weird?" Ford asked.

"The weird is holding steady," I said.

"She seemed very nice," Yarin commented.

I sighed. "I mean...she *is*...I'm just...probably getting paranoid."

He nodded, face growing serious. "It's good to be cautious, you never really know who you can trust."

His tone worried me. I nodded back, unsure what else

to say. I remembered his story about the doctors and my stomach twisted. People had used kindness and protection to trap Yarin and get close to him—I had to be cautious that the same thing didn't happen to me. Or to Yarin again, for that matter; if Elixabete was a danger to me then she was probably a danger to him, too.

Ford led us to his van and we climbed in, Yarin insisting I take the passenger seat and climbing into the back. As we drove, I glanced back at him, wondering how he was doing. It felt like an awkward thing to ask, but I did find myself worried about him and wishing I could do more.

Instead, I asked, "What are you reading?"

He looked up and smiled, holding his book so I could see. "*Nightfall.* It's by one of my favorite authors, Isaac Asimov. I started it before but never got to finish it, but then Ford found it for me. When I first read it, it was only a short story, but now it's a novel! It's very good, have you read it?"

It was the most he'd ever said unprompted, and the way he lit up made me smile. I glanced at Ford, who was grinning too.

"I haven't, but maybe I can borrow it after you're done. What's it about?"

"It's about people who live on a planet with six suns, so there's no concept of 'nighttime' to them. There's a myth of a doomsday that is set to come soon, and they're trying to prevent it, while others are trying to prove it's all superstition."

"Wow, I had no idea he wrote stories like that," I admitted. I had never read anything by Isaac Asimov, but I knew my dad liked a few of his books.

"You can certainly borrow it when I'm done," Yarin said, settling back into his seat and returning to his reading.

I looked over at Ford, wondering how getting those books had gone. Had he asked Yarin what he wanted and just gone to the bookstore and loaded up? Had he had some of them in his family's library already? I decided to ask later.

A few cop cars raced by while we were stopped at an intersection, and I glanced at Ford. It was probably unrealistic for me to take any indication of a problem as 'ghosts are tormenting people' but it was hard not to.

"I'm sure it's nothing," Ford said quietly, glancing over at me.

"Yeah. Probably," I said.

Ford pulled up to the restaurant and parked the van and we climbed out; the boys made their way to the doors while I trailed behind them. My mind kept going over Yarin's experiences with the doctors who had trapped him, and Elixabete, and how I really couldn't know if she was being honest with me or not.

Today is a bad anxiety day, I thought to myself—something Dr. Thompson had told me to do to clarify that I was experiencing heightened anxiety and not genuinely under threat. I ignored the nagging voice that whispered that I was, in fact, under threat, and followed Ford and Yarin into the restaurant.

The others weren't there yet, and the boys were talking—discussing sci-fi books, it seemed, and having a good time from what I could tell. I didn't want to interrupt them, especially since I didn't think there was anything they could do about my spiking anxiety.

Besides, I often asked Ford for help with that, even if I did so indirectly. I needed to get better at managing it myself. That was hard to imagine when I could feel my heartbeat in my throat, and my hands were sweating, and everything seemed too loud and close and too... *much*.

What had Dr. Thompson taught me to do? I scrambled momentarily, trying to remember her techniques.

Breathing. Right.

Inhale for four seconds. Hold for seven. Exhale for eight.

I did this a few times, feeling my heartbeat steady little by little with each repetition. It didn't completely calm me down, but it had taking me from 'rapidly becoming more distressed' to 'mildly nervous' and that shift alone felt like a huge improvement, even if I still wasn't feeling *good*.

There was another exercise, something about my senses, but I couldn't remember what I was supposed to do, and looking around trying to figure it out was only making me feel worse, so I stuck with breathing.

We got to the front of the line and Ford asked what I wanted for lunch. I glanced up at the menu, realizing I had completely forgotten to pick something out.

"Um. What are you having?" I asked.

Ford glanced at me, seeming to catch that I was a bit off. "Teriyaki bowl for me, grilled steak wrap for Yarin," he answered.

"Um. The bowl, teriyaki bowl, that sounds good," I said. It wasn't a lie—I generally liked teriyaki, so it felt like a safe choice.

Ford's eyes lingered on me a moment longer, like he wanted to ask if I was okay. I turned away quickly, saying, "Um, why don't I find us a table?"

I picked a booth by the window and sat down, only realizing then that I'd let him pay for my food without offering to cover my share, and in fact acting like it was obvious that he would pay for my food. Well. That was rude. But he hadn't argued, so I just made a mental note to pick up the tab next time.

Before I could slip into too much social awkwardness, though, a pair of strong arms wrapped around me and I was crushed in a big hug.

"Hi Roz!" Hazel—the only person on Earth who could get away with that without being instinctively swatted away—said.

"Hi Haze," I answered. I would usually tease her or make a joke, but honestly I kind of needed the hug today, so I just leaned into it.

She seemed to notice, but didn't say anything. She hugged me for a moment longer, then gave a little extra squeeze before untangling from me, settling into the booth beside me.

"Don't you need to order?" I asked.

She held up her phone. "Already ordered, I just need to give them my table number."

"My, aren't we prepared?"

"I'm a regular boy scout."

"I'm so impressed," I said, feeling more myself with her there.

Ford and Yarin joined us, and we talked a bit about Yarin's new accommodations. He was still very worried about his brother and still very confused by new technology, unsurprisingly, but he also seemed thrilled with his new space. I imagined that, after accidentally time-traveling and finding yourself in a forest being hunted by some unknown horror, having a quiet, safe room to yourself with plenty of books and food would be like a dream.

That wasn't even getting into what his life had been like before coming here.

Emily and Derek arrived, ordered, and joined us. Hazel's food was also ready, and with all of us present, conversation quickly turned to business.

"Any ghost issues for you?" I asked Yarin.

He shook his head, considering. "No, not particularly. But I don't see as many ghosts as you seem to."

"Roz seems to act like a kind of...beacon to them," Derek said. "I'm curious as to why it seems to be different with you, especially since you've already said you two have different strengths. Your powers are so similar, but they seem to present in opposite ways."

Yarin nodded.

"Do we have any theories why?" Ford asked.

Derek glanced at Emily, who shrugged.

"Not particularly," Derek said. "I've done a little research but I can't find much about this kind of ability anyway—at least nothing *real*, it's mostly either theoretical or largely told like a myth. So...not many answers. But it seems like its an inherited trait, so I see it kind of like any trait we might inherit from our parents. Emily and I both have dark hair, but it's different." He shrugged. "I mean, kinda dumb example, but it's the best I can think of."

"No, no," Ford said. "That's actually a great analogy.

And you're probably right. Similar traits but a little different from person to person. Kinda makes sense."

We ate a little more and Hazel steered the conversation back to more casual topics. Yarin told us about his room, and how he and Ford had set it up. Derek talked sci-fi books with him and offered to loan him some long series that sounded complex but fascinating. The prospect of sharing books excited Yarin and he agreed to lend Derek a few of his book, in return. I hadn't realized Derek was such a big reader, but he'd read almost all the books Yarin liked and had a lot of additional suggestions for him.

"Veering slightly back to business," Derek said, glancing at Emily before turning to look at Yarin and I. "Emily and I were thinking we should do some practice with your powers. If we're going to try and get you home, we need to get a better handle on how that might look, and what each of you can do."

Yarin nodded, considering it. "I don't know much, but it would seem you have learned quite a bit, so it is probably wise to get more experience managing these abilities. Although..."

He trailed off, and I looked at him, nodding in understanding.

"You're scared. I get it. Last time you used them it brought you here. I...I get scared, too, but maybe together we can help each other?" I offered.

He nodded, still looking a bit anxious. I couldn't blame him—this all terrified me, too.

But I wasn't alone anymore, and there was a strange comfort in that. I just hoped it would be enough to keep us from destroying ourselves with these powers.

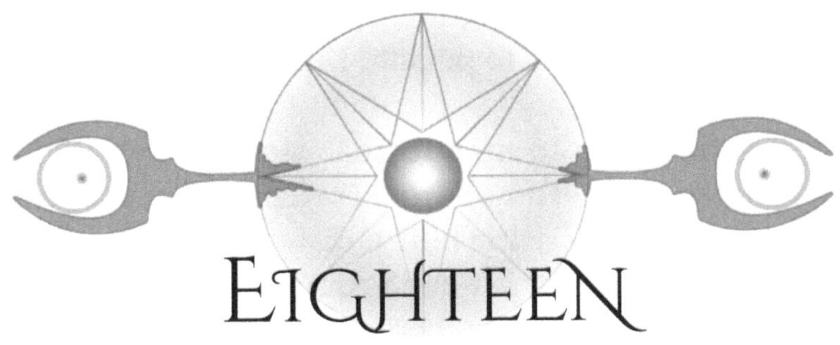

Eighteen

It was becoming habit for Ford to pick me up and drive himself, Yarin, and I to our various group meetings. I didn't mind—I liked Ford's van and being around them was a good distraction from whatever dark thoughts I tended to be dwelling on. I had recovered from the previous day's general anxiety, but not quite from the fear of my friends all becoming too busy to help me, or too tired of the constant drama.

I figured I needed to talk about that with someone, but I had no idea how to broach the subject, least of all with my friends. Briefly, I considered asking my therapist, but what could I tell her that would make sense?

I didn't want to completely write that off, though, so I decided to try and find a way to ask her about it without bringing up the ghosts.

And this was why driving with Ford and Yarin was better than driving alone. I got to interact, to take my mind off things, and to spend a little time with friendly faces where I actively couldn't be working, so I pretty much just had to engage in normal conversation.

Yarin had finished *Nightfall* and moved on to a Jules Verne novel about a Venezuelan expedition. He told me a bit about it as Ford drove, and I showed him some of my saved sketches on my phone. He had adjusted to the idea of smartphones quicker than I'd expected, though he still seemed fascinated by them, and had a lot of questions about them. I supposed, in a strange way, being a science fiction fan had prepared him for this a little better than if he'd stuck to fantasy or contemporary literature—as shocking and unexpected as all this was, he at least seemed able to adjust to new technology relatively fast, and have some mental framework for the things that were different now.

Or maybe it was just the adaptability of the human spirit. We seemed, as a species, strangely resilient.

None of us had been to Emily's house before, so I was navigating for Ford as he drove. We usually met at my house, but that was harder now with Elixabete around all the time, and it seemed the grid she'd made kept ghosts away (mostly), which was great for sleeping and terrible for practicing my powers.

If we had any chance of helping Yarin get back home and putting a stop to the constant hauntings, it would depend on my ability to control these powers. And Yarin's ability to control his. I still wasn't sure if we had the same exact abilities, or just similar ones with different strengths, but I supposed we would find out.

When we got there, I saw Derek's car already in the driveway. Both Emily's parents were at work, and Emily was an only child, like me, so we'd have the place to ourselves.

I took in the house as I got out of the van, certain I'd have to use it in a comic someday. It was two stories, with stonework up the front, framing the windows. The top half, where the stone ended, was a light, buttery yellow. Round and peek-a-boo windows, also framed in stone, added a uniqueness to it. Somehow, Emily's family had managed to keep climbing vines alive and strong enough to creep up the sides of the house.

The lawn was plush and green, with fanciful ornaments, a stone birdbath, wind chimes, and a few little stone statues of children. It had a whimsical feel—something that belonged in Ireland, among the rolling hills, not in the middle of the Mojave Desert.

I rang the doorbell, which chimed musically, and Emily threw it open with a smile. "Hey! Welcome!"

"Hey Em," I said. "Your house is really cute."

"Thanks!" she said, ushering us inside and closing the door. I noticed a mat with shoes on it, and slipped mine off. Hazel's family also had a shoe-free house, so I was used to it.

"Hazel will be here soon," I said. "She just needed to cover the store for a bit while her mom was busy."

Emily led us into the living room, which had the same whimsical, cottagey feel. I was looking around, taking it all in, when I noticed a picture of two very blond people standing on either side of a younger Emily, hugging her affectionately.

"Are those your parents?" Ford asked.

"Yeah, why?" she said.

Ford shook his head. "No, no, I just...I had no idea you were adopted."

"What? I am?" she said in alarm.

We stared at her for a moment before she broke down giggling.

"Oh, your faces were priceless. Yes, I am indeed adopted."

Ford laughed. "Okay that was good. I respect that. Also, how have you never mentioned this?"

"Yeah, how has that *never* come up?" I asked.

Derek, on the floor setting things up, rolled his eyes. "Emily never tells anyone. I found out when her dad picked us up for a classmate's birthday party in fifth grade. She likes to spring it on unsuspecting people and watch them be confused."

Emily was still giggling. She had even managed to get Yarin to laugh.

I snickered, too. "That sounds about right."

Ford nodded appreciatively. "A brilliant move. And you can keep doing it to new people—that well really never runs dry."

She nodded. "I thought you of all people might enjoy that, Ford."

"Wait," I said, my brain catching up to what Derek had said. "I thought you guys met in eighth grade?"

Derek and Emily both shook their heads and said, at the same time, "No, fifth grade."

Emily laughed and mussed Derek's hair, then sat down across from him to set up her tablet. As she worked, she said, "Eighth grade is when we had our paranormal project, but we were already friends. We met when Derek moved to my school the second week of fifth grade. He was really quiet and shy so I decided to be his guide and we've been friends ever since!"

"That's cute," I said. I didn't have a 'how we met' story for my best friend; Hazel and I had known each other since we were babies. I knew I'd remember when and how I met the rest of them, though—there would be no forgetting this summer.

When we had settled in, Emily and Derek explained this plan; summon a ghost, then banish it. We listened to them talk about how they were going to measure our progress with their equipment and try and see if they could pinpoint what was working and what wasn't. Yarin looked determined and a little worried.

After warming up with some simple summoning, we'd try dimension stuff. I was a little more nervous about that, since I didn't fully understand it, and there was such a risk of getting permanently lost, but I refused to back out. I couldn't be afraid of my abilities forever, and after learning what had happened to Yarin, I was more determined than ever to get control of them. I wanted to help him. I wanted to save myself from ever having to go through something like that. And I had kind of started to accept that if I was ever going to have a life outside this, I'd need to be able to control these abilities better.

For instance, going back to school.

I listened to Derek explain his new RGB camera, and how it had a special sensor and the ability to project infrared light. Apparently, instead of seeing things as a flat image, it processed images as 3D, so it could capture depth like sonar. It was supposed to make picking up on otherworldly entities easier. He went on like this for a while as he sorted his notebook and equipment out neatly on the table. I was trying to figure out his order—alphabetical? By size? By frequency of use?—when Hazel arrived.

Like the angel she was, she had brought coffee for everyone. I took the cup offered to me—my preferred order, of course—and sipped it appreciatively. I would need a little boost if we were going to intentionally bring ghosts here and then banish them away.

"So we're really doing this?" she asked, sounding a bit unnerved.

"Yeah. I mean. We kind of have to. I can't keep getting caught off-guard by things, I have to start learning to control it so I can stop it from hurting anyone."

Hazel nodded, biting her lip. "Yeah. Yeah I guess. But I mean...it's not going to hurt anyone, right? It hasn't...it hasn't caused too much damage yet..."

I knew why she was saying that—she was worried about me. I glanced at Derek's cast, then back at her. It was true that things could have been much worse, but they could be much better. And maybe by doing this, I could *make* things better.

"It'll be okay, Haze," I assured her.

We put our research away and I got down to summoning ghosts and pushing them back. It was getting easier, and I was definitely feeling more in control of what I was doing. In part, I think it was just because it was something clear and precise and technical to focus on—I couldn't think about Yarin getting lost in time or my mother's death, which I now suspected was related to all this, or how terrified I was when I did this work. I had to set all that aside and just be in the moment. It was nice to forget about all of them and do something I actually had *power* in.

At first, Yarin would summon a ghost, then banish it, then I would do the same. After a while, we started switching off—he'd summon, and I'd banish, or vice versa. I noticed a strange resistance when sending his ghosts away, and he seemed to struggle similarly with the ones I called up.

Then it was time for *me* to move around. My hands shook, getting clammy just thinking about it. I had never liked this aspect of my abilities, but the thought of getting lost in time was horrifying. It made it so much harder to handle.

I tried to ignore the churning in my stomach and focus on the task at hand.

"Okay. Here goes," I said. I had volunteered to go first, since this still seemed to freak Yarin out a bit. Not that I could blame him. It scared me and I wasn't the one who'd lost everything to it.

I closed my eyes and recalled the 'slipping down' sensation I always got when I dropped into that dark place. When I opened my eyes, I was still in Emily's living room.

"Well, *that* worked well," I muttered. The others chuckled.

"Try again. Take your time. And try to relax," Hazel said. I shot her a look and she shrugged apologetically. "You know what I mean," she said, giggling a bit.

I let out my breath in a huff, then concentrated once more. I didn't feel anything shift, so I opened my eyes again.

"This is *not* working," I muttered.

No one answered.

"Well, looks like it worked," Derek said. I glanced over and saw them sitting just where they had been, but fuzzy, unfocused. I hadn't fully transitioned, it felt like, but I had slipped into something else. It almost felt like a space *between*.

Yarin frowned. "I can almost sense her...but...I can't see her...she's still partially here, though."

I focused again, and slowly, the others faded. I saw everything darken. The shadows deepened until they overtook the room, and it seemed to be stripped of all the elements that gave it character. I was left standing in a plain, almost empty, dark room.

I nodded to myself, shaking a bit. "Okay. That worked."

I decided not to stay long—I tried moving up, but just like climbing is harder than falling, moving back to my own dimension took more effort. I remembered being *very* tired after returning in the past, but I hadn't paid attention to the work required to draw my way back up. I wasn't usually doing this while calm and rational.

Concentrating, focusing on my breathing and whatever ability it was that pulled me from dimension to dimension, I resurfaced in Emily's living room, stumbling and falling to my knees.

"Are you okay?" Ford asked, immediately at my side.

I chuckled weakly. "Yeah, fine, just lost my footing a little. Without panic to motivate me, it's harder to get back here."

"Yarin, you ready to try?" Emily asked.

He looked between us, face drawn. "I think so."

"Want me to take you through it?" I asked. "So you can get a feel for it?"

He nodded and I went to his side, linking our arms. "Stay close, and pay attention," I said. It was tiring, doing it all over again, especially with another person, but I drew us both down, through the fuzzy, hazy halfway point, and then into the dark place.

He tensed beside me, clinging like a fearful child. "This is where I was trapped," he whispered.

I nodded. "It's a creepy place. Okay, now back up. It's a little harder, but just follow my lead."

I went slowly this time, so he could track what I was doing. It was a lot harder than before, and this time, when we reemerged in Emily's living room, I all but fell over. Yarin still had my arm and held me up, but Ford was there to help catch me.

"Okay, time to sit," he said, leading me gently to the sofa. I didn't fight him. Hazel handed me a bottle of water and I drank gratefully from it.

Yarin went alone this time. Much like I had, he disappeared from my vision before I lost track of his energy. I told the others a little about this, and Emily immediately told me how I could use it to spy on people.

"Why is that the first place you go?" Derek asked.

"I'm not saying she *should!* I'm just saying it's an option!"

We waited for a moment, Yarin's energy too far away to sense anymore.

"Think he's okay?" Derek asked.

I stared at the spot he'd occupied a minute before. It was hard to gauge how long I'd taken to drop down and come back up, but I felt like this was taking too long.

"Oh, man, what if he gets trapped again?" Ford asked.

Just as I was about to go in after him, the air rippled and he appeared before us, gasping and shaking.

I blinked. I had never seen it from this side before, and frankly, it looked weird.

Emily clapped. "You did it!"

"Hah, yes..." Yarin said. He was sitting on the ground, head in his hands. I had a light headache, too, but nothing like I used to get when switching dimensions. I supposed that must be because of all the practice I'd gotten.

I stood up, moving back to the center of the room while Yarin sat.

Despite not agreeing that I should use that halfway ability to spy on anyone, I was curious about it. It seemed almost like what had happened to me on the Strip, though that had been a bit more complete as I'd stopped seeing all the people and many of the more transient physical objects in the area. I wanted to see if I could replicate that, and see how it worked more, because it seemed to me to be how the ghosts followed me around without being visible.

I tried to recreate what I'd done before, but felt like I was slipping too far, too fast. I quickly pulled back, but again felt that resistance of going *up* instead of *down*. It wasn't as hard as before, but it was still tricky, especially since I was trying to go to some middle ground, rather than completely one way or another.

Finally, I landed in that space, and when the dizziness passed, I looked around, taking it in.

The room was still mostly the same, save for a few things that had disappeared. The shoes by the door were almost all gone, with just a pair of flip-flops that looked like they belonged to Emily's dad remaining, though they were blurry and semi-transparent.

I looked for my friends. I could still sense them, but I couldn't see them. Wait. I kind of could, actually. They were just showing up as vague, faintly glowing shapes. I could miss them with my eyes, as they looked almost like forms of weak light, but if I felt for them, they became clearer.

Curious, I took a few steps closer. Yarin was clearer than the rest of them, and he felt a little different. Then again, they *all* felt different—it was like when we'd gone after the monster, but I could sense their different energies much more intensely now.

Can I move around this physical space and resurface in a different area? Yarin had gone in at one point and come out at a very, very different point—I didn't want to mimic his results exactly, but the notion seemed like it could be valuable.

I wandered out of the living room, to the dining room, then the kitchen. It was a cute little kitchen, cottagey and homey, to match the rest of the house, and I chuckled at what a warm, whimsical house Emily lived in. It was somehow the exact opposite of what I expected *and* a perfect fit.

When I'd had a good look around, the world a still a little bleary and hazy from being in this half-space, I went back 'up' to my dimension. There was that little tug, but it was much less than usual, further solidifying my theory that this wasn't a full 'step' down.

I looked around—I was still in the kitchen, but I couldn't be *positive* I was back until I got confirmation from the others. Another thing I needed to work on, I realized. If I was ever on my own, it'd be good to be able to tell without asking someone else.

"Guys?" I asked.

"Roz? Where are you?" Hazel called. "I can hear you but I can't see you!"

"Maybe something went wrong..." Derek said.

"I can sense her here," Yarin added. "We should be able to see her."

I popped my head around the corner and grinned. "Hey, it worked!"

"How did you get over there?" Emily asked. They all looked a little nervous. I hadn't considered that my exploration might startle them.

"I was testing," I answered. "To see if I could move around in this dimension by moving around in the other one. Usually I can't—at least I don't think so—but if I go a half-step down I can."

"Interesting," Emily said, and Derek jotted some notes down. Ford looked thoughtful, and Hazel just looked worried. I glanced at Yarin. He looked...like he was somewhere else. Figuratively speaking.

"You were gone for longer that time," Derek said. "Usually it's only a few seconds between when you disappear and reappear, but if you walked into the kitchen to test that, it seems that played out in real-time, rather than whatever time dilation happens regularly."

I nodded. That made a vague kind of sense, at least when matched with what I was starting to learn. For some reason, the phrase 'time dilation' made me think of Rowan, and I wondered again what she might know.

"Well, should we wrap up for today? You two look

beat," Emily said, looking between me and Yarin.

I glanced at him, then nodded. I didn't feel dead-tired yet, but I had a feeling it would settle in once the excitement of exploration and new things wore off.

We said our goodbyes and Ford drove Yarin and I home, chattering excitedly about planes of existence and dimensional rifts and everything else he'd been researching.

I felt like I should be the one doing all this research, but quickly caught that thought—*no, I'm dealing with enough, it's okay if I use my down time to rest instead of doing more work*, I corrected the rogue thought. It hadn't quite been self-criticism, but it was close, and I was trying to stop that the second it started—at least when I noticed it.

The notion made me smile; I was making progress, both with my weird powers and with my overall mental health. It wasn't much, but it was a start.

Nineteen

When I arrived home, Elixabete was sitting at the kitchen table sorting through some paperwork, organizing a few files. They didn't look like ours—I couldn't imagine my dad asking her to go through his work folders, and I knew he kept those drawers locked for liability reasons—but I still peeked, just to make sure. She was doing *something* secretive, I knew, I just didn't know *what*.

"Hello, Rosalind," she greeted me cheerily. "Did you have fun with your friends?"

"Yeah. What are you working on?" I asked. No need to be sneaky.

"A filing system for the household. Your father had one somewhat started, but it hasn't been updated for some time. It's a good way to keep manuals, warranties, receipts for services, and other such things organized should you ever need them."

I nodded. I remembered my dad working on something like this—I had even helped a bit—but with work and school we'd both dropped the ball, and since the move there had been no updates whatsoever.

I thought of what my dad had said, about getting to know her better, and decided maybe I should try. She was still suspicious, but maybe if I learned more about her, I could get some answers.

So I sat down at the table across from her and said, "Is there anything I can do to help?"

She glanced up, smiling. "Oh no, dear, don't worry—I'm almost done. Though I suppose, if you want to, you can look through this," she handed me an old folder that was stuffed with papers, "and create a pile for anything that's expired or outdated,"

I accepted the task, sorting through a bunch of old warranties. Many were, in fact, expired, and I set them aside like she'd asked. We worked in silence for a while.

"So, were you born in Nevada?" I asked, trying to sound casual.

"I was," she said. "But not here in Vegas. I was born up in Northern Nevada, in Winnemucca."

"Oh. I've been up north but not there. What's it like?"

"It's lovely. A small town, not even eight thousand people, and smaller when I was growing up there."

"What was that like?" I asked, mimicking how I'd seen my dad engage with people.

Elixabete continued working, her hands moving smoothly through the motions. "It was farm life, really. The farm has been in my family for a long, long time. My great-great-great-great grandparents started as sheepherders there back in the 1860s."

"Wow. That's cool. I have no idea what my great-great-great-great grandparents were getting up to," I said.

Elixabete chuckled. "That's understandable. I only know because they stayed there, in a small town, for so long that their history became somewhat interwoven with the town's."

I enjoyed hearing about how her family moved to Northern Nevada from the Basque region of Spain, and settled there just before the town of Winnemucca was founded.

It was interesting to hear her speak of her family and her history. It wasn't giving me too much in regards to whether or not I could trust her, but it was helping me feel a little less suspicious of her overall. I considered that this could all be a ruse to trick me into trusting her more, but I didn't want to dwell on that. I was very aware that I was being paranoid, and could be being very unfair to a perfectly nice woman who'd done nothing to wrong me, and in fact had been quite warm and friendly despite me being weird and shady.

I finished sorting through the paperwork, and Elixabete thanked me, suggesting I go do something fun.

Instead, I went up to my room and worked on my computer for a bit, sifting through the emails I hadn't finished dealing with before and doing my best to prepare for the start of school. There wasn't much I could do, but organizing emails, looking over my schedule, and making lists of school supplies gave me some semblance of control and productivity.

The thought of Rowan nagged at the back of my mind again. She had wanted to know about dimensions, and I had been practicing moving between them earlier. She might have more information for me, or theories, or new research. She might be scary as hell, but she also might be able to help. I bit my lip, wondering if I should reach out to her again.

As a kind of compromise, I snatched up my dog-eared copy of Rowan's book, *Between Worlds*, and my mother's journal, skimming through them. In *Between Worlds*, Rowan had expanded on the possibility of energy changing forms and shifting after death, and there being a dimension where such energy was rampant. Next, I checked my mother's notes. There was no talk of dimensions, though she did write extensively about the 'ghost world'—that place where the ghosts seemed to reside, and where they stayed unless the veil between their world and ours got too thin.

So she *had* experienced the shift...but she hadn't really understood it. It reminded me of how Yarin had spoken of it; confused, and afraid, and aware they were somewhere else, but not understanding how or why. Not that I did, either, but at least I had a term for it. Both my mother and Yarin spoke of it in mystical terms; something magical and inexplicable.

Emily seemed to be closer to that mindset, but she was also confident in the rules and that they could be learned and understood.

And Ford...Ford saw this as scientific. Quantifiable. Able to be tested and understood and proven or disproven.

I still wasn't actually sure where I landed on all this.

Flipping through my mother's entries, a word that seemed completely out of place caught my eye: *Assassin.*

I blinked, my mind flashing immediately to the giant, shadowy figure that had turned out to be a humanoid being who had come to kill me.

Was that who she'd meant? Did she think of the Shadow that had come for me as an assassin?

Was he an assassin?

My mouth was dry. The word triggered something in me, and a puzzle piece clicked into place. The Shadow...the doctors who'd imprisoned Yarin... Elixabete suddenly showing up at my house, unafraid of ghosts...they had a similarity that shook me. A dangerous, inexplicable nature. The angles of the Shadow flashed through my mind again, and I shuddered. I knew it was stupid to compare a human to whatever was hunting me, but hadn't Yarin been captured by other humans? Was that so far-fetched an idea, that some people out there might know about all this stuff and come after me?

I tapped my finger against the word 'assassin,' thinking of the being that had attacked me. My mother hadn't just recognized the Shadow, she'd seemed to have *known* him. She'd stopped him from killing me. And...he seemed to have *known* her. He had spoken to her, said her name.

I decided to actually *read* the entry. It was short, most of the page dominated by a rough sketch that had a basic semblance to the first Shadow that had come after me. She'd used up a whole pen coloring it in, I could tell that much.

I ran my fingers along the sharp edges of the sketch, then forced my eyes back to her writing—I'd always had a harder time focusing on words when there were images—and read:

The Dark One is still following me. I'm almost certain it's trying to kill me. This isn't random. I caught one and killed it, but I got some information first. It's an assassin, and someone sent it after me.

I froze. How had I missed this entry? It was toward the end—dated around five years ago.

She had *caught* it? And *killed it*? That struck me as incredible. And bizarre. As did the confirmation of the Shadow being an assassin specifically sent after her. Who was sending assassins after her—after *us*? Why were they trying to kill us?

And, most upsettingly, it lent credence to my fear that she hadn't died by suicide, but by murder. I thought back to her death. An overdose. But weren't those rather easy to fake? How well had they checked what was in her system, with her history, and the note?

I shook my head. I needed to focus. Getting caught up in that was only going to make me emotional, and if I was going to avoid her fate, I had to stay on task.

I turned the page and found a diagram. And instructions. It was a detailed description of how she'd captured the assassin. I read the directions twice. At first, it sounded like a spell, but Ford's words popped into my head; *Everything is science, we just don't understand it all yet, and that makes it look like magic.*

"Science..." I muttered, scanning the words again. Not a spell. Not magic. A scientific method. A formula. "How did you find this, Mom?" I whispered.

I picked up my own journal and opened it, flipping through the pages quickly. I found the page I'd devoted to a rendering of the Shadow. 'The Dark One', my mother had called it. An assassin. Sent to kill us.

I drew the diagram and copied down the instructions. Then I tapped my pen against the page while I thought. I had already known the Shadow from before was after me, knew my mother, knew of me...I just hadn't thought of him as an *assassin*. I wasn't sure *what* I'd thought, but assassin felt so...official. So intense. I guess I'd thought perhaps that had been some rogue individual out to get us, or some isolated incident, but an assassin was... planned. Structured. On a mission. It felt strangely real.

Inescapable.

It also felt incredibly organized. And if they—whoever 'they' were—had sent one assassin...what was to stop them from sending another? And what was to stop them from trying a new approach?

I dropped my head on my desk, grumbling. Why were there so many questions and so few answers? Why did I keep going in circles?

I needed a distraction. Picking up my phone, I decided to see what Ford was up to.

TWENTY

"Hand me that?" Ford said.

I handed him the tool he was searching for, sitting back against the shelves lining the wall. We were in his garage, the bay door open, letting in the warm summer air.

I'd called Ford to see what he was up to. He'd been working all morning with his lawn care business, but now he was free, doing some maintenance on his van. I'd decided to join him. When I asked where Yarin was, he surprised me by telling me that Derek had picked him up earlier to take him to the bookstore and the café during Derek's shift. Apparently, Derek and Ford had started coordinating on this without even telling me, and were working together to make sure Yarin got to go out of the house a bit. It was oddly adorable, and the thought made me smile.

While he worked, I flipped through some old car manual Ford had on his shelf. It wasn't entirely random; I wanted to do a car-engine-mechanics related piece, and I was looking for cool diagrams to give me some inspiration.

That idea had been completely derailed when I'd come across a page detailing all the various warning lights. They were numbered, with their explanations listed in order on the opposite page, but I ignored that information. I mean, I knew what most of them meant, but they'd always looked so funny to me. I remembered some of the weird things I'd thought they were as a little kid, and I was using my pencil to write in my own explanations.

Ford rolled out from under the van and asked, "What are you doing?"

"Labeling the car warning and signal lights," I answered, keeping my face serious.

Ford peeked over my shoulder, then frowned. "What? That's the check engine light."

"No, it's a wonky helicopter." I was trying really hard not to laugh at this point—I'd never caught him off guard and without a witty comeback before.

He looked at me. "Why would a car have a warning light for a wonky helicopter?"

I shrugged, fighting back a grin. "I don't know, why would it have a light for Summon the Genie?"

"That's the check oil light!" he said, and I burst out laughing at how seriously he was taking this.

Ford was laughing too, now, looking at me with a grin and mock annoyance. He pointed at the 'headlights' symbol and said, "Okay, then. What's this?"

"Beware of comets?"

He rolled his eyes. "And this?" He was pointing at the high-beams.

"Beware of *super-fast* comets."

"I'm gonna have to ask you to leave," he said.

I laughed harder at that and he made a big show of snatching the manual away from me.

"Hey! No!" I cried, trying to get it back.

He held it out of my reach, falling back as I scrabbled for it.

"I won't let you deface the honorable..." he checked the cover of the manual for the name, and as he did so, I grabbed at it, almost getting it back. "Ranger! I won't let you sully the good name of the Ranger manual!"

I gave up and sat back, still snickering. When he sat up, I made another grab for it, but he yelped and threw the booklet across the garage. That made me crack up all over again, and Ford gave me a light push, also laughing.

"You are so weird," he said, still grinning.

I had calmed down a bit, but I was still grinning, too. "That's what I thought those things meant when I was a little kid. I'd look at them on my dad's car and make up all these stories for each of them. I thought the battery was a winky robot, and the airbag thing meant like, holding a beach ball. Oh, I also thought the low gas light was a robot with a long, weird arm."

Ford laughed at that. "That's awesome. I should ask Oops what she thinks all those lights mean."

My phone beeped then—a calendar reminder. I groaned. I knew what it was reminding me of.

"What?" Ford asked.

"I have an appointment with my therapist today," I

grumbled, my good mood deflating a bit.

"Oh. Want me to drive you?" he offered.

I was about to tell him no, but I realized that I would actually love to have his company.

"Are you sure?" I asked. "It's an hour of sitting there doing nothing. Won't you get bored?"

He shrugged. "I can entertain myself. And, uh, we could get lunch after or something. I mean, I guess it'd be late for lunch. Early dinner?"

"Yeah, maybe," I said, scowling at the notification on my phone. It wasn't so much that I didn't want to go, it was just that I'd been having a good time here, and I really didn't want to leave.

Ford washed up and I went to get the manual. I took a picture of the page with all the car signal lights. I still wanted to use them for something. Besides, I knew I'd find the picture in my gallery later and it'd make me smile again. I tried to leave myself nice little surprises like that sometimes, especially now that everything was so weird. Then I put the book back on the shelf and got into Ford's van. He made sure everything was in order, then climbed into the driver's seat.

Part of the drive was taken up by me directing Ford where to go. My doctor's office was pretty far, though, apparently she was one of the best, so I was stuck driving across town twice a week.

"Turn left at the next light," I told Ford.

"I should have you record a bunch of phrases like that and use you for my nav app."

"What?" I asked, turning to him. It was such a weird thing to say, I couldn't come up with a witty response.

"You sound nicer than my navigation app. She always

sounds like she's upset at me. Or like, judging me. I'd rather have you giving me directions," he said, grinning at me.

I chuckled, shaking my head.

Ford parked in front of my therapist's office and we went inside. He found a place to sit and pulled a tablet out of his backpack, starting to flick through things while I signed in and greeted the receptionist.

"What are you working on?" I asked. He had the look of someone concentrating on a project.

"Sorting through my notes," he said.

"Notes?" I asked.

He looked at me, then laughed.

"Yeah, Roz, I keep notes on all this ghost stuff, too," he said, dropping his voice a little so no one else could hear.

I blinked in surprise and he laughed again, shaking his head.

"Sorry, I guess...I mean I knew Emily and Derek took a lot of notes, but it didn't occur to me you did, too," I admitted.

Ford shook his head. "You're not the only one working on this group project, Roz. I mean I know you're doing most of the work, since none of the rest of us can do anything cool and superpowered—well, except Yarin now—but...yeah. I'm not gonna let you do *everything*, I try to keep track of stuff so it's not all on you."

He grinned, clearly meaning it as a joke and focusing on the 'group project' aspect of his teasing, but I felt an odd relief at his words. I wanted to say something—to thank him or express some kind of appreciation, but just as I was opening my mouth to speak, the door behind me opened and my therapist smiled at me, welcoming me in.

"Oh, I um, I'll see you after my appointment," I said to Ford as I stood up, fidgeting with my bag and making my way across the room.

He gave me a little salute and turned back to his tablet, and I greeted Dr. Thompson, following her back to her office. The Offspring-shirt ghost was standing in the hall, watching me again. He didn't speak or move, but his eyes followed me as I stepped into her office, and I wondered if he'd been a former patient of someone here, or if he was one of those newly called-up ghosts with no connection to the place he haunted.

"It's so good to see you Rosalind," she said as she held open her office door for me. "How have you been since our last appointment?"

"Good," I said, and despite everything happening, it didn't quite feel like a lie. Maybe an exaggeration, or a simplification, but not a lie.

"Was that your friend Ford I saw out there?" she asked.

I nodded, taking my seat. "Yeah, he drove me today. We were hanging out earlier."

"He seems nice," she said. "So. Any paranormal activity troubling you?"

I considered how to answer this. The truth was 'yes, lots of trouble' but I honestly didn't feel like getting into those details.

So I just said, "No, though I have been having some...anxiety...episodes? Not really anxiety *attacks*, but..." I shrugged. "Plenty of anxiety."

She nodded. "Have you been able to remember to use the steps I've given you?"

"Yes. And they do help, actually. But it's tricky to remember..."

She nodded. "Do you think it might help to have something physical to remind you? Perhaps a necklace or bracelet or something that can go with you everywhere and serve as a kind of anchor and reminder to use those strategies?"

I blinked, thinking that over. It was actually a really good idea.

"Yeah. I like that. I'll find something...that would probably work."

She smiled. "Good, I'm glad you like that suggestion. Anything else? How is your new housekeeper?"

"She's..." I almost outright lied—'she's fine, it's going well'—but why? Who was I protecting here? Dr. Thompson was *my* doctor, I could tell her whatever I wanted. Even if it was stupid.

I cleared my throat. "She stresses me out. Maybe it's just having someone new in my house, since she moved in recently, my Dad hired her as a live-in housekeeper, but...I'm still adjusting to her."

Dr. Thompson nodded, understanding. "That can be quite stressful, especially with how much change you've had in your life recently. Do you find you at least get along with her well, or do your personalities clash?"

That question made me pause. I had never actually had a direct problem with Elixabete, it was really just that with all the ghost stuff—and how differently she responded to it—I got nervous about what it could mean.

"She's nice," I said slowly. "And we always seem to get along well. But...she still makes me feel uneasy."

We talked for a bit about Elixabete, then my upcoming school year. She suggested I call or email my counselor and express some of my concerns about starting at a new school, even giving me a little script to follow and customize with my own ideas, and assured me I'd do well. I still wasn't sure about that, but having a few small actionable steps to take did make me feel a little better.

The hour flew by, and it took me a moment to realize as we were saying goodbye that there had been no paranormal activity through the whole session. Nor while I sat in the waiting room, or even at Ford's garage. It was surprising. A relief. Also a little confusing. We said goodbye and I headed back to the waiting room, thinking over the oddly peaceful day I was having.

I found Ford sitting right where I'd left him, now watching videos on his phone. He pulled an earbud out as he saw me approaching.

"Done already?" he asked.

"Yeah. Thanks for waiting. I hope you weren't too bored."

He waved his phone. "Who can be bored with the entirety of human nonsense at their fingertips?"

"Fair," I said, following him out to the van.

We stopped to get chicken nuggets and frostys at Wendy's, and Ford parked in a neighborhood I hadn't been to yet with lakes and trees and grass. I was surprised it was here in Vegas, but I enjoyed it. There were ducks swimming and flying and just lounging around on the grass, people out walking their dogs, toddlers picking flowers...it was nice.

"All right," he said, consolidating our trash into one

bag. "I gotta get home—I'm supposed to game with Sean tonight."

"You haven't seen him in a while, have you?" I asked. I had all but forgotten about him, save for Hazel's occasional complaints of missing him. They seemed to text fairly regularly, though, which I figured was a good sign.

"Yeah. He goes to this camp every summer, but we can usually sneak in some games here and there," he explained as he shifted his van into gear and started the drive home. We stopped to pick up Yarin, and they dropped me off at my house—Yarin once again insisting on them getting out and walking me to the door—before circling the cul-du-sac and pulling up to Ford's house.

I watched them go inside, then turned back to my own home. It was late afternoon, my dad wasn't home yet, but Elixabete was there, as she always was now. I thought about my conversation with Dr. Thompson; it was entirely possible that I *was* just anxious because there had been a lot of changes in my life, and Elixabete was the most recent in that string of changes. She was also the easiest change to be frustrated with—the easiest person to direct that fear at.

My stomach twisted a bit. There was still... *something*...about her that bothered me. Something that I didn't understand, that didn't make sense.

I took a long, hot shower. After that, I sat down at my computer and considered sending that email to my school counselor. Something about it twisted in my gut, though, and I decided to do it the next day. I had felt relatively tranquil today, I didn't want to shatter that fragile peace just yet.

While pulling things from my pockets so I could drop my clothes in the hamper, I found the crystal that had been perched on my window frame. I rolled over in my hands, wondering if I should go ask Elixabete about it.

No. Not now. I didn't want to deal with whatever her answer would be. Either she'd tell me no, she wasn't putting crystals around the house, and ask what I was accusing her of, and I'd have to explain myself...or she'd say yes, and I'd have to deal with *that*.

I slipped the crystal into my pocket and tossed my clothes into the hamper.

Standing in my bedroom, I wondered what to do. There was plenty to read, draw, write, and watch, but I didn't know where to start.

Background noise. I grabbed my laptop and pulled up a show. A show I'd seen before, and liked, and could zone out of if I needed to.

Then I laid on my bed with my phone and messed around on that for a while. I made it a point not to do any paranormal research, instead just sticking to stupid, pointless things. I watched a lot of videos, scrolled through a lot of posts, and overall just wasted time.

Part of me wanted to go do something productive and creative, but trying to decide what, and how, was mentally draining. Wasting time on my phone seemed like the only thing I had energy for, and my therapist had encouraged me to relax, and not worry about how productive that relaxation was. Rest, she'd said, wasn't supposed to be productive, it was supposed to be *restful*.

She'd also pointed out that my compulsion to be *doing something* all the time was a result of being anxious and feeling out of control, and thus trying to control something in my life by overworking.

So I was trying not to do that now.

Every time I found something funny, I sent it to the group chat, or whichever friend it specifically reminded me of. I liked the thought of the others' phones blowing up from notifications from me and it just being a bunch of memes and stupid videos.

When I got bored of that, I just laid there watching my show until my dad came home and it was time for dinner.

I wasn't terribly hungry, as my snack with Ford hadn't been that long ago, but I could eat a little dinner and spend time with my dad. He seemed tired when I went down to greet him—not in his behavior, as the things he did and said were all the same. I could just tell from something about the way he carried himself, about the way he moved. His eyes looked a bit wary, and again I wondered what was going on at work.

Elixabete joined us for dinner again, and I found myself glancing across the table at her, wondering if I'd ever stop feeling this uneasy around her.

"Glad you could join us," my dad said as we all sat down together. He sat at the end of the table, and I was on his right, Elixabete on his left, across from me.

"Yes, sorry I haven't been able to much lately—I've had some personal business to attend to in the evenings this week," she said, beginning to serve herself.

"Oh, do you need some time off to take care of that?" he asked. "We can manage without you if you need to tend to anything."

Elixabete waved her hand. "No, no, that's very kind of you, but that won't be necessary. It's not so pressing or difficult, just something occupying my down-time."

I wondered what it was, but of course my dad was too polite to pry—she'd said 'personal business' and offered no further details. That meant it was the end of the discussion.

"Well, if you ever do need some time off, please don't hesitate to let me know," my dad said.

She smiled. "Thank you."

We finished serving ourselves and started to eat, and as usual, it was delicious. My dad and Elixabete chatted about the meal, and how she learned to cook from her mother and grandmother. I listened, trying to find anything that was a hint about...whatever I was trying to sort out about her. But she and my dad were just discussing being born in Nevada, and comparing the southern part of the state to the northern part of the state.

"How was your day, Roz?" my dad asked.

"Um, good. Hung out with Ford a little. Went to see Dr. Thompson," I answered. Both were true, and just to round out my account of the day, I added. "It was a good day. I need to reach out to my counselor at school about a couple things, though."

We made plans to go shopping for school supplies, and my dad offered to read through the email I wanted to send and help me articulate my questions and concerns. It was nice to have a plan, and to have help.

With dinner finished, we cleared the table and I went to the kitchen to clean up. It was technically my chore to load the dishwasher, but Elixabete had been covering for me lately. I appreciated it, especially with how stressed I'd been, but sometimes it was nice to have a sense of normalcy, and I found my head was clear enough today that cleaning the kitchen seemed very...comfortable.

"I could do that, Rosalind," Elixabete offered, stacking some dishes by the sink.

"It's okay, I'm supposed to do something around the house," I said.

She chuckled and nodded. "Fair enough. Do you need help?"

"No, but thank you."

She nodded and made herself a quick cup of tea, then left. I put my music on and cleaned the kitchen, putting leftovers away and loading up the dishwasher. A few things weren't dishwasher safe, so once I had that set, I washed them by hand and placed them on the drying rack.

I stood there, looking around the kitchen to make sure I hadn't missed a stray pan or measuring cup, but everything was clean. As I surveyed my work, it occurred to me that I *still* hadn't really seen any ghosts today. In fact, I had barely seen any ghosts around the house since...

...since Elixabete moved in.

My dad was in his room. Elixabete was sitting in the dining room, sipping a cup of tea and looking at her phone. I went over to where she was, watching her for a moment before speaking.

"Elixabete?"

"Hello, Rosalind. Can I get you anything, dear?" she asked, looking up from her phone.

I shook my head absently. My dad seemed to trust Elixabete. Was that a good sign or a bad sign? He usually had good instincts about people, but he'd been wrong before. Everyone could be wrong sometimes.

My attention shifted back to Elixabete. A question was forming in my mind, but I wasn't sure how to ask it.

"You know about the ghosts, don't you?"

Apparently, I was going with the 'blurt it out tactlessly' method.

Elixabete was as surprised by my question as I was, but she didn't look confused; just caught off-guard. She met my gaze, then sighed, pushing back the seat beside her with a nudge of her foot.

I sat tentatively next to her, watching her closely the whole time.

"Yes. I know about the ghosts," she said. Her honesty surprised me. A million more questions surfaced, and I didn't know where to start.

"How?" I finally croaked out.

She looked at her hands, then got up, getting me a tea cup and coming back to sit beside me. "I can see them, like you can," she said, pouring a cup from the pot she'd made.

"And you can ward them off," I said, not asking this time.

She raised her eyebrows. "Yes, I can. How did you—" she chuckled then. "No, wait, I remember—you found my crystal grid."

"Well, yeah. I also noticed how all the ghosts were gone."

Elixabete laughed at that. "I knew you'd found the crystals—I went to check and found one missing. Had to replace it for the grid to work properly."

I nodded, pulling the little stone from my pocket. "What is it? What does it mean?"

She picked up the small crystal, turning it over in her nimble fingers. “It’s agate. For healing. You seemed... unwell, and I thought it would give you peace.”

I was quiet for a moment while I considered my next question.

“Why...why didn’t you say anything to me?” I whispered.

Elixabete sighed, taking a sip of her tea. “Drink—it’ll make you feel better.”

I took a sip, still watching her.

“Honestly, I didn’t know how to bring it up,” she said. “I knew right away there was a haunting—a good client with no specific complaints, but high turn-over? I recognized the signs right away. And when I got here...it was obvious. There was...a *lot* of ghost energy in this house.”

I kept quiet, waiting for her to say more.

“It took some time to clear it up, and the upkeep has been intense, but...I thought I could help.”

“And...that’s why you came here? And wanted to move in? Because you...wanted to help us?”

“Yes, mostly. I could tell they were wearing on you the worst.”

I stared at her, perplexed.

She laughed. “Is it really so strange that I’d be inclined to help? Wouldn’t you, if you knew how to ward off ghosts, want to help others suffering with hauntings?”

She had me there. That was exactly what I’d been doing the past couple weeks. I had another appointment in the morning, in fact.

I nodded. “Yes, I would.”

She smiled.

"Speaking of which...how did you learn to do that?" I asked.

"My mother," Elixabete answered. "It's an ability that runs in my family. Over the years, we've learned a few tricks on how to keep the spirits at bay. We don't usually discuss it with others, as it's not always well-received, but I don't mind telling you."

I nodded, unsure what to say. "Well...thank you. It's... a relief."

She smiled again. "You're welcome."

We drank our tea in silence for a while. I had a sudden, wild impulse to tell her about Yarin, but I suppressed it. I didn't think that accepting the existence of ghosts was the same as being ready to face time-travelers. Instead, I listened as she told me a little more about her history with ghosts, and how I could ward them off. I had another question, though.

"Elixabete?" I asked.

"Yes?"

"Is there...could I let *one* ghost through all the warding? To-to talk to them?"

She frowned. "I suppose. Why?"

I hesitated. I hadn't told her almost anything to do with my own ghost experiences, and I didn't want to reveal too much to her. I got a strange, confusing sense from Elixabete, even now. I felt I was safe with her, but also that there was more still that she wasn't telling me. Besides, my situation was a lot more complicated than just 'I see ghosts.'

"Um..." I said. "I have a question for one. I...I need to ask them something."

She nodded. “I could work something out, sure.”

“Okay. Thanks.” I expected her to ask follow-up questions, but she didn’t, and I was grateful.

We finished our tea and we said goodnight to each other. It wasn’t terribly late, but the day was winding down, and I was happy to just go up to my room and continue to do nothing in particular. I knew if my dad needed me, he would come find me, but he had seemed tired—it was entirely possible he needed a little down time himself, or that he’d fallen asleep already.

That was fine by me. I was content to lay on my bed and play games on my phone while listening to *East/West* episodes. Someone in a nearby town claimed to have seen a werewolf.

I was so relaxed that, at first, I attributed the shift in the air to the air conditioner kicking on, but it didn’t take long for me to catch the subtle energy and sit up, alert.

Send it away, I ordered myself sternly, but my eyes landed on the impossibly dark figure standing at the foot of my bed, and I froze in terror. Clearly, this being had no problem getting through the warding.

This Shadow was smaller than the last one, but still massive. A slimmer build, but still far too powerful. I pushed back and the being faltered, seeming to lose its footing for a moment.

I leapt up, racing for my door, but the creature took a swing at me.

“No!” I screamed, and though it charged at me, its attack went right through me, harmlessly.

We both paused, confused for a second. It lashed out a second time, but again, the attack was ineffective.

“How are you doing that?” a metallic voice demanded.

"I-I don't—I'm not..." I was so scared, I could barely think. I didn't know if I *was* doing this or not. And having this thing *speaking* to me was surreal.

It grabbed for me again and again, and I ducked out of instinct, but the creature couldn't make contact. No matter what it tried, I was untouchable.

I heard it growl something that sounded like another language.

"Why are you after me?" I whispered. I hated that, for all my supposed abilities, I had still ended up cowering on the floor, completely at its mercy.

I couldn't see the eerily human face that I knew hid behind the mask, but I could feel its eyes lock on mine. It didn't say anything, it just stared at me. I held its gaze.

After a second of this, I concentrated, pushing back. I couldn't make it leave, but I saw it move—I flinched—and it pressed its hand to its shoulder. The Shadow before me dissolved into nothingness, and I was left trembling on the floor.

When I was sure it was gone, I crossed my room on shaky legs and snatched up my phone, sinking to my bed. I hadn't told anyone but Ford, as I hadn't been completely sure, but after the energy I'd felt on the Strip and this most recent encounter, I knew.

So I typed up a text with trembling hands on my group chat:

Guys, we have a problem. Another one of those Shadows is trying to kill me.

TWENTY-ONE

We had a few more ghosts to get rid of, so I got up and got ready right away. The crystal I'd fallen asleep clutching was on my bed, and I grabbed it before heading out. It was odd, how comforting the crystal felt, even before I had been sure of its purpose, but I liked having it with me.

My phone was full of messages from my friends—concern, questions, suggestions, all worried about the new Shadow. As much as I wanted to resolve the issue of being hunted again, I didn't want fear over that clouding my mind today while I worked, so I sent a quick acknowledgement, then suggested we table that until after we'd finished our banishings for the day. I wanted to get this all over with and then approach the new Shadow with a clear mind.

It was a weird thought but that was my life now.

As had become our habit, Ford picked me up, with Yarin in tow, and we met Emily and Derek at the address she'd sent.

Today we were at a house rented by three twenty-something guys, and they informed us that their landlord was going to kill them if things kept getting broken. I tried to be reassuring, but Emily was a much better saleswoman than me, so I let her take the lead on talking to them while I felt out the ghostly presences.

Hazel wasn't here yet, but I wasn't sure she could make it anyway—which I was both glad for and sad about. I didn't like bringing her into these potentially dangerous situations, but I did like having her with me for emotional support.

These ghost-banishing sessions always made my anxiety spike, despite how much better I was doing with handling ghosts overall. The idea of failing somehow and letting my friends get hurt, or even just not being able to banish the ghost and letting down the people I'd come to help, was terrible.

Emily had offered to stop bringing me on these, but I refused. I knew there were other ways to get rid of ghosts, and that she and Derek knew enough to implement them now, but I also knew that my way was much more effective.

It was getting oddly routine though—despite my nervousness whenever I set out to do this, more and more I found I was able to resolve the issue rather quickly. It was still tiring, and still took a lot of focus, but it *was* starting to feel easier. Or at least, doable. That was a nice change.

Yarin had joined us today, and was going to observe

what we were doing. If he could do the same, it would be a huge help. We could split these calls and get rid of even more ghosts.

I still didn't know what to do about other things, like crime going up or potential future monsters, but there had been no new reports that hinted at unknown monstrous creatures, and crime seemed to be slowly returning to normal on its own—Hazel kept me updated on the news and it seemed like things were calming down little by little. There had been a spike following the fire on the mountain, but all things considered, that was probably just a result of the stress caused by more ghosts around. It still bothered me, but 'getting rid of the ghosts' still seemed to be the best thing to focus on.

"Have you ever sent away a ghost before?" I asked Yarin as we headed towards the house.

"No," he said. Then he frowned, and said. "Well...yes, actually. My brother and I stayed with a cousin for a few months, but the only room he had for us was a storage room he rarely went into. His children thought it was haunted. I thought they were joking, until..."

I nodded. "Didn't believe in this stuff until then?"

"Not really, no," he said. "My brother was frightened and I could...sense...something. One night it lingered for so long. I couldn't see it, but I could feel it in the room with us. And my brother...he didn't understand it like I did but he knew something was wrong, and it scared him. I kept wishing it would go away, leave us alone, and then...it was gone."

"It's odd," I said, thinking of my first experiences with ghosts. I was impressed that Yarin had been able to send one away like that, and hoped that was a good sign for our upcoming task.

"Is that how it feels for you?" he asked.

"Kind of. I'm not sure, each one is different, but yeah...that sounds familiar." I had another question that I was mulling over, but I knew it could be painful for Yarin.

So I tried to lead into it gently. "Feel free to not answer this question, I don't want to...stir up any painful memories or anything, but...could anyone else in your family do things like this?"

Yarin considered my question. "My grandmother. She...she used to tell me that she had friends no one else could see...spirits from another world...or that she could still talk to loved ones who had died. She told me not to fear death because it wasn't the end, and that she was curious to one day go beyond the veil..."

He seemed lost in thought, so I didn't interrupt, but then he turned to me.

"Do you think we could talk to her? Ask her what she might have known?"

"We could try," I said. "It sounds like she could do what we do, that might be where you inherited it from."

He nodded. "I think my father might have had the gift, also, but he never admitted it—he told me that my grandmother was mad and not to listen to her stories."

I considered all this new information as we walked into the house and set up. Yarin was still fascinated by the technology Emily and Derek used to detect and track ghosts, and he had learned fast about each piece—more than I had, in fact. He went straight to them to discuss what they were doing as we entered the house.

I made my way to the sofa and sat down. I felt a bit lazy and unhelpful, but I needed to conserve energy, just in case this was a difficult ghost to deal with.

Ford sat on the sofa with me, but didn't say anything. It surprised me whenever he was quiet, but it was still nice. I liked being able to just sit quietly with someone. He gave me a smile but turned back to his tablet quickly, working on whatever he was doing with his research and notes.

I almost wanted to ask him what he thought things would be like when school started, when there was so much more to do and he was too busy to keep this up, but there was something nice about this moment. Derek and Emily setting up, Yarin sitting by Derek, asking questions and appreciatively listening to the explanations, Ford beside me with that focused look on his face.

Hazel even joined in with a text just then: *You should start offering crystal-grid setup services*

I typed back, *YOU should do that, you know way more about that than me*

Oooh, side-offer for my own little business

I smiled. *Emily isn't charging*

Yeah but I can

I laughed and told her, *Nice. Right. Anyway, I gotta go get rid of a ghost*

Have fun! I'll be at the next one!

I put my phone in my pocket and was about to say something to Ford when I felt another presence join us on the couch.

It was so soft, I thought at first it was another ghost, but when I turned...

"Oh!" I said, surprised. "Hello," I reached out slowly to the cat that had sprung up on to the sofa beside me, gently scratching its ears. "Aren't you a pretty kitty." It was a Siamese cat, with white fur along its body and black fur around its tail, paws, face, and ears. It also had stunningly blue eyes, which gazed up at me for a moment before closing, a purr rising in the cat's chest as it lightly headbutted me.

Ford leaned forward and smiled. "Hey, I didn't know they had a cat."

"They do?" Emily asked, getting up and crossing the room. "I asked them if they had any pets, they were supposed to disclose that. Or at least take the pets with them."

The cat purred as I continued to scratch its ears, leaning into my hand and laying against my side.

"You're so friendly," I said, stroking its soft fur.

I realized I hadn't yet told the others about Elixabete and decided I should update them, just in case they were worried.

"Oh, so get this, apparently Elixabete knows about banishing ghosts and that's why she took the assignment at my house," I said, scratching the cat's head as it crawled onto my lap.

"Really?" Ford said.

"Yeah. I guess it's something that her whole family can do."

"Huh," Derek said, itching absently at his cast. "So she kinda did for you what you're doing for everyone else."

I hadn't thought about it that way. "Yeah, I guess so."

"Oooh, Roz, do you think I could interview her too?" Emily asked.

"Uh...maybe?"

"Okay," Derek cut in. "All set up. Are you ready?" Derek asked, glancing at me.

I sat up a little straighter, looking over at him. "Yeah, yeah, I'm good."

I stood, stretching my fingers a bit. Yarin stood as well, following me to the center of the room. Technically, I probably didn't need to be in the center of the room, but it made me feel ready for whatever was coming next.

The presence of a ghost hadn't been hard to pick up on as we'd approached, but it wasn't a particularly powerful ghost. It seemed agitated, though, and as I felt it out I heard cabinets slam in the kitchen.

Derek said something, but I missed it, because for once I could hear a whisper, and I was trying to focus on it.

It wasn't unheard of that ghosts might speak—I'd heard whispers and cries and muttered words—but it still felt odd. Most of them were pretty quiet, and didn't seem interested in speaking to the living. Or maybe they just assumed we couldn't hear them and had learned not to bother. Other than Diego, I hadn't really *talked* to any ghosts.

"Strange...hideous..." it whispered. There was more, but that was all I heard.

A bit rude, but ghosts also weren't known for their manners.

I glanced at Yarin, and he looked alarmed—he'd heard it too. His eyes met mine and widened in question. I shrugged slightly.

In turning to see him, I saw the cat out of the corner of my eye. It was still on the couch where I'd left it, but now it was alert, its large eyes wide, pupils dilated, seeming to stare at nothing. I followed its gaze and found a presence lingering there. The ghost seemed to be trying to conceal itself, which also wasn't strange—sometimes ghosts wanted to get a look at you without being seen.

The presence shifted and the cat hissed, its ears flattening against its head. I spun, holding my hands out and pushing back. The hand gestures weren't necessary, but I always did them without thinking.

The ghost grumbled, annoyed. *"Stupid girl,"* it said.

"Roz, how we doing?" Emily asked, watching closely.

"He's not very considerate," I said, and they all looked at me in confusion.

I almost had the ghost through whatever barrier I was trying to get him to cross when a tremendous force threw me back, and I stumbled into the wall. I hit hard enough to rattle the shelves, knocking the wind out of me and leaving me disoriented.

"Roz!" Ford said, jumping to his feet.

I held a hand up to them, signaling them to wait. The ghost didn't have a lot of power, he just seemed to be using it strategically.

"Just leave me alone," the ghost said.

It was so strange to hear a ghost speak to me—I'd heard them say things before, but this one was much more vocal than I was used to.

"Leave the people who live here alone, then," I said.

"No, no, no...they want trouble, they can have me," the voice said.

I didn't know what that meant, and while part of me

wanted to ask, I mostly just wanted to get rid of this ghost and go home.

Rather than responding to what the ghost—who was becoming clearer to see and hear, and also seemed to be a young man, around the same age of the guys who rented this house—had said, I concentrated on the ghost's presence. It was kind of like getting a good grip on something heavy before hefting it up.

Once I had that 'grip' in place, it was easier to get him through the 'doorway' I'd opened. It was hard to think of in normal terms, but I had discovered that doing so helped me understand what I was doing a little better. In essence, it seemed I was like a doorway between the dimension the ghosts inhabited and the dimension humanity lived in. I preferred to think of it as me having the *key* to that doorway, since it was weird to think of myself as the doorway, and it made the visualization tricky.

So, I had the key. There was a doorway. All I had to do was unlock the door and guide (or usher, coerce, push, or force) them through, then I could close that door again and they would, hopefully, stay there. I could go through the door myself, but I could come back, because my key worked from either side.

It wasn't quite that simple, in principle or execution, but it was an easier way for me to think of it.

So I 'gripped' the spirit, who was cursing and yelling at me—*"Let go of me, you idiot! What the hell do you think you're doing?"*—and shoving him as hard as I could through the doorway. Visualizing it that way was also kind of funny because, in reality, I probably couldn't have shoved people with as much force as I sometimes did the ghosts, but physical strength wasn't the deciding factor here, and somehow I was much stronger than the ghosts I dealt with. They were quicker, more experienced, and some were very feisty, but once I had a handle on them, it seemed I had more overall raw strength than they did.

I wondered, idly, why that was—being alive? This strange ability I had? Having a physical form?—but with the ghost thrashing and snarling at me, I was a little distracted.

He fell through to the other side, and I effectively 'closed' the door.

I stood, panting, a little shaken. The cat sprang off the sofa and threaded around my legs, meowing and looking up at me with its wide blue eyes. I looked down at it, wondering what it wanted.

"Wow," Yarin said, looking at where the ghost had disappeared, then back at me. "Was that very hard?"

"You get used to it," I said, running a hand back through my hair to smooth it out. "And it gets easier. He wasn't too bad."

Absently, I picked up the cat, scratching its ears. It closed its eyes and purred, seeming content.

"Nice work, Roz," Derek said, looking over his readouts. "We even picked up some of what he said."

"He was chatty, wasn't he?" I asked, sitting down on the sofa again.

"We don't get a lot of talkers," Emily mused. "I wonder why."

"Well," Ford said, scratching a finger across the cat's head. "It is entirely possible that, since most of these ghosts were drawn out because of that weird explosion on the mountain, they're disoriented. Maybe a lot of them don't know how to talk in this form."

I turned to him. "How do you have theories for everything?"

"My brain is just so good at thinking thoughts," he said.

"How are you feeling, Roz?" Derek asked.

"Less exhausted than usual, still kinda tired though. It does feel like it's getting easier."

Yarin was still looking at where the ghost had been, seeming to scan the area. I wondered what he was looking at, and if he was still seeing something. Then I realized I could just *ask him*.

"Do you see anything?" I asked, pulling him from his thoughts.

"No...just..." he gestured towards where the ghost had been. "There's a lot of leftover energy, and I can see it much better now."

I blinked, turning back to where the ghost had been. I still felt something...odd...a fuzzy, hazy distortion that was common when dispelling ghosts. I had always thought that was just me being tired and dealing with brain-fog after ghostbusting.

Yarin said he could see it, but I didn't see anything as I peered at where the ghost had last been. I felt it, though. I felt a lingering energy that seemed to be fading, but slowly.

"There is something there," I said, turning to Derek and Emily. "What would that be?"

Derek was looking at the same spot I was, brow furrowed in contemplation.

"I'd say it's most likely residual energy from opening

those portals," he said after a little thought. He glanced at Ford. "Ghosts usually do leave some traces behind, but we have to factor in the portals here."

Ford nodded.

A little *prrp!* interrupted my thoughts as the cat jumped lightly onto my lap. It looked up at me, its bright blue eyes almost seeming to study me, then rubbed its head against my chin, purring.

"That cat really likes you," Derek said.

"Maybe it's a familiar," Emily said with a laugh.

"What's a familiar?" Ford asked.

"You know," Emily answered. "Like a witch's familiar —the magical animal companion that helps witches with their spells and stuff."

"Oh! Like Joanne!" he said.

I rolled my eyes. "Ford she's not a witch, she's just an old lady with a cat. It's not that deep."

"It could be!" he argued.

"You used to think she turned *into* the cat!" I accused.

"You don't know," he said.

"I've been to her house a bunch of times, I think I know better than you," I teased back.

"Do you really think this cat is something supernatural as well?" Derek asked. I appreciated his ability to stay on-task while the rest of us spiraled off onto tangents.

Emily shrugged. "Not really, I was just kidding. In reality, cats are just known for being pretty sensitive to supernatural energy, so it's probably just sensing that. Or it likes how Roz smells, I dunno."

"Cats usually like me," I said, scratching its ears. It was true—Joanne's cat, which was apparently notorious for avoiding people, even came to say hi to me from time to time, so I mostly figured it was just my general appeal to cats. Which, I realized, could actually have to do with the supernatural anyway, as apparently I'd had some ties to it all my life.

Derek and Emily finished their scans and, along with Yarin and I, confirmed that there were no more ghosts in the house. As we tidied up, Emily called the guys who lived here and told them we had successfully exorcised their house. They arrived a few minutes later, apparently having just gone around the corner to wait for the all-clear.

"Thank you so much," one of the guys said to Emily as the other two looked around, almost like they expected someone to jump out at them. "It was hell the last couple weeks."

"There's been a lot of that going around," Emily said.

I listened to their exchange, absently scratching the cat's head. It was sitting on my lap now, eyes closed, purring softly.

"It even feels different in here," one of the other guys said. He was the tallest of the three, and wore a hockey jersey for Vegas' team.

"There's some lingering effects but all supernatural entities are gone now, so you should see your home return to feeling like normal pretty soon," Derek said.

As we were getting ready to leave, I picked up the cat to set it down, and the guys turned to me.

"Oh, damn, you guys brought a cat with you?" the guy in the jersey said. "That's wild, does it hunt ghosts or something?"

"Crap. I'm crazy allergic to cats," the first guy said. "It

didn't sit on too much stuff did it?"

I blinked, holding the cat up to look at it, then towards the guys. "This...isn't your cat?" I asked.

"Nah, no pets allowed. Plus, Kyle is allergic to everything," the jersey guy said.

"Oh. I thought it was yours," I said. "It just came over to me."

The first guy—Kyle—smacked one of his roommates on the arm. "Dammit, Ralf, you left the bathroom window open again, didn't you?"

"It gets stuffy in there, man!" Ralf said, hitting Kyle back.

The third guy shook his head. "Sorry, this happens sometimes with neighbors' cats, and occasionally pigeons. Anyway, never seen that cat before, but thanks for getting rid of the ghost."

I nodded, pulling the cat back towards me to hold it against my chest. It seemed content enough, but now I was wondering whose cat this was and how to return it to them. It didn't have a collar, but it looked clean and well-cared-for.

Just what I need, I thought as I looked down at the cat. *Another lost soul to worry about.*

TWENTY-TWO

We left, and Ford drove us around the neighborhood looking for signs. When we spotted someone out walking, we'd roll down the window and ask if they knew anyone missing a Siamese cat, but no one did.

I resolved to post a picture of it online and take it home with me for now. My dad probably wouldn't mind and it seemed happy enough with me.

At home, I looked at the cat, unsure what to do with it. I had taken pictures in Ford's car and posted on some local 'lost pet' pages while we were driving over, so now that that was done, I just had a cat to look after.

"Hm, you're probably hungry," I mused aloud to the cat, who still sat contentedly in my arms, purring softly, eyes closed.

I set her down and grabbed a small bowl from the kitchen cabinet, filling it with water and setting it in a corner where it was unlikely to get kicked over by accident. Then I found another bowl and dug around in our pantry until I found some tuna.

The cat ate appreciatively while I sat on the floor watching. She was a pretty cat—young-ish looking, but not a kitten—and seemed to have a nice temperament. I checked my phone, but I had no responses to my posts yet.

"What should I call you for now, huh?" I asked.

She looked up at me and meowed once, then returned to eating.

"I don't speak cat, so I don't know what you just said."

She continued to eat, ignoring me. When she finished, she stretched, her back arching in a dramatic curve. Then she trotted over and looked up at me curiously, almost studying me before exploring the house a bit.

I had texted my dad and Elixabete to let them know I was bringing a cat I'd found home. My dad had simply responded "*ok*"—likely he was having another hectic day at work—but Elixabete had told me she'd get some cat supplies while she was buying groceries.

So there wasn't anything else for me to do, really. The cat was fed and had water to drink, I had done everything I could think to let her owners know I'd found her, and told my dad she would be here. Cat food was even on the way.

I got up and went to sit on the sofa. The cat was still exploring, wandering around. She looked over at me occasionally, though, like she was checking on me regularly. I opted to mess around on my phone; Hazel had gotten me hooked on some stupid little game that was just connecting dots by drawing a line between them, but was somehow addictive. I played for a while, and the cat leapt up onto the sofa beside me, curing up on my lap. I pet her absently as I played. She was curled in a way that she almost looked like a little hill of light sand.

Dune, I thought, stroking her fur. That had a nice ring to it. It was a book my dad liked, and I'd always thought the word itself was just...pretty.

"How about I call you Dune?" I asked her as I scratched her ears.

She purred, twisting to get better scratches.

The garage opened, and a few moments later Elixabete walked in carrying some bags.

"Ah, you're home," she said, setting the bags down on the counter. She came over to look down at the cat. "She's beautiful. Does she have a name?"

"I don't know, she doesn't have a collar. I'm thinking of calling her Dune," I said.

Elixabete reached into one of the bags she'd set down and retrieved a little mouse toy, tossing it to me to dangle in front of Dune. I held it out for her and she stared at it, sniffing at it a bit before turning away.

"Fine, ignore the nice present Elixabete got you," I said, setting the mouse aside.

Elixabete chuckled. "Do you think your father will mind?"

"No," I said, stroking her fur. "He likes cats. We used to have one but that was when I was really young. Anyway, I think he'd be okay having another one around for a while."

Elixabete nodded. She seemed to study the cat for a

moment, then picked up the rest of her bags and went to the laundry room.

I sat there for a while, just petting the cat and zoning out. When I finally came back into focus, Elixabete was in the kitchen preparing dinner.

The cat sprang down from my lap and began to explore again, and I stood up, stretching out and checking my phone. Still no responses to the 'found cat' posts, though they had been viewed a few times. A few offers from people willing to take her in if her original owners weren't found, but no one claiming her as theirs.

My dad got home a little later, and surprised me by sitting down on the floor with me and Dune to play with the cat a bit. She took to him immediately—animals always did—and kept jumping onto his lap and purring loudly.

"Anyone claiming her yet?" he asked.

I shook my head. "No one."

"She's pretty—be on the lookout for people who just want a free cat," he said, scratching her ears.

"A few have already offered to take her in, but yeah, I could see that."

"What do you want to do with her if you don't find her original owner?" he asked.

"Keep her?" I blurted out without thinking.

My dad laughed. "That would be nice. Been a while since we've had a pet. We should take her to a vet, though, see if she has a microchip."

My heart sank a little. I had forgotten about microchips in pets—a surefire way to find their owner if they had one.

"Yeah. We can do that tomorrow," I said.

We played with Dune a little longer until it was time for dinner. The rest of the evening was largely uneventful, though I did keep wanting to get Elixabete alone. I had so many questions to ask her, and I noticed she kept looking at Dune in a way that felt more significant than, 'Ah, yes, I see a cat over there.'

Maybe she doesn't like cats? I wondered to myself, but she had seemed friendly and sweet towards the cat every time she'd encountered it. Her look didn't seem disdainful at all. Just...noteworthy.

When my dad got a work call and ducked into his office, I had my opportunity. Elixabete and I were cleaning up the kitchen together again, and she had some calming guitar music playing as we worked, making it feel safe to talk.

"Elixabete?"

"Hmm?"

"Um...is there something...something about the cat that I should know?"

She glanced at me, then over at the cat, who was sleeping on the sofa, curled into a little fluffy ball.

"I can't be sure just yet," she said, turning back to me. "But I think this cat came to you. Much like I did."

I blinked, not fully tracking. "Wait...how? Why? The ghosts?"

She nodded. "Cats are very sensitive to supernatural energies. And this cat..." she glanced at it again as it rolled over a bit, still sleeping. "I can't say for certain, but I think she's more than just an ordinary cat."

"Like...a witch's familiar?" I asked, grasping at the only knowledge I had on the subject, which had all come from books and movies and Emily.

"Something like that."

I had expected Elixabete to laugh a little at my childish suggestion, but she seemed to be mulling it over instead, like she was seriously considering the possibility.

I looked down at Dune, who was now looking up at me with a calm, steady gaze. There certainly was something about this cat that felt different from other animals.

The rest of the evening was relatively quiet. I would check the listings I'd posted once in a while, but there was nothing new on any of them. Ford texted to ask how the cat was and I told him what Elixabete had said, deciding to send a similar message to Hazel. I also sent her some pictures, since she hadn't been there to see the cat in person. And because the cat was being cute.

My dad emerged from his work call, and as he rounded the corner it occurred to me how...tired he looked. The call had gone pretty long, and it was almost nine at night. It wasn't unheard of for him to have to work round the clock, but it wasn't very common, either.

"Everything okay?" I asked.

He looked at me, then smiled, sitting down on the sofa. "Yeah. Just had to answer some questions."

The cat purred and jumped onto his lap, and he chuckled, scratching her ears.

He went to bed not long after, and Elixabete retired to her room. I sat there, holding the cat, deciding whether or not I was going to actually go snoop through my dad's office.

I had tried to see things here and there when I'd been in his office with him, but I hadn't really gone and actually invaded his space like this yet. I was vaguely aware that, as things calmed down with the ghosts, I was almost actively *looking* for more trouble.

But I had to know.

Setting Dune aside on the sofa, I got up and headed down the hall, trying to sneak while not looking like I was sneaking anywhere.

I reached his office and opened the door quietly, stepping inside and closing it behind me, but not before Dune darted inside, giving me a look and a little "*mrow!*"

"Don't give me that," I said to her, closing the door and turning on the light on his desk. I didn't turn the main light on, hoping to prevent anyone from noticing I was in here.

I felt bad. It was a weird thing to do, but he wasn't telling me anything, and I knew myself—the less I knew, the more my imagination would run away with it. I knew he was trying to protect me, but I also knew he had no idea what I could handle, or how much worse my own theories would be than whatever was actually happening.

It wasn't the best excuse for spying on my father, but I pressed on anyway.

There were some papers on the desk, but nothing was particularly clear. It occurred to me that I didn't know enough about law to even really know what I was looking for. My dad talked to me about his work plenty, but it's not like I sat there reading contracts and briefings regularly.

Before touching anything, I took a picture of how his desk was laid out. Then I moved the pages on his desk carefully, keeping everything in the correct order as I looked through them. My dad would *know* if anything was even a little out of place, so I had to put everything back just right.

Most of the stuff on his desk was uninteresting—there was a memo for his office reminding everyone of various policies, an update from the LA office about some 'big wins' that they were congratulating various employees on, and a few bills that needed to be paid. Nothing interesting. Nothing to explain his secrecy.

There was one document with a few hand-scrawled notes in the margin. The original printout was talking about some business—a corporation called The Moretti Group—and some investment purchases they'd made. But from what I could tell, nothing about it was illegal. The notes in the margin were just a couple dates. I frowned. It was probably important for *something,* but I had no idea what.

Frustrated, I put all the papers back how I'd found them.

Well of course he wouldn't leave it lying around, I thought. I opened a drawer that was just pens and pencils and other office supplies, and another that was full of wires and chargers neatly rolled up.

I checked a third door and found it locked. I frowned. Clearly that was where the information was. There was a fourth drawer, and it, too, was locked.

I sat there at his desk, drumming my fingers on the armrests of his big leather office chair.

It made sense that the important information was locked up. He was a lawyer, a lot of what he did was confidential, so keeping it secure was important. Logical.

But it made my task a lot harder.

I put everything back how I found it and opened his laptop. It was password protected, of course, and when I tried all the passwords I knew, it informed me that none of them were correct.

So. His work computer had a unique password that he had never told me. It made sense, but still upset me. Not at him, just in general—at my own helplessness, at how little power I still had in so many ways.

Dune jumped up onto my lap and I stroked her head, sitting there for a moment contemplating what other possible avenues I could take to find out more. The reasonable answer was just to drop it, to respect that he didn't want to tell me about this and move on. It wasn't like I was bored or lacking things to do; I had more than enough on my own plate, but here I was, digging around for more things to be stressed about.

I sighed, standing up and pushing the chair back in place. My hand was on the switch to turn the light off when I heard movement in the hall.

I froze. I didn't know who was out there, but I didn't want them to see any change—the light turning off would be more of a giveaway than the light just being on.

So I waited, listening. The sound was coming closer. And the walking pattern, muffled though it was, definitely sounded like my dad.

Crap! I thought, scrambling, looking around for a place to hide, but there was nowhere. My dad kept his office tidy and minimalistic—there weren't any convenient little hiding spaces for me.

The doorknob turned. I could make an excuse—like looking for office supplies or some other equally inadequate lie—or...

I concentrated, closing my eyes and praying this would work. And then I felt the familiar slip *down*.

Not too far, not too far, I chanted to myself. I opened my eyes just as my father stepped into the room. I held my breath, waiting, but as I watched him, I could see the strange refracted light that told me I'd gone into that halfway point, where I was still technically in my dimension, but not enough to be seen.

My dad didn't see me. That was immediately apparent, because I was standing right in front of him and he wasn't even looking at me.

He did look confused, though. Dune mewled at him and rubbed against his legs, and he chuckled, picking her up and scratching her chin.

"How did you get in here?" he asked. Then looked at his desk, frowning.

While he contemplated how the cat got into a closed room and turned the light on, I slipped out the open door behind him, darting up the stairs to my room. I collapsed on my bed, returning to my normal state of 'being' in this dimension, shaking with adrenaline. I sat there, trying to look like I'd *been* sitting there for a while, and waited.

As expected, a few moments later my dad knocked at my door.

"Come in!" I called. I had arranged myself so I was lying on my bed, hoping I looked like I had been lounging there for a while.

My dad opened the door, holding the cat in one arm.

"Hey, I found her wandering around," he said, setting her lightly on my bed.

Dune made her way to me and I scratched her ears.

"Oh, thanks," I said. "Are you headed to bed?"

"Yeah. You?"

"I'll be up a little longer," I told him.

He came closer and kissed the top of my head, bidding me a goodnight. I returned the sentiment, then waited until he'd closed my door behind him.

Then I let out a sigh of relief and flopped back on my bed. Dune walked up onto my chest and sniffed at my chin.

"Sorry for leaving you behind back there," I said, scratching her ear. "In fairness, you won't get in trouble for being in there, but I might. Thanks for being a distraction."

After a moment, it sank in what exactly I'd managed to do. I'd used my weird ability to move between dimensions to...sneak around. Like Emily had said, to *spy*.

That fact sat uneasily in the pit of my stomach. There was something underhanded about that. And I considered how easy it would be to start using powers like this to do bad things.

I should tell the others. It was a useful skill, even if it was kinda shady. I grabbed my phone, then stopped—would they be worried I'd use it against them? I wanted to say I wouldn't, but the fact was I already *did*. I used it against my *dad*. Not maliciously, not even intentionally, really, but that's what had happened.

I set my phone aside. I needed to be careful. My dad had always told me that power didn't change people, it just amplified them. He had meant normal power—money, influence, connections, all that—but I had a feeling the lesson applied to strange supernatural abilities, as well.

"You always get a say in who you choose to be, the trick is to catch yourself if you start going down a path you don't like. And be brave enough to admit that you made a mistake. Or that you didn't like what you saw. You always have the power to alter your course, you just have to have the awareness and courage to see it, admit to it, and act on it."

He'd told me some variation of that numerous times over the years, and it had never meant too much to me before, but now...

Now, I realized, I had a decision to make. Who I wanted to be, how I wanted to act, and what I wanted to do with the power I had.

I'd been so caught up in thinking how I didn't want this power, how cursed I felt to have it, that I hadn't really thought about what it meant, or how I should use it. Well, that wasn't entirely true, I realized. Some credit, at least, was due to me: I was trying very hard to help others with ghost issues, and that was good. I thought.

And...I had caught myself, I supposed. I had used this ability in a questionable way *once* and caught myself.

That was also good, right? Or at least better than nothing?

I laid back, Dune curled up on my chest and purring as I absently stroked her fur. I would tell my friends in the morning. For now, I just wanted to be alone for a little bit. I hadn't felt alone in so long, since there was always *someone* (human or ghost) around anymore. And I liked to be alone.

I wasn't entirely alone, but somehow Dune seemed to enhance the solitude, rather than detract from it.

So I stayed as I was, the cat purring softly as my mind wandered. And for the first time in as long as I could remember, it didn't wander anywhere dark or miserable. And I felt alone, and safe, and relaxed.

I knew it wouldn't last, but it was very nice for the moment.

Twenty-Three

"Do you really want to come to a different café on your day off?" Emily asked.

"The coffee is better here," Derek said.

"No it is not!" Emily said, almost sounding offended.

"Fine. I don't have to make it or feel like I made it. That makes it more enjoyable," Derek amended. He took a sip, then added. "It's probably about the same if I'm being honest, but let me have my lie."

"...Fair," Emily allowed.

I snickered. Sometimes I just wanted to film the two of them and turn it into some kind of comedy stream. 'The Misadventures of Derek and Emily.'

We were at a little place called The Cuppa. It had a cozy, welcoming feel to it, and I liked it. It was quieter than Derek's work, which was a plus.

When we'd gotten our drinks, we took one of the bigger tables and sat down together, spreading out our notes. I took a sip of my chai, pleased to discover that it was really delicious. I was ever in search of a good chai latte, and so far I hadn't found my spot in Vegas yet. This might be it. Hazel was having the same, and it had gotten her seal of approval, which meant it was good.

"Okay, so," Emily said. "Refocusing here: Roz, what can you tell us about this new Shadow?"

"What is a 'Shadow'?" Yarin cut in, looking at me.

I bit my lip, then showed him the drawing in my mother's journal. "It's this...creature...it looks like it's wearing darkness, but it's really just some kind of armor. It has a humanoid face under that," I said, tapping the empty-looking head of the sketch. "It's trying to kill me. We encountered one before...that night...with the fire."

"It's horrifying," Hazel whispered.

He nodded, frowning.

"Anyway," I said, returning to Emily's question. "This new one is smaller and, it seems...sneakier? I don't know, that's the sense I get. I feel like the last one was more blunt-force—he'd just show up and attack. This one...seems more calculated. Seems like they're doing more recon, observing me a lot. Probably trying to figure out what went wrong with the last one so they can..." I didn't finish that thought. I didn't think I had to.

Derek nodded. "Makes sense. Smart strategy. So this one hasn't attacked you at all yet?"

I shook my head. "It tried once. But...it couldn't. *They* couldn't," I amended, reminding myself that these Shadows, whatever they were, seemed to be people. Or at least some variant of 'people'. "I think it was whatever

Elixabete did. That crystal grid thing?"

Hazel nodded. "If she's as skilled as she claims, and seems to be, then she might have been able to do something to limit the access spirits and other entities have to your house."

"Well, whatever she did, I appreciate it," I said.

Emily opened her laptop and started to do something, then paused, frowning.

"What?" Derek asked.

"We need to do school stuff," Emily said with a light tinge of disdain.

"Oh yeah..." Ford said, sounding a little disappointed.

Derek sighed.

Hazel looked around at us. "You guys haven't done that yet?" she asked in alarm.

"Stop shaming us, Miss Perfect," I said, and Emily snickered lightly.

"We should work on that," Derek said with a sigh.

Not all of us had brought laptops, but Emily had hers, Ford had his tablet, and the rest of us decided we could make do with our phones.

Yarin watched us curiously as we logged into our school's portal, checking classes and assignments. Ford made it a point to show Yarin what he was doing and how it worked. Luckily, my dad had gone over electives and such with me. I had gotten into graphic design, which I was looking forward to. I drew a lot with paper and pencils and other real-world materials, but I had never really learned digital art. I was curious about it, but I had barely dabbled in it and always felt a bit intimidated by the whole idea.

I had an assignment from my English class—I had to

read *To Kill A Mockingbird* before the semester started, and I had just a month to complete this assignment. That didn't sound too hard, but I never knew how calm or crazy things were going to be.

"Ooh, maybe I can write about ghosts for the school paper," Emily said.

We finished checking in and getting our assignments logged away, then finished our drinks and snacks.

"Yarin, what will we do with you while we're at school?" I asked, knowing he didn't have an answer but wanting to include him—I didn't want to talk *about* him while he was right there.

"I'm not sure. I suppose I'll need to find a way to do *something* productive while you're all away..." he said, contemplating his situation.

I felt bad. He was in such a strange predicament and I didn't know how to help him. He couldn't hide in Ford's attic forever; we needed a long-term solution for his situation and I had no idea what that might be. Especially since 'sending him back to his own time' carried so much risk. If we even *could* do such a thing, would that be right?

I supposed that it wasn't really for me to decide, and his brother had been left behind. I didn't have my own siblings, but I'd learned from Hazel and Ford that even when their siblings drove them up the wall, they likely wouldn't abandon them. I could relate in that I didn't think I could abandon one of my friends like that, let alone a family member. Hazel was the closest example I had and I knew I could never leave her in danger like that.

Thinking too far ahead, Roz, I told myself. Dr. Thompson had told me people with anxiety tended to try and think of *everything*, when in reality it was much more manageable and realistic to try and think of the next step, do what needed to be done, and keep working out from there. It sounded very practical, and I had no idea how to go about implementing it.

"I could work," Yarin offered.

I wasn't quite sure how I felt about that, but it would give Yarin some power in his own life. That would be good. Maybe a job was a good idea. I wasn't quite sure what he might do, but I'd help him any way I could.

We mulled over job ideas for Yarin, as well as alternatives for what he could do. The debate about how to best help him was a tricky one; we didn't want to tell any of the adults in our lives, not because we didn't trust them, but rather because they would all want to do the safe, responsible thing. They would want to call the authorities, try to find his parents, all that. Then they'd discover that he wasn't on the record as existing at all. Best case scenario, he'd end up in some foster home. Worst case...I wasn't sure what happened to time-travelers when they were caught but it didn't sound good.

They won't believe him.

My stomach twisted at that thought. I didn't want what had happened to my mom to happen to him. Or anyone.

Getting ahead of yourself again.

It was occurring to me that I didn't really know *how* to fully relax. To take it one step at a time. I was so desperately trying to do everything at once, and since that was impossible, I always felt like I was messing up.

Dr. Thompson had probably said this to me at one point, but it was hitting me a little differently now, thinking of Yarin and how much I wanted to help him. How powerless I felt to do so. And how I simultaneously also felt like the only person who *could*.

It was a lot of responsibility, and if I couldn't help him, I was setting myself up for a lot of guilt.

Knowing all this was one thing. Learning how to feel it was still far out of my grasp.

We decided that Yarin couldn't really get a job, as that required paperwork and proof of identity, but Ford told him he was welcome to join him with his gardening business once in a while. Yarin seemed excited about that, probably eager to have something to do, some way to feel productive. I knew when I didn't feel like I was contributing it made me antsy and uncomfortable.

I listened to my friends talk and sipped my chai, only half-aware that I was scanning the coffee shop. I didn't sense any ghosts, which was almost weirder than sensing a ghost nearby anymore, but I tried not to worry about that. Maybe the ghosts were calming down. Maybe they were used to me. Maybe things were going to go back to normal-ish soon.

Probably not, but I could dream.

I decided to go to the bookstore before going home. Hazel went with me. It was something we used to do all the time before everything got so...weird.

We wandered around, looking at the journals and sketchbooks (which were always so tempting) then moving to the various books we liked. I wanted to expand my collection of classics, and also get some new comics. I wasn't an *avid* comic reader, but I did like getting stand-alone comics sometimes. Especially since being a comic artist was something that intrigued me. I wasn't sure if I'd really end up pursuing that, but it was fun to think about.

"I feel like I haven't actually read a *book* in forever. I get so much digitally now," Hazel said, holding a novel I remembered her recommending to me. Or rather, a series she'd recommended, the book she was holding being one of the volumes. I should see if I could borrow the first one from her. Not that I'd had a ton of time for reading lately, but I should be trying to make time for things like that.

As was my habit now every so often, I checked my phone to see if anyone had reached out about Dune. I did so now with increasing apprehension, because the longer she stayed with me, the longer I wanted to just...keep her. She was sweet, and cute, and I hadn't had a pet in so long; I'd forgotten how nice it was.

A few more offers to adopt her. But no one claiming her.

Good.

I got a few comics and then found myself standing near the 'Magic & Mysticism' section, which was not far from the comics in this store.

"Should we look in there?" I asked Hazel, who turned and followed my gaze.

"Yeah, why not?" she asked, leading me towards the aisle. I trailed behind her, looking at the assorted books. I wasn't sure *why* I was interested in looking at the books when I'd researched everything happening to me online, but truth be told I had always been a bit drawn to books, even if everything could be found on the internet.

The books on crystals caught my eye. I considered that, yes, the internet had guides for them...but a reference book might be nice. They were easy to flip through on the fly, and something about the tangible book I could hold in my hand made the information feel more *real*.

I picked up a couple books on crystals, flipping through them. The second one I'd grabbed had minimalistic, glossy pages with large color-pictures of each gem and neatly sectioned-off bubbles describing each one's various properties and abilities.

I felt a little silly, looking over this information. I wasn't even sure this was the *right* information—while there was no denying that something was going on with the crystals (since Elixabete had been able to successfully ward off ghosts with the crystal grid, even with me there acting like a ghost magnet), who was to say that these silly mass-produced books were the correct crystal guides? Maybe I should ask Elixabete.

Despite this thought, I held onto the book. Hazel grabbed a few others—on ghosts, paranormal phenomenon, and cryptids.

"Why cryptids?" I asked. "Isn't that a different category?"

She shrugged. "We saw a freaking...tree-monster, I dunno, I'm not writing anything off at this point."

Well. That was fair.

Hazel laughed and grabbed something off the shelf, dropping it onto the stack I held.

"Here, Ford would recommend this."

I looked down at the book and smiled. It was titled *All About Aliens*.

"Yeah, okay," I said with a laugh.

We went to the little café area of the bookstore and sat down with our books, going over them and discussing which ones we should get. Hazel insisted on getting snacks, bringing us each a coffee and some kind of cookie cheesecake thing to share, despite us just having left a café not that long ago.

"Okay. Sugar and caffeine, check! Research materials, check!" she said brightly.

"The research materials were an afterthought," I pointed out, glancing at the pile at the side of the table, which neither of us were touching.

Hazel shrugged. "It's the illusion of productivity, Roz. Go with it. The mission of this was the relaxation more than anything, so," she held up the manga she'd grabbed. "Also check!"

We sat together, sipping our drinks and nibbling at the dessert. I had a comic I was terribly behind on and eager to catch up with.

But I kept...feeling guilty. Like I should be looking into dimensional stuff for Yarin. Or ghost stuff for all the people still calling Emily for ghost-removal services.

I knew I shouldn't. But it didn't change that I did.

Hazel looked at me, eyes narrowing, and—not for the first time in our lives—I wondered if she was psychic.

"Roz. Are you feeling bad about relaxing?" she asked.

No use in lying. I nodded, not looking up from my book.

"A little," I added after a moment. I glanced up at her,

now feeling a little guilty about feeling guilty.

Hazel sighed and set her book down, folding her hands on the table and looking at me.

"Roz. I know you're hyper-responsible and think everything is your problem, and I know you feel like the only one who can solve all these problems, but...please go easy on yourself."

"I know. I just. I feel so useless already, like I can't fix all the things I should be able to. And the on top of it I'm taking breaks?"

"Be nice to my best friend!" Hazel said, quietly but fiercely, pointing at me in a mock-threatening way.

I chuckled. It was something she and I always said to each other when one of us was being hard on ourselves. It made me smile now, especially with her expression.

"I'm trying," I admitted. "But I still worry."

"I get it," she said, a little softer, sitting back. "But you can't put all this on your shoulders. You're a teenager, you're supposed to be doing normal stuff. School starts in a few weeks! That sucks enough as is, what about all this ghost crap?"

I shrugged, setting my own book aside finally.

"I have no idea, Haze. I don't know what I'm gonna do if the ghost stuff stays as...bad as it has been. I don't know what to do with Yarin. I don't know how to keep more ghost stuff from happening. I don't—"

My voice caught. I was about to cry, the tears suddenly brimming in my eyes as my throat tightened.

Hazel got up and sat in the chair between us, hugging me. I didn't fight, even though part of me was aware that this probably looked very dramatic to anyone watching. I took a few deep, steadying breaths while she hugged me tight, a few tears slipping free from my eyes.

"I don't know what *we're* gonna do, either," she said. "But it's *us*, we're in this together. Whatever happens, I'm gonna be right here with you."

I nodded, hugging her tighter.

As nice as it was when Ford said stuff like that...it meant the world coming from Hazel. She had been with me through everything, all my life. I didn't know how I would have gotten through all the horrors of what happened with my mom without her. Even normal stuff, boring stuff.

She stayed there until I evened out, sitting up straighter. Then she smoothed down my hair in a pretty motherly way and I laughed.

"Thanks, Haze."

"Yes, I am wonderful. Now eat your cake."

We resumed reading, talking casually, and I felt a little lighter after my outburst. I didn't like how my eyes felt after crying, but ignoring that was easier when I was drinking coffee and talking to Hazel.

After we finished our snack, we sorted through our books, deciding what to buy.

"Should I get any of these?" I asked, glancing at the stack of books from the 'magic/mystic' section. I had barely skimmed them, but they might have good information...

Hazel shrugged. "Just come to my house. My mom has a ton of books like that. Well. Except that one," she said, tapping the spine of the book about time travel I'd grabbed.

So I bought that one, putting the rest back. I also got the comics. I wasn't finished with them and I was determined to do some reading for *fun* at some point.

We went to Hazel's house to peruse her mom's collection, finding that it was indeed very full of useful books. I wasn't too surprised, Hazel had told me I should stop by for this reason, but I had forgotten to. Or rather, I had been busy and every time I went to Hazel's I either got distracted by my aunt and uncle, ended up goofing off with Haldi and laughing at his bickering with Hazel, or just...laying there trying to relax because her house had always made me feel calm.

But the rest of the family was out today, so the house was—oddly—quiet. Still nice, though. Because my house was just my dad and I, and because we were both pretty neat and tidy and quiet, the house tended to be all those things—neat, tidy, quiet. And I liked that, honestly.

But there was always something so...warm and welcoming about Hazel's house. It was a little messier, a little more lived-in. There was usually *some* noise—food cooking, people talking, music, the TV, *something*—and it always smelled like food and incense. And it was all so familiar and safe.

So after going through her bookshelves, we curled up in the big cushy armchairs with blankets and tea and read.

It was much more pleasant to study all my creepy ghost stuff like this—I should keep that in mind for future research sessions.

The book I'd bought on time travel was complicated. I had expected more new-age mumbo-jumbo, but it seemed like the author was really trying to back up their claims and theories with science. I wondered what Ford would make of it. I'd have to lend him the book and get his take on it.

The idea of portals seemed to kind of come up, but not as blatantly as I was hoping. Not that I'd expected much—our situation *was* pretty odd.

I sighed, frustrated. "Why is going *forward* in time so much easier than going *back*?" I demanded to no one in particular.

But Hazel was there, so of course she answered: "Because that's the direction we usually go?"

I threw a pillow at her.

"Linear time is a scam!" she yelled, bringing up an ongoing joke between us.

"Yes! That's why I'm trying to break it!"

"Don't break time, Roz. I already can't keep track of it," she said, giggling.

"Yeah, yeah, well if I break it you won't have to."

She threw the pillow back at me and I laughed.

I tried to read for a little longer, but eventually just set the book aside, resolving to go over it with Ford later. For now...I closed my eyes, letting myself drift off. I wouldn't have done that with almost anyone else, but this was Hazel. I didn't mind sleeping around her.

When I woke, it was to Haldi babbling happily about his soccer camp—which he went to each year—and Aunt Fiona asking what they should cook.

"Roz! I didn't see you there. Will you be staying for dinner?" she asked brightly.

I stretched, trying to look like I wasn't still half-asleep. "Yeah, that'd be great."

Even though I was awake now, I stayed in the armchair where I'd fallen asleep, listening to the family activity. Hazel was also still in her chair, looking at her phone. I pulled mine from my pocket and checked the time, then let my dad know I'd be having dinner with Hazel tonight. He had a dinner tonight anyway, so it worked out well. Even if it was probably with Veronica. I texted Elixabete next to tell her we'd both be out this evening.

Then I put my phone away, getting up to see if I could help in the kitchen. Aunt Fiona *loved* to cook, and loved to get pretty elaborate with it—she'd try new recipes, make up her own concoctions, and present it like she was a gourmet chef. It was really cool. When I was younger, I had seen cooking only as a chore, so the idea of my aunt loving it so much surprised and confused me. I thought she just slaved away in the kitchen because she had to.

But now I saw it more like how I would draw or paint—it was a creative endeavor, an expression of ideas. And I liked the thought of being able to create in a way that nourished others. It was cool.

Tonight, though, was one of the nights my aunt didn't feel like cooking something elaborate—which again fit with the idea of it being a creative outlet—so she was just throwing a few frozen pizzas in the oven and tossing a salad.

"If you want to help, Roz, you can make us tea," she said with a smile.

I nodded, heading over to the area of the kitchen that was entirely devoted to tea. There were a lot of options, but mint seemed to be a crowd-pleaser, so I made that. They made their mint tea with real mint, the whole green leaves still attached to the stalks floating in the cup. I liked it. I needed to remember to get real mint for home.

Maybe we could plant an herb garden, I thought, surprising myself with how normal and calm the thought was.

I had become so used to fixating on ghosts and other paranormal problems that normal thoughts felt alien to me.

Alien. The word made me laugh. Ford and his theories.

Dinner was quiet and nice. We ate, the family talked. My aunt and uncle tried to include me, but I was honestly just happy to listen and soak up the normalcy.

It had been a quiet day. I tried not to get too comfortable, to settle in too much. As pleasant and fun and relaxing as it had been, I knew it couldn't last. Knowing that made some little part of me nervous. Like I was just waiting for the next terrible thing to happen.

Unsurprisingly, I didn't have to wait long.

I stayed the night, a little warily because I was still waiting for something bad to pop up, but aside from a ghost appearing—one who didn't really seem to notice us or care about our presence, instead preoccupied with practicing what appeared to be a dance routine—and me having to send it away (which was surprisingly easy; I was getting better at this), it ended up being uneventful.

I had brought my research and notes to review, but we ended up ignoring that. We watched movies and shows, Hazel finally got me to watch some silly ghost-hunting show that mostly felt like two guys running around in the dark being snarky, but managed to make me laugh a bit. I found myself critiquing the show like some kind of expert—"That isn't how that works," "What's their plan here?"—which, I supposed, I was kind of becoming. But it was still funny. The fact that they were mostly spooking themselves (well, the one guy got spooked, the other clearly didn't believe in any of this) and running around interesting locations while making amusing commentary was more than enough to carry the show for me, even if the 'ghost hunting' element felt a little weak.

When we were tired enough to sleep, I got nervous again, but still, nothing happened. I was wary. But things were...quiet. Almost, I thought as I drifted off, suspiciously quiet. That unnerving silence that comes before something bad happens.

But even if that was the case, I had also learned that I was going to have to take the quiet moments I could get. Overall, things *had* calmed down, which was good. I had been able to find time to do...nothing. I had found time to play on my phone or doodle in my notebook or do things around the house that were mundane and boring and wonderfully normal.

And more bad stuff would happen. But right now, nothing bad was happening. In fact, it had been a *good* day. A calm day. And I had to enjoy those when I got them, because things clearly weren't ever going back to normal.

I laid there in Hazel's dark room, turning over these thoughts. They weren't exactly new—the idea of taking it one day at a time, enjoying the good moments, and trying not to let the terror of looming future 'bad things' ruin all your happiness was something I'd been taught as a kid with my first therapist. I had learned this stuff when my mother was sick, while her mental health deteriorated, and finally...maybe most of all...after she died.

Her death felt like a question to me now. Like I wasn't quite sure what *had* happened, but I knew I was missing details. It had felt so certain and final before, but now everything was up for debate, and I couldn't be sure about anything until I could talk to her.

Are you out there, Mom? I asked silently into the night.

No reply came, but I felt like the answer was *yes,* and that I was going to find her.

Twenty-Four

A couple days passed with relative calm. I was still busy, but I was able to be busy with normal life-stuff, and it felt oddly wonderful.

I had therapy, I had a painting lesson with Joanne, my dad took me out for lunch one day just because we hadn't done so in a while. We took Dune to a vet to check if she had a microchip, but found none. And since the message boards had dried up on responses, I had kind of settled on just having a cat now. Which I was pretty happy about; I had grown attached and wanted to keep her.

I finished getting all my stuff lined up for school, and my dad and I went shopping for everything I'd need. For whatever reason, shopping with him in particular felt so...normal. Like I'd gone back in time to a point when nothing weird was happening in my life.

Only one ghost showed up in my house, and Dune amazed me by chasing it off the second it showed up, successfully scaring it away, then prancing back over to me like nothing had happened and going right back to cleaning her fur.

I was even able to start watching a show with Hazel. Sometimes we watched in person but sometimes we watched while on a call, and it reminded me of when we'd lived in different states and called each other to sync up pressing play on whatever we were watching together. We'd done that so often that I couldn't remember what shows we'd watched together in person and which ones we'd watched long-distance. Either way, they were nice memories.

We were chatting online one night—Hazel was in the same room as Haldi and hated when he invaded our calls, so we were keeping our contact written—getting ready to start an episode of our new show when I caught the presence of *something*. Beside me on the bed, Dune lifted her head from dozing and looked suddenly alert, her eyes wide, fixed on me. Her ears were straight up, flicking from side to side.

I frowned; Elixabete's crystal grid had been working well, and I hadn't really encountered any ghosts in the house. Feeling around, I tried to determine what I was sensing.

Hold on, picking up on something, I sent to Hazel, setting my laptop aside and sitting forward a bit.

It was late. Not *terribly* late, but late enough that my dad, who had an early flight for his business trip, was already asleep. Elixabete was out of the house—she'd said she had something she needed to do this evening, and left just as my dad was getting home from work.

So, realistically, I shouldn't really be sensing any other *people* around the house. Not that it felt like anyone I knew.

At that thought, I realized it didn't feel like a *ghost*, though.

A flashing on my computer screen alerted me to a new message from Hazel. I checked it, unsurprised to find a string of increasingly-frantic questions.

I'm fine, I typed back, sending it before I read what she'd sent, which was:

What?

What is it?

YOU CAN'T JUST SAY THAT AND STOP RESPONDING.

About what I expected.

Investigating but still okay. Please hold, I sent after reading through what she'd sent.

I stood there, feeling out the room.

The Shadow.

I recognized it now. Faint, but present. On my bed, Dune's eyes were wide, pupils fully dilated, ears pressed back against her head and hissing at the dark presence.

I thought again of how this Shadow was different... how it seemed to try and sneak around, rather than coming at me outright.

Why? Why was it *watching* me, when I knew it was sent to kill me? Was it also studying me? Trying to learn about me? Had it decided it needed to figure something out about me before it killed me? Or was its mission...different?

I turned, spotting it. Or at least spotting a place where

the light seemed to bend and disappear. Again, I noted how my eyes almost couldn't hold onto it—how they seemed to slip past it, unable to focus on the presence.

My ability to *feel* the Shadow helped me maintain a lock on it. Whatever struggles my physical senses had with it, this new sense was unaffected.

It shifted, moving quicker than I'd think a being of that stature could, and coming around to the other side of the room, sidling up behind me before I could turn my body.

A tight grip closed on my arm, pulling me back towards it. I spun, pulling away. In reality, there was no way I could have wrenched free from that powerful hold, but paired with my ability to slip through dimensions, I was able to escape their grasp. My momentum, plus suddenly being free of the thing I'd been straining against, threw me to the floor, and I scrambled back desperately.

Dune was standing now, hackles raised, hissing furiously at the Shadow.

I tried to focus on the Shadow, which was more corporeal now, making it slightly easier to see.

I staggered back, mind reeling.

Focus, focus!

Dune sprang from the bed, moving between us and snarling, swatting at the Shadow.

Oddly, it attempted to side-step the cat, giving her a wide berth, but still moving lightning-fast to reach me.

I pushed back, trying to do as I did with the ghosts, but it was always so much harder with the Shadows. They were different. Powerful. And much more prepared for me.

The Shadow sprang forward, and—fully corporeal now—hit me, knocking me to the ground with surprising force. It had done so carefully, though, not crushing me, just pinning me down.

It was much, much stronger than me and no matter how I strained, I couldn't escape its grasp.

The Shadow pulled something from its belt with one hand, holding whatever it was just over my heart.

And...then it didn't do anything.

I stared up at it, helpless, certain that this time, I would die.

But nothing happened. I could *feel* its cold stare on me, somewhere behind that mask, but I had no idea what it was waiting for. Was it savoring the moment before the kill? Or did this weapon work slowly and I was already dying? Was it waiting for me to do something?

Slowly, the Shadow returned the unknown device to its belt. It stood, taking a few steps back.

Then it was gone.

I laid there on the floor, shaking, confused. Dune—who had been circling us the whole time, swatting at the Shadow and hissing angrily—pounced onto my chest, purring loudly, headbutting my chin to rub her head affectionately against me. I scratched at her ears, distracted, looking around. I always felt so strange when the Shadows showed up, and even more so when they disappeared. The fact that this one had left on its own made this all the more confusing.

Holding Dune close and listening to her purr, I gave myself a moment to just...sit. To just breathe, and recover from...whatever that had been.

Once I was composed enough to move, I carried Dune

to my bed and grabbed my laptop.

The new Shadow came back. Had to fight it off, I messaged Hazel. Though...that wasn't entirely true. I hadn't really fought it off—it had just left.

Immediately, my phone rang, and I was not at all surprised to see my cousin calling.

"Hey," I said, trying to sound steady as I answered.

"You can't just send me a message when something tries to kill you, Roz!" Hazel chastised.

"Sorry," I said, giggling. Nervous energy was still flitting through my body and I shook my free hand aimlessly as I paced around my room.

"Are you okay? Should I come over?" she asked.

"No, no, I'm fine, it's gone," I assured her. I would have loved to have Hazel with me, but if the Shadow came back, I'd be putting her in danger.

"God, Roz, this is ridiculous," she said, angry on my behalf. I could hear her moving around, probably also pacing.

"Yeah, I know." I kept glancing at the spots where the Shadow had been, thinking how it had swallowed up the light wherever it went.

"We have to *do* something, but...I don't know what to *do!*" she said. I rarely heard Hazel upset. But her frustration was almost palpable.

"Me either," I said, sinking into my desk chair.

My mother's journal was there, the bird-in-flight symbol that adorned the Shadows' armor sketched on the cover. I still didn't know *why*. Nor did I know what it meant.

While Hazel and I talked, I flipped through the journal, looking for...what? For an answer? For solace?

My mother had done all this, and she'd still been killed in the end. What made me think it'd go any differently now?

I had tabbed off several pages, but now I was looking between those. There was a lot in the journal I still hadn't read, mostly because it was so messy and disjointed and I always, *always* got a horrible headache when I looked at it too long.

I still didn't know why that happened, either.

Annoyed that I wasn't finding anything concrete, I flipped to the first page and used my conversation with Hazel as a distraction from the pain while I turned each page—one by one—scanning for hints or mentions of the Shadow. I knew my mother had encountered them, even *caught* one, but I needed information. Concrete actions I could take.

It was tedious, but being on the phone helped a bit. I kept talking to Hazel, letting the conversation bounce between 'important ghost stuff' and 'whatever random nonsense came to mind' until I interrupted myself by going, "Aha!"

"Found something?" Hazel said, completely unsurprised by my outburst.

"Yeah. A...oh. Oh! A summoning ritual! For the Shadows!"

"Why would you want to *summon* one of these things?" Hazel asked, then sighed, answering her own question. "Of course. To trap it. And interrogate it."

I looked at my phone, perched on my desk, set to speakerphone, incredulously. I hadn't mentioned my mother catching a Shadow to Hazel.

"How are you always right?" I asked.

"I know all!" Hazel said, laughing. Then she said, "Wait is that really it?"

"Yeah?" I said, a little uncertainly. "I mean...my mom does talk about catching one."

"*What?*" Hazel said.

I paused for a moment, considering, then said, "We should do this."

"I'm sorry, I think I had something *stupid* in my ear, what did you just say?"

"It could give us answers!" I argued.

"Roz! It could get us killed! *You* specifically, since you seem to be the one it's after!"

"Emily would be on-board," I whined.

"Emily is totally obsessed with this stuff and it makes her reckless," Hazel said. "Stop making me be the reasonable one, I don't enjoy it."

"Sorry, *Mom*," I said.

"I'm not your mom because if I *was* your mom, I would ground you from ghost stuff for even considering this."

"But you realize I'm gonna do it, right?" I asked.

Hazel gave a long, tired sigh, then finally said, "Yes."

I knew it wasn't the best idea, and there were a lot of reasons not to, and I understood Hazel's fear, but I also knew that if we didn't do *something*, I was never going to escape this nightmare.

I had to do *something*. And this was the only thing that I had any ability to even attempt.

"All right," I said, trying to sound more confident than I felt. "Let's call the others."

"Do you think this is a good idea?" Derek asked.

"No," I admitted. No sense in lying.

I had told the others what I'd found in my mother's journal, and I was buzzing with anxious energy. I had a plan: Capture the being that was after me—the Shadow—and find out what they wanted from me. I knew they wanted to kill me, but I didn't know *why*. And this was the second Shadow...*assassin*...that had been sent after me. If they were just going to keep sending them, I had to learn more about them, or I'd never be free.

Besides, if anyone would know anything about helping Yarin get back to his own time, it would likely be the Shadow.

All in all, as stupid as this idea seemed, I didn't feel like we had much other choice.

In preparation for this, I'd deconstructed part of Elixabete's grid. As far as I understood, removing one crystal from its place nullified the whole arrangement. I'd removed three and put them in my desk drawer—according to Hazel, that was enough to break the grid.

Everyone was at my house. Elixabete was out running some errands, and my father had flown out this morning for his business trip, so we were guaranteed some time alone. I needed to do this, and I needed to do it now.

We were hurriedly setting up; rearranging the furniture, discussing the plan, laying out the equipment, and going over my notes a few times to make sure I knew what I was doing. Which, for the record, I definitely did not.

I was a shaky mess already. Could I do this? Probably not. So much hinged on it. And I might get people killed. It was a tad stressful.

Normally, I tried not to draw directly on the floor, but this time, I didn't want to take the risk of the paper tearing or moving, so I was drawing on the hardwood, hoping it would wash off later. I had no plan for what I would tell my dad if it didn't—I hadn't thought that far ahead. At least this part of the floor was usually under a rug.

I was drawing a summoning circle I'd found in my mother's journal; two circles with two squares within them, a smaller circle within that, and a starburst pattern in the very center. From four of the starburst points, these things that looked like staffs extended outwards. Those were supposed to point north, south, east, and west, so I had a compass out as I drew, careful to make it precise.

When I was done, I stepped back, making sure it was correct. It was actually quite beautiful, but it was hard for me to appreciate the artistry of these things when they had such dangerous meaning.

"Do you need my help?" Yarin asked. He was so eager to be of use, but I didn't know if him drawing energy in would help or hurt.

"I might," I said. "Later. This part is probably safer if I do it myself."

He nodded and stepped back, looking fearfully at the circle I'd drawn out. I realized it probably seemed somewhat satanic from his perspective. I would explain, but I was too frantic to get going with this plan. I had to do this before I had a chance to think it through and realize I was being ridiculous.

"Ready?" Derek asked.

I sighed, swallowing the lump in my throat. "No, but

let's do this anyway," I croaked, my voice hoarse.

Hazel lit the herbs she'd placed in a bowl, and I stepped into the circle. It reminded me of the séances we'd held, though hopefully this would go better.

I closed my eyes and concentrated. My mind was swimming with a million different fears and questions and emotions. Intentionally bringing my attacker to me, to all my friends, seemed like a terrible idea, but what else could I do? I pushed all my doubts down, forcing them out of my mental line of sight.

I stayed like that for a long time, concentrating, trying to draw the Shadow forward.

But nothing happened. Yarin joined me in the circle and we tried together, but still nothing.

Despite my stubbornness, no matter what I tried or how long I stood there, nothing happened. Finally, I conceded that—for whatever reason—this wasn't working. It was back to the drawing board.

The others helped me put my house back in order and I dropped heavily onto the sofa, frustrated and tired despite the whole thing having not worked at all. And the summoning circle had *not* washed off, so I would have to ask Elixabete to help. Which would involve me explaining what I'd been trying to do (or at least coming up with a convincing lie), so I was feeling completely defeated as I sat there.

"Roz?" Emily asked. "You okay?"

"Yeah," I said with a sigh. "I just...really wanted to get this handled."

"Maybe here isn't the best place for summoning the Shadow," Hazel said. "I know we deconstructed the crystal grid, but what if she did more to protect you?"

"But the Shadow has shown up here before," I countered.

"True, but it's possible she's done more stuff that we don't know about since then. Or maybe it was accidental. But it might be hard to force it to happen."

Ford nodded. "There are too many variables that could interfere with this; we probably need to try this somewhere else."

"But where?" I asked, my mind racing as I tried to think of any possible options. I wouldn't use any of the others' houses, so that was out. And everywhere else felt too open. Too exposed.

"Outside the city?" Derek offered. "Maybe the desert somewhere?"

"That could work," Emily said.

Ford nodded.

I frowned, unsure—it was a better idea than doing it at someone's house or in some public area, but it inevitably reminded me of last time we'd ventured out into nature to deal with one this kind of thing. It had gone badly.

"Yeah. But nowhere that can catch on fire," I added quickly.

The others nodded solemnly. None of us wanted to repeat the mountain fire.

We made plans and packed up, the others hanging around for a while, since they'd blocked the whole afternoon for this.

"Where should we try this next time?" Yarin asked.

Ford considered that, then answered. "There's a lot of desert outside the city. Secluded areas you can go that are really far from civilization."

"That's probably a lot smarter than forcing the Shadow out in the middle of a suburban area," I said, thinking maybe it was lucky this *hadn't* worked. If I didn't completely contain the Shadow, they might get loose, destroy the house, kill my friends, kill other people. I shuddered.

Going outside the city—in the desert where there was nothing to burn—was the right move.

Ford pulled up a satellite map on his tablet and we scanned the surrounding areas for the best options, since none of us knew where exactly to go. To the west were a lot of hiking trails and mountains. To the east was Lake Mead and a lot of recreational spots. Both meant *people*, and I wanted somewhere with no one. North and south of the city were about the same, but North seemed to have more areas between other small towns that were just empty, expansive desert.

"Do you think it's an issue that there's an Air Force base up north?" Derek asked.

"Maybe," Ford mused. "Area 51 is up north too."

"Really? Where?" Emily asked, leaning closer to the map. "I've never actually known where it is."

Ford zoomed out a bit and scrolled up, moving the map to the north and a bit to the west. I had no idea what he was looking for, but he seemed to find it fairly easily, zooming in on what looked to me like a big, blank white patch on the map. As he zoomed closer, I could start to make out the squares and lines of manmade structures—little roads and buildings becoming clear.

"What's that big blank space?" I asked.

"Salt flat," Derek answered. "Used to be a lake."

Ford nodded approvingly. “Yup. There are a few of them up there.”

I wasn’t sure what I expected, what with all the mystery and intrigue surrounding Area 51, but it just kinda looked like an airport with some extra buildings surrounding it. I could even make out what kind of looked like a baseball diamond, which made me laugh, though it did make sense for the people stationed there to have recreational options.

“In any case, it seems like that’s far enough away for it to not be a problem,” Emily said, zooming the map out a bit to show how far it was from the city. She was right—there was plenty of space between Area 51 and Las Vegas, more than enough for us to find a quiet little patch of desert to trap the Shadow in. Idly, I wondered how they might look in the blazing sunlight. I’d seen the last Shadow surrounded by fire, but it had still been nighttime, and in fairness I hadn’t really *looked* at them—I’d been panicking and running far too much to really remember details like that.

We decided “north” and I left it to Emily and Derek to pick where, exactly, since they were the paranormal experts.

Then I sat back, frustrated that I couldn’t resolve this now, but a little relieved that I didn’t have to face the Shadow just yet.

TWENTY-FIVE

I sat with the others in the Abramovich library, which was a perfect place for a large group to do study and planning. Ford and Derek sat at one end of the table with a map pulled up on a tablet, narrowing down the best place for us to go.

Hazel and all her scholarly prowess sat beside me as she looked over my journal, organizing my notes into a binder that she was putting together. Across from her sat Emily, who was switching between looking stuff up on her laptop and calibrating the equipment we'd be using when we summoned the Shadow. Yarin and I were at the other end of the table, my mother's journal lying open between us. He was flipping through it, telling me what he had experienced and comparing it to what I had gone through.

We were trying to learn all we could about the

Shadows, and figure out a good time to go out and summon this newest one. We needed a day when no one had to work, no one had any family things going on, and—if we could swing it—a day that wasn't outrageously hot and sunny. We were going to be out in the desert, probably for hours, and too much heat and sun could be dangerous all on its own. I didn't need to narrowly avoid the Shadow killing me only to get sun poisoning.

We also had to make sure we were ready, hence Yarin and I literally comparing notes and making sure we were on the same page.

He studied the sketch of the Shadow that I had done, as well as the one in my mother's journal.

"I do feel like I saw such a being once," he said, frowning. "But it didn't pursue me long."

He looked through my mother's journal for a bit before setting it back down on the table and rubbing his temple.

"It gives you a headache, too?" I asked.

"Yes. What is that? Why does it do that?"

I shrugged. "No idea, but I can't read it too long without hurting my brain."

Yarin chuckled lightly at that and folded his hands on the table. I realized, watching him, that he was the first person to really try and read it—I had mostly kept the journal to myself and *told* the others what it said, maybe showing them a page or two on occasion. I wondered if it gave *everyone* a headache, or just us.

"I'm sorry I don't have more experience with these Shadows," Yarin said. "But I will do my best to help you when it's time to summon it."

I nodded. "Yeah. I don't know how to practice this—I

definitely don't want to try summoning it *here*—but..." a thought occurred to me.

"I wonder...I wonder if that Shadow didn't *want* me to summon it...and resisted me."

Yarin nodded, considering this. "It is powerful, and more knowledgeable than we are, it could likely do so."

"Oh! If that's the case, then maybe we can do a thing where like..." I waved my hands, trying to put my weird theories into words. "Where *you* lend some...strength? I guess? Some strength to the summoning, and *I* direct it. We might be able to overpower it that way."

"That could work," he said, brightening a bit.

"Do we know how to do that?" I asked.

"I might, actually," Yarin said. "When I was with those...doctors...they tried to make me direct my abilities many times. There was a device they wanted me to power. Apparently, I was the only one who could. I was able to do so a few times, but their machine didn't seem to work right, even when fully powered. It made them quite mad but even they had to admit that the flaw was with their design, not my abilities."

I frowned as I listened to him speak. "What was this... device? Machine? What was it supposed to do?"

Yarin's brow furrowed as he thought. "I...I don't know for certain. I believe it was intended to...direct my ability. To open doors at will. But not just any doors...or...portals, I suppose. I..." he shook his head. "They never spoke directly to me about it, but occasionally I'd hear them bicker. I think they were trying to open...one *specific* portal. They were trying to...to go somewhere, though I don't know where or why. All I know is that it was harder to reach than most other places—I could open many portals, and the machine could open more still, but it never seemed to be the one they wanted."

We sat in silence as I mulled this over, wondering who these people were, and where they were trying to go. If we *could* get Yarin back home, perhaps I could corner these two. Ask them some questions of my own. Ensure they left Yarin and his brother alone forever.

"That's...horrible. I'm so sorry," I said.

I bit my lip, worrying about the implications of Yarin's story. I hadn't even considered the possibility of *other people* becoming a threat to me because of these powers. I'd been so worried about the ghosts and the Shadows that I hadn't even considered that *humans* might try to capture and use me. It sent a shiver down my spine. I'd have to keep an eye out for that.

"Well...I suppose that experience with directing your raw power can be helpful for this," I said. I felt bad. I didn't know *what* to say about his imprisonment.

"With any luck, it'll help both of us," he said with a tight smile.

I nodded.

"Ha!" Ford declared triumphantly. We all looked over at him and he turned the tablet to face us. "We found the perfect spot! I knew it was out there somewhere," he declared, grinning broadly.

I looked at the map, then laughed. It was a featureless stretch of desert with nothing around, save for the thin line of a dirt road in one corner.

"Well. We did ask for secluded," Emily said.

"I think you'll find that this is the ideal level of secluded," Derek said, matching her tone.

"We can't go *too* far off-road; none of our cars are really cut out for that," Ford said. "But I know this area all right, it should be drivable in my van but still well away from prying eyes."

I nodded, still studying the nondescript patch of dirt. Ford had the satellite view pulled up, showing the features of the terrain. There were no trees and almost no plant life around, and I breathed a small sigh of relief.

"Okay, let's get ready," I said.

The spot we'd picked was about forty minutes outside Vegas, so while the drive was longer than usual for getting around town, it wasn't too bad.

As we drove, I realized what had looked fairly remote on the map was *incredibly* remote in real life; there were no towns in sight. Barely any cars passed us as we got further and further outside the city. Pretty soon it was just us, the open road, and the endless expanse of desert spreading out in every direction.

Ford pulled us off the highway and onto a smaller road, following that until we reached a dirt road, which we took deeper into the desert.

If my goal was to be far away from people, we had succeeded—there was no one. No buildings, no cars, barely even any desert plant life. It was featureless, nothing but the hard, dry ground of the desert and, far off in the distance, the mountains that surrounded us.

We had waited for an overcast day. This, thankfully, hadn't taken too long, as it was technically monsoon season in Las Vegas. It didn't mean a *lot* of rain, but there were rainy days, and today was one where the sun was a bit obscured by the clouds, so at the very least we weren't baking in the direct rays of the summer sun.

It was humid, though, which was odd to feel in the typically dry desert.

The few days we'd waited had given me time to study my mother's journal a bit more—to prepare, to theorize with the others, to discuss strategy.

And to overthink. To worry. To doubt.

But I had to know more. The Shadow was somehow linked to all this, and ever since that day on the mountain it had been affecting other people. I prayed this wouldn't cause more trouble for anyone else; the goal was to *stop* the problems, not cause more.

The only way I could think to do so was to speak to this Shadow and try and find out what was going on. I had no idea how to make them talk to me, or how to tell if they were telling the truth if they even did, but I couldn't keep living like this. I had to do *something*.

Ford parked the van and we piled out. Yarin looked around, seeming a bit intrigued, and I realized he'd probably never seen a desert like this until he wound up here, and it must still feel a bit strange to him.

We found a relatively flat, clear place to work and hauled the equipment over.

I had bought some craft supplies, and so drawn the summoning circle with fabric paints on a big square of cloth, which I opened and spread on the ground like a picnic blanket.

Hazel and Yarin helped me find some rocks to weigh down the corners. Then we went to where Derek, Emily, and Ford were setting things up. We had loaded Ford's van up, and it took a while to get everything in place. We had a couple plastic folding tables on which to set all the equipment. We also had battery packs for the things that needed to be plugged in. It was kind of an elaborate setup, and out here in the desert it seemed terribly out of place.

"Ready?" Emily asked.

I nodded, taking a deep breath and stepping into the circle. Yarin silently followed. We were both nervous, I didn't need any weird new senses to know that. My hands fidgeted, scratching nervously at my cuticles. I balled them into fists and took a deep breath.

Standing within the circle, I concentrated, clearing my mind as much as I could, and thought of the Shadow. The assassin. It took a while, but I was used to that by now. I kept my eyes closed, breathing evenly. It was hard, but I held out.

I thought of the Shadow's energy—the way they had followed me, haunted me. It was kind of like remembering the sound of someone's voice. I focused, but that seemed to make it even harder to grasp. I tried what my Aunt Fiona had taught me about meditation, to hold the thought gently, not with a clenched fist, but with an open, relaxed hand—the way you'd hold a baby bird.

When I tried that, the feel of the Shadow became clearer, and I found myself able to recall it easily. The energy became stronger and stronger. It was so strong now, it was almost like the Shadow was standing right beside me.

A quiet gasp made my stomach flutter. I opened my eyes. The Shadow knelt on the ground between Yarin and I.

Their hand shot out, but we stepped back quickly,

exiting the circle. They launched, but when they reached the edge of the circle, they were abruptly stopped, a crackling spider web of silvery energy spreading out from where they had made contact. The light shimmered in the air for a moment, then dissipated as it rippled outward, vanishing again. The circle I'd drawn glowed with a soft, pulsing light.

Yarin and I stared in disbelief at the Shadow. I glanced back at my friends, to make sure they were seeing this, too.

Everyone looked stunned. The equipment was going wild.

I swallowed hard. The trap had worked.

"Roz," Ford whispered. I shot him a glance and he gestured toward the Shadow. "What now?"

The Shadow stood up, and for the first time, I could *really* stop and look at them.

This one was definitely smaller than the last one. Narrower, too, but with that same absolute darkness that made them look like a cartoon silhouette. They stood out in an almost comical way against the bright, plain backdrop of the desert. The armor was less angular than the first Shadow's. When I looked closely, I could see an insignia on the breastplate, barely visible against the nightlike armor, only distinguishable in that it had a slight sheen in contrast with the matte finish of the suit. I couldn't tell if it was the same as the other Shadow's insignia, but it looked similar, and that only served to confirm my fears that this being was coming from the same place.

I scanned the pitch-black armor for any more clues, or anything distinct at all that could give me some idea of what I was dealing with. There was something on their hip much like a weapon, and I shivered despite the hot, humid air.

As I studied the weapon, the Shadow pounded against the invisible barrier, sending shocks of slivery light spiraling around the cylindrical field containing them. They growled, their metallic voice sending chills down my spine. The rest of us were still, silent, a bit at a loss now that we'd actually managed to catch this thing. Though I couldn't see their face, I could tell they was turning their head, looking around.

"Uh..." I cleared my throat to get them to look at me. "Hey. Hey!"

They paused, and I felt their cold gaze on me, just like before.

"Who...who are you?" I asked, unsure what else to say.

The Shadow was silent, watching me.

"Why do you want to kill me?" I demanded.

She's too dangerous. The words echoed in my mind.

Shut up, I thought to myself, uncertain who I was directing that at, but simply wanting the accusations of the last Shadow to leave me be.

The towering figure before me remained silent, standing still as a statue. While they might have been smaller than the previous Shadow, they were still massive, probably over seven feet tall. Their suit was so completely, absolutely dark that it was hard for my eyes to hold onto it—my gaze kept shifting to the side, as if my brain couldn't even process it.

"Why are you trying to kill me?" I repeated, my voice stronger now.

The Shadow sat down, and again, became motionless. The suit was so dark, their arms disappeared against their body like a silhouette.

I glanced at my friends, then grabbed my mother's journal. She had pages upon pages of details on how to get the Shadow—I saw the word 'assassin' in her notes again and swallowed hard—to talk. Spells, I guessed, or rather, 'scientific processes we didn't understand yet,' as Ford would say. Either way, they involved using my powers. The idea of using most of these methods was repulsive to me, and I was alarmed to find that my mother had even considered them, let alone that she might have used them, but I supposed if things got desperate enough, I might be pushed to do things I couldn't imagine now.

That thought was unpleasant. I shook it off and returned to the task at hand.

The Shadow's gaze lingered on me, heavy, almost tangible. I stared them down, clutching the journal and wondering if I had the guts to go through with any of this.

When they continued to remain silent, I opened the journal to the pages I'd marked and read through my mother's notes. The armor was strong, but not impenetrable.

Hand shaking, I reached out and touched the barrier, little silver sparks of light emanating from where my fingertips made contact. Contrary to my expectations, it felt cool to the touch, causing me to shiver.

I concentrated, focusing on the forcefield created by this particular summoning circle. I could feel it, and I could make it contract, increasing the pressure within.

The Shadow hissed, but did not relent. I kept it going

until I heard them groan, then sigh. They reached up and clicked something on their neck. The blackness surrounding their head pulled apart, folding back on itself to reveal the same kind of humanoid face I'd seen on the last one. They had similarly pale, almost greyish skin, as well as alarmingly light eyes. They were somehow reminiscent of the last Shadow, but this one had softer features.

Our eyes locked and a cold chill ran down my spine. I could...*feel*...their mind, but not in the way I had with my friends—this was deliberate. And it was not under my control. The assassin was reaching out, just a bit, communicating a few things to me.

And suddenly, I *knew*.

I knew she was a soldier—or at least that was the closest equivalent I could comprehend to what she was—and she had been sent for me. I knew that she had been monitoring me, that she had been sent after the last Shadow disappeared, and that more would come after me if she did not return.

I shook my head, taking several steps back as I started to shake. The journal dropped from my hands and I felt Ford and Hazel draw closer, grabbing the book for me and trying to comfort me, asking if I was okay, if the Shadow was doing anything to hurt me.

I couldn't make sense of their words at first—words, spoken aloud, which felt oddly clunky and imprecise after the clear drop of information from the assassin. It was efficient, but it also made my head spin.

Recovering a bit, I stepped back up to the circle, assuring the others that I was okay and looking at the assassin where she sat.

"If you've been studying me..." my voice wavered, and I swallowed hard. "Then you know English. Just *talk* to me."

She watched me for a moment, then said. "It is a crude, inefficient form of communication, but if you insist, little human, so be it."

I blinked, and in the midst of all my shock about everything happening right now, I very deliberately did *not* look at Ford—she had said 'human' and she very clearly was not one. I knew that already, but hearing it spoken gave it an odd gravity.

"I'm not letting you out until you answer me—*why* do you want to kill me?" I practically screamed.

She sighed, "Have you not realized by now? You are a threat, Rosalind Petronilia Weissmandl," she said, drawing out my full name. I shuddered in response.

"A threat to who?" I asked.

She looked up at me, her eyes glinting dangerously, and said, "To all of existence."

Twenty-Six

I froze, staring at her. I wanted to look at my friends, to see what their reactions were, but I couldn't. My eyes flicked to Yarin. His face was pale, eyes wide, and he looked over at me, mirroring my shock and horror at her answer.

Trying to regain some control over the situation, I pressed on. "And who are you?"

Her expressions were hard to read—subtle and unfamiliar. She seemed to be frowning, though.

"I am A'lna Isht-Har. I am...you would use the word 'assassin' though it's a bit more complex than that." She spoke with a bit of an accent—almost Russian, but also very different. "And unless you want your friends to suffer your inevitable fate, you will ask no more."

I glanced at the others.

"You can leave if you want," I whispered to them.

"No way," Emily said, determined.

No one else moved.

I nodded, then returned my focus to the assassin. She had confirmed that was what she was, no use denying it now.

"How do we send him back to his time?" I asked, pointing to Yarin.

Her pale eyes drifted over to him, appraising and harsh. "Yet another thing you cannot do. And before you ask, no, I will not assist you. I was sent to eliminate you. It is already in your favor that I have elected to capture you, instead, but that is as far as I will go."

"Well, good luck with that, because I have you contained," I said, almost sounding convincingly bold. "Plus, we're recording this. On several devices. We've set up a live upload, meaning that this is being saved online as we speak. It's going to all our storage accounts. So if you kill us, people will know. You'll be exposing yourself, and you seem like you're working pretty hard not to do that."

She continued to watch us. I almost sensed reluctance.

"I do not fear what the humans think or know."

Humans. There it was again, and this time I was prepared, "Where are you from? What are you?"

She was silent. I studied her, trying to get some kind of read on her.

"A'lna, please. I'm not a threat. I know—I know some weird stuff has been going on, but it's not—"

"It *is* your fault," she cut me off. "Perhaps not by choice, but by *existence*. You are a danger simply by living. As was your mother," her sharp gaze turned to

Yarin. "As is he."

"So you just...you killed her?"

"Not I."

"But someone *did* kill her," I insisted.

She was quiet.

"Answer me!"

"Her death was at the hands of another." Her voice was oddly quiet.

My blood ran cold. My mother *had* been killed. It wasn't suicide. It was murder.

I wasn't sure what I'd expected, but it didn't make me feel better. I threw a quick glance in Yarin's direction.

"What about him? Did your people ever hunt him?"

"We hunt all of your kind," she said. "I will capture him, as well."

"Because—because we...open these doorways? Between...dimensions?"

"You *are* doorways. It is your nature to disrupt the natural order. We terminate all such threats when we discover them."

I gritted my teeth. "So you *killed* my mother just so she wouldn't disrupt your way of life?"

A'lna barked out a cold laugh. "Disrupt? Your kind can annihilate entire planets."

I fought back tears. My breath was shaky and uneven. I had no idea how we could be that catastrophically dangerous, but I wasn't going to let it get to that. "Well, you're not gonna kill me," I said, all bravado, no ability to back it up.

"No, as I said, I am here to collect you. You are to be studied. We've not yet taken one of your kind alive—it is time."

"Why not...why not teach us how to *not* be destructive?" I asked. I was desperate for any alternatives. I had her captured now, yes, but what would I do with her from here? I couldn't hold her forever.

A'lna's head tilted to one side, studying me.

"I understand that you do not want to be destroyed, nor captive," she said. "But it is necessary. It must be done." Her tone was a bit different now—before she'd sounded more formal, almost like she was reciting a code. Now she sounded a bit...softer. Like she took no joy in this.

I opened my mouth to ask another question when I heard the sound of a car tearing through the desert. Fear spiked through me and I whipped around.

"Oh no," I whispered, dread washing over me as the car came into sight along the dirt road.

It was Elixabete's.

My mind raced, wondering how she knew and why she'd come and what was going on, but my thoughts were abruptly cut off by an explosion. Small, but big enough to throw me to the ground, knocking the wind out of me. My ears rang and I scrambled back, coughing as smoke and dust filled my lungs. Around me, the others cried out in alarm, though I couldn't see them for all the smoke obscuring the air and stinging my eyes.

The circle I'd created had been broken, and I could *feel* the defenses fall.

A'lna stepped out of the smoking circle, moving toward me.

"I only want to *take* you. Do not make me do more." Her eyes flicked to my friends. "Perhaps I can wipe the memories of the others and leave them be. At least, the dimensionally-locked ones."

She drew her weapon in one swift motion, but before she could do anything, a large rock smacked against the back of her head.

"Get away from her!" Hazel screamed. A'lna turned and Hazel threw another rock, which slammed against A'lna's chest. Not enough to knock her out or bring her down, but enough to give us a split second of stunned, confused silence before all hell broke loose.

I leapt onto A'lna's back and tried to grab for her weapon as she turned and trained it on Hazel. But I was too late. She opened fire on my cousin, striking Hazel and...

...Wrapping her in a thick black net. I blinked. She was trapped, flailing and struggling with the net, which appeared to be quite heavy, but she was alive, and seemed unharmed.

Ford and Derek both rushed forward, tackling A'lna and throwing her off balance while I grappled with her weapon. Emily grabbed the remains of my cloth summoning circle and tossed it over A'lna's face, temporarily blinding her, then raced to help Hazel out of the net. Yarin darted over, gripped A'lna's other arm, and concentrated. I felt her body waver, becoming less solid.

Taking advantage of her distraction, I pulled as hard as I could, trying to get the net-gun from her.

A'lna managed to wrench her arm away from me and hit something on her belt. All of us were thrown back by what felt like a light electric shock and a blast of wind. I had been on her back, and fell far, slamming into the ground on my left side and groaning. Ford and Derek had bene thrown back against our tables of equipment, crashing into them and sending devices flying. Yarin had rolled across the ground, landing not far from me, but regaining his footing faster than I had.

The assassin leapt nimbly after me, net-gun aimed, but a blast of light struck her mid-air, and she fell hard to the earth, groaning in pain, dropping her weapon.

I stared at her in shock, then turned to see what had hit her.

Elixabete. She had jumped out of her car, door still open, racing towards us at an alarmingly quick sprint, blasting the assassin once more. The assassin pulled another, smaller weapon from her belt and shot at Elixabete, who narrowly dodged the blast, holding out her hand and hitting A'lna with a brilliant beam of energy. It wasn't enough to kill the assassin, but it was enough to hurt her. She stumbled back, growling while I stared in awe at Elixabete.

While they fought, I crept across the ground, reaching for the fallen weapon. Yarin had seemed to have had the same idea, because he was moving towards it, as well.

The assassin leapt, tackling Elixabete to the ground, then pouncing away like a jungle cat. She cleared the distance and was on Yarin and I in an instant. I fought back with the only power I had, trying to get her out of this dimension. It worked enough that her point-blank shot—this time from the *real* weapon—passed through me. It wasn't harmless, though; it was strong enough to burn, and I screamed in agony. She caught my wrist and wrenched me off the ground.

Elixabete blasted the assassin again, but A'lna didn't release her grip on me. It was like when the ghosts had grabbed me; weak, but present and unrelenting and oddly terrifying.

I tried again to push her down, push her away.

We slipped, and I saw the darkness envelope us. She released me in the confusion, and I fell back. In this dimension, she was all but invisible. All I could see was her alarmingly pale face.

She hit the control on her suit and the helmet folded out around her head once more, hiding her from me completely.

My chest still burned from her earlier attack, and I wondered if any permanent damage had been done. Would I die from these injuries later? I could barely breathe, and I couldn't move as quickly as I should. Her next shot narrowly missed my shoulder, and in my attempt to evade it, I stumbled and fell hard to the ground.

"I thought you didn't want to kill me," I managed to gasp.

"I do not," she answered. "But I will if I must."

A'lna grabbed me again, and I scrambled, pulling us back up to my own dimension. Elixabete was ready for us. She had pulled out a baton and struck the assassin in the head. She hit her again and again, adding a few kicks to the mix, hitting hard enough to throw the assassin back, even in her armor.

"Go! Run!" Elixabete shouted at me, turning back to release another blast of light at the assassin.

I scrambled to my feet, racing to the others, who had taken shelter behind the piles of broken equipment.

No, not all of them. Where was Yarin?

I looked around frantically, spotting him crouched not far off, holding A'lna's net-gun, which I'd entirely forgotten.

A'lna kicked Elixabete back and Yarin jumped up, still holding the net-gun. He fired, hitting her with shocking precision. The net wrapped her up, and she fell to the ground with a heavy *thud.*

We all stood, shocked, still, staring at A'lna as she scrambled and struggled to break free.

Elixabete pulled a device from her pocket and moved forward, nimble and quick and incredibly precise. She pressed the device to A'lna's head and the assassin twitched, going limp and lying still.

"Is...is she dead?" I whispered.

Elixabete shook her head. "No. But she will be unconscious for quite a while."

She pocketed the device, collapsed her baton, and walked over to us.

She placed her hands on her hips, surveyed all of us, and said, "What the hell did you think you were doing?"

"I—we—" I stammered.

Elixabete shook her head and checked us over quickly, then pulled another small device from her pocket.

"This is Agent Zatarain, badge number 47135. I require an emergency pick-up crew for immediate assistance at my location. Mark is secure. H.D. asset has been captured."

A crackling confirmation came through the radio and she put it away.

I pulled myself up, still dizzy.

"How did you do all that?" Emily demanded, staring

hard at Elixabete, apparently the first of us to recover her faculties.

Elixabete ignored Emily, surveying the assassin, the broken equipment, and the general disarray of the whole scene. Systematic. Professional.

"You fought that—that *monster*. How?" Emily insisted.

When she still didn't answer, I said, "Elixabete?"

She turned to me, her dark eyes flicking quickly between us.

"I'll tell you later," she said, "After..." she glanced at my friends.

Realizing what she meant, I shook my head and forced myself to my feet. "No. You tell me now. I'm telling them either way, you may as well say it in front of them."

Elixabete frowned, then sighed. "Fine. But first-aid takes priority. Who's hurt?"

Twenty-Seven

Elixabete went down the line with us, tending our wounds. They were mostly light, but Ford had hit his head pretty good when he'd been blasted back, and we were all scraped up. Hazel was actually the least hurt, and started picking up the mess of broken and scattered technology, almost like she just needed something to do with herself. When we were all patched up, we started helping, trying to make sense of what remained—not everything was broken, but the equipment had seen better days for sure.

Two very big black vans pulled up, and a few people who looked like they were on the SWAT team piled out of one. The other was opened to reveal something that looked like a containment cell.

Four of the black-clad people hoisted A'lna up and carried her into the van, placing her inside. A kind of force-field was activated and the doors shut, making a sound as if they'd been hermetically sealed.

Elixabete turned to us as we loaded things into Ford's van.

"Do you still want me to tell them?" Elixabete asked me.

"Yes," I said.

She nodded. "Right. Then follow my car, we can leave the rest to the clean-up crew."

We looked at each other in confusion, then piled into the van and drove behind Elixabete as her car turned and pulled back onto the highway.

The drive was silent. It was strange, but the whole day had been strange, and a bit of quiet was a welcome relief.

She led us to a secluded diner, which confused me, but I was too stunned to ask questions. We parked beside her and followed her inside, the whole time wondering why we were here. Elixabete's demeanor was strange, different. I watched her with fearful curiosity the whole time.

The diner was largely empty, and neither the patrons nor the staff seemed fazed by our appearance.

The girl behind the counter looked us over, then glanced at Elixabete and said, "Booth or counter?"

"I'd prefer a table in the back," Elixabete said. The waitress nodded and gestured for us to go ahead. Elixabete led us to a few booths in the very back, but we didn't sit down. We walked past them, to the door that said 'Restrooms & Exit.' Past the bathrooms, there was a third door that said 'Employees Only' that Elixabete knocked on twice, then unlocked and guided us through.

Beyond the door was small, hospital-looking room,

complete with four hospital beds.

"Brooks," Elixabete said. She was still using that clipped, professional tone from before. I wasn't used to hearing her voice like that.

A tall, thin man with thick glasses peeked out form the small doorway at the very back of the room. It looked like he'd been in a broom closet with half a desk and a computer shoved into it, but I guessed it was supposed to be an office. The man, Brooks, hurried over to us and Elixabete gave him a brief run-down of what kind of injuries we had. She'd been able to do some quick patches, but getting proper medical attention probably wasn't a bad idea.

He looked us over, then glanced at Elixabete and said, "Wasn't this the exact *opposite* of your mission?"

Elixabete rolled her eyes. "Don't start with me. I've had a bad day."

"Clearly," he said, coming over to us and examining our wounds.

"What the hell is this place?" Emily asked, somewhere between horrified and fascinated. She, at least, was clear-minded enough to still demand answers.

"And, seriously, who *are* you?" Ford asked.

Brooks ignored our questions, instead surveying us, then leading Yarin and I each to one of the beds and motioning for us to sit. He indicated that Ford should take the third, and the other three turned the remaining bed into a place to sit so they were out of the walkway.

Elixabete sighed, glancing at Brooks. "I'm gonna explain this to them. Do me a favor and don't tell Eldridge."

Brooks didn't even look up from selecting a few tools.

"You know I never offer more information than I have to. Or want to. Or should."

Elixabete half laughed, half shook her head, then turned to us and said, "My name is Elixabete Zatarain. Codename Otxoa. I'm—"

"It means 'wolf'. Fitting, really," Brooks cut in.

Elixabete raised her eyebrows at him. "What happened to not offering more information than you have to?"

Brooks shrugged as he tended to Yarin. "It comes and goes."

She rubbed the bridge of her nose and plunged on: "As I was saying, I'm a special agent. But not with any division you've heard of. We work with paranormal and supernatural phenomenon. I am trained in espionage, martial arts, and weaponry, but also in...well, you would likely call it magic. I was sent to protect you, Rosalind. Your mother was supposed to be under our protection, as well, but we lost track of her after she was taken as a baby—"

"Taken?" I asked.

Elixabete nodded. "We'll get to that later. I was sent to protect *you*."

I had even more questions now, but my head was aching.

When Brooks finished with Yarin—surprisingly quickly, with the result that Yarin was sitting up straighter, looking alert and perfectly healthy—he came to me. He positioned his hand so two fingers fell on my left temple, while his thumb resting against the center of my forehead. I was about to ask what he was doing when he said, "Okay," to himself and moved his hand to my throbbing shoulder. He muttered something, and the pain was suddenly gone. I had been unable to properly move that arm, but now I flexed it and found it was as good as new. I realized that the burning sensation in my chest had completely faded, as well.

Before I could ask him how, he said, "You have a couple broken ribs. May I?"

"Uh, s-sure," I said, and he gingerly placed his fingertips against my lower ribs, muttering again. Once more, the pain suddenly evaporated, and I was able to breathe without pain.

He sealed up my cuts in a manner of seconds and moved on to Ford. When he saw Derek, he looked at the cast, rolled his eyes, and said, "Hold out your arm." A moment later, he was cutting away Derek's cast and tossing it aside with disdain, like it was some medieval torture device.

Derek flexed his arm and looked at Brooks in amazement. "How did you do that?"

"Practice," Brooks said.

When he was done with us, he gave a little salute to Elixabete and headed back into his claustrophobic closet-office. We all stared after him, then looked at Elixabete for answers.

"Ignore Brooks. He's...weird. Come on, let's get you some food."

She led us back out to the restaurant, and we sat in one of the back booths. Elixabete refused to answer any more questions until we'd all ordered a meal, so we did, all still totally perplexed by the turn this day had taken.

Once we had ordered, Elixabete looked sternly at me and said, "What were you thinking, calling that beast to you? I did so much to ward it away from you and you drew it right to your location."

"I wanted to get answers, and to try and help Yarin," I said. "And...ask about my mother," I added, looking away.

She nodded, then turned to Yarin. He withered a little under her stare.

"I didn't realize you were mixed up in all of this," she said, her tone softening a bit.

"Y-yes, ma'am," he said.

Elixabete appraised him for a moment longer before asking, "Where are you from, Yarin?"

He glanced at me, then answered, "Germany... 1942..."

She nodded like this was not so much shocking as it was inconvenient.

"I'm sorry," Ford said. "There is a secret government agency dedicated to fighting the paranormal? Like... Men in Black? X-Files? Is that what I'm learning right now?"

Elixabete chuckled. "Not quite, but yes, of course there is. If it exists, if it is in the known world, then there is invariably a branch of the government dedicated to it."

"And this place?" Derek asked.

"A safehouse, so to speak. It's where agents come to lay low, receive medical care, or just exchange news. It's also just a place to eat, to recuperate. With our work, we usually cannot be ourselves—we must always be on the job. This is one of the few places we can visit where the mask can come off."

"How did you even find us? How did you know to come after us?" Emily asked.

Elixabete looked at all of us in turn, then sighed. "I placed a tracker in Rosalind's phone, and I've been tracking the assassin; whenever Rosalind goes anywhere, I try to stay close. When I saw you and the assassin converging on the same point..." she shrugged.

Everyone was silent. I looked at my phone in alarm.

My thoughts were starting to collect into something I could make sense of, and frankly, I didn't like them. "You were...assigned to me?"

"The agency tracks all supernatural activity. That little 'Area 51 Breach' event—which clearly had *nothing* to do with Area 51, isn't even *remotely* close to it, but I suppose to the general public, that's 'close enough.' Anyway, it set off all our alarms and many of us were assigned to this area, to help with the overflow," she gestured to the diner, and its other patrons. "I was assigned to you. Before that, we knew you were somewhere in the States, but hadn't been able to locate you. Your powers were dormant, and we couldn't pick up enough of a signal to know where to look. After all that happened, though, it wasn't hard to find you. I chose the role of housekeeper so I could get as close to you as possible without it seeming suspicious."

"Why wouldn't you just...tell me this?" I asked.

Elixabete raised her eyebrows. "Think back to when you first met me. Would you have believed me? Or trusted me? I didn't know you yet—I had to learn about you before I could know how to approach you with this."

The fact that that made sense irritated me.

"And what about..." I gestured vaguely to the north, thinking of the patch of desert where we'd fought A'lna. "What about that...assassin?"

"We've only encountered a few higher-dimensionals before, but we should be able to contain her."

Higher-dimensionals, I thought, turning the phrase over in my mind.

"Wait, wait, wait," Ford interrupted. "What exactly is a 'higher-dimensional' and would you say it qualifies as an alien?"

I swatted at him but he was undeterred, his eyes fixed on Elixabete.

"I...don't really know," she said. "They're not human, and they do live elsewhere, so in a sense I suppose some might define them as 'alien'."

"Yes!" Ford said, raising his arms like he'd just scored a winning goal.

"*However*," Elixabete said. "Their physiology is similar enough to ours that there is some possibility we're related. In which case, I'm not sure if that would count as an 'alien' or as simply a related species."

"Hmm," Ford said, calming down a bit. "Much to consider."

I rolled my eyes. I was never going to hear the end of this.

"What's going to happen to her?" Derek asked, getting us back on track.

"I don't know. She's a prisoner now. We can't just let her return—she'll come for you again if we do," Elixabete said, her eyes drifting to me.

I wasn't sure how I felt about that, but considering the only alternatives were 'kill her' or 'let her go and allow her to capture or kill *me'* I didn't know what to say.

Another thought nagged at my mind, but our food came then, and all conversation screeched to a halt as we devoured our meals. I don't think any of us had realized how hungry we were until we were eating.

When were finished, Elixabete answered more questions, but I could see everyone growing weary. We'd had a long, exhausting day, and now that the adrenaline was wearing off, and our stomachs were full, we were all ready to go home and recover.

We drove back to my house, and Elixabete rounded us up as we piled out of Ford's van to stand around her in a close little huddle.

"Before you go," Elixabete said. "You must all swear to me that you will not tell another soul. I have already revealed myself to my ward, which is trouble enough, but to five others? Children, no less? I am choosing to trust you with this information, because you're all involved and you've all shown yourselves to be strong and determined. I feel like you've earned my honesty here. But you must return my trust with your discretion. No one else is to know. *No one.*"

We all agreed, and the intensity of this new situation settled on my shoulders as I considered her words.

Ford opened the back of his van and sighed at the wrecked equipment we'd hastily packed up. Emily and Derek looked on sadly.

"Well. At least we have backups," Emily said.

"How are we gonna replace all that?" Derek groaned. "It took us *years* to save up for this stuff."

"We can catalog the damage tomorrow," Ford said. "Just get the stuff that's still intact now and we can sort out the rest after we've gotten some sleep."

They gathered the few items that hadn't been wrecked and I looked unhappily at the wreckage. I couldn't afford to replace all of it, but I would do my best. They had been helping me, and I wanted to return the favor.

The sun was starting to set, and I knew my dad would be home soon. Hazel hugged me and told me to rest, and the others all said their goodbyes.

"Where are you staying?" Elixabete asked Yarin.

"Oh...I've been..." he looked at Ford uncertainly, like he wasn't sure if he should say.

Ford also looked a little stunned. So I cut in, deciding there was no sense lying to Elixabete at this point.

"He's been staying with Ford. But...secretly. We're afraid to tell any of our parents...we don't want him to be taken by the system or anything. We're the only ones who can help him and..." I looked at him. "He's our friend, we need to look out for him."

Elixabete nodded, again having a far more relaxed reaction than anyone else likely would have.

"I'll see what I can do to help with that situation," she said. Yarin looked at me nervously, but I nodded reassuringly. I had a feeling Elixabete's version of helping wouldn't be like anyone else's.

The others all said goodbye and went their separate ways, heading home. I looked at Elixabete.

"What now?" I asked.

"Now? Well, your father will be home shortly, so we go inside and I finish dinner."

I blinked at her attitude, which was somehow both surprisingly calm and intensely protective. She went inside and I followed her into the house.

"I got this for you, by the way," Elixabete said, holding out a necklace.

I accepted it, studying it in the dim light coming from the hall. It was a new crystal, inlaid with a beautiful, intricate pattern in a dark metal, possibly pewter.

"Thank you. What is it?"

"That will protect you—shield you," she said. "It will function much like the grid I've set up here, but it will go with you."

I nodded. "It's beautiful." I slipped it over my head and looked down, admiring how it hung right over my heart.

"I'm guessing you have more questions?" she asked.

"I do."

She nodded. "Well, come on. We can talk while I cook."

I followed her inside, a nervous flutter in my stomach—but this time, it wasn't a sickly twisting, it was an electric kind of excitement.

Elixabete was smart...and skilled...and she seemed to know a lot about all the impossible things happening to me.

She had been sent to protect me, and so far, she'd proven rather capable of it.

The feeling, I realized, was hope, and it had been a while since I'd truly felt it.

Twenty-Eight

As soon as I walked through the door, Dune leapt at me, slamming into my chest and climbing her way up my body. She perched on my shoulders, yowling at me a bit before aggressively headbutting my cheek with her head and purring loudly in my ear.

"Hey," I chuckled, reaching up to scratch her ears. "What's wrong?"

I tried to pull her off my shoulders and hold her in my arms, but she scrambled back up and perched there, her front paws on my right shoulder and her back paws on my left, her tail flicking about, her blue eyes wide and, I could swear, *worried*.

"She was *not* happy when you left," Elixabete said. "She kept crying to me, right up until I followed you."

Elixabete came over and stroked Dune's head a bit, then headed towards the kitchen. She started preparing tea and motioned for me to sit at the counter, setting out the teapot and two cups, then joining me.

By the time Elixabete sat down beside me, Dune had calmed down, slinking down to my lap and curling up on me, purring contentedly. I continued to pet her while Elixabete poured our tea.

"Drink, you'll feel better," she said.

I took a sip of the tea, and she was right, I did immediately feel a little calmer.

Elixabete nodded towards Dune and asked, "How did you get her again?"

"Huh? Oh, I found her on one of my—" I stopped, realizing I hadn't been entirely honest with Elixabete about what I'd been doing. "I, uh, I've been going around getting rid of ghosts haunting people. And she was at one of the houses I went to. I thought she belonged to the people who lived there, but she wasn't theirs. I...I don't know where she came from or why she came to *me,* but..."

Elixabete nodded, sipping her own tea. "Ah, that would explain it then."

"Explain what?"

She gestured to Dune. "She's your familiar."

"Wait what? Those are *real*?"

Elixabete nodded, chuckling lightly. "She's no ordinary cat. She came to you, to help you."

I stared down at Dune. My friends had joked about just that, but I hadn't considered that it might be true.

"Why...why would a familiar come to me?" I asked.

"*Your* familiar. And she came because you are brimming with power. And because you need help."

Elixabete said it so simply, like it was so obvious and normal.

After staring down at Dune for a moment, I asked, "How can she help me?"

"Hmm. That will depend on the two of you, but familiars have a habit of surprising us. Keep her close. She might be a valuable asset. And if nothing else, a source of comfort."

That was true. Dune continued to purr, and between that and the tea, some of the tension from before was starting to unravel.

We sat in silence for a moment while I tried to figure out what to ask next. I had a million questions, but I couldn't think of any of them.

"You said...that my mother was taken," I finally said. "What happened?"

Elixabete frowned, looking down at her cup of tea. When she spoke, her voice was quiet.

"We don't really know," she said. "One of our operatives was assigned to her, but they were killed, as were her parents, and she was taken. She was just over a year old."

I kept petting Dune, focusing on the feel of her soft fur.

"What about after? Did your agency ever send another operative after her?"

Elixabete nodded. "They tried. But we could never find her. We barely found *you,* it wasn't until the event on the mountain that we knew where to look."

"Those...things...they killed my mother," I said. The words were hard to get out. My throat was tight.

"They did."

"They want to kill me."

"I won't let them."

There was a ferocity in her voice that caught me off guard. I looked up to meet her eyes, and found I believed her, impossible as that promise seemed.

I tried to say something—"What if you can't?" or "How?" or just "Thank you"—but no words came out. Instead, a strangled little sob escaped, and Elixabete put an arm around my shoulders while I took a few deep breaths.

When I'd calmed down and wiped away the tears that had formed in my eyes, Elixabete patted my shoulder a few times.

"Go get cleaned up, I'll finish dinner. We can talk more later, if you'd like."

I nodded, scooping Dune up in my arms and standing to go. Just as I was turning away, I remembered something.

"My mother kept a journal," I told Elixabete. "It...she logged almost everything that happened to her. I don't know if it'll help you, but it's been useful to me."

"I'd like to see if you're willing to show me," she said.

I nodded. I hoped Elixabete could help me make sense of it. And sort out what I should be doing.

I turned to go again, but remembered something else.

"Oh...also..." I glanced towards the living room, and the carpet that concealed the circle I'd drawn there. "I drew a summoning circle in the living room. And I couldn't get it off the floor. So, uh, sorry. And also do you know any ways to get it removed?"

Elixabete raised her eyebrows, but an amused smile tugged at her lips. "I'll see what I can do."

"Thanks," I said, finally heading off.

Upstairs, I set Dune on my bed, relieved to see that she'd calmed down enough to allow me to step away from her now. I took a hot shower, scrubbing away the grime and sweat and stress of the day. Usually, I tried to be quick about my showers, but I let myself take a while this time, trying to forget everything and just enjoy the warmth of the water hitting my back.

But I couldn't forget today. I found myself wondering what had happened to A'lna—where she was, and what the agency was doing with her. Would they ever let me see her? Talk to her? Try to get more answers? I knew they'd interrogate her, collect data, but I wanted to know for myself. I wanted to learn about the people—or whatever they were—sending assassins after me, and how I could fight them.

There was no guarantee she'd tell me, but there was always a chance.

When I was done with my shower, feeling refreshed and renewed and almost like myself again, I went downstairs and had dinner with my dad and Elixabete. He asked what I'd done with my friends today and I did my best to tell the truth while skirting around the more alarming details. I told him about driving a bit outside the city, looking around at small towns, and getting lunch at a diner. It was all technically true, but again I felt that odd sorrow of lying to him.

Maybe someday I could tell him the full truth.

After dinner, we watched a show together. Elixabete left, and I realized that all the nights she went out were likely when she'd go report with her agency. Yet another strange development in my ridiculous life.

In any case, Elixabete had a hell of a status report to deliver after today.

"Is Yarin available to meet today?" Elixabete asked as soon as my dad left for work.

I looked up across the table, still strewn with the remains of breakfast. "Uh. I think so? Why?"

"I have an operative in place to take custody of him," she said, taking a sip of her tea. When she saw the alarmed look on my face, she shook her head and waved her hand. "That sounded bad. They aren't taking him *away*, they're just going to act as his legal guardian and provide him a place to stay. We'll keep him nearby—it actually does make sense to keep the two of you close. I'll even get him enrolled in your school, I think he needs the community you and your friends have provided him."

Relief washed over me. Yarin would have his own home, his own place in the world, even if it was temporary. And his own version of Elixabete to look out for him. I liked the idea of him having a place that was his, where he didn't have to sneak and hide and live in secret. He'd had enough of that already.

"He likes sci-fi books," I blurted out. "Isaac Asimov. Jules Verne. All of them."

Elixabete chuckled and nodded. "I'll pass that along. We'll make sure he's comfortable, don't worry."

I nodded. "Okay. I'll let Ford know."

I sent a text on the group chat, figuring it was easier to notify everyone at the same time. It had been active all morning, with everyone checking in as they woke up and asking follow-up questions about the events of the previous day. We were going to get together to try and sort through the remains of the damaged equipment anyway, so I'd see them all soon.

"When will this...person...be ready to take Yarin?" I asked Elixabete.

"Today."

I nearly choked on my coffee. "Today?" I sputtered.

She grinned. "We work fast."

"Yeah, no kidding."

Elixabete laughed and got up, gathering the dishes. I helped her and we cleaned up together.

Then I got dressed for the day and went over to Ford's. The others weren't there yet, but I figured it made sense for me to be early, as I had the shortest commute.

"Hey guys," I said as I approached. Like he so often did, Ford had the garage door open, his van parked in the driveway. He'd backed it in so the equipment wasn't facing the road, which was probably for the best.

"Hey Roz!" Ford said. He had already set up the folding tables from yesterday—which were remarkably intact—and started removing broken devices from the back. Yarin was there helping, and greeted me with a smile.

I helped them lay everything out and watched as Ford surveyed the damage.

"Is any of it salvageable?" I asked.

"Some of it," he said, picking up Derek's fancy new sonar reader, which looked like it might be one of the items that was *not* salvageable. "I can probably replace some of it."

"You don't have to do that," I said.

He shrugged. "I feel bad, I know they saved a lot to get this stuff, took them years to get it all..."

I felt bad, too. "Maybe we can all pitch in to replace some of it?"

He nodded, setting the sonar reader down and looking over at me. "So. How are you this morning?"

I shrugged. I had no idea how to answer that. In many ways, I felt better than I had in a long time—the assassin hadn't killed me, it was in custody, Elixabete was far more proficient in dealing with all of this than I could have imagined, and I had more answers than I'd expected to get.

And in some ways...I felt a little lost. Adrift.

"Better than I expected," I answered honestly. "Even if there's still a lot to sort through."

He nodded. Then he grinned.

I rolled my eyes. "Oh god, *what*, Ford?"

"I mean. Secret government agencies? Aliens from another dimension? Do you really have to ask?"

"Oh, shut up," I said, but I couldn't help but smile. I turned to Yarin then, watching him fiddle with a broken tablet.

"Yarin?" I asked. "How about you?"

He looked over at me, pulled from some other thoughts, then looked back at the cracked black screen of the tablet. "I'm well, thank you Rosalind. Ford mentioned that Elixabete has...made arrangements for me?" he sounded a bit nervous.

I nodded. "Don't worry, I don't think she'd let anyone but the best take you in—she's got a protective streak."

He smiled at that, returning to taking things from the back of the van, but looking a bit more relaxed than when

I'd first arrived.

By the time Hazel showed up, we'd gotten everything out and mostly sorted. When Derek and Emily got there, Ford had figured out what could be repaired—a cracked case here, a bent antenna there—and what needed to be replaced.

"I'm sorry your tools got destroyed," I said, surveying the damage. "And...I'm sorry you guys got thrown into the table of equipment in the first place," I added, looking at Ford and Derek.

"It was kinda cool, honestly," Ford said.

I expected Derek to have a little more sense, but he nodded in agreement and I rolled my eyes at them. Emily was giving them a similar look of derision while Hazel giggled.

"Anyway," I said. "We'll pitch in, help you replace what was broken."

Emily shook her head. "You don't have to do that, Roz."

"But I want to. Please. You've all done so much for me, it's the least I can do."

She sighed, putting her hands up in surrender. "Okay, fine, I accept. But you *really* don't have to—it wasn't your fault and this is part of the risk of paranormal investigation. Hell, you're not official until something supernatural breaks your stuff, it's like a rite of passage."

We were all silent for a moment, looking at the destroyed tech splayed out on the tables.

"So. Summoning the Shadow worked," Derek finally said.

We all burst into nervous giggles at that.

"Yeah. Yeah it did."

"And Elixabete is some kind of...operative?" Emily asked.

"Apparently?" I said. I told them what she'd shared with me, and tried my best to answer their questions, which were much the same as the ones I'd had.

I glanced at my phone and saw a message from Elixabete.

Meeting for Yarin set at 1. Can you both meet me at Sambalatte on Rampart?

Yes, I sent back. Then I checked the time—we had just under an hour.

"Yarin," I said, looking over at him. "Elixabete has your agent ready to meet you at one."

The words were so strange and I found myself saying them so casually. It was further evidence of how weird my life had gotten and how quickly it had done so.

"Can we meet them too?" Hazel asked brightly.

I shrugged. "Sure, why not."

Elixabete probably didn't expect me to bring everyone along, but I figured she could work with it. I had been honest with her when I'd said whatever she told me I'd end up telling the others, so including them in this seemed fitting.

Besides, it might be a bit easier for Yarin if we were all there—we hadn't known him long but I, and I suspected the others, had grown rather protective of him, and I didn't think it would go over well if I tried to tell my friends we were handing Yarin off to some stranger and they weren't invited to meet them.

So it was the six of us who pulled up to the coffee shop just before one o'clock, and Elixabete took one look at us, sighed, and said, "I'll find a bigger table."

The bigger table ended up being upstairs, in a little loft-like area lined with bookshelves. Elixabete got us all drinks and we sat up there, sipping our various coffees and teas.

From that vantage point, we could see the door rather well, so I kept peeking over every time someone walked in. A man pushed the door open and Elixabete sighed. I glanced at her, then back at the newcomer. He wore jeans, a black shirt, and a leather jacket. He snapped stylish aviator sunglasses off and slipped them into his jacket pocket, then looked up and caught sight of Elixabete. A wide grin broke across his face and he gave a jaunty little wave, then headed to the line to order a drink. I lost sight of him then, then turned back to Elixabete.

"So. Clearly you guys know each other."

"I've worked several cases with Agent King, yes."

Yarin was peeking over curiously, but didn't say anything.

I decided to ask on his behalf. "Is he nice?"

Elixabete chuckled. "He's...a lot. But yes, he's nice." She caught my eye, then looked over at Yarin, growing more serious. "He's one of the best, he'll take good care of you."

The man—Bryce—came up the stairs then, taking them two at a time. When he reached the loft, he grinned again, striding over and setting his coffee on the table. He put his hands on his hips and surveyed us, then turned to Elixabete.

"Damn, Ixi, you brought a whole party," he said.

Elixabete rolled her eyes but didn't comment on the

nickname, nor did she look upset. Instead, she sipped her tea.

I glanced over at Bryce, trying to get a read on him. He was tall, and handsome in that kind of typical action-movie-hero way. I realized, getting a better look at him, that while his outfit was simple, it was still high-quality. He looked more like someone I'd have seen in Hollywood.

"Bryce, this is my charge, Rosalind," Elixabete said, indicating me. "These are her friends; they've seen too much for me to effectively lie to them and, well, Rosalind tells them everything anyway. This is Hazel, Ford, Emily, Derek, and your charge, Yarin," she said, nodding to each of them in turn.

Bryce surveyed us all, then held out his hand for Yarin to shake, "Good to meet you, kid."

Yarin shook his hand tentatively. Bryce gave a quick nod to the rest of us, pulled back a chair, and sat down. He had a very relaxed demeanor, and compared to the seriousness of the whole 'secret agent' thing, it was throwing me off. He acted more like he was catching up with an old friend than taking on a new assignment.

"So," Bryce said, his voice slightly lower now. "We got...ghosts, time travel, and a higher-dimensional in custody." He looked around the table at us. "I'm impressed. You've done more than some field agents do in their entire careers."

"Yeah, we've been keeping busy," Ford said.

"I can see that," Bryce said with a laugh. "Well, I'm Bryce King, secret agent in the paranormal division, blah blah blah." He waved his hand. "Way less interesting than this...little collective you got here," he said, indicating us. "Elixabete has told me a little about your...exploits. You're a talented bunch."

"We manage," I said. "So...you're going to be looking after Yarin?"

He nodded. "That I am. Usually I do this in secret, kinda weird to talk so openly about it but...kinda nice, too."

"Where will he be?" Ford asked.

"I'm renting an apartment not far from here—spacious, furnished, real nice. Two beds, two baths," his tone softened a bit and he looked at Yarin. "I know you've been through a lot, so mostly this is just gonna be keeping things calm and stable for you," he said.

"I've helped Bryce ward the space—no ghosts or other spirits will disturb you there," Elixabete added gently. "Nor should anyone else searching for you be able to track you."

Bryce nodded. "Yup. So it's nice and safe and quiet. And anything you need," he pointed to himself, "I got ya covered."

Yarin nodded.

"Can we see this place?" Derek asked.

I smiled a little at how concerned everyone was, casting a glance at Yarin. I supposed we couldn't help but be a little protective after everything he'd been through. He looked between all of us, glancing at me, then returning his focus to Bryce.

"Yeah, happy to have you guys over," Bryce said. "Nice thing about our job is I'm not *really* hiding you from humans, so it's not like I need to keep the place on complete lock-down. At least not from anyone Elixabete has cleared."

The way he said it made it sound like he *had* protected people from other humans before, but I decided not to ask. At least not now.

"What if we need to get ahold of Yarin?" Hazel asked.

"Ah, yes," Bryce said, reaching into his pocket and pulling out a phone. He handed it to Yarin. "Elixabete mentioned you didn't have a phone, so here you go."

"How are you...putting all this together?" Emily asked, looking between Elixabete and Bryce. "Apartment, phone, Roz mentioned enrolling him in our school...how does all that work?"

Bryce smirked. "We've got some connections. It's not hard for us to whip up official documentation, or get funds for a relocation like this. It's all part of the program. We got a new identity all set up, I'll be acting as your legal guardian—anyone asks you can say I'm your cousin."

Yarin, still studying the phone, nodded in agreement. Finally, he asked his own question: "Will I go by another name?"

"We kept Yarin, but chose the last name 'Brodsky' so we don't trip any searches for your true identity. Just in case," Elixabete said.

"Yup. So," Bryce said with a little salute. "Bryce Brodsky at your service."

"You did that on purpose," Elixabete said to him.

"You know I love my alliterations, Ixi."

She shook her head, chuckling, then turned to Yarin. "I know this is a lot to take in. And after you've already dealt with so much. Are you doing all right?"

I glanced at her appreciatively, then looked back at Yarin. We were all looking at him, and I felt a little bad—

he must feel so put on the spot.

Yarin was still looking at the phone, but it felt more like he needed something to focus on rather than everything else around him.

After a moment, he nodded, saying, "Yes. Thank you. I'm...very grateful for your help."

Yarin's only possessions were what we'd given him. And that all fit in one piece of carry-on sized luggage, which Ford had provided and helped him pack up. It was in Ford's van, and we went with Yarin to retrieve it.

"How do you feel about this guy?" Ford asked, looking at Yarin but also over at me.

"I don't know," I said. "He seems nice enough... Elixabete trusts him."

"Do you trust her?" Emily asked.

I nodded. "Yeah. I do." It was surprising to be so certain.

Yarin, still looking over at Bryce—who was standing a bit away, talking to Elixabete—said, "He's trustworthy. Odd...certainly...but...he has a good heart."

"I guess. If he gives you *any* trouble, though, you call us," Derek said. Yarin nodded seriously.

"Speaking of which, here, we'll put our numbers in your phone," I said.

He handed his phone to me and I programmed my contact information in, then passed it to Ford. We sent the phone around to each of us, and when Hazel finally added her number, she used Yarin's phone to send a text to all of us.

"There, now you're in the group chat *and* we all have each other's numbers," she said, handing it back to him.

"Thank you," he said.

We said our goodbyes and he promised to let us know when he'd settled in and update us on everything, then he climbed into Bryce's car—a matte black Mustang—and drove off.

The others climbed back into Ford's van, but I stayed outside with Elixabete a moment.

"This Bryce...he's a good guy, right?" I asked.

"One of the best. And a good friend, truly," she said. She smirked at me, "Do you think I'd let anyone near you or any of your friends if I didn't trust them with my life?"

"I guess not. How long have you known him?"

"Oh, long time," she said. "Since he joined, actually. I was a couple years in already but still fairly new. He was just a kid, really, but he had the skills and he's a hard worker. He's also very kind. Yarin is in good hands, I promise."

I nodded, relieved to hear that. Bryce had certainly seemed nice, but my paranoia hadn't eased up much, and with how stressful things had been—and after everything Yarin had been through—my protective instincts were in hyperdrive.

We went home, and I started messing around on my phone to pass the time.

I checked my email, still wary after ignoring all those school messages.

But there was nothing about school.

There was, however, an email from Rowan.

I stared at it, confused. The subject read 'New Activity'.

I opened the email.

Rosalind,

My instruments picked up new activity in the desert north of Las Vegas.

Was that anything to do with you?

- *Rowan*

I stared at the email, unsure if I should reply. Instead I took a screenshot and sent it to my friends.

I was about to call Elixabete over when I paused. Should I tell her about Rowan? Glancing over my shoulder, I caught sight of her in the kitchen and wondered what to do.

For now, I would keep it to myself. I had more pressing matters to discuss with Elixabete, and I didn't want to let myself get distracted.

Rowan could wait, and maybe if I waited long enough, Rowan would just forget about me.

Twenty-Nine

The apartment Bryce and Yarin were sharing was nicer than I'd anticipated.

They were in a small complex not far from my house, a newer development that had a sleek, modern feel to it.

Their unit was on the third floor, the highest up, with nice views. Yarin was excited to see us and show us around, and Bryce sat with Elixabete in the living room, seeming to be discussing work.

Yarin showed us his bedroom, which had been decorated with bookshelves stocked full of books. A queen bed was tucked into one corner, and a reading chair sat beside the window, providing him a comfortable space to curl up with a book. There was even a small desk by the foot of his bed with a laptop resting on it.

"This place is great," Emily commented, looking around.

Yarin nodded. "It's wonderful. This is the first time I've ever had my own room."

"Hell of a selection," Derek said, going to the shelves and looking through them.

"Oh, yes, Derek I have a few books to return to you," Yarin said, indicating a little stack on his desk. "Thank you for lending them to me."

"Anytime—I might wanna borrow some of yours."

Yarin nodded eagerly.

Ford tapped the laptop. "You tried this thing out yet?"

Yarin shook his head, his face paling a bit. "I...I really don't know how to use it."

"I can show you if you want," Ford offered. "I mean I'm sure Bryce can, too, but if you have any questions just call me up."

"Rosalind," Yarin said, his tone growing more serious. "Have you heard any news about the assassin?"

I shook my head. It had only been a couple days since we'd captured the assassin, and I'd asked Elixabete before we'd left, but she said she had no updates, other than that they'd placed A'lna in long-term containment and had successfully managed to disarm and hold her captive.

"Sorry, no news yet. But I'll let you know as soon as I have any new information."

He nodded. I looked around the room, then added, "And, uh, no news on time-travel yet...but I'll let you know about that, too."

"Thank you. For everything," he said.

"Hey, I barely did anything," I said. "Mostly I just got us all in trouble."

"In fairness, we were pretty willing to follow you into that trouble," Emily said.

"Yeah you guys are *very* on-board with the troublemaking, it's worrisome," I replied.

"Hey guys, pizza's here," Bryce called from the living room.

Ford and Derek were the first out the door, seeming to race each other. Emily rolled her eyes and Hazel laughed as they followed the boys out.

I glanced over at Yarin. "You still doing well? Bryce still good?"

He smiled. "Yes. He's very kind. Sort of...odd. Silly. But in a fun way. He reminds me a bit of Ford."

I laughed and nodded. "I can see that."

We joined the others at the dining table and Bryce set the pizza boxes on the counter. We all grabbed some pizza and sat down.

"So. I'm assuming you all have questions?" Bryce said as he sat down.

We looked between each other. To my surprise, Derek spoke up first.

"What's your track record with successfully protecting people?" he asked.

"So far I've never failed anyone I've been assigned to protect," he said. "Which isn't to say I haven't messed up on missions before, but I've never messed up with a charge."

"And you've had a lot of assignments?" I asked.

Bryce smirked, looking at Elixabete. "They're good interrogators, we should recruit them."

"They're concerned for their friend," she said mildly. "Answer Roz's question."

Looking back at me, Bryce grinned and said, "My fair share, yeah. Not as many as Elixabete, but yes, I've successfully guarded twelve marks."

"What do you guard them from?" Emily asked.

"It varies from person to person," Bryce said. "Malevolent spirits, lower-dimensionals, assorted ghosts and ghouls and other spooky things."

"Ever any of...those...higher-dimensionals?" I asked.

He glanced at Elixabete.

She answered. "No. We've encountered them before...but we've never had to guard anyone from them."

"But we can," Bryce said quickly. "And we will."

I thought of my mother, but didn't say anything.

"How do you even get involved in this line of work?" Derek asked. We all looked at him, then between the two adults. It was a fair question.

"Well, for me it's kinda a family tradition to serve," Bryce said. "My mother was an agent—she had the same abilities as I do."

"What abilities?" Emily and Ford said at the same time.

Bryce grinned. "Well, I think a demonstration is in order."

Elixabete gave him a look. "Bryce, please—"

"C'mon, it'll be good fun!" he said.

And with that, he picked up a fork and stabbed it into his hand.

Cries and shouts and gasps erupted around the table, save for Elixabete, who just looked amused. Bryce winced, but laughed, pulling the fork free. It had punctured the skin, deep, and he was bleeding.

And then, before our eyes, the wounds closed up, healing without a trace, leaving a little blood on his completely unmarred hand.

"Bam, super-healing!" he said happily, using his napkin to clean his hand. "I can also do this paralysis-shock thing that makes a person unable to move, but I'm guessing none of you want to volunteer for a demonstration of that."

"Whoa," Ford said appreciatively. "So...you're Deadpool."

Bryce grinned broadly.

"What about you?" Emily asked Elixabete. "What can you do?"

"I can speak to ghosts, and over the years I've learned to banish them," she answered. "But I can also produce fairly powerful...well..."

"Those energy blasts!" Hazel said brightly.

Elixabete nodded. "Yes. Very handy in combat. The ghosts are less useful for combat but surprisingly useful for reconnaissance."

"And giving me a chance at a full night's sleep," I added.

She laughed. "Yes, that as well."

We stayed for a bit longer, eating pizza and discussing ghosts, time travel, and some of their past work. It was an oddly lovely afternoon, and for the first time in weeks, I felt like maybe things would be okay.

In Elixabete's car on the way home, I turned to her, remembering one of the questions I'd wanted to ask.

"How did you get rid of the ghosts that day in my

room, when they were attacking me?"

Elixabete didn't take her eyes off the road, but she answered right away. "Ah, that. I didn't actually do much—I just startled them. They were focused on you, so the...I suppose you would call it a kind of 'psychic blast'. Mostly it was just loud and bright and unexpected, but I think since you were trying to push them away, once they got distracted, you were able to send them off."

I nodded. That made sense. It was weird, but it made sense.

We drove for a little longer before I remembered another question I had.

"Um, so...that journal of my mother's I mentioned? Every time I read it I get this horrible headache and I can't read it for long without needing to rest."

Elixabete glanced over at me, then returned her eyes to the road. "Does this only happen with the journal?"

I nodded. "Yeah. I can read other stuff, books or articles on my computer or anything else. It's just the journal. And it happens really fast, I'm lucky if I get ten minutes before my skull feels like it's being split open."

"Hm. I might be able to help with that."

At home, I ran up to my room and retrieved the journal, bringing it downstairs. Handing it to Elixabete felt odd. I had been so intent on hiding it from her, presenting it willingly now was the complete opposite of how I'd been acting just a few days before.

But she might be able to help, and if she could do that...who knew what I could discover within these pages.

Elixabete looked the journal over, turning it around in her hands and running her fingers along the cover and spine. She traced the etched-in insignia my mother had added, then opened it and flipped around the inside for a bit.

"Ah. Here we are," Elixabete said. She set the journal down on the table and pointed to a symbol scribbled in the corner. "See that? And these?" she indicated more symbols, one at each corner of the inside cover. I hadn't really noticed them before, in part because they were small, and also because my mother had drawn all over the journal, so a lot of it just kind of blended together.

"What are they?" I asked.

"Seals. They're not very good ones, but enough to deter most people."

"Can they be removed?" I asked.

Elixabete nodded. "They can. Give me a moment."

She laid the journal flat and held her hand over the first symbol. It sizzled and sparked, and when she pulled her hand back, the symbol was gone—burned away, leaving a scorched patch where it once had been. She repeated this for each of the symbols, then flipped through the book again, like she was checking to make sure there weren't anymore.

"There," she said, handing it back to me. "Should be fine."

"Thank you," I said.

"Oh, and I'll work on permitting your mother through. I can just set it to where, if there's a ghost you *want* to see, you can bring them here."

"Like how you have to invite vampires in or they can't enter?" I asked.

Elixabete laughed. "Yes. Just like that."

I meant it as a joke, but I found myself wondering if

vampires *did* exist. It was strange, how much felt uncertain now that I knew ghosts and weird 'higher-dimensional' people existed. As well as monsters like the one I'd fought in the forest. I'd have to ask her about that, too.

I had a painting lesson soon, and by the time that was over my dad would be home, so as excited as I was to dive into my mother's notes—now headache-free—I knew I should wait until I could do so uninterrupted. I had made it a point to never read the journal, or even have it out, around him; I was afraid he'd recognize it, or even just my mother's writing, and start asking questions.

So I tucked it away in my room and came back downstairs, Dune right on my heels, to help Elixabete with a few chores and gather my supplies before I left for Joanne's.

On my way out the door, I caught Elixabete staring at her phone, her brow knit.

The dome in Joanne's studio was finally repaired, and she was happy to be back in her favorite place.

I was hesitant, but it did have a magnificent view. And it was good to be back up here—it made even my painting lessons feel like they were going back to normal.

"Don't you love this weather?" Joanne asked as she looked up at the sky, watching more storm clouds roll in. "It's so unusual this year, but it's beautiful."

I looked up, frowning at the grey clouds. I was still wary of them, but as a light rain began to fall, I had to admit that watching it from within this dome was truly stunning.

We painted, her working on a new piece, a couple holding hands and walking through a field of tulips.

I decided to paint a smaller canvas, and somehow ended up painting a bookcase packed with novels. It was kind of like the one in Yarin's new room. The sight had just been so...homey, so sweet. I liked it.

I saw my dad's car pull up to the house, and through the window, I caught a flash of long blonde hair.

Ugh, Veronica.

I'd almost forgotten she was coming over. I wondered what Elixabete would make of her. I returned my attention to my painting, trying not to let her sour my mood.

When we were finished for the day, I helped Joanne clean up, thankful there had been no incidents this time. We set our unfinished canvases aside to return them at our next lesson.

"I think, once you're back in school, we should create a more regular schedule for your lessons—that should make it easier for you to structure your weeks."

I nodded. "Yeah, that's a great idea." A thought I'd had before occurred to me, and I turned to Joanne, unsure if I should ask.

But what was the harm? So I asked, "Joanne? Why... why did you offer to give me these lessons?"

Joanne stopped in the middle of cleaning her brushes, glancing over at me.

"I lost my mother young, too," she said. "And when I met you...I don't know what it was, but I sensed that same sadness I felt—I still carry with me—in you. And I wanted to offer some...solace. Some joy, if I could. This seemed like the best way to do so."

I didn't know how to respond to that. I was stunned, and grateful, and touched, but all of that swirled together and I couldn't quite put it into words, so I just nodded.

"That's...thank you," I said, my voice thick.

I stayed a bit longer with her, enjoying a cup of tea before leaving. She showed me a few new art pieces she'd acquired, and a couple she was working on to add to her gallery.

As it always did, the huge, grim painting over her staircase caught my eye. It stood out among her art, most of which was bright and colorful—though, when I looked closer, there was a morbid sense to some of them, and I supposed that was perhaps just a style she liked.

We said our goodbyes and I went home, bracing to see Veronica.

But when I walked through the front door, Elixabete caught me and motioned for me to follow her.

Confused, I looked towards the living room, then darted after Elixabete, down the hall that led to her room.

When we were well away from the rest of the house, she turned to me, her face drawn.

"What's wrong? Is it Veronica?" I asked, unable to hide my suspicion.

"What? No," Elixabete said, shaking her head. She looked at me for a moment, then said, "Rosalind, my agency contacted me while you were gone."

My mind raced with panic—was she being reassigned? Was there some new emergency? Had there been a problem with Yarin?

"The assassin...she hasn't spoken once since we took her in," Elixabete plunged on, "but...today, she finally said something. She made a request."

Elixabete hesitated. She looked torn, like she wasn't sure she wanted to tell me this or not.

"What is it?" I asked.

"She..." Elixabete sighed. "She wants to speak to you. She said she'll *only* speak to you."

I stared at her, my heart hammering.

"You don't have to if you don't want to," Elixabete said. "My superiors are against it, but I..." she sighed. "I wanted to give you the option. I know you wanted to speak with her, and this might be the only way for us to get answers."

"No, no..." I said. "I...I think I need to."

She nodded. "Okay, I'll set it up."

Elixabete turned and walked back to the kitchen, leaving me alone in the hall, mind racing, a strange mix of fear and excitement coursing through me.

I had wanted to speak to her...and now she wanted to speak to me. Would *only* speak to me.

What did that mean...and what would she tell me?

But if I could speak to her again...it opened so many doors. It carried the possibility of promise. Of answers. Of closure. Or perhaps none of that—perhaps something far worse.

I supposed, I thought as I made my way down the hall, that I would have to wait and see.

Sneak Peek:

Dark Sentinels – The Labyrinth

"Rosalind, darling!"

My grandmother crushed me in a tight hug, and I laughed. People were arriving to the barbeque and I was already wondering what the hell I'd been thinking when I suggested this.

"Hi, Grandma. How was your trip?"

My grandmother had been in France for some conference for the past two weeks, which wasn't terribly surprising. She was involved with several big charities, and sat on the board for a large corporation. She was fifty years older than me and I couldn't keep up with her schedule.

"It was wonderful. I should bring you along next time," she said brightly, after telling me a bit about France.

I didn't like the idea of being 35,000 feet up with

vengeful spirits, but I kept that thought to myself.

My grandmother spotted Hazel and Haldi then, heading over to greet them. I followed her, listening to her going on about Paris and Évreux, and how much she enjoyed getting out of the country.

So far, Hazel was the only member of our little ghost hunting club to arrive. My phone had been blowing up with texts from Emily, but they had been largely unhelpful for my current predicament.

"You know dreams. What did that nightmare mean?" I asked, leading Hazel aside and skipping all greetings or social niceties.

"I don't know for sure. I don't think normal dream interpretation works in your case anymore."

"Why not?"

She shrugged. "Last dream you had like this ended in a forest fire. That's a little unusual, Roz."

"Well, yeah, but isn't the basic *meaning* the same?"

Hazel shook her head. "Not if spirits or something else are trying to give you a message."

"Something else? Like what?" I demanded.

Haldi cut in then. "Hey, so I hear your dad's hot new girlfriend is coming today. Is she really a model?"

I sighed. "Yes, Haldi."

"Sweet. Does she hang out with other models?"

Hazel rolled her eyes. "You are the actual worst," she said to him, taking my arm and puling me away.

I let her guide me, still rambling. "So if my dreams are freaky ghost dreams, how do I figure out what they mean? I mean, if I'm being...told...something, then how do I decode it?"

"Roz. I have literally zero information about this,"

Hazel said, looking at me pointedly.

I sighed. "I know. I just...things have been so *weird* lately."

"Like accidentally capturing a 'higher-dimensional being'?"

I frowned. "Yeah. Exactly like that."

"Ford is thrilled," Hazel said. "Emily probably doesn't love the 'aliens' explanation as much."

I scoffed. "Emily doesn't care, she's just thrilled she's gonna have the best grant proposal of all time."

Hazel laughed, and I ended up laughing, too.

Almost as if he'd been summoned by the humor, Ford appeared, his trademark smirk in place. I wondered why, until right behind him came Veronica and her older brother, Victor.

"Hey," Ford said, sidling up to us.

"Hi. Why are you so amused?" I asked.

"Top secret. Above your paygrade."

I pushed him lightly.

"Okay, okay," he laughed. He pulled something from his pocket and showed it to me. "It's a code grabber. Picks up frequencies."

"And...?" I asked, still unsure why he was so proud of himself.

"And I got Veronica's when she locked her car as she was walking up to your house. I was waiting on your porch and snagged it. And even if her car uses rolling codes—which I think it does, based on the make—I've made some modifications so it'll..." he caught sight of my expression and realized he was in techno-babble mode. "Anyway. We can get into her car."

I stared at him, slack-jawed.

"What?" Hazel asked, looking between us in confusion.

"You're crazy," I whispered, still looking at Ford.

"But very efficient," Ford said, grinning more broadly.

Hazel looked at him, then at me. "Oh, no, Roz—"

I cut her off. "Don't 'oh no Roz' me, *there is something wrong with that woman.*"

"So you're gonna what?" Hazel demanded in a frantic whisper. "Spy on her? *Break into her car?*"

"No!" I insisted. "Just some...light...investigative snooping."

Hazel smacked me on the arm. "No. Bad Roz! And you!" She turned, smacking Ford. "Encouraging her when she's fragile!"

"Ow!" he said, accosted.

"Hey! I'm not fragile!" I said.

"Roz?"

I spun around. My dad was standing there staring at us.

"Oh. Hey, Dad," I squeaked.

"Wanna come say hi to Victor and Veronica?" he asked.

I nodded and shot Hazel a *don't say a word* look before following my dad. Ford trailed behind me, slipping his practicing-for-a-life-of-crime device into his pocket.

"Hi, Roz," Veronica said, hugging me. I froze. We were standing by the pool, and I was flashing back to my nightmare. Veronica had been wearing the same shade of green, and it made me queasy.

"Hey," I said, shaky, returning the hug despite my churning stomach.

"Rozzy!" Victor boomed, giving me a big bear hug. I returned the hug with a laugh. I knew Victor well. He travelled a lot for work, but he had always made it a point to visit for my dad's birthday, special occasions, or any time he was in the area.

"Hi, Uncle Vic," I said as he released me.

"I see you've finally met my sister," he said, patting Veronica on the shoulder.

I nodded. From the way he'd spoken of her, I'd always thought of his sister as a rambunctious tomboy who got into good-natured trouble. I still hadn't quite made the mental connection between the Veronica of my father and Victor's childhood and the Veronica who stood before me now.

Hazel came over to greet Victor and introduce herself to Veronica, and with Ford lingering just behind us, I had no choice but to introduce him, as well. He was surprisingly gracious and normal, mature and respectable, even. It was something I'd seen him pull a few times around adults, but still hadn't gotten used to.

"This your boyfriend?" Victor asked.

"What? No, no—Ford's just a friend," I said. I was running low on sleep, freaked out from a nightmare, and now blushing in front of half my family. I could see Haldi laughing and made a mental note to have Hazel smack him later.

Ford, though, still in 'impress adults' mode or whatever, just laughed it off and commented on Victor's Princeton t-shirt. They talked about schools and majors for a while, giving me a chance to recalibrate.

It also gave me a chance to notice that, while Veronica was smiling and accepting a drink my dad was handing her, she was also scanning the yard. I focused on her, catching her looking towards the house, the side gate, the walls, and the neighbors' houses. It seemed...intense. Appraising. She wasn't a party-goer casually observing her surroundings, she was a woman with purpose, actively studying the lay of the land. Her mouth was a casual smile, but her eyes were sharp and alert.

She caught me watching her and I turned away in a rush, muttering something about greeting guests.

People filtered in until the backyard was full of chatter. Friends and colleagues of my father's, a couple neighbors, family friends, and some people Hazel knew from school.

When Emily and Derek arrived, I cut through the crowd to reach them.

Emily was grinning. "Hey! The food smells amazing. What is all this?"

"Em. Focus," Derek said.

"*Right*. Ghost stuff," she said, winking. We moved a little away from the rest of the party, taking a seat under one of the larger trees in my yard.

"So," Emily started. "Derek seems to think that dream was trying to tell you something."

I sighed. "I don't know. I mean, last time I had a dream that felt like that, it wound up being...*bad*. But this doesn't make sense. Veronica's not dead."

"Maybe she is," Ford chimed in, grinning.

"I already told you," I said through gritted teeth. "No one we know has secretly been dead the whole time."

"Well maybe *we're* all dead and the ghosts are—"

I rounded on him. "*You're* gonna be dead if you don't knock that off."

He just laughed. I sighed—half annoyed and half amused—and turned back to Emily.

"Prophetic dreams aren't unheard of," she pointed out. "The problem is deciphering them. We should see what Yarin says when he gets here. He's got the same abilities as you, he might know more about dreams like this."

"Are you sure it wasn't just stress about today?" Hazel asked gently.

Derek shook his head. "So far, we have more reason to believe Roz's dreams are sending messages than to think it's just random or emotional."

"Do we?" I asked. "I mean, it's frustrating, but..." I looked at Elixabete across the yard, then at my ghost-filled house. "I think we have bigger problems."

I wasn't being completely honest. I *was* worried about Veronica. Some instinct I couldn't name was sounding the alarm, but while part of me wanted the help, I didn't want to get too deep into this with my friends. Ford was already involved, but it was hard to keep him at bay, and honestly, I liked the company.

"Look," I plunged on. "I was freaked last night, but now...I dunno, let's just try to relax and have fun. We have a meeting this evening, right? We'll talk then."

The others nodded, but Ford raised one eyebrow at me. I ignored him until they left, and he scooted a little closer.

"We're not really ignoring this, right?"

I glanced at him. "Of course not."

He grinned. "Okay, good, because I'm *dying* to do

some spying," he said with a wink.

"Don't make me push you in the pool."

He snickered and I sat back against the trunk of the tree. "Okay, so..." I started, not knowing where to even begin. "How do we get to her car? People will notice. It's not exactly hidden. And Elixabete is inside. And astute. She won't approve."

He slipped his little car-hacking device into my hand.

"They'll notice if we *both* leave, but if one of us stays here—say, me, being talkative and distracting—then I can cover for you."

I nodded. "Okay. Thanks."

He showed me how to use the device and we formed our plan. We decided I'd hang out a bit longer, mingle, and make sure I was seen by enough people before slipping off.

I still didn't know what I expected to find, or what I thought I was doing, but after my latest nightmare, I knew I had to do *something* about Veronica. She was only getting more suspicious, and I wouldn't be able to shake this anxiety until I confirmed that it was all unfounded.

I made my way into the house and out towards her car, promising myself I would find nothing unusual or suspicious, and that all my fears would be proven false.

I was wrong.

Acknowledgements

We have a lot of people to thank for helping make this book what it is today. Writing can sometimes feel like a lonely pursuit, but in reality it took the support and contributions of so many to take this story from an idea to the book you're holding in your hands today.

Since we're a team, we'll both be thanking the people who helped us get to where we are today!

But before we get to any of that, thank YOU, the person holding this book right now (in digital or physical form), for buying this, for reading it, and for getting this far—we hope you love reading this as much as we loved writing it, and we hope you'll come back for the next book in the series.

Naturally, we owe a huge "THANK YOU!" to Tim Baughman, Jr., our talented editor. He has been one of the biggest champions for this book, and a more supportive friend and surprise marketing team than we could have ever asked for.

Big thanks to our critique group partners, Ann Kimborough, Michael Harley, and Eddie Carroll—you are all so talented, and not only did we get to read your great stories every couple weeks, but your feedback and encouragement helped us get this book to where it is today. Same for our beta readers—Murphy, Amy, Steve, Julia, Jas. Thank you for lending us your eyes and your opinions.

Matt Davis and Cait Greer both worked on the cover art, and we're thrilled with how it came out. Cait Greer also did the formatting for the book—inside and out!—and it came out beautifully. Thank you so much for lending us your talent and skill to make this book look and feel the way we dreamed.

You have all given us so much to help create the book you're holding in your hands now, and we are eternally grateful.

P.E. Crawford

When it comes to writing books, it takes time, effort, energy, and many hours of research—staying up late because you're bursting with ideas, and passion for the stories aching to get out.

Too many times we can't go to bed, until we write this one last sentence, or read just one more article for research, or work out a twist you want to get just right.

Having a supportive, caring, and understanding family is imperative for us authors, and that my friends I am happy to say, I have when it comes to my family.

Let me start by acknowledging E.V. Jacob, my daughter, who is the main reason I get to be creative and do one of the things I love the most: tell stories. If I were to detail my gratitude for all you do, for everything you are, and all my love and admiration for you, I would be writing books full of lovely things about you. So, let's keep it brief, shall we?

Thank you for being a wonderful daughter and friend, and a great business and writing partner! Thank you for the support and encouragement, in helping me open up, and feel confident enough to share my ideas with the world!

To David Crawford, you have been such a supportive husband, and I'm grateful to you for that. While I was sad to leave behind my career when our younger ones were born, I was grateful for the opportunity to work from home and take care of the little ones while doing so. I've never worked so hard in my life—I was on call 24/7! But at the same time, it was so rewarding!

Thank you for the opportunity to do what I love doing, which is work together with E.V. and write our stories.

William, and Emma, aka "the Babies." What can I say that you and the world already don't know? I'm so happy and grateful for the two of you, for being so wonderful, understanding and patient with me, for those days I'm distracted, busy, and running around, or taking a nap, because I slept late the night before. Thank you for making me tea, or a flat white. You are both AMAZING people!

William, I love you so much for our intelligent conversations, and keeping me abreast of global issues, and keep me entertained with history facts. You are awesome! Thanks Sweetie!

Emma, you are an amazing artist, a great student and you are super funny. Thank you for sharing your beautiful creations with me—your talent is astounding. Thank you for being you!

There's no way I can forget to acknowledge my parents-in-law, Dad and Mimi, who are like my own parents. I am always so appreciative, for your gifts, your words of wisdom, your encouragement, and especially your love. Thank you, Dad, I love you. Thank you, Mimi, I am absolutely grateful for all you do for me and my family. You are the BEST!

I would also like to acknowledge my parents for my richly diverse and worldly childhood. Sadly, Papie, I lost you on Christmas morning of 2019. Needless to say, it broke my heart. I'm grateful for your kindness, your love and your lessons. Because of you I learned so much about life and the world—you were brilliant and amazing, and you will always be in my heart! Mamie, being your daughter has taught me many things in life, and I thank you for your humor—you made me laugh so much, and that means a lot. Thank you for teaching me so much about my own creativity and being my own person.

E.V. Jacob

First and foremost—thank you, Mum, for always believing in me, encouraging me, and writing with me. We make an awesome team, and I love that I get to work with you and create these amazing worlds. Your unending support, in my writing and everything else I've ever pursued, has made me who I am today. It's a joy to tell this story with you and I can't wait to get all the other books out there!

Then of course my younger siblings, William and Emma, who are still teenagers and therefore still useful for asking questions like "is this something you and your friends would do?" They have been incredibly supportive, helpful, and kind.

William, you are so smart and gentle and I love that we can have in-depth conversations or just sit in comfortable silence together. You're an amazing young man and I'm so proud to be your sister.

Emma, what a wonderful friend you have become. I love the time we spend together, and I love that I can geek out about our favorite stories with you. Being your big sister is a joy and a privilege.

(Pro-tip for fans: Emma is not above being paid off to harass me into working, so do with that information what you will.)

Thank you, Dad, for loving and supporting my work, for being understanding when I have to work endlessly on editing and revising, and for bragging about your daughter, the author. Thank you for all the help you've given me over the years.

Papa and Mimi, you are both so encouraging and wonderful—I am lucky to have you as grandparents and to get to share so many lovely experiences with you. Thank you for your love and support, and for

To the #WritingCommunity on Twitter, there are too many of you to list at this point but you have all done so much for me and I'm so grateful. Especially to my RPG gang—KT, Allison, Jas, Kait, Bryan, you've all helped me improve my writing so much, and in such a fun way, and I'm incredibly grateful for your friendship and the inspiration you provide.

And finally, an immeasurably large thanks to my Best Friend, Mhage, for simply being you, for being there, and for loving what I create as much as I do. You are in so much of what I write and in so much of who I am. We've been through so much together and I'm so grateful to have you by my side, even when we're thousands of miles apart.

About the Authors

Jacob Crawford is the pen name for a mother/daughter writing team consisting of *E.V. Jacob* and *P.E. Crawford.*

P.E. Crawford is a mother of three—E.V. being her eldest—and spends her days philosophizing, studying quantum mechanics, and asking impossible questions. She likes to drink tea and has a habit of overthinking things.

When she's not looking after her family, she can be found watching documentaries, reading articles, and expanding her very eclectic and unique knowledge base.

E.V. Jacob is a philosopher some days, a scientist others, and a writer always. It's a wonder that such a scatterbrain ever gets anything done, but based on the existence of this book (and several others in various stages of editing), she can at least jot down some of the ideas bouncing around in her head.

She lives in Las Vegas, where she spends her time planning to take over the world. She is a fan of tea, a hopeless geek, and an Oxford comma enthusiast.

You can find her on Twitter and Instagram @EveyJacob.

www.ingramcontent.com/pod-product-compliance
Lightning Source LLC
Chambersburg PA
CBHW030524310726
48979CB00010B/1795/J

* 9 7 8 0 9 9 9 6 1 0 6 6 4 *